THE PROMISE
OF A LIE

Also by Howard Roughan

The Up and Comer

HOWARD ROUGHAN

THE PROMISE
OF A LIE

Copyright © 2004 by Howard Roughan
All rights reserved.

Warner Books

Time Warner Book Group
1271 Avenue of the Americas, New York, NY 10020
Visit our Web site at www.twbookmark.com.

Printed in the United States of America
First Printing: March 2004
10 9 8 7 6 5 4 3 2 1

Library of Congress Cataloging-in-Publication Data

Roughan, Howard.
   The promise of a lie / Howard Roughan.
      p. cm.
   ISBN 0-446-52943-5
   1. Psychotherapist and patient—Fiction. 2. Manhattan (New York, N.Y.)—Fiction. 3. False testimony—Fiction. 4. Psychologists—fiction. 5. Deception—Fiction. 6. Widowers—Fiction. I. Title.

PS3568.O883 P76 2004
813'.6—dc22   2003018910

Book design by Giorgetta Bell McRee

For My Mother and Father

ACKNOWLEDGMENTS

Many people to thank so let's get started.

First and foremost, my wife, Christine. For every moment we have together, and for understanding when the work keeps us apart. Trevor and I are two of the luckiest guys around.

Shari and Marc for your love and support. Shari, I've never been more proud to be your brother.

Barbara, Will, Jill, Mitch, and Lisa—for that same love and support.

And Elaine, you continue to be the greatest inspiration to us all. Here's to your eternal strength, and always making me laugh.

From family to my extended family . . .

At William Morris, my agent and Top Dog, Jennifer Rudolph Walsh. The bark, the bite, and the brains to back it up. My sincere thanks for looking out for me. As well, I'm truly grateful to Alicia Gordon on the filmic front-line.

At Warner Books, the list is long—but that's what happens when so many people go to bat for you. Larry Kirshbaum, Maureen Egen, Jamie Raab, and Nancy Wiese. Harvey-Jane Kowal (my goddess of grammar), along with Shannon Langone. Jimmy Franco, Erika Riley, Ann Schwartz, and Jason Pinter.

Now a few glowing words for my editor, Rick Horgan. (There were actually a lot more but, of course, he edited them down.)

Rick, your guidance on this novel made such a huge difference; I simply can't thank you enough. You're a true talent, and it continues to be a spectacular pleasure working with you.

Without slowing down . . .

The incomparable Brian Lipson at the Endeavor Agency—a class act if there ever was one.

Michael Douglas, Marcy Drogin, and the rest of the outstanding people at Furthur Films. Also, the very gifted John Polson. Never a dull moment, huh, buddy?

My amazing "technical advisor," Rick Whelan, for being there at the beginning and coming through for me at the end. You're a wealth of knowledge, Rick, and a helluva guy to boot. Thanks for being so generous with your time.

A big *dekuji* to Jara Burnett. Where would I be without your *Czech*pertise? Your always-quick answers—diacriticals included!—truly made Mamka come to life.

As with my first novel, I again owe a debt of gratitude to the legendary lawyer, trusted compadre, and short-game specialist, Scott Edwin Garrett. Imagine that, I just used *lawyer* and *trusted* in the same sentence.

Thanks as well to . . .

Dr. Jeffrey Blum for the wisdom and insight out of the gate, and Ben Cruz for delivering in a pinch. Also, my friends at the Poisoned Pen in Scottsdale, AZ; R.J. Julia's in Madison, CT; Books on the Common in Ridgefield, CT; and the Open Book Shop in Wilton, CT.

Finally, a special thank-you to James Patterson. Jim, the more I listen to you, the smarter I get.

PART I

ONE

To be perfectly blunt and unprofessional, my lineup that day read like the maladjusted all-star team of Manhattan.

My nine o'clock was a bulimic, twice-divorced executive who was having an affair with her married boss.

My ten o'clock was a guilt-ridden kleptomaniac who could never keep what he stole. He was always revisiting stores in order to put things back.

Then came my eleven o'clock. So to speak. A sexually compulsive cellist who, among other things, liked to masturbate in the backseat of cabs. I suppose it goes without saying that she lived well beyond walking distance to my office.

A couple of hours for lunch and paperwork, and it was time to reload.

Two o'clock: a soap-opera actor who could no longer distinguish between himself and the character he played.

Next up was my three o'clock. On second thought, don't get me started on my three o'clock.

Finally, there was my last patient of the day. My four o'clock. The main reason I remember that day at all.

His name was Kevin Daniels.* A struggling young writer who'd written seven spec screenplays and had yet to sell any of

*In the interest of patient privacy, all names have been changed.

them. Unable to drop the word *aspiring* from his desired profession, Kevin's frustration had manifested in a deep and bitter hatred of the very people he so much wanted to impress. To Kevin, Hollywood wasn't just populated by mere assholes or idiots. Rather it was infested with, and I quote, *culturally retarded wayward whores destined to make feel-good-movie johns out of all of us.* End quote.

I could only imagine how his screenplays read.

But on this particular afternoon, an overcast Thursday in the middle of October, Kevin arrived at my office with an uncharacteristic smile. He professed to having significant news.

"I've had a moment of intense clarity, an epiphany," he said. He leaned forward and lowered his voice to a whisper. "I need to be in the belly of the beast."

He stopped and stared at me.

"So you—"

"That's right." He plowed on. "I'm moving, David. I'm going to Hollywood."

"The belly of the beast, as you say."

"You got it."

"To fight the battle from within."

"Exactly," he said.

I nodded, my face giving away nothing. "Are you sure this is a move you want to make?"

"Not only am I sure, I've practically already done it," came his answer. "I flew out there last weekend and rented a place in Hollywood Hills. I'll be heading back there for good the day after tomorrow."

"You're not wasting any time, are you?"

"Not if I can help it."

"Have you told your parents?" I asked.

"They cosigned on the new apartment."

"I take it that means they approve?"

"I wouldn't go that far," said Kevin, his palms raised. "My parents know they can't stop me, so they haven't bothered to try.

What about you, though, David? Do you approve of my moving?"

I cautioned myself. Much about psychotherapy, or at least the way I approached it, was predicated on the belief that an opinion should never do more harm than good. My job was not to ferret out right from wrong in any absolute sense. Only what was right or wrong for a particular patient.

Kevin was waiting for my answer.

"Do I approve of your moving?" I said slowly. "To be honest, I'm not sure my thoughts have anything to do with approving or disapproving. The important thing—and this is something you and I have been talking about for quite some time—is that no one has more control over your life than you do. While that fact alone won't guarantee you success, it will guarantee you the right to make your own decisions. For better or worse."

"In other words, fuck anyone who disapproves," said Kevin.

"More or less."

He shrugged. "I can live with that."

After looking at each other in silence for a few seconds, we both realized that continuing to talk merely because we had time left in the hour would be silly. Kevin told me I should still charge him for a full session.

"No, this one's on the house," I said.

"Really?"

"Sure. Buy two hundred, get one free."

He laughed and we shook hands. I wished him luck. After taking a few steps toward the door, Kevin turned and looked back.

"The belly of the beast," he said. "That's where you can find me." Then he left.

And that's how it came to be. Why I remember that day so well. I'd told Kevin what I'd been telling him repeatedly over four years: that no one can have more control over your life than you do. It was pretty good advice, I thought.

Too bad it was wrong.

Dead wrong.

I know this because Kevin's leaving created an opening in my schedule . . . and the person who filled it was going to be all the proof I needed.

TWO

The very next night around eight o'clock.

I watched as Parker reached out and poked his index finger at the doorbell. As the three of us stood there waiting, I took the opportunity to complain one more time.

"I can't believe I let you two talk me into coming to this thing," I muttered.

"Nonsense," Parker replied. "You wouldn't be here unless you wanted to be."

"That's very shrink of you," I said.

"And that's a *nondenial* denial," said Parker.

I chuckled. "There's the lawyer I know and love."

Parker's wife, Stacy, gave him a nudge. "Will the lawyer I also know and love please ring the doorbell again," she said. "I don't think anyone heard us."

Parker rang the bell again as I weighed the option of making a mad dash for the stairwell. Too late. The door opened almost immediately.

"*Omigod!* Will you look who's here," she practically shrieked. Cassandra Nance, all ninety-eight pounds of her, stood before us with a bony hand slapped over her mouth in mock surprise. A little black dress draped her shoulders as if it were still on the hanger. The woman was thin. "Come in, come in," she said.

Air kisses, initial pleasantries, and the customary bottle-of-wine handoff. A rented man in a tuxedo stepped up and took our coats. We were officially in. Cassandra led us through her foyer and into the party. As she did, she locked her arm around mine and whispered in my ear, "It's really great you could make it, David."

At least one of us thought so.

Nonetheless, by that point I was resigned to the situation. This was the appearance to keep up appearances, and I was wholly prepared to put in the good effort. Perhaps even enjoy myself. But before that could ever happen, I needed to say hello to someone. *Hello, Mr. Bartender.* After a very brief, one-sided conversation with the guy, I was handed my bourbon and water. Two quick sips and I was ready. Any notion that David Remler had become a complete social recluse was about to be unequivocally dispelled.

I looked around. The circle-of-friends legacy of two rich ex-husbands, numerous patron-of-the-arts type endeavors, and Cassandra's current stint as a fashion editor at *Vogue* meant a most eclectic gathering. Seemingly every ethnicity, ideology, and sexual orientation was represented—all happily conversing with one another and all somehow connected to our hostess.

As for my connection, it was originally through Parker and Stacy, my escorts for the evening. Quick background. Parker Mathis was my freshman-year roommate at Columbia. Call it luck of the draw, but we became fast friends and, over the course of four years, best of friends. Had we gone our separate ways after graduation, we still would've been close. That we'd each decided to remain in the city practically made us brothers. I had even forgiven Parker for growing up to be a criminal defense attorney.

But to the extent I could kid him for his lapse of judgment in choosing a career, I had to hand it to him for his success in choosing a bride. Stacy Mathis was smart, witty, attractive, and the founder of a women's crisis center in Harlem. The complete package topped off by a halo. Indeed, as Parker himself would often concede with a slow nod, it was only on the coattails of Stacy's social conscience that he had any real chance of getting into heaven.

Anyway, as for my said connection to Cassandra, its origins were geographical. Up until the previous year, Parker and Stacy had lived in the same building as Cassandra, two floors below. They'd struck up an elevator friendship, which spawned back-and-forth social invitations. That translated into her being a regular at Parker and Stacy's annual Christmas party. She never missed it. She also never missed the opportunity to corner me—another regular—in conversation once she learned I was a psychologist. Over the years and a plethora of eggnog, I'd managed to hear Cassandra's entire life's story. I think all she wanted was some validation for her decisions. I gave it to her. In appreciation, I suppose, I had become a permanent fixture on her guest list.

So there I was. Reasonably dressed up and ready to mingle. And what a backdrop to mingle against. Italian marble, Persian rugs, French doors, and English furniture. *The American dream.* At least on the Upper East Side. For the next couple of hours I made the rounds, shaking hands and trading anecdotes, happy to discover that my group social skills, while a bit rusty, hadn't completely deserted me.

Then, en route to another bourbon and water, I felt a sharp tug on my arm courtesy of Cassandra. She was standing with a few other people. "David, dear, you absolutely have to hear this!" she announced.

"Hear what?" I asked, obliging her.

"Nathan's theory, that's what. It's positively Neanderthal."

I waited a moment as feet shuffled left and right to make room for me in the conversation. The Cocktail Two-step.

"Oh, c'mon, Cassandra, you can't pretend to tell me you disagree," said the man I presumed was Nathan. We hadn't met.

"Nathan Harris," he said to me, quick to remedy that. He shifted the highball in his hands so we could shake.

"David Remler," I told him.

"Yes, I know. I read your book."

Cassandra, ever the hostess: "And, David, you've met Jane and Scott Wallace, right?"

"Yes," I said, smiling at the other couple rounding out our circle.

"Good," she said. "So go on, Nathan, tell David what you were saying. I'm curious what our resident psychologist will make of it."

"Only if he promises not to bill us later," joked Nathan.

"Not to worry," I assured. "I'm taking my usual fee in hors d'oeuvres this evening."

"Fair enough," he said, humored. I watched as he took a long sip from his drink. He was fortyish, thin, and tan out of season. He was also impeccably groomed. The word *dapper* immediately came to mind. So did *pompous*. "What I was saying," began Nathan in a measured tone, "is that I have this theory about the true difference between men and women. Very simply, I believe men are superior to women when it comes to all things tangible—things that we can actually touch and get our hands on. For example, men are far better than women when it comes to building things. I don't just mean in terms of physical construction; I'd include the planning and design as well. Think about it. All the great architects throughout history have been men. And while we're at it, consider the arts, at least those with a tangible component. Holding a brush and palette, molding clay— all the great painters and sculptors throughout the ages have been men as well. The better surgeons? Men. The better chefs? Men. Even when it comes to making money in general—cold, hard cash—men are better at it than women."

Nathan paused and took another long sip of his drink. While he did, I glanced at his hands. Much to my surprise: a wedding band.

Nathan went on. "Ah, but women," he said, wagging his index finger in the air. "When it comes to the intangible—the things you can't touch—women have us men beat by a mile. Feelings. Emotions. That's what women are all about. That's what defines their world and what motivates them more than anything. As far as women are concerned, men can have their buildings, their statues and canvases; men can even have their greater earning power. Just so long as women have their intangibles—their feelings and emotions. Because when it comes to that, women rule and men are powerless. And don't think for one second that women don't know this. They know it all too well and take full advantage; often luring us men into a serene sense of being in control, only to suddenly turn the tables."

"So," said Cassandra, turning to me with a frown. "What do you think of Nathan's theory?"

"I think it's very interesting," I answered, completely aware that that alone wasn't going to get me off the hook.

"You'll have to do better than that, David," she said, shaking her head. "You've already had far too many of my hors d'oeuvres to be so evasive. You have to tell us what you really think."

What I really thought at that moment was that I should've taken a different route to the bar.

"Well, let's see," I began. "You seem to be saying, Nathan, that while men are the hands of our collective culture, women represent the heart. Unto itself, numerous exceptions notwithstanding, that's a pretty tenable idea. Take one thing you didn't mention, for instance. Sex. Not who's better at it, but the widely held belief that men view sex as a physical act, while women view it as an emotional one. I think that kind of supports what you're talking about.

"However, here's where you lost me. The notion that women use this difference as a way of tricking and deceiving—sort of like, if you'll pardon the pun, men are from Mars and women are Venus flytraps. With all due respect, I'm afraid I don't really buy that. To me that paints a rather unflattering, not to mention inaccurate, picture of what I've always considered the more compassionate sex. Wouldn't you agree, Cassandra?"

She looked ready to kiss me. "I couldn't agree more."

"Sold!" I announced. The only thing left was my exit line. I shook the empty glass in my hand. "Now if you'll all excuse me, I seem to need a refill."

Not so fast, David.

Nathan Harris, hardly shaping up to be my new best friend, couldn't leave well enough alone. I'd tried my hardest to appease both Cassandra and him with my assessment of his little theory. Yet Nathan was clearly the type who took no pleasure in partial victories.

"Interesting," he said, scratching his temple. "Let me ask you something, though, David. Can you honestly say that you've never been taken advantage of emotionally by a woman?"

"I don't think so," I answered without hesitation. Deliberately, I looked at my watch and smiled. "Of course, the night is still young."

Everyone found that amusing except Nathan. Like a pit bull, he'd latched on to the idea of goading me and wasn't about to let go. "With all due respect, I'm afraid I don't really buy *that*," he said, throwing my exact words back at me. "Somewhere along the line surely you've been the victim of a woman."

Jesus, Nathan, isn't there a tanning salon appointment you're late for?

A little help, please. I looked over at the other couple standing with us, Jane and Scott Wallace, hoping one of them would say something, anything, to change the subject. No such luck. They were being highly entertained and had no intention of talking during the middle of the show.

"Nathan, my dear, don't you think we're getting a little bit personal?"

At last, Cassandra had come to my rescue. The party's hostess was informing one of her guests that he was perhaps in bad form. Certainly, Nathan Harris, with all his pretensions of being a gentleman, would cool it now and back off.

No such luck again.

"I'm not asking him to name names or reveal intimate details," said Nathan indignantly. "I'm simply asking him to be honest." He turned to me. "You can be honest with us, David, can't you? I mean, you're capable of that, right?"

That about did it. Overt condescension. My mind raced with possible comebacks, not the least of which was informing the guy that I recently had an opening in my schedule and that, in my most *honest* opinion, he currently ranked as the person most in need of therapy on the entire East Coast. I figured the gloves were off. Nathan Harris was becoming far less dapper and far more pompous by the minute. It was time to put him in his place. A thought was jelling and words were forming, and I was about to say a few things I knew I'd later regret.

"Excuse me, do you mind if we borrow David for a moment?"

It was a welcoming and familiar voice. Parker, with Stacy by his side, had leaned in over my shoulder. I was being sprung. Parker already had ahold of my arm and was pulling me away.

"I'm afraid I've been summoned," I told the group, which was all that needed to be said. It happened so fast that Nathan could do nothing except stare helplessly as I backpedaled.

A safe distance later, I thanked Parker and Stacy for their timely appearance.

"We figured as much," said Parker. "You looked almost constipated standing there."

I performed an exaggerated deep sigh and kidded, "Like I said, I don't know how I let you two talk me into coming to this thing."

"Oh, c'mon, David," said Stacy with a push on my shoulder. "You've had a good time tonight, admit it."

"If I do admit it, can we leave?"

Stacy's eyes rolled. "Why is it that men always have to get something in return?"

"Because apparently all men are based in the tangible," I answered.

Blank stares.

"Never mind," I said.

Soon thereafter, the three of us shared a cab home. We discussed (read: *gossiped about*) some of the people we'd encountered that evening. No shame to be had. That's what cab rides home after parties are for.

Stacy told of being introduced to a recently married couple who had the distinction of meeting while taking part in a Spencer Tunick photograph. Apparently, mass public nudity was the ultimate icebreaker.

As for Parker, he recounted his discussion with an older woman who'd bent his ear about a Holocaust documentary that had recently aired on public television. The woman's obvious passion for the program was muddled, however, by her inability to distinguish between a notorious secret police force and a certain chilled soup. "It was almost surreal," claimed Parker. "This woman kept referring to the scare tactics of the German *gazpacho*."

Even our cabdriver laughed at that one.

For my part, I gave a quick synopsis of Pompous Nathan and his little theory about the difference between men and women—the tangible versus the intangible.

"Personally, I would've given the guy a very tangible kick in the ass," said Stacy, having what would appropriately be the last word on the subject.

Other than that, the only remaining business was our ever-diminishing hostess, Cassandra. Unanimously agreed: the woman could really stand to eat a Twinkie or two.

At Sixty-ninth and Third, the taxi pulled over to let me out. As I opened the door, I thanked Parker and Stacy again for not taking no for an answer when they asked me to join them for the party. Persistence is the hallmark of friendship, I declared. Or something like that. They got the point.

Once out on the sidewalk, the autumn night air crisp and biting, I watched as their cab sped off, fully aware of the inevitable. Now it was I who'd be discussed by Parker and Stacy. But don't read *gossiped*. To know them as I did was to know their words would be kind, their faces ones of concern. They'd talk about me and continue to wonder as they surely had since the day it happened: *in missing her as I still did, would I also miss out on the rest of my life?*

At the time, I was kind of wondering that myself.

THREE

I didn't do the silly things. The things that screamed for help. I didn't continue to set a place for her at the dinner table. I didn't talk to her as if she were still somehow in the room. Yes, I visited her grave, but I did that once or twice a year, not once or twice a week. As for her clothes, they'd long since been donated to Goodwill.

It had been nearly three years since my wife, Rebecca Remler, died at the age of thirty-one. She was four months' pregnant at the time.

Talking about it didn't really bother me. To do so was to switch on the autopilot and engage in rote recitation, the facts and details of her death so ingrained in my memory—so ingrained in me—that I didn't ever have to think about them. It was almost as if I was telling another guy's story. His sorrow, not mine.

A few of those facts and details.

Rebecca and I owned an apartment in Manhattan. In addition, we owned a small cottage out in Connecticut on Candlewood Lake. Our weekend retreat. The cottage was intentionally rustic, but being city dwellers, we didn't go overboard. The wood beams, Buck Stove heating, and hanging lanterns were more than neutralized by a small satellite dish and a digital thermal coffeemaker that cost four hundred bucks. It couldn't be helped. I loved watching the Yankees, and she loved her caffeine.

In fact, that was the only thing Rebecca complained about after becoming pregnant. The occasional morning sickness; the extra pounds beginning to round out her slim, athletic frame—those things she could handle. Not having her coffee was another story. At one point, I gently reminded her that the doctor had said it was fine to have a cup a day if she really wanted to. No harm to the baby. In return for my reminder, I was given an immediate look of exasperation. Said Rebecca: "It wouldn't work; I couldn't enjoy just one cup. I'd be too busy thinking about the others I couldn't have."

I'm pretty sure there's a life lesson in there somewhere.

Often, Rebecca would get a jump on the weekend with a Thursday-night drive out to the cottage. As a freelance writer, she made her own hours. Summer Fridays were a fixture in her work schedule. So were fall, winter, and spring Fridays. Hardly the case for me. As a psychologist I may have made a good living, but I still only got paid by the hour. I'd work a full day on Friday and join Rebecca that evening at the cottage after taking the train up to Danbury.

Such was the case that second weekend in November. Or at least it was supposed to be until everything changed. On the Friday of that weekend, I only worked a few hours. I took an earlier train. And instead of Rebecca picking me up at the station as she usually did, a policeman was there waiting. His job was to take me to the county coroner's office.

I think his name was Bill.

Earlier that morning, a freezing rain had fallen all around the lake area. Rebecca had left the cottage during the worst of it to pick up groceries. (She cooked Fridays; I cooked Saturdays.) Given what we drove, an Audi A_4 Quattro, she probably figured she'd be okay on the slick roads.

It was a head-on collision. An eighteen-year-old kid behind the wheel of his parents' Lexus. He hadn't been drinking or smoking pot or whatever other youthful indiscretion pops to mind when you hear *eighteen*. The kid was just a kid, driving far too fast when he really shouldn't have been driving at all. He lost control of the car coming out of a sharp turn and spun right into the oncoming lane. Right into Rebecca.

Yes, in time I found I could deal with talking about her death. It was *thinking* about it that I couldn't handle. Thinking about it was the impromptu conversation with myself, and for that there was no autopilot, no rote recitation of the facts and details behind which to hide. I could easily disengage from the concern and curiosity of others; the caring questions and the postmortem rubbernecking merely disguised as caring questions. But I couldn't escape my own thoughts . . . and the frequency with which they'd turn to Rebecca.

And our baby.

It was too early to know if we were having a boy or a girl. I suppose that's good if you believe in a hierarchy of anguish. Rebecca, though, had every intention of finding out the sex as soon as she could. As she explained to friends and relatives alike, she was very uneasy about having an *it* growing inside of her. That was too impersonal, too unattached for something—some*one*—who was very much the opposite. The sooner Rebecca could say he or she, the better. Having no strong opinion either way, I left it up to her.

In the meantime, we didn't discuss names. That was my suggestion. Waiting until we knew the sex meant 50 percent less arguing, I joked. With the knowing look that could only come from a wife, Rebecca agreed. Agreeing not to discuss names, however, didn't mean we weren't thinking about them. I know I was. I was sure she was as well.

A few weeks after Rebecca died, I was looking through the closet for a pair of gloves. What I found instead was one of those baby name books. I never knew Rebecca had purchased one, and given the hiding place, I guess that's how she wanted it. Of course. How could you have something like that lying around and *not* get into a name discussion?

I sat down on the floor in front of the closet, taking a few seconds before opening the book. In the movies the bereaved husband would've found a lost Christmas present or secret diary. Heavy-handed, tears never in doubt. But reality is usually more subtle. Still, I didn't know quite how to react. I began flipping through the pages, glancing at a circled name here, a checked name there. It was the kind of book that also included supposed meanings. I read a few. *Shayna* meant "beautiful." *Trevor* meant "prudent." *Jake* meant "held in esteem."

Then I came across it. Tucked in the page that ended the *S*'s and began the *T*'s was a little piece of white paper. On it was a list. Not of potential baby names, though. This was different. Rebecca had written a sentence near the top. It read, *Things we will teach our child . . .* Underneath, she'd jotted down the following:

To love.
To laugh.
To laugh some more.
To listen and learn.
To say please and thank you.
To have opinions.
To respect those of others.
To be honest.
To be a friend.
To be yourself.

How long I stayed there on the floor I can't remember. I read what Rebecca had written over and over until I memorized it. I even put the paper down at one point to test myself. When I passed, I picked the paper up and put it back in the book. The next day, I went to a bank and rented a safe deposit box. I placed the book in it. I told myself that if I ever forgot any part of Rebecca's list, I'd come and remind myself.

I've yet to go back.

FOUR

There was a brief message waiting for me when I arrived at my office Monday morning. It was from Mila, or *Mamka* (Czech for *Mom*) as I was fond of calling her. I think she was fond of my calling her that as well. She'd never had any kids.

Mamka, aka Mila Benninghoff, was my secretary, bookkeeper, insurance company liaison, and all-around godsend. At seventy, she made it look easy. Then again, having lived in Prague for both the Nazi and Soviet invasions, she knew from hard.

The setup the two of us had was ideal, albeit a little unorthodox. Mila oversaw the scheduling of my appointments, my correspondence, my billing, and pretty much everything else going on in my day-to-day life. All from her apartment. Which was fine by her and exactly how I wanted it. Two reasons. One, the workload didn't mandate someone's sitting out in my reception area full-time, particularly since I never took calls during a session. Two, it had been my experience that receptionists tended to make some people in therapy uncomfortable, and those people generally had enough to be uncomfortable about on their own.

So from her rent-controlled, one-bedroom apartment near Gramercy Park, Mila would call me in between my appointments to pass along any messages—those she fielded herself and those forwarded by my answering service. As for Mila's message that afternoon, it regarded the opening in my schedule created by Kevin Daniels's departure for Hollywood. I'd told her about it, and she was going to get back to me after checking the waiting list.

A lot of therapists have waiting lists. But of course, a lot of prospective patients don't wait around on them. Manhattan offers its citizens a bevy of professionals to treat every ailment from head to toe. Especially the head. The number of shrinks alone numbers well over a thousand. Which means that no matter how highly recommended a doctor may be, there's always someone else equally as recommended. Besides, waiting around for a new refrigerator or car is one thing. Waiting around for a new outlook is quite another. Still, the occasional holdout isn't that uncommon. As was the case that morning.

"David, it turns out there is someone on the list," began Mila's message. "His name is Sam Kent, and he'll be your Thursday, four o'clock."

I wrote it down in my calendar.

Right this way, sir.
Being on *The Charlie Rose Show* doesn't get you a better table at a New York restaurant. What it does get you is a few curious stares from the people actually seated at those better tables. They think they know you from somewhere, only they can't figure out where. You can see it in their eyes. You walk by and they stare, and for a moment you're the center of their attention. But only for a moment. Because when they inevitably—and it is always inevitably—can't put a name to your face, they return to their meals without giving it another thought. Like they never saw you in the first place. Such is the limbo of being quasirecognizable.

However, that particular afternoon, the reservation wasn't in my name. It was under Coyne, as in Debra Walker Coyne, my esteemed literary agent. I was meeting her for lunch at the Four Seasons to discuss the outline for my second book. Debra, it

should be noted, had eaten lunch in the Grill Room at the Four
Seasons at least twice a week for the past seven years. She also
tipped like a rock star. Consequently, her table didn't come any
better.

The published psychologist . . .

The reason there was going to be a second book was due to
the surprise success of my first, *The Human Pendulum*. It spent
eleven weeks on the *Times* nonfiction bestseller list, which, in
turn, prompted a fair amount of publicity and interviews, including my chat with Charlie Rose.

If I believed in such things, there'd be significant temptation
to ascribe my book's success to cosmic reparations. Meaning that
were it not for Rebecca's death, I never would've written the
damn thing. When she was alive, I had no desire to be an author.
When she was dead, I still had no desire. What I had, however,
was time. Suddenly, lots of time. And just enough sense to realize that filling this time would require a better hobby than grief.

So I wrote a book. It was safer than taking up hang gliding. It
was also a distraction that still afforded me privacy. A welcome
paradox.

Did I fully know what I was doing? Absolutely not. In fact,
had I even a smidgen of knowledge about publishing—what
generally sold and what didn't—I would've nixed the idea at the
outset. How many people, after all, could've been seriously interested in David Remler's sardonic take on human behavior?

Plenty, it turned out.

Though not without a lot of help from the gods of timing. It
happened like this. Months before my book was published, a
rabbi from the Upper West Side was arrested for murder. Not
quite your everyday event, even in Manhattan. According to the
district attorney's office, the rabbi, who was married, was supposedly having a sexual relationship with a female member of
his congregation. When the affair went sour and the woman
threatened to expose him, he allegedly went to her apartment
and strangled her.

At first, the evidence seemed overwhelming. The rabbi's fingerprints were at the scene and a nosy neighbor had seen him leaving. On top of that, the woman was strangled with wire, the gauge of which matched that of a half-used spool found in the rabbi's home.

Finally, there was the diary. The woman had kept a detailed—one might say obsessive—daily account of her relationship with the rabbi. Apparently, it was a creepy read. Like *Fatal Attraction* with a yarmulke. Particularly fascinating were the numerous references to the rabbi's threatening to harm the woman if she betrayed his trust. The last entry—the smoking entry, if you will—was dated the morning of the woman's death. It read, simply: *I think he's going to kill me today.*

Needless to say, the arrest of the rabbi and the ensuing trial were perfect fodder for every news outlet in the city. The case also attracted some national attention. Why not? It was a whopping good story. It had murder, it had sex, it had religion.

Then, before I knew it, it had me.

All thanks to one Ethan Greene. Ethan was a very enterprising young prosecutor with the Manhattan D.A.'s Office. He was also on the spot. His superiors were convinced they had their man, rabbi or not, and in Ethan Greene, they believed they had the right prosecutor to nail him.

Ethan was intuitively smart, incredibly polished, and had no reservations about putting a rabbi away for life. Best of all he was Jewish. The image of Ethan fighting for not only justice but the sanctity of his own religion was deemed to be just the right touch—both in the courtroom and in the court of public opinion.

Despite all the evidence, though, the case turned out to be anything but a slam dunk. The rabbi claimed the woman was very unstable and had somehow decided the two of them were destined to be romantically involved. In fact, she spoke as if they already were, often referring to conversations and secret meetings between them that had never happened. That would explain her diary.

The rabbi said he'd tried to counsel the woman, while also being quite clear about the impossibility of his ever being more to her than a spiritual adviser. As for his being at the woman's apartment, he was merely making a house call. The woman had become increasingly belligerent over the previous weeks, and he was trying one last time to help. It was no use, though. On that day, said the rabbi, he left the woman's apartment firmly believing she needed psychiatric care. He went so far as to call a hospital to inquire about a program. Phone records indicated as much.

Was the rabbi telling the truth?

Or was he lying to save himself?

No matter how the jury was digesting the rabbi's story, the defense would still have to address the question: *Who, then, killed the woman?*

Simple. She killed herself.

It could've happened. Or so suggested a medical expert put on the stand by the rabbi's defense team. Suicide by self-garroting. Physically achievable, claimed the expert. He'd read the autopsy report, and in his opinion the self-garroting scenario couldn't be ruled out. Especially with there being no real indication of a struggle. The expert went on to cite two other cases in which the same type of suicide was thought to have occurred. He also managed to remind the jury three times that he was a professor at Harvard Medical School. His bow tie was blue with yellow polka dots.

The defense lawyers strutted as if they had it all figured out. The woman had strangled herself with a strip of picture wire common to a million households. She was despondent over being romantically rejected. She was also angry. Enough to want to make the suicide look like a murder.

Suddenly, things were looking up for the rabbi.

That's when I got the call from Ethan Greene.

Having read a little about the trial in the paper, I thought I knew immediately what he wanted. A way to come back at the defense. Testimony from a psychologist saying that the woman's profile made her incapable of inventing a love affair, let alone ending her life in such extreme fashion and with such malice. That had to be it, right?

Wrong.

Profile *shmofile*. Ethan Greene's problem wasn't the woman but the jury, he said. Above everything else he had to convince them it was *okay* to convict a rabbi. That none of them would suffer from any plagues. That they'd still be able to sleep at night, having put away a "holy man."

"Fair enough, but why me?" I asked.

Ethan explained. He'd first heard of me over a plate of spaghetti and marinara. A dinner with an old college friend, the two discussing the dilemma presented by the rabbi. Ethan's friend, who himself was a budding psychologist, mentioned my book and how it might apply. Ethan purchased *The Human Pendulum* the following morning. He liked what he read.

He loved one part in particular.

> I'm reminded of the woman who killed her children the same month she won a "Teacher of the Year" award. Then there's that nice family man who raised millions of dollars for charity yet one day dragged a guy out of his car and kicked him to death—all because the guy had the temerity to honk at him after the light turned green.
>
> These are stories we hear from time to time and will continue to hear time and time again. They won't go away. Nonetheless, we persist in thinking of them as aberrations. Anomalies to the spectrum of human behavior.
>
> Quickly, we try to ascertain the mitigating factors. Medication the person was taking. A suppressed trauma from childhood. Postpartum depression, excessive stress, the playing of violent video games. Anything and everything. Just so long as we don't have to confront the disturbing reality head-on: *good people can do very bad things*. Because to accept that notion is the

ultimate self-indictment. It means we're all capable of doing the unspeakable.

It means that we're all at risk on the Human Pendulum.

Pride and hubris. Anger and frustration. Love and obsession. Fear and anxiety. Jealousy and spite. Sadness and depression. The list goes on. Feelings that are universal to the human experience and can exist in nearly endless combinations and potency. They can blur the sense of right and wrong, and they can affect someone's ability to cope no matter how resilient—how "good"—that person might appear to be. Fortunately, the vast majority of these feelings rarely have dire consequences. But look out for that very stubborn minority.

Which is not to say that your friendly, law-abiding neighbor will be chopping up his entire family with an ax anytime soon. Only that out there somewhere, *somebody's* friendly, law-abiding neighbor will be. And right now he doesn't even know it. As troubling as that may sound, it could be worse.

You could be that neighbor.

My initial response to Ethan's plea for help was a polite yet firm no. He persisted, though, pointing out that my testimony could be crucial in getting the jury to accept what they already knew—that the rabbi, like the rest of us, wasn't impervious to temptation. The man had made an all-too-human bad decision and in his efforts to conceal it had made another bad decision. Really bad.

Still, I continued to say no to Ethan—and he continued to implore me. Back and forth we went. Eventually, I figured he'd get the point. That's when the real point was made clear. Ethan wasn't exactly *asking*.

"The fact is, Dr. Remler, you will be testifying in my case. The only question is whether you'll be a friendly witness or a hostile one. Personally, I don't like subpoenas. They're a lot of paperwork and a pain in my ass. But if that's what it's going to take, so be it."

Well, when you put it that way . . .

Two days later I got called to the stand and somewhat nervously spoke to the unfortunate but undeniable reality that there's no tenured status for do-gooders. Human behavior, I said at one point while quoting from my book, is like the fine print of a mutual fund prospectus: *past performance doesn't guarantee future results.*

I never once looked at the rabbi. For the most part, I fixed my gaze on Ethan while intermittently acknowledging the jury. To my eyes they seemed as if they really didn't give a damn about Dr. David Remler and his precious little book. My wish not to partake in the undoing of the rabbi was, by all appearances, going to be fulfilled. When I stepped down from the stand, Ethan gave me a shrug that I took to mean "Well, it was worth a shot."

Closing arguments came the next day. The verdict three days after that. When the jury had asked for a transcript of the testimony from the Harvard professor and his self-garroting scenario, the smart money was on the rabbi. The legal pundits on cable were pretty much all in agreement. Not guilty. I was prone to agree.

Of course, I of all people should've known better than to try to predict human behavior. *This just in,* announced the radio host of the jazz station I listened to when eating lunch in my office. I sat there at my desk with half a tuna sandwich and stared at the small stereo on my shelf, waiting to hear if it would be one word or two. It was one.

Guilty.

Ethan Greene had prevailed. Later that night, I'd watch on the news as he stood in front of the courthouse after the verdict was read and spoke to reporters. He chose his words carefully. He praised the work of his department and the wisdom of the jury. He answered, "Satisfied," when asked how he felt, and cautioned that "happy" could never be used to describe his feelings in a case like this. A woman had died, after all, and the man who killed her, a onetime pillar of the community, had now left that community searching for answers. There could be no happiness in that.

Then it happened. The footage of Ethan switched to footage of some older Hispanic woman. She looked familiar. It took me a second before I realized where I'd seen her before. Yes, of course. She'd been in the first row, third from the right. Like it or not, we were in the age of the postverdict juror interview, and here was this woman, one of the jurors, telling the reporter what had really influenced her decision. She mentioned briefly the facts of the case and how the prosecuting attorney had been very persuasive. "But I guess what really made the difference for me was that psychologist witness. The one with the book."

Ditto, said the young man in a business suit standing next to her. He'd sat somewhere in the second row of the jury box; I couldn't remember exactly where. While the Hispanic woman nodded, he claimed it was my testimony that helped him overcome what had been one of his main obstacles: *believing a rabbi could ever do such a thing.*

Ten seconds later, my phone was ringing. I picked it up to hear Parker howling. He and Stacy had been at home watching the same news channel. "Congratulations," said Parker. "You're about to become a bestselling author."

"What makes you say that?" I asked.

"Because you just single-handedly diminished, if not demolished, one of the oldest tenets of trial law: the character witness. Now every attorney and law prof in the land will have to read your book to see what all the fuss was about," he said. "You wait."

I didn't have to wait long. Within a few days, my editor called to say that an immediate second printing of the book had been ordered. The sales reps were getting inundated with calls from law school campus bookstores. The major chains and independents were beginning to ring in as well. They all wanted more copies of *The Human Pendulum*. ASAP.

Cut to my esteemed literary agent, Debra Walker Coyne. She was fielding calls from a horde of news programs, all wanting me to make an appearance. To Debra this meant one thing and one thing only: more books sold. So it was a no-brainer. I would naturally say yes.

"*What, are you fucking crazy?*" she yelled at me through the phone.

"Maybe I am," I told her. "All I know for sure is that I'd rather have the book speak for itself."

"David, it's a book. BOOKS CAN'T SPEAK! It's their authors who can, and when they do it sells *more* of their books. What part of this are you not understanding?"

I got the same treatment from my editor. Frustration. Bafflement. Profound disbelief. The kind of laughing that had nothing to do with funny. I couldn't blame them. They were both trying to do their job, and I wasn't letting them. To my agent I was the pain-in-the-ass client. To my editor I was the pain-in-the-ass author. I had some nerve.

Ultimately, I relented. I agreed to do one show. Debra called to say she could get me on with Charlie Rose. Before I could say yes or no, she added that if I turned it down she'd come over to my office and knee me in the balls so hard I'd need a crowbar to take a piss. The woman certainly had a way about her.

"Tell me where and when and I'll be there," I said.

By the time the show aired, Parker's prediction had come true. I was a *New York Times* bestselling author.

Skip ahead to the Four Seasons.

"Are you going to eat that?" asked Debra. She'd polished off her salade Niçoise and was now lunging forkfirst into my risotto with white truffles, a specialty of the house, or so the waiter claimed.

"You really do get fifteen percent of everything, don't you?" I joked.

Debra laughed. It was her most recognizable feature. Like a PEZ dispenser, she'd snap her head back as she emptied her lungs of every last breath of air, the resulting sound falling somewhere between that of a hog caller and a train whistle.

"Agent humor. Very fucking funny, David," she said as her fork went in again for my risotto. That was Debra all right. A Prada-wearing, profanity-spewing tornado of a woman who could make coffee nervous. "So talk to me," she continued. "Tell me what my bestselling author has planned for his second book."

I put my utensils at three o'clock, took a sip of water, and told her what I was thinking.

There's still a chance I'll write it one day.

FIVE

The American Blind Spot continues to grow and fester as if it were a plague," said Marcus, pissed off as usual. "My latest example: drivers who say thank you to toll collectors. Like those people in the booth are doing us a favor by taking our money. I mean, David, is that ridiculous or what?"

"Maybe it's just friendly," I offered.

"Ah, fuck friendly," he said with a dismissive wave.

My Thursday, three o'clock. Marcus Owen. An established sculptor with a touch of hostility. Under the guise of learning to be tolerant, he was basically paying me so he could vent. With two ex-wives, one estranged teenage daughter, and zero friends to speak of, that's what it had come to.

Every week Marcus would jump-start our session by giving me his latest example of people who are unable to see how stupid, rude, or pathetic they really are. The American Blind Spot, he named it. One time, after Marcus had made a rare sojourn out of Manhattan to visit his sister in Denver, the example he cited was people on airplanes. *Why does everyone think it's okay to use the back of my seat to help them get out of theirs? Don't they realize I'm connected to the seat they're pushing off of?* Another time he railed against actors who get involved with each other while filming the same movie. *Dammit, that's not love. That's proximity.*

Tough to disagree.

Somewhere along the line I commented to Marcus that the vast majority of his examples could apply to people anywhere. I asked him why he referred to it as strictly the *American* Blind Spot.

Marcus considered the question. He scratched his head, shrugged his shoulders. *I don't know. I guess it's because I've never been out of the country.*

At ten of four I said good-bye to Marcus and spent the remainder of the hour taking notes on the session. I'd long since figured out that learning to be tolerant is like learning to be tall. You either are or you aren't. So helping Marcus was a matter of perception, not reality. It was all about appearances. If they can sell shoe inserts to make a man look two inches taller, I could instruct Marcus on how to appear more understanding of others. Some would call that disingenuous. I would call it Marcus not dying a very lonely man.

At four on the nose, I double-checked my calendar for the correct name of my new patient. Mr. Sam Kent, according to Mila. My Thursday, four o'clock. I got up from my desk and opened the door to the reception area. What I saw wasn't quite what I expected. I hesitated.

"Is something wrong?" she asked.

Sitting on the couch against the wall was a woman, a black shoulder bag by her side. She was wearing a long raincoat with a high collar, and a Yankees baseball cap, the rim barely clearing her eyes. A soft blue.

"I'm sorry," I answered. "You're not—"

"I am," she said. "Sam Kent. Short for Samantha." She stood and we shook hands.

"Dr. Remler. But call me David."

"Okay, David."

I hesitated again. "You don't have a deep voice, though."

"Excuse me?"

"My secretary told me you were *Mr.* Sam Kent," I said. "The Sam name notwithstanding, I assume you spoke with her."

"E-mailed, actually. When I first called a few months back, I got your service. I gave them my e-mail address because I was moving and my phone number would be changing. Your secretary and I ultimately traded e-mails."

"Well, that explains it," I said. "Come on in." I motioned with my arm, and Sam Kent stepped into my office. She removed her raincoat. She had on blue jeans and a red sweatshirt.

"Where should I sit?" she asked. They always did.

"Sofa or chair, whichever you prefer."

She preferred the chair, a wingback opposite mine. We both sat. I crossed my legs and looked at my new patient. A sudden change. She was now visibly upset.

"I'm sorry," she said, wiping away a tear. "I promised myself I wouldn't do it, but I still did. Right off the bat, no less."

"You mean cry?"

"No," she said. "Lie."

"What about?"

"You asked me whether I had talked to your secretary. I told you about my e-mailing, why I didn't give a phone number. I said it was because I was moving." She wiped away another tear. "I was never moving."

I got up, grabbed a box of tissues off my desk, and walked it over to her. She took one and dabbed her eyes.

"Okay, so you were never moving," I said, returning to my chair. "I take it there was some other reason you didn't want to give out your phone number."

"It's the same reason that I'm here," she said.

"Which is what?"

She took a moment. "My husband," she answered softly. "It's because of my husband."

I sat there thinking about how to go forward. It's always about going forward. Usually, a first session is nothing more than an extended introduction. A relaxed atmosphere with the implicit understanding that there's plenty of time in the weeks ahead to "get into" everything. The immediate concern is getting to know each other.

Or maybe not.

Occasionally, a patient delves right in to things. Whatever it is he or she is carrying around has grown beyond heavy. It's high time to unload. This was one such occasion.

"Your husband . . . what is it about him, Sam, that brings you here?"

She reached for another tissue. Wiped her eyes. Proceeded to look right into mine. "I'm here because I want to kill him," she said.

I didn't flinch. Language and meaning have a way of betraying each other. "When you say you want to kill him, are you speaking literally or figuratively?" I asked.

"Both," she said. "Though as you might imagine, it's the *literally* that has me worried."

"That you might actually do it?"

"That, and how I could be so crazy even to think such a thing."

"Believe it or not, that doesn't make you crazy," I told her.

"I beg to differ."

"Yeah, on second thought, you're right. You're probably nuts."

It was all I wanted, and I got it. A smile. Brief but definitely there.

I continued: "Let's put your murdering ways on the back burner for a moment. I'm still a little confused about how your husband has anything to do with not giving out your phone number."

"That's easy," she said. "Say your office calls and he picks up or he hears a message. I couldn't have that. He simply can't find out I'm seeing a therapist."

"Why's that?"

"Because he'd know I'd be talking about him."

"He wouldn't like that, huh?"

"You have no idea."

She was right. I had no idea. That would have to change. While there was no rush, I chose to seize the opportunity she was giving me. "Do you mind talking a little more about your husband?"

"What do you want to know?"

"Anything you feel like sharing."

"I'd do better if you asked me questions."

"Okay," I said. "What does he do for a living?"

"He's a venture capitalist. He and a partner have a firm downtown."

"Wall Street?"

"That's where the money is, he likes to say."

"Does he work a lot?" I asked.

"All the time."

"Is the firm successful?"

"Very," she said. The subtext being *very* very.

"What about children? Do you have any?"

"A little boy," she said, her expression warming. "He's two."

"How is your husband with him?"

The warm expression disappeared. "Like I said, he works all the time."

"Did he want to have children?"

"I think what he wanted was an heir," she said.

"And how many years have you been married?"

"Five."

"Do you love him?"

"I just told you I wanted to kill him. What do you think?"

"I think you haven't answered the question."

"No, of course not," she said. "I don't love him."

"Did you ever?"

She thought about it. "I believe I did once. Early on."

"If you had to tell me why you think you loved him then, what would you say?"

"I'd say he was handsome, rich, and charming."

"The trifecta," I said.

"So I thought. He's still handsome and rich. Turns out he's not so charming."

"Do you fight a lot?"

"Not anymore," she said. "Fighting assumes you still care."

"Which I guess begs the question: why haven't you left him?"

"Because if I did, he'd be the one killing me."

Here we go again, I thought. "Literally?" I asked.

"Figuratively," she answered. "He told me that if I tried to divorce him he'd make sure I'd never get custody of our son."

"How would he accomplish that?"

"Do we have to talk about it now?"

"Not if you don't want to."

"I think I just need a little time with that one."

"Fair enough," I said. "As for my next question, you can chalk it up to professional obligation. Has he ever hit you?"

She laughed, shook her head. "No. He's too smart for that. Any man can hit a woman. But only he knows how to render one helpless."

"Which is how?"

"You name it," she said. "Condescension. Ridicule. He belittles my every move, questions my every motive. He's turned my family against me, as well as most of my friends. He has no problem telling me I'm not as pretty as I once was. Or as thin. Would you like me to keep going?"

"Not for my benefit," I said. "However, when he says and does these things, what do you say and do in return?"

"That's the problem," she replied. "I wish I could say I gave it right back. I wish I was that strong. I'm not. It hurts too much. And the worst part is, he knows it. It's like he feeds off of it."

With that, the timing seemed right. At some point during every first session I asked the same question. So it was with Sam Kent. "What do you want to gain by coming here?"

She looked away for a few seconds and stared at the wall. When she looked back at me, her eyes were on the verge of more tears. "The strength to stand up to him," she said. "Once and for all."

She reached for another tissue, and I decided to keep the remainder of the session as light as possible. We talked about her background. A topline with no probing. She'd been raised in

Larchmont, north of Manhattan. Only child. Parents retired in Tempe, Arizona. Dad called her Sam for short and it stuck. She graduated from Brown. Worked in fashion. Dreamed of being a designer. Ended up working as a buyer for Bergdorf's. Met her husband at a trunk show. Zegna. Or was it Armani? She couldn't remember.

After fifty minutes, we agreed to meet once a week. Same day and time. Thursday, four o'clock. The subject turned to payment. She reiterated how important it was that her husband not know she was going to a therapist. "Everything's joint with us moneywise. He sees all my checks and credit card charges," she said. "Can I pay you in cash?"

I told her I didn't see why not.

She reached into her shoulder bag and removed a bank envelope. Three crisp one-hundred-dollar bills were taken out and handed to me.

"I have to admit, this is a first," I said.

"I'm sorry."

"Don't be, it's fine. Though if you don't mind my asking, wouldn't your husband notice the bank withdrawal?"

"A girl has to have her walking-around money, doesn't she?" Sam put her raincoat back on and adjusted her Yankees cap. It was one of those fashionable kinds, styled to look as if it were old. Instead of the traditional dark blue with white lettering, it was made from gray flannel.

"Are you a fan?" I asked.

"My uncle was a season ticket holder while I was growing up. He took my dad and me to a lot of games. Pretty good memories."

"I bet."

We shook hands.

"So I'll see you next week," she said.

"Absolutely."

Sam Kent. Samantha Kent. Mrs. Samantha Kent. She left my office, and I sat behind my desk to jot down notes. I always wrote. Never typed. Even my book was written in longhand.

Yes, I owned a computer. I also owned a waffle iron. Both items were used with the same frequency.

I recorded the bare essentials. A physical description of her: early thirties, attractive, affluent without pretense. A few facts about her background: places lived, jobs, anything else that could've possibly shaped who she was. Finally, a summation of the issues touched on. Some patients took months to open up. Sam had taken minutes. In bullet-point fashion, I recounted the conversation about her husband.

Her *husband*.

I never once asked his name. That was intentional. If she'd offered it up, fine. My experience, however, was that it was harder for some patients to be as forthcoming about their problems when discussing others by name. Fact was, Sam Kent was going behind her husband's back. That he might have deserved it made the situation no less stressful. Her husband, therefore, would remain "the husband" as far as I was concerned. Be it consciously or not, that little shred of privacy she could afford him would in turn afford her the opportunity to be more honest.

The mind works in mysterious ways. So must a psychologist.

SIX

"Hello, David."

"Hi, Mamka," I said. "Rád teˇvozím."

Mila chuckled. "You just told me it was good to drive me."

"Damn. I thought I had that one. How do you say 'It's good to see you'?"

"Rád teˇvidím," she replied, her accent kicking in perfectly.

"Isn't that what I said?"

"No, you said *vozím* instead of *vidím*."

"Vozím . . . vidím . . . potato . . . pot*ah*to. You have to admit I was close, though, wasn't I?"

"Yes, you're getting much better, David."

"And you're a lousy liar, Mamka."

She had come to my office for her regularly scheduled visit. Every other Tuesday at five o'clock. The main purpose of our meeting was for me to sign checks she'd brought along. Utilities, the lease, and other things relating to the practice. Occasionally, I also signed books. People would call and ask Mila if they could send a copy of *The Human Pendulum* for me to autograph. Some wanted it for their library. Others, while never admitting it, wanted it for eBay. Either way, like a commercial for a K-TEL product, Mila would tell all of them to include two dollars for shipping and handling, and allow four to six weeks for delivery.

"By the way," I said to her after signing the last of the checks. "My new patient, Mr. Sam Kent? He's not a he. He's a she."

"You mean he's a transvestite?"

Mila had perhaps lived in New York too long.

"No," I said. "What I mean is, Sam Kent is actually a woman. Sam is short for Samantha."

"I'm sorry, I just assumed—"

"Don't worry about it," I told her. "I would've done the same thing. Anyway, for reasons I can't go into—you know, patient privacy and all—she's going to be paying me in cash. So if you could deposit this with the rest of the checks," I said, handing her the three hundred dollars Sam had given me.

"Sure." She took one of the bills and held it up to the light.

"What are you doing?"

"You can never be too sure," she said, staring at the bill.

Mila had *definitely* lived in New York too long.

"Does it look real?" I asked with mock concern.

"As far as I can tell." Mila put the cash in a folder she used for the checks. "Oh, one other thing," she said. "Don't forget, you've got the Kesper Society cocktail party this Friday."

I frowned. "Can't you write me a note? You know, say I'm too sick to attend?"

She frowned back. "Now what kind of Mamka would I be if I did something like that?"

"The best kind."

Two days later and Marcus was at it again. His latest installment of the American Blind Spot. "You know what really bugs the shit out of me?" he said with a slight snarl. "All these rap stars who get famous singing about killing cops. Then they go ahead and get parts in movies and TV shows. What do they end up playing? *Fuckin' cops.*"

I had to admit it. It was definitely one of his better ones.

At four o'clock I welcomed Sam Kent back to my office. Her jeans and sweatshirt were replaced by a sharp-looking gray flannel suit. There was makeup and jewelry. Her blond hair, which had last been tucked beneath a Yankees cap, was now straight down and long. A very polished look.

"I think you've exceeded the dress code," I said.

"Fancy lunch with a girlfriend," she explained while dropping into the wingback chair opposite mine. "By the way, I confided in her about coming to see you, and she knew exactly who you were. Apparently, she read some article on you."

"Is that right?"

"Yes, and to listen to her talk I think she has a crush on you," she said.

"I'm flattered."

"You should be. She's very attractive and very single."

"Then I'm doubly flattered," I said.

"I'll relay the message. In the meantime, can I ask you a personal question?"

"I thought that was my job."

"I know," she said. "It's just that my girlfriend mentioned you lost your wife a few years back. Is that true?"

"Yes, it's true."

"I'm so sorry."

"Thank you."

"I was wondering . . ." Her voice trailed off.

"What is it?"

"Well, did it help or hurt more that you were a psychologist? What I mean is, given what you do for a living, I'd think you'd be almost too aware of your emotions, or at least your expected emotions, to grieve as one normally would."

A lot of patients did this. Assumed that because they were revealing their deepest, darkest, most intimate secrets they were entitled to know anything and everything about me. It was an occupational hazard that required me to walk a fine line. I couldn't tell them that my personal life was none of their business even though it was. That would jeopardize the trust and openness all therapy is based on. So, instead, I became a master of the seamless segue. I'd throw out an honest tidbit about me that related as much if not more to them. I was about to do exactly that when Sam caught herself.

"What am I *doing*?" she said with a gasp. "This is *so* none of my business. I apologize; I don't know what I was thinking."

"It's okay," I said. Which it was. It was also pretty refreshing.

"This is about me and let's keep it that way," she said. "What should we talk about today?"

"Anything you want."

"That's too open-ended. Like I told you last week, you need to ask me questions."

"Okay, here's one," I replied immediately. "You mentioned that if you tried to divorce your husband he'd make sure you'd never get custody of your son. My question again is, how would he do that?"

"So much for easing into things."

"You plan on telling me eventually, don't you?"

"I suppose."

"Then why wait?"

"Because I don't like to think about it," she said.

"Perhaps by telling me you—"

"I tried to kill myself," she said, her voice remaining calm.

I expected to see tears from her. There weren't any. Her face was expressionless.

"When did this happen?" I asked.

"A few years ago."

"Before you were pregnant?"

"*God*, yes."

"What is it you did?"

"I swallowed thirty Halcions with a bottle of wine," she said. "Pinot Grigio, I think."

"Yet, here you are today," I said.

"My husband found me. He was supposed to be out to dinner with a client. The client called him at the restaurant to cancel—some type of emergency at home. Ironic, huh? Anyway, my husband came back to our place and there I was."

"Lucky for you."

"At the time I didn't see it that way."

"I can imagine," I said with a nod. "Tell me, what did your husband do?"

"You mean after he broke down the door to our bedroom to get to me? Well, let's see. He saw the empty bottle of pills near the bed and asked how long it had been since I took them. I told him it had been long enough, or something like that, which it clearly hadn't because I was still pretty lucid. My husband then went to the medicine cabinet and grabbed a bottle of ipecac. I didn't even know we had something like that in the house. He obviously did. He force-fed me a couple of ounces, and the next thing I knew I was puking my guts out. Thirty pills had gone down; twenty-eight came back up."

Sam Kent folded her legs and stopped talking. I had been waiting for the part about her husband calling the hospital. She hadn't mentioned it.

"What happened next?" I asked.

"I slept like a baby and woke up the next morning."

"You didn't go to the hospital?"

"No."

"Why not?"

"I knew I was going to be all right. At least physically," she said. "That night, a hospital wasn't going to do anything for me mentally. I assured my husband I didn't need to go."

"He was okay with that?"

"More than okay, I think. I'm sure he felt relieved," she said. "In fact, this is him in a nutshell: better to have a wife who committed suicide than a wife who's known to all his friends and associates as the one who'd *tried* to commit suicide. Going to the hospital meant there was a good chance the story would get out. Serious dirty laundry. Bad for business and really bad on the cocktail circuit."

"So you never told anyone about that night?" I asked.

"Not until this moment, no."

"And your husband?"

"Not a soul. Or should I say, not a soul *yet*. Because that's his leverage. It's also the answer to your original question," she said. "If I ever file for divorce he swears he'll tell the court about my trying to kill myself. Which means there goes my son." Her eyes narrowed and her jaw tightened. "Courts don't award custody to suicidal mothers."

"It's not as cut and dry as you think," I said. "Determinations have to be made. Usually by folks like me. In your case, you weren't a mother when this happened. It was a few years ago. Things change. People change. Ultimately, a court might trust that you pose no risk to yourself."

"That's the problem. The word *might*. There's too much at stake for me to put faith in a word like that."

"So instead you've been living the alternative—a compromised life with your husband."

"Because it meant being with my son, yes."

"Now you see and feel the consequences," I said. "How it's no life at all."

"That would be an understatement."

"It's strange, though, Sam. The more I listen to you, the less I understand your husband and his possible motivations. What's in it for him?"

"The ultimate freedom, that's what," she replied. "He does whatever he wants, whenever he wants. He even does *who*ever he wants."

"You're saying he's had affairs?"

She nodded.

"You sure?"

"As sure as I need to be," she said.

"Have you confronted him about it?"

"What for? He'd just deny it and accuse me of being paranoid. That's the way it is with him."

I had no follow-up to that. Not a single comment. I simply sat there looking at Sam Kent, seeing the obvious: a woman who needed out of her marriage, and fast. She knew it too. That's why she'd come to me. To give her the strength to walk away, she'd said. The only real question remaining was how I was going to accomplish that.

"What are you thinking, David?" she asked, breaking the silence.

"I'm thinking you deserve better," I said.

SEVEN

Free legal advice. That's why it's good to have at least one friend who's a lawyer. I'd sometimes shared that observation with Parker just to tweak him. Or, at other times, as a segue into asking him for what I wanted. Which was, of course, free legal advice.

I dialed his office the next morning, a Friday, between my ten and eleven o'clock sessions. His secretary put me through.

"Can I pick your brain for a minute?" I asked.

"There's not much left by the end of the week but go ahead," he said.

"It's about a patient of mine . . ."

"Whoa, it must be serious."

"Why do you say that?"

"Because you've never once told me anything about any of your patients. Not that I ever asked."

Parker was right. I'd never before talked to him about someone I was counseling. Not even in the most general, keep-the-patient's-privacy-intact kind of way.

"Well, consider this your lucky day," I said. "To hear about one of my patients is to realize how good you've got it."

"Excuse me while I withhold judgment," he said. "So what's the deal?"

"It's a woman who wants to divorce her husband," I began. "They have a two-year-old son. Before the kid was born, and before the woman knew she was pregnant, she tried to commit suicide. An entire bottle of sleeping pills in one gulp. Minutes later, though, her husband found her and got her to vomit everything up. She ended up being fine. Physically, at least. Now here's the tricky part. Not only did they not go to the hospital after it happened, they never sought out any professional counseling."

"Why not?" he asked.

"You got an hour?"

"Never mind."

"Let's just say neither wanted to deal with the aftermath," I told him. "Except now the husband is threatening to spill the beans to keep her from the kid. That is, if she tries to divorce him. So the question I've got is, if she goes through with it and files, what chance does she have at custody? How much of a role will her attempted suicide play?"

Parker sustained a low grunt. It was his official sound for mulling something over. "First off, this is family law, and I'm not," he said. "Then again, far be it from me not to think I know everything. So here we go. Will the suicide play a role? Yes. How much? Like everything else in life, it all depends. A custody case, as it should be, is geared entirely toward the well-being of the child. Anything that even hints at jeopardizing that well-being is fair game. My first question back to you is, do you think your patient is still a threat to herself?"

I thought about it for a second. "Personally, I don't," I answered. "Professionally, though, which I suppose is all that matters, I couldn't say for sure. We've only had two sessions, and making that determination hasn't been my focus. On the plus side, the suicide attempt was three years ago."

"A point in her favor," he said. "Though here's the real question: does the husband have money?"

"Yeah, why?"

"Quality of representation. Plain and simple. A good lawyer won't be banking on some doctor saying she's unfit to be a mother. He'll assume she gets the medical thumbs-up going in and make it his mission to redefine the battlefield."

"Which would be what?"

"The rest of her behavior," he said. "Specifically, those things that either show or promote questionable judgment on her part. Example: does she drink, is she taking any antidepressants, has she ever been arrested? Nothing goes unscrutinized. Everything gets magnified. One speeding ticket, okay. Two speeding tickets, and she's got a death wish. From there, the husband's lawyer will be begging the court. The words won't be this but the message will be: *if we can't even let the kid be in the same car with his mother, how can we consider letting him live in the same house?*"

I snickered. "That's brutal."

"That's family law," said Parker.

"Let's assume for a second that my patient is otherwise a model citizen," I said. "Then what?"

"Then she's got a fighting chance. Given that she's got good lawyers on her side, they'll be digging up the same dirt on the husband. Even if he's a Boy Scout, they'll be nailing him for his lack of judgment when his wife tried to check out. It was his responsibility to get her to a hospital. That he didn't take her goes beyond stupid." Parker laughed. "Suicidal mother, idiot for a father. The kid's going to grow up to wish he was adopted."

"Wonderful."

"How old did you say the kid was?" he asked.

"Two."

"Silver lining, I suppose. He won't actually remember the proceedings. You know, if you want, I can put you in touch with a guy who handles nothing but custody cases."

"I might take you up on that later," I said. "For now, what you've told me is a big help. One last thing, though. Absent of all the facts, give me her odds . . . ballpark."

That sustained low grunt from Parker again. Like the hum of a vacuum cleaner in a distant room. "Absent of all the facts? Sixty percent," he said. "Sixty-five if she's pretty."

What if she's very pretty? I wanted to ask but thought better of it. Instead, I remarked, "Those aren't such bad odds."

"No, they're not," he said. "No matter what, the mother is always the incumbent. Hey, are you sure you don't want to talk to a family guy?"

"Yeah, I'm sure. Thanks, though."

I hung up the phone and remained seated behind my desk. I stared at nothing and thought of everything.

Two sessions. That's all I'd had with her. A combined total of an hour and forty minutes. Yet there she was in my head. Sam Kent. Her voice telling me her story, the details of a life in retreat. She didn't have a marriage; she had an arrangement. A rather lopsided one at that. I could hear the sound. The catching of her breath as Sam cried in my office that first day. The gasping. It was the sound of suffocation.

I wanted to help her. In the shadow of her husband her self-esteem could barely clear a curb. I would change that. I'd help restore her confidence. Yes, I wanted to help, and there was nothing wrong with that. I wanted to help all of my patients. That was my job.

But this was different, and I knew it.

The wall was beginning to be chipped away. It had been built over years of schooling and experience, and ensured a proper separation between patient and doctor. Nothing was personal. Everything was professional. That's the way it had to be.

So put down the chisel, David. That's what I tried to tell myself.

Let the wall stand.

EIGHT

The charity function. How the haves do for the have-nots without having to look at them. A very cynical view of philanthropy and one that I was trying to shake. Unfortunately, the Kesper Society cocktail party wasn't making it any easier.

Briefly. The Kesper Society was started by one Arnold Kesper. As in the satellite-hoarding conglomerate, Kesper Communications, and as in more money than God. The man was somewhat eccentric—a personality trait not uncommon among billionaires—and he rarely missed an opportunity to reinforce the image. Countless examples could follow, although, in my opinion, not a one could match the report that Kesper had his own food-taster. I kid you not. A young man of Danish descent whose entire job was making sure no one was trying to poison his boss when he dined out.

Not exactly your résumé stuffer.

Fittingly, Kesper managed to be eccentric even with his charitable giving. In effect, he held competitions. Under the guise of better acquainting himself with all of the world's problems, he, along with his wife, would throw huge, lavish cocktail parties twice a year and invite representatives from various causes. He'd mingle with them, listen to what they had to say, and then, after presumably giving it some thought, decide how much to bestow on each cause.

The good news was that being invited to one of these parties was to know you were getting some funding. The bad news was that the exact amount could vary greatly and was a function of the impact you made in those pressure-filled few hours. Word had it that the more you kissed Kesper's ass, the more zeros were added on to your donation check.

"Pucker for the fucker, will you, David?"

That was Bennett Larson on the phone to me. He'd called two days prior to let me know he was going to be out of town for the event. I wasn't happy to hear it. Not your typical psychologist, Bennett Larson was an all-smiling, joke-telling, natural schmoozer in the "Damn glad to meet you" tradition. In other words, he was everything required to separate fat cats from their money. And he was great at it—by far, Crescent House's top "financial lobbyist." Or, as he freely admitted, the Money Whore.

Anything for a good cause, though.

Which was precisely what Crescent House was—a free psychotherapy and analysis clinic for the poor and uninsured that I'd recently been named a board member of after having volunteered there for more than two years. With only one location, in Queens, Crescent House had set its eyes on expansion. First to the other boroughs and eventually to other cities. There were plenty of therapists willing to donate their time. Some even their money. But securing the bricks and mortar, not to mention the real estate on which to break ground, required a much higher level of generosity. The Arnold Kesper variety, to be more precise.

So that Friday evening, sans Larson, I, along with some of the others filling out the Crescent House board, descended on the Great Hall at the Metropolitan Museum of Art, the site of the latest Kesper Society cocktail party. That Crescent House had been invited in the first place remained no small achievement. We'd previously tried to get on the guest list for at least three previous Kesper parties, failing each time.

Then Larson had the idea of sending Kesper a phrenology head with the inscription DECIDES TO HELP CRESCENT HOUSE placed in one of the sectioned-off squares. Why a phrenology head? I didn't know. It seemed silly and unconnected. "Precisely," said Larson to me at the time. "Silly and unconnected. Not unlike Arnold Kesper himself." Sure enough, not long after the phrenology head went out, the invitation from the Kesper Society arrived in the mail. Go figure.

"That's the thing about capitalism, really. It necessitates there be an underprivileged class. That's why those who succeed—the fortunate who flourish under capitalism—have a responsibility to give back and try to minimize the disparity and, if you will, the despair. I'm sure you'd all agree."

I nodded willingly for Arnold Kesper, as did the others from Crescent House standing with me. We were an hour and a half into the cocktail party and were finally getting our audience with "the man." One of his minions, a petite and humorless-looking woman clutching a clipboard, had rounded us up one by one out of the throng of guests. She had us all gather in a designated area before bringing over Kesper. "Mr. Kesper, may I present the representatives from Crescent House," said the woman, with a stiff arm extended. Then, in a hushed tone, she introduced each of us to her boss by name. We might as well have been at the Vatican.

Given that, maybe the question he threw at me wasn't from so far out of left field.

Up until that point, the conversation had been relatively innocuous. Kesper asked about what we did at Crescent House, and we answered the best we could. What were some of the typical problems our patients had? Did we feel we were making a difference? Where did we see Crescent House down the line? Softball lobs for the most part. Kesper expressed his admiration for our efforts and genuinely seemed to understand our objectives. He was affable. He was congenial. I was beginning to think his reputation was unfounded. Then a woman came by holding a tray of appetizers. Before Kesper reached out for one, he glanced over at a tall, blond-haired Scandinavian type standing off to the side. The guy nodded discreetly. Clearly the salmon canapés were okay to eat.

Let the weirdness begin.

As the woman and her appetizer tray moved along, Kesper spun on his heels and looked directly at me.

"Tell me, Dr. Remler, did you think he was guilty?" he asked.

"I'm sorry?" I said.

"The rabbi in that trial," said Kesper, his voice deliberate. "Did you think he was guilty? Because I'm not so convinced, to tell you the truth. I tend to think he was innocent. Though from what I understand your testimony sure did him in."

I was slightly taken aback, and I was sure my expression said as much. My involvement with that trial was the last thing I expected to be discussing with Arnold Kesper. Yet there we were, doing just that. Normally, I couldn't have been bothered by what a guy like him thought of me. But as I glanced at the other board members from Crescent House, who were collectively looking my way with a nervous "Don't blow it for us, Remler" gaze, I decided to tread lightly.

"I think it was certainly possible the rabbi was guilty," I told Kesper. "Though it was hardly a clear-cut case."

The billionaire shook his head. Mock disappointment. "That's far too diplomatic of an answer," he said. "Stop me if I'm prying too much, but I'd have to believe that deep down, you have a very strong opinion one way or the other. Am I wrong?"

"You're not wrong," I said. "I'm just thinking that it might be better if that strong opinion remained that way. Meaning, deep down."

Kesper pursed his lips. Shifted his jaw. "I suppose this is the part where I tell you how I can respect that, Dr. Remler," he said. "Though I must confess, I'd be dismayed to learn that your reticence is on account of not wanting to appear disagreeable with me. Maybe you'd like some assurance that speaking your mind will have no bearing on my intentions for Crescent House."

"I don't think that's really necessary," I said.

"Oh, come now, of course you do. It's quite well known that I'm a man of curious motivations, to say the least. The fact is, as much as this shouldn't be the case, I'd be lying if I didn't admit the following: your not indulging me about that rabbi—not revealing your innermost thoughts on his guilt or innocence—would indeed adversely impact my feelings toward Crescent House. What can I say? That's just the way it is. Perhaps, given your vocation, this isn't as shocking to you as it would be for others." Kesper turned up his palms as if feeling for rain. "Hey, I agree it might not be fair. Nonetheless, it's honest. So I'm afraid that puts us at an impasse."

All eyes settled on me, waiting for a response. I had no idea why the guy was fucking with me, but I decided to take one for the team. Damn all integrity—there were more Crescent Houses to be built. I cleared my throat. "Guilty as sin," I crowed.

"What's that?" said Kesper, who no doubt heard me perfectly.

"I said I believe the rabbi was guilty. Guilty as sin."

"Yes, that's what I thought you said." He stuck his hands in his pockets and hunched his shoulders forward. The edges of his mouth curled up high and wide. It was a physical preface to the moral of his story. In a whisper he let go, "It's amazing what we'll do for money, isn't it?"

I said nothing. Everyone said nothing. So Kesper continued, his voice now relentlessly cheerful. "Though at least in your case it was for a good cause. With most people it's usually not." His hands reappeared from his pockets, and he clapped two times loudly. "Thank you, Dr. Remler. Thank you, Crescent House. Thank you very, very much."

I watched as he backed up a few steps before walking away. His grin. His satisfaction. My utter bewilderment.

And that was Arnold Kesper.

I stuck around after that just long enough to polish off three bourbon and waters in ten minutes. Those, combined with the three rounds I had prior to meeting Kesper, meant I was extremely good to go.

Out the front of the Met and into the brisk night air. I stood there under a streetlamp for a moment, breathing it in. A moment became a minute. That's when I heard the voice over my shoulder.

"Fancy meeting you here."

NINE

I turned around and saw a figure coming down the steps. A long black dress and a red shawl draped over her shoulders. A purse held in her hand. It took me a second. A familiar person in an unfamiliar setting. Then I realized. I was looking at Sam Kent.

She negotiated the last step in her heels and walked up to me. "For a moment I thought you didn't recognize me," she said.

"For a moment I didn't," I told her. "I think this is what you call 'out of context.'"

"I know, isn't this funny? The two of us being at the same function. Though I'm surprised I didn't see you inside."

"Me too," I said. "So what wonderful cause were you shilling for?"

Sam rolled her eyes. "I should be so lucky that this would be a onetime event for me," she said. "No, I'm afraid I'm a regular at these things. My husband's firm handles the charitable trust for the Kesper Society. According to philanthropic etiquette, that makes me a member."

"Where's your husband?" I asked somewhat warily.

"Singapore," she said with a strained smile. "He always manages to be away for these things, which leaves it up to me to represent the both of us. Any other event and I'd take a pass. But for all of Arnold Kesper's eccentric, ego-driven ways, he really has helped a lot of people. Plus his wife is a hoot."

"I didn't meet her."

"That's too bad. She's very down to earth. A great counterbalance to Arnold," she said. "Nice suit, by the way."

I instinctively looked down at myself. "Thank you."

Good form would've had me returning the compliment, telling Sam she looked nice herself. Which she did. But she was a patient. At that moment I was trying hard to remember that.

"So is this uncomfortable for you?" she asked.

"What do you mean?"

"Bumping into a patient in public."

"No," I replied. "Why do you ask?"

"I don't know. Woman's intuition?"

"A highly overrated sense," I said. A wisecrack.

"Maybe for those who don't have it," she countered.

We both smiled.

"You look very nice as well," I told her.

"Thank you."

We had a small patch of silence. It occurred to me that Sam was sounding a little different that evening. A little more free and easygoing. Maybe she'd had a few drinks. Maybe it was the moment itself, our chance encounter.

She looked at her watch. "So where are you off to now?"

"I guess home," I said.

"You know, that's what I hate about these parties. They dress you up, ply you with booze, and give you just enough finger food to make you actually hungry before throwing you back out onto the street without dinner. It's a crime, really."

"I suppose it is, isn't it?"

"Absolutely." She glanced around. "Hey, you know what I should do?"

"What's that?"

"I should buy you dinner."

"You should?"

"Yes."

"And why's that?" I asked.

"Because you've been helping me. I feel I owe you," she said.

"Not with my rates, you don't."

"Money well spent, David. Which is why you should let me buy you dinner. What do you say?"

She was determined. I was hesitant. It showed.

"Wait, don't tell me," she said. "*Of course.* You're thinking how that wouldn't reflect too well upon you, the two of us being seen together. Socializing with your patients must be a no-no."

"It is kind of frowned on."

"By whom, if you don't mind me asking?"

"Those who actually care about that kind of thing."

"Does that mean you don't?"

"No, I do. I'm simply not as fanatical about it," I said. "But as far as going to a restaurant is concerned, I'm afraid appearances do come into play."

"There you have it. That's our solution."

"What is?"

"Not being seen," she said. "Instead of buying you dinner, I'll cook it for you."

"Sam, I'm not sure that—"

"What? We're two adults who happen to be hungry. There's nothing wrong with that."

"Yes, I know, but—"

"Actually, it's pretty funny when you think about it. To avoid the suggestion of impropriety we're forced to do something far more suggestive." She put a hand on her hip. Then, tongue in cheek: "So what will it be, David . . . your place or mine?"

I waved a hand in front of my face. "Am I here right now?"

"Yes, but if I let you get a word in edgewise you'll try to talk me out of it," she said. "Wait a minute, I just realized something." She stomped a heel in disappointment. "We can't go to my place. Celeste, our nanny, is there watching my son tonight. She's quite the talker, if you know what I mean. A blabbermouth, to be more precise. Her seeing you would *really* not be a good thing. Hmmm. So it looks like it's your place."

She stood there and stared at me.

At last, I had the chance to say something. It was the exact moment in which to do it. I'd give a deft explanation. Make a graceful exit . . . alone.

Instead, I said nothing. Not a word. I was too busy noticing the things I shouldn't have. The sheen of her hair. The snugness of her dress. The fact that I was seriously considering her offer.

Cool it, David.

I was a man who knew better. But I was also another man. One who hadn't felt anything for another woman in quite some time. That man had also drunk six bourbon and waters on an empty stomach. The checkpoints were lax. The alarm bells temporarily out of order.

"There's really nothing in my refrigerator," I said.

She smiled. "Don't worry, I'll make do."

Sam immediately went to the curb and began hailing a cab. Had it taken a few minutes for one to come along I probably would've got cold feet. Nixed the whole idea once and for all. But, of course, a cab rolled up within seconds. I did my best not to read too much into that.

Fate was such a big word.

T E N

Thirty blocks of pleasant conversation between the two of us and some spectacular rationalization all on my own. That was the ride back to my apartment with Sam. I kept telling myself I hadn't done anything wrong. Nor would I. Still, the red lights were a bitch, being a less than subtle implication of the need to put a stop to this.

Ten minutes later we arrived.

Doormen in New York City can be counted on for two things. The first is saying what is pleasant and expected; the second is simultaneously thinking otherwise. "Good evening, Dr. Remler" was all the one on duty said to me as Sam and I walked into my building. But to read his mind? *Hey, maybe that poor son of a bitch is finally going to get laid.* Either that or *I guess he's not gay after all.*

Sam and I had the elevator to ourselves. "I kind of miss not having them," she said after the doors closed. "Doormen, that is."

"Your building doesn't have them?"

"No, we live in a town house," she said. "When I was single, though, I lived in a doorman building. Made me feel safer."

"I'd say the same, but any time I happen to come home really late, the guy here has usually nodded off."

"That must do wonders for his Christmas tip."

"Actually, last year, instead of money I gave him a pillow."

Floors ten, eleven, and twelve. A led-crystal display charting our progress.

"How long have you lived here?" she asked.

"About three years."

She nodded slightly while appearing to put one and one together. It made three. As in how many years it had been since my wife died. Safe assumption that I would've moved to a different place in the aftermath.

Floors twenty and twenty-one. Then mine—the twenty-second.

Once in my apartment, I took off my coat and Sam handed me her shawl. I hung them both up on a hallstand. While I went to turn on some lights, she immediately disappeared on a self-guided tour. I stayed behind in the living room, stacking some newspapers and scooping up a few empty bottles of beer. For the most part, though, the degree of mess seemed well within the acceptable range for a man living on his own.

Sam called out from my library. "I guess I pictured more wood paneling," she said.

"I hope you're not disappointed."

"Quite the opposite," came back her voice. "In fact, I told myself that if I spotted a pipe rack I'd leave immediately."

She walked out of the library, turned a corner without looking at me, and headed down the hallway to the bedrooms. First the guest's, then mine. Meanwhile, I just stood there. A guy who didn't know what to do with himself in his own home.

She reappeared. "I like your place," she said. "No pretensions."

"Is that polite for 'no discernable style'?"

"No, it simply means you're not a cliché."

"Thank God for that."

She eyed a picture frame on an end table next to her. She picked it up. "Are these your parents?"

"Yes."

"They're adorable. Where was this taken?"

"On the back deck of their house out west."

"Whereabouts?"

"Santa Barbara."

"That's nice." Sam stared at the photo a little more. It was of my mother sitting in my father's lap. A couple of seventy-year-old lovebirds.

"You told me your folks live in Arizona . . . Tempe, right?"

She didn't respond.

"Sam?"

She looked up at me. "I'm sorry, what?"

"I was just saying that when we first met, you told me your parents had retired out in Tempe, right?"

"Oh," she said. "Yes."

The way she replied made me think she wanted to add something. Or, maybe, had left something out. I looked at her as she continued to stare at the picture frame in her hands.

"Is everything all right?" I asked.

Again, she looked up. "God, I'm sorry; I get this way sometimes when I look at other people's parents."

It was tempting to ask the obvious. *Why?* I was hoping, though, that she'd tell me on her own. She did.

"My parents out in Tempe are actually my adoptive parents. I didn't mention it at the time because . . . well, I just didn't."

"That's okay; you don't have to explain," I said. "Besides, you know how therapists are, we think everything has to do with parents. That would've given me twice as much to nag you about, so, really, I don't blame you."

She smiled. "That's a pretty good habit you have."

"What's that?"

"Always saying the right thing."

"Nah, I just get lucky once in a while," I said, smiling back. "Though at the risk of ruining your impression of me, do you mind if I ask you something?"

"It's about my birth mother and father, right?"

"Yes. Have you ever met them?"

She shook her head. "No. Apparently, my father died in some

factory accident before I was born. As for my mother, all I know is her address and that she's really poor, which was why she had to give me up."

"You've never wanted to make contact with her?"

"When I was younger I was far too angry about the whole thing. As I got older I started to think about it more."

"And?"

"I guess I always thought it was too complicated—and these days, as you well know, that's the last thing my life needs."

"I can see why you'd think that, but you might be surprised. Taking care of one unresolved issue can often do wonders for working out another."

"I don't know . . ."

"Just something to consider."

"It's been so long, though. I can't help thinking I'd only be meeting a stranger and not my real mother."

"Perhaps at first. In time that would change."

I could see how uncomfortable she was getting. This was turning into a session, and that was wrong. I was about to change the subject when she saw fit to change it on her own. She put the frame down. Next to it happened to be the phone.

"Do you mind if I call home?" she asked. "I want to let Celeste know where I am."

"Sure. No problem."

Sam picked up the phone and dialed. I went into the kitchen to get rid of the beer bottles. While in there I could hear her telling the nanny that she'd dropped by a friend's apartment and wouldn't be home for a bit. Sam called out to me again. "David, what's your number here?"

I walked to the entrance of the kitchen and told her. She repeated the number back to Celeste.

"I always feel I've got to give her two ways to reach me," said Sam after hanging up. "She's got my cell-phone number, but I still don't trust those things. Half the time you can never get through to someone."

"I know what you mean."

She glanced over my shoulder. "So is that the kitchen?"

"Ready and waiting," I said.

"Good. Then let the magic begin."

I followed her into the least-used room in my apartment and watched as she took a few seconds to size it up before heading for the refrigerator. "You weren't kidding," she said after opening it and taking a look.

"I know. I told you; it's a barren wasteland."

"The takeouts in the neighborhood must love you."

"Yeah, they are rather fond of me," I admitted.

Sam pivoted on her heels and eyed the cabinets. "Pasta," she said. "Tell me you've got some type of pasta."

I went and opened a cabinet by the stove. On the top shelf, behind some microwave popcorn and a couple of cans of soup, sat a box of linguine. For all I knew, it came with the apartment. "Does Ronzoni go bad?" I asked while pulling it out.

She came over and took the box from my hands. She flipped it around, ingredients-side up. "Hmmm. Does Ronzoni go bad?" she echoed. "Let's see . . . ferrous sulfate, thiamin mononitrate." She gave me a deadpan look. "Not in our lifetime, it doesn't."

We were in business. She went back to the fridge and grabbed a few things. Eggs, butter, a jar of capers I didn't know I had. She opened the freezer and started poking around.

"Your freezer burn has freezer burn," she said.

Before I could compile a witty retort, I heard an *Aha*! She stepped back and held up a package of chopped sirloin. "This will do," she said. "Now all I need is a big bowl and half your spice rack."

I got her the bowl and opened a lazy-Susan cabinet littered with various seasonings. "Do you want an apron?" I asked.

"Probably a good idea," she said.

I dug one up and gave it to her. "So, what are we making here?"

"It doesn't really have a name."

"Interesting. *The no-name linguine*. I like the sound of that."

Sam tilted her head. "Me too," she said. "It implies no responsibility on the part of the chef."

Smiling, I leaned back on the counter and watched as she got busy. Meat in the microwave to defrost. Egg whites, spices, and some capers in the bowl. "You actually know what you're doing," I said.

"It's all a facade," she replied. "Though I'm happy to learn I've got you fooled."

"Completely," I said. "Can I help in some way?"

"Nope. Remember, the idea is that I'm cooking for you."

"Give me *something* to do at least."

She thought about it for a moment. "You can open up some wine, how about that? You do have a spare bottle lying around, I hope?"

"I think so," I said. Truth be told, I knew so. Wine happened to be the holiday gift of choice for many of my patients. Over the years, I'd been given more bottles than I honestly knew what to do with. So at that moment I was quite content to know what to do with at least one of them. Nonetheless, the irony—or whatever you want to call it—was hard to ignore as I went to my dining room to fetch a bottle. Wine from one patient was about to be poured for another.

I decided on red. A Joseph Phelps '97 Cabernet that I brought back into the kitchen and uncorked. I filled two glasses. "To the no-name linguine," I said, toasting.

She raised her glass to mine. "That and to better days ahead," she added. "Much better days."

It was a natural opening.

"Listen, Sam, normally I'd be discussing this with you in my office, but given the circumstances, it makes sense to bring it up now."

"Uh-oh. Is this good news or bad news?"

"Good news," I said. "What I wanted to tell you is that I spoke to a friend of mine about your situation. He's a lawyer and—"

Her face immediately flushed with concern. "You didn't mention me by name, did you?" she asked, her voice nearly pan-icked.

"No, no, my fault," I said quickly. "I should've made that clear right away. I apologize. Not only wouldn't I do that, I couldn't."

"I'm sorry, it's just that . . ."

"No, I don't blame you for reacting that way. There's nothing I told my friend that could betray your privacy. The thing is, I wanted to get some professional advice about what you said the other day, about your husband using your suicide attempt against you to get full custody of your son."

"You mean, if I try to divorce him?"

"Exactly."

"What'd your friend say?"

"Well, first off, while he's a very good attorney, he doesn't practice family law. So this isn't definitive by any means. His take was that you stood a decent chance of winning if you went to court."

"How decent?"

"Better than a sixty percent chance," I said.

"Based on what?"

"A few things. The amount of time that's passed since the at-tempt, your not being a mother when it happened, and the most important factor of all—that you *are* a mother now." I gave her a reassuring smile. "And a good one at that, right?"

She nodded slightly. She seemed somewhat dazed.

"What is it?" I asked.

"The whole thing," she said slowly. "The prospect of having to be judged, of having everything dragged out in a courtroom. I don't know if I can handle that."

"I think you can. What's more, I think you have no choice. To listen to you these past couple of weeks is to know for sure what you *can't* handle . . . and that's your life as it is now. Wouldn't you agree?"

We were interrupted by three loud beeps. The microwave over the stove. The meat had defrosted, and I walked over to take it out. One hand pulled the door of the microwave open while the other—*shit!* I grabbed my left hand, writhing in pain.

"What happened?" she said with a gasp. Then she quickly realized. The burner was on. "Oh my God, I forgot to put the pot on it."

She felt awful. I didn't feel so good myself. I looked down at the inside of my throbbing hand. I'd been branded by a GE Profile Range.

Sam rushed to the freezer and got some ice. "I'm so sorry," she said as she began gliding a cube in circles on my palm. "I am so, so sorry."

"It's okay," I told her. "I'll be all right."

"Wait . . . butter," she said.

"What?"

"You're supposed to put butter on a burn. Here, hold this," she said, leaving the ice in my hand. She went back to the refrigerator and found a tub of Country Crock. She scooped some out and began rubbing it into my hand. "I'm such an absent-minded idiot," she said, shaking her head.

I tried to reassure her it wasn't as bad as she thought. She still seemed flustered.

"You know, technically I don't think that's butter," I said.

She looked up at me. "Huh?"

"Country Crock. In fact, I don't even think it's margarine. What's it say on the label?"

Sam picked up the tub and spun it around slowly. The more she turned it, the more befuddled she looked. "That's weird. It just says *Shedd's Spread Country Crock.* It doesn't say what it actually is."

"See, I told you. Pretty interesting choice too, their using the word *crock.*"

"Hold on, here's the good news," she said, now looking at the lid. "Whatever this stuff is, it says it's got one third fewer calories than margarine."

I glanced back down at Sam still basting my palm. "Great. We certainly wouldn't want my hand to get fat."

She laughed out loud. Kind of what I was going for. A little levity.

I was feeling better, and it appeared she was as well. That's when we both noticed. We were standing six inches apart. Facing each other. Our hands touching and our eyes locked. Staring.

She was beautiful skin. She was full lips. She was so close I could hear her breathing.

I was a decision waiting to be made.

I wanted to kiss her. Badly. And who knows, maybe I would have. Maybe loveliness—and yes, desire—would have impelled me to forsake my professional responsibilities and do exactly what I shouldn't. But at that moment, something caught my eye. I looked down and noticed the embroidered words on Sam's apron. *Kiss the Chef!* I realized it was the same apron I'd originally given Rebecca.

I backed away. Sam let go of my hand.

"Are you okay?" she asked. "You look like you've seen a ghost."

I had.

ELEVEN

It could've been awkward after that. It wasn't. Sam could've pressed me on what appeared to be my change of heart. She didn't. Instead, she finished cooking while I set the table and put on some music. *Lay It Down*, from the Cowboy Junkies. We ate, talked, drank the wine, and acted as if nothing had happened. Which it hadn't.

Still, temptation would get a second chance.

After heaping praise on Sam's no-name linguine and insisting I'd take care of the cleanup, I watched as she tried to suppress a yawn.

"I think it's past my bedtime," she announced. "Are you sure I can't help with those dishes?"

"I'm sure."

"But if you let me, I won't feel so bad asking you for a favor."

"Don't worry about it," I said. "What's the favor?"

"Seeing me into a cab downstairs."

"I'm insulted," I announced, my smile making it clear that I was also kidding. "You actually thought I wasn't planning on doing that?"

She demurred. "I didn't want to assume."

"In that case, I'll go one better," I said. "I'll see you all the way home."

"Don't be silly. You don't need to do that."

"But I do. In the name of gentlemen everywhere. So don't even think of trying to talk me out of it."

She squinted at me and cocked her head. "Okay. But just so you know, I live over on the Upper West Side."

"Oh, *now* you tell me!"

She laughed and grabbed her purse. I fetched my coat as well as her shawl, handing it to her. Out the door, down the elevator, up to the street corner, and into a cab.

"Fifty-six West Eighty-first. Right off of Central Park West," Sam told the driver. I added that we'd be making a round trip. He grunted, and we were off.

We talked about current movies. She'd seen a lot; I'd hardly seen any. We talked about the coming winter, both agreeing it was probably going to be a cold one. Then I asked the wrong question. "When does your husband get back from Singapore?"

She turned to me. "To think it was almost a perfect evening."

"I'm sorry."

"I'm kidding," she said. "He gets back tomorrow night."

"He travels a lot, huh?"

"Yes, thankfully."

A few blocks of silence. We stopped at a light. I looked out the window at some sign for a yoga studio.

"I really do hate him, David," she said as the light flashed green and we turned.

"I know."

"I mean I *really* hate him."

"Which is why you've got to seriously consider what we talked about before. You can win. You can get out . . . with your son."

"I want to believe you."

"Then do," I said.

"You make it sound so easy."

"It won't be; I know that. But I can help you through it."

The cab came to a stop. Fifty-six West Eighty-first Street. Right in front.

"Home sweet home," she said sarcastically, looking out the window at her town house.

I leaned over to take a look. It was quite the building, actually. Brick with columns. Tall windows. Beautiful flower boxes. Right over the entrance was a stone statue of an eagle with its wings spread. I stared at it. The thing was gigantic.

"Yeah, I know the bird is huge," she said, still looking out the window. It was like she was reading my mind. "Let's just say I'm not the one who picked it out."

She turned back to me. And there it was—that moment repeated. Close together, face-to-face. Temptation all over again. Though it was easier this time to turn it down. I had practice.

"Thanks again for dinner," I said.

"It was the least I could do."

"So I'll see you Thursday, right?"

"Yes, Thursday," she said.

"In the meantime, do some thinking, okay?"

"I will." She reached for the door handle.

I reached for mine. "Wait, let me walk you to your door."

"No. It's okay," she said. "In fact, the way Celeste's radar operates she probably has the curtain already pulled back to see if it's me. Best if we make sure it's *only* me."

"Beware the nosy nanny."

"I know, it's a little silly. I'm sorry."

"Don't be. I'll wait until you get inside, though, okay?"

"Of course," she said. "We wouldn't want to jeopardize your standing as a gentleman." She was about to exit the cab. "Oh, I almost forgot. Let me give you money for the ride."

"Not necessary."

"Are you sure?" she asked.

"Definitely."

She smiled and put her hand on top of mine. "Thanks, David. Thanks for everything."

I watched as she stepped out and slowly walked up the entrance to her town house. She reached into her purse, found her keys, and waved. That was good enough for the cabbie. He sped off, but not before I got one last look at her. Sam Kent. Beautiful. Vulnerable.

My patient.

Two nights later I was watching a cable show on one of those house and garden channels. I'd seen it before. It was sort of a reality series based on real estate.

The cameras followed around a different couple and their broker each week as they tried to find a new home. Since no one had any theatrical training whatsoever, all the dialogue and movement was hilariously stilted. Maybe that's what made it so entertaining.

It certainly wasn't the surprise factor. Every episode seemed to unfold the same way. The broker would take the couple to the first home, and for any number of reasons, they wouldn't like it. The broker would take them to another, and again, the couple wouldn't like it. Then, just when things were looking bleak, the broker would say something like "There's one more home I want to show you, and I really think you're going to like it." Sure enough, that's the one they'd end up falling in love with. They'd make an offer—which was accepted right away, of course—and live happily ever after.

If only real life were so predictable.

After watching the scenes from the following week's show and lying to myself that I wouldn't tune in, I went to bed. Counting FOR SALE signs, I was asleep in no time.

But not for long.

A few hours later, I was awakened by a phone call. It was around 2:30 AM. My eyes half closed, I answered it. "Hello?"

I heard nothing on the other end.

"Hello?" I said again.

Finally, a voice. Barely recognizable. "I did it," she said faintly.

"Sam, is that you?"

"I did it, David."

I shifted the phone in my hand, trying to hear her better. "What are you talking about? What did you do?"

Silence.

"Sam, talk to me. *What did you do?*" A thought occurred to me. "Did you leave your husband?"

"No, David," she said, giving way to another pause. "I killed him."

I shot up in bed, jolted by what she'd just said. But there was something else. The *way* in which she'd said it. How she sounded. Drained. Listless.

Tired.

"Sam, where are you?" I asked.

I could hear soft crying.

"Sam, where are you?"

"Home."

"Listen to me. Have you taken anything? Have you taken sleeping pills?"

No reply.

"Damn it, Sam. Answer me!"

But she didn't. Or wouldn't. At that point it didn't make a difference. So I yelled, at the top of my lungs, wanting to know if she was trying to kill herself . . . again. Eventually she spoke.

"It was the only way, David," she whispered. "The only way." Then I heard a thump.

It was the phone hitting the ground.

PART II

TWELVE

Pants, sweatshirt, socks, and sneakers. It felt as if I was putting them all on at once.

This can't be happening.

I reached for my wallet on the bureau and instead knocked it onto the floor. I kneeled down quickly to pick it up and smacked my head hard against an open drawer. I felt nothing. There was no time to feel pain.

Could she really have done it?

Ready to go. No, wait—keys. I dashed out of the bedroom straight to the sofa table in the living room. A little ceramic bowl from Mexico. That's where I always kept them. The keys. *Shit.* Where were they? I checked the kitchen. I checked the library. I checked back in the bedroom.

Of course she could've done it. She goddamn told me she wanted to.

So much for always being in the last place you look. I found the keys when I went back to search the kitchen again. The second place I'd looked. They were sitting by an empty glass of what had been a double bourbon and water. My homespun version of Sominex. How fitting—*sleeping pills.* "It was the only way, David," Sam had said on the phone.

She was dying with each passing second.

I yanked an overcoat off my hallstand, slammed the apartment door behind me, and cursed the elevator for not arriving fast enough. Down twenty-two floors and a sprint past the door-man who—big surprise—was asleep behind his desk. Out on the street I didn't so much hail a cab as jump in front of one.

"Eighty-fifth and Central Park West," I barked at the driver. No, wait, that wasn't the address. "Actually, make that Eighty—" I stopped. Eighty-what? I couldn't remember. I *had* to remember. Was it Eighty-fifth or Eighty-first? The driver, a fat guy with crumbs in his beard, stared at me with growing impatience. "Just head to Central Park West in the Eighties as fast as you possibly can," I said. He flipped the meter, and we were off.

I leaned back in the seat and tried to catch my breath. Up ahead the light turned yellow. If the driver had hit the gas we could've made it. Instead, he slowed to a stop before it went red. What part of *as fast as you possibly can* did he not understand? Clearly some additional incentive was in order.

"Two dollars for every red light," I told him.

The driver looked at me in his rearview mirror. "Huh?"

"I said, I'll give you two extra bucks for every red light you don't stop for."

He scratched his beard, shaking loose a few crumbs. "No, not worth the risk . . . don't think so," he groused. The accent was foreign though not thick. Most likely Russian.

"Make it five bucks then," I said.

That seemed to alter things a bit. He glanced back my way. "I'll see what I can do."

Two blocks later, he did pretty well. Swerving into the bus lane to dodge a line of cars stopped at a light, the driver made his first five bucks. I held on tightly and watched as his head whipped back and forth through the intersection to check for crossing traffic. Not to mention cops.

Fuck.

The police. Granted, the circumstances weren't exactly con-ducive to clear thinking. But in all the haste I'd neglected to call them. That was a mistake. Understandable, perhaps, but still a mistake. The fact was, I'd reacted as David Remler, the guy who'd been with Sam in his apartment two nights prior. Not the David Remler who'd seen her as a patient for the past two weeks. David Remler, the psychologist, had a professional obligation. To inform the "proper authorities."

I quickly checked my pockets. Sure enough, there was something else I'd neglected to do. Bring my cell phone.

We made a left turn heading west on Fifty-seventh Street. Already the driver had an extra fifteen coming his way. We zipped past two pay phones, and I thought about yelling for the guy to stop. I would get out and call the police. Tell them what had happened and to send an ambulance, that I would meet them at Sam's town house.

Sure, David, if you could only remember where the hell it was.

I remained silent in the backseat trying to remember. We sped along, approaching Columbus Circle. I knew I could've figured something out for the police regarding the address. I'd give them the vicinity and mention the one thing about the town house that really stood out—that huge eagle with its wings spread over the entrance. Eventually, they'd find it.

No. The real reason I wasn't at a pay phone right then was there on my watch. Time. It had been ten minutes since Sam called. How many minutes before that had she taken the pills? The way she sounded, it had probably been a while. Stopping to make a call would only make me later. As it was, I couldn't help thinking I'd be too late anyway.

I would get there, and she'd be gone.

"You're bleeding," he said.

"What?"

"You're bleeding," the driver repeated. I watched in his rearview mirror as he pointed. "There, on your forehead."

I reached up above my eyes and felt around. Dry, dry . . . then wet. Mushy and warm to the touch by my right temple. I brought my hand down and saw the blood. A dark redness, dull and opaque in the stingy light of the cab's backseat. With my other hand I checked my pockets again, one after the other, for a tissue or napkin or anything. There was nothing.

"Here," said the driver.

I looked up to see him passing back a crumpled ball of paper towel. I thanked him and took it. Unraveling it, I ignored what appeared to be mustard stains and folded it into a square. I wiped my forehead a few times, soaking up the blood. There was lots of it. I pressed the paper towel against the gash to try to stem the bleeding. The longer I pressed, the more I smelled pastrami.

We were getting close. North on Central Park West in the Seventies. The Driver Red Light Bonus was now thirty bucks . . . and climbing. I peered out my window to the left, waiting to see something other than that eagle that would jog my memory. A store. A building. Some type of sign.

I saw it. Right before the corner of Eighty-first Street, an actual sign. It was tucked inside a second-story window. Big with all caps. GO YOGA! plus a phone number to call. I remembered seeing it that night riding back with Sam. We'd turned immediately after.

"Eighty-first Street!" I practically yelled at the driver. "Turn on Eighty-first!"

Three seconds and five more dollars later he did. It was a steering-wheel spinning, bald-tire screeching left on red that nearly plastered me against the right side of the cab.

"What's the number?" the driver immediately asked as we straightened out.

"I'll know it when I see it," I told him. Then: "There! On the left, past the streetlamp; that's it." Sam's town house. Brick with columns. Tall windows. The flower boxes.

That unmistakable statue of an eagle.

The driver hit the brakes and flipped the meter off. A total of $8.50, it read. "Plus nine red lights," he reminded me.

It was really only seven, but I wasn't about to argue. I was already halfway out of the cab, sixty bucks pulled from my wallet and tossed over the partition. The universal definition of airborne money: keep the change.

He kept it all right and sped off the moment my door closed. In between he mumbled something about "thank you."

I stood there on the curb looking up at Sam's town house. It was completely dark. I rushed up the steps three at a time and reached the front door. Make that double doors. I pounded on them with my fist. I abused the knocker. I spotted a buzzer to the side and hit the thing like a kid playing a video game. It was all wishful thinking. As much as I had to try, the prospect of getting Sam to let me in seemed altogether nonexistent. Assuming, of course, she was even able to at that point.

Plan B.

As in breaking in. I rushed back down the steps and eyed the tall windows in front. But this was New York, not Iowa. Sprouting up from behind those flower boxes were iron bars. I swore and began to pace. Out of frustration, I ran back up the steps and began pounding on the doors again. More abuse of the knocker, the doorbell pushed to a cacophony of chimes. I grabbed the cold brass of the doorknob and was about to—

What the . . . ?

Around went my wrist. The spring latch retreating back into its cylinder with a forceful *snap*! Just like that. No resistance. The door had been open the entire time. I couldn't believe it. A little bit of Iowa, after all. Or maybe it was something else. Yes. That's what I told myself. Sam had called me. She'd wanted me to come to her. To save her. The front door had been left open on purpose.

In I went.

To near total darkness. The only light being what was filtering in from the street—enough to create a few shadows, nothing more. But what I couldn't see I could feel. The hollow expanse of a large foyer . . . and the underlying stillness of the rooms around it. I groped for a light switch, finding it in the shape of a round dimmer knob some ways in on the wall. A chandelier, dripping with crystal, lit up above me.

"Sam?!" I yelled out.

No answer.

I yelled her name again, louder.

The same result. Nothing.

There were archways to other rooms on my left and right. A huge, curving mahogany staircase in front of me. A hallway extending underneath it that trailed off into pitch black. I ventured to think. *Where would I be if I'd just killed my husband and tried to commit suicide?*

Upstairs, my gut told me.

I ran, nearly tripped twice, and actually did trip once, my shin slamming into the lip of one of the stairs. Mahogany shared a lot of properties with concrete, not the least of which was how much it hurt when you fell on it. Sometimes you can just feel a bruise forming.

I was a search party of one, all the while screaming Sam's name. I reached the second floor and hit another switch for more light. There was a wide hallway before me with two doors on each side. At the end of the hallway, another door. All were closed.

Anxiety, adrenaline, impatience, and, most of all, fear. Fearing the worst behind each door. First up, a guest room. It had that minimal, barely used look. That's all it had, however.

I darted across the hall and barged through door number two. It was a small study. I turned on a light and saw a couch, a chair, a lot of books, and a desk. The clutter of someone busy. But no Sam. No husband.

The next door over—door number three—and another bedroom. Slightly larger, though no more lived in. I yelled out Sam's name for what was maybe the hundredth time. My throat was raw. I was short of breath. There was sweat running down my forehead, and I went to wipe it. Instead I was wiping blood. A wide red smear left on the back of my hand.

Across the hall again. I stormed in on a bathroom. A sink, a toilet, and an immediate sense of foreboding. There in front of me was a shower curtain, glossy white and pulled taut from one end to the other. I froze. It was my own personal horror flick. The required slow walk up to the curtain. The bracing for what lay in wait. The quick grab and pull back. I did it all. Only to find an empty tub.

Four doors down; one to go.

It was the one facing me when I got to the top of the stairs. Presumably the master bedroom. I breathed in, exhaled, and reached for the knob, turning and pushing at the same time. But I went nowhere. The knob barely moved. The door moved even less. It was locked.

"Sam!" I called out one last time. I pounded with my fist.

Nothing in return.

She had to be in there. Then another thought—they were *both* in there. Sam and her husband. The only question was how the story in the papers would read. A murder-suicide. Or a murder with an attempted suicide.

I took a few steps back and steeled myself.

It was time to find out.

THIRTEEN

Everything I had left I put into the heel of my right foot. Over and over I kicked. I aimed for the doorknob, hoping to splinter the wood around the cylinder. My first few attempts were futile. Then came progress. A crack and a buckle.

I wound up again with my foot. *Wham!* More cracks appeared. *Wham!* The wood shuddered with each successive kick until the door finally ripped open, flying on its hinges and slamming against the wall. I stepped in. An immediate rush of cold air hit me as I stood amid shadows of billowing drapes. Every window was open. Instantly, I could see my breath.

The light from the hallway spilled in over my shoulder, and my eyes adjusted. On the wall there was a lone switch. I flipped it, and the room appeared in a soft hue. Frantically, I scanned past a dresser and a night table. Across an unmade bed and over to a chaise lounge. I was about to check the closets when something caught my eye. It was the bed again, thick with covers.

Too thick, I realized.

That's when I began to see. The shape of a head . . . possibly an arm . . . what looked to be a pair of legs. Undefined yet unmistakable, a body beneath the sheets. Sheets I'd have to pull back. It was déjà shower curtain. Except this time there was definitely something there. Make that some*one*.

I was shaking. From the cold and from what I was about to do. An immediate swish of bile flooded my stomach. There was dizziness. A sense of watching myself from afar.

It would only get worse.

The drapes continued to ripple from the windows. I approached the bed and placed my hand on the corner of the duvet, gripping it tight. There would be no countdown, no extra breath taken. Just a swift and determined yank. And me staring, riveted.

Sam Kent. Samantha Kent. Mrs. Samantha Kent.

It was none of the above. Lying there facedown on the bed was a man. A very dead man. I wasn't that kind of doctor, but I was sure of it. There was blood all over and all around him. He was wearing a pair of sweatpants and a T-shirt. The T-shirt was riddled with tears. Each one being where a knife had entered his body. It didn't matter that there was no knife to be seen. It was that obvious.

"I killed him," Sam had said. "I killed my husband."

Many times over, it appeared.

My heart pounded away while my mind grappled with images of what must've happened. The anger being unleashed by her. The violence of it all, and how it was so incongruous with the woman I was getting to know. Therein lay a real regret. That I hadn't got to know her well enough. Or fast enough.

I continued to stare. Somewhere there was a manual that warned against touching the body at a crime scene. I hadn't read it. I was looking at what was the back of Sam's husband, unable to see his face. That didn't seem right. For whatever reason, I felt as if I needed to see it. His face. As if none of this was really happening until I did. I reached down under his right shoulder and began to lift. *So that's what they mean by dead weight.* It would take both of my hands along with a second push. Finally, the body rolled over.

Unbelievable.

I had my pick of things to make me shudder. The excess blood that had gathered on his chest, thick and sticky. The fact that his eyes were open, fixed with fear and panic, and seemingly boring into mine. But of all the things, the most unsettling was this: when I looked at the face of Sam's husband, I couldn't help thinking, *I somehow know him.*

Maybe there's a phenomenon in which you see a dead guy and immediately think he looks familiar. Some weird trick the mind plays on itself. Confusion in the name of sympathy. I didn't know for sure. I just had this feeling, fast and full, that it wasn't the first time I was seeing this guy. Not in a picture but in person. I couldn't remember when and where exactly. Only that it felt very real.

That thought immediately took a backseat. It had to. I'd found Sam's husband but not Sam. There were more rooms to search. An entire first floor. So goes the mantra of the battlefield medic: save the ones you can save; don't linger over those you can't.

I bolted out of the bedroom and down the stairs. I bounced from room to room, a human pinball, going everywhere.

The library off the foyer.

Back out and over to the living room and the dining room off of that.

Over to the den with a large-screen TV.

Into the kitchen and a walk-in pantry.

I covered every inch of the place. I searched every room and opened every door.

Except that one.

On the far side of the refrigerator, tucked away in the corner, I saw it. A narrow door. Another pantry, I assumed. When I opened it, though, there were no canned peaches. No cans of anything. Rather, what I saw were stairs, steep and descending into darkness. There was one more floor to search. The basement.

An exposed bulb beckoned with a pull chain a few feet in. I grabbed it and was rewarded with just enough light not to fall and break my neck—an otherwise safe bet given that there was no handrail.

Down I went. With each and every step the wood slats beneath my feet creaked their age. It was a prewar building all right. The question being, *Which* war?

I reached the bottom. The air was musty, damp, and smelled of pine-scented laundry detergent. I could make out a washer and dryer with a large folding table nearby. There was a furnace and a water heater. Some metal shelving with odds and ends. Yet no sign of Sam.

I looked for another pull chain or a switch, anything to provide additional light. I was sure it was there—I simply couldn't find it. Just as I was convinced Sam was there in the house—but I simply couldn't find her. I knew I was desperate when I checked inside the Maytag.

Where the hell is she?

The possibility sank in. She'd left the house. It didn't make much sense, but in the context of murder and a suicide attempt, who was I to look for logic?

Maybe she didn't want me to save her after all. Perhaps she'd walked out of the town house and neglected to lock it, home security not exactly being a priority at that juncture. *That* actually did make some sense. If it were true, the front door's being open had nothing to do with me.

It was all speculation. Truth was, I hadn't a clue. The one thing I was sure of was that Sam wasn't in that town house. She could've gone anywhere. A place she knew or nowhere in particular. At that very moment she could've been lying in the fetal position on a sidewalk or in an alley, drifting off to a permanent sleep. If that were the case, I was wasting even more time. A bigger search party was needed. What I'd opted not to do before was now an absolute necessity. I had to call the police.

I turned and climbed back up those narrow stairs as fast as possible. Reaching the kitchen, I saw a cordless phone sitting on the counter. I took a step toward it, then another. That's as far as I got, though. I was about to dial 911. Apparently someone had beaten me to it.

"Freeze!"

I spun around to see two cops at the entrance of the kitchen. One was short, the other tall. Beyond that they had a lot in common. Both looked very pissed off, both had their guns drawn, and both barrels of those guns were pointed directly at my chest. That probably explained why the first words out of my mouth didn't go over very well.

"Thank God," I said, with a deep exhale.

"Put your fucking hands up!" the first cop barked in response.

"Officers, I—"

Their feet shuffled, and their hands twitched. They both took a few fidgety steps forward.

Point taken. Up went my hands.

"Do you live here?" the second cop asked me. He was the tall one.

"No, I—"

"Who are you, and what are you doing here?" he asked rigidly.

"My name is Dr. David Remler, and I'm a psychologist here in the city," I said, attempting some degree of calmness. Then, a total rookie mistake: I started to reach for my wallet.

The two officers cocked their guns and took a few more fidgety steps forward. "Keep your fucking hands in the air!" was the gist of what they both shouted.

"Sorry! Sorry!" I shouted in return while cowering. I raised my hand back up and swallowed hard. "I only wanted to show you some ID."

"Just tell us what you're doing here," said the first cop. In fairness, only next to his partner did he look short.

"I got a call . . . one of my patients . . . Sam Kent," I began. I was sounding like a telegram, but I couldn't help it. The more I stared at the guns, the more out of breath I became. I started to ramble. "Actually, Sam is short for Samantha. It's really Samantha Kent; she's a woman, that is. Anyway, she told me she'd killed her husband and—"

The two cops exchanged glances.

First cop: "Wait a minute, *who* said this?"

"Her name is Samantha Kent. This is her home," I said.

"She told you she killed her husband?"

"Yes."

"Where is she?" asked the second cop.

"That's the thing; I don't know," I said. "I thought she was here. That's why I'm here. But I've searched absolutely everywhere in the house, and I can't find her."

Second cop: "What about the—"

"He's upstairs," I said with a grimace. "I'm afraid she was telling the truth. It's pretty bloody."

That last word was barely out of my mouth before I saw both cops look me over again, the blood on my forehead and right hand particularly. Red flags in the most literal sense.

"How'd you hurt yourself?" the first cop asked, his suspicion more than palpable.

"Oh, this . . . ," I said glancing up above my brow. "No—this is from my hitting my head back at my apartment in the rush to get over here. It's not what you think."

"And what would that be?" intoned the first cop. "What would we think?"

"I don't know exactly. Maybe that I had something to do with—"

The second cop jumped in. He was either very impatient or had a much better understanding of Miranda rights. "What'd you say your name was again?" he asked.

"David Remler," I answered. "Dr. David Remler."

He nodded. "Dr. Remler, what I think right now is that you should go ahead and show us that ID," he said. "Slowly, though."

"Yes, sir," I told him. And like a bad mime, I reached for my wallet. I pulled out my driver's license. Then came the cards. My business card. My American Psychological Society card. I nearly pulled out my gym membership card. Pure nerves.

The second cop approached me, his gun still drawn and aimed at my chest. He looked everything over and gave a quick "he is who he says he is" head bob to his partner.

I gave a sigh of relief. It was short-lived.

I realized my need to find Sam as fast as possible had been slightly drowned out by another need—not getting shot. My immediate health apparently in check, the thought of Sam quickly resurfaced.

"There's something else," I said. "It's why we've got to hurry. I'm pretty convinced that wherever Samantha Kent is right now, she's got a handful of sleeping pills in her."

"What makes you say that?" said the first cop.

"Number one, the way she sounded on the phone," I said. "Number two, I'm her psychologist."

"You're saying she's suicidal?" said the second cop.

"I'm just saying that I'm her psychologist," I replied. It was instinct. Later I'd be amazed that I could retain doctor-patient confidentiality at a time like that.

First cop: "You sure she's not here in the house?"

"Almost positive," I said. "Can we go check around the neighborhood?"

"First things first," said the second cop. "You show us where the husband is upstairs."

FOURTEEN

The rhythm and routine of a murder in Manhattan.

Or at least what happens after the murder. When the victim is found. When the system kicks in. When a bunch of people show up who make their living off of other people dying. It's a dirty job, all right, and I was amazed at how many somebodies there were who had to do it.

I saw it all firsthand. In one sense it was the epitome of order. In another, utter chaos. I likened it to an elaborate jazz piece, one performed by a resolute ensemble of notepad-toting trench coats and a whole string of people wearing latex gloves. These were guys—and they were indeed all guys—who walked and talked the part. And to a man, they had that tired look to them that no good night's sleep could ever cure.

But for a time it was just me and the cops.

At their request, I'd led them to Sam's husband. Up the stairs and down the hallway. En route I was neither friend nor foe. I was somewhere in between, a "yet to be determined." Which meant one of them had his eye on me at all times. If not his gun.

I turned back to them at the entrance of the master bedroom. "It was locked," I said in response to their curious looks at the smashed-in door. "I had to kick it open."

They didn't comment.

We went in. The room felt even colder than it had before. A bitter October night had continued to be sucked in through the open windows. Despite my coat, I let go with a few shivers. Not so my escorts. They didn't seem to mind. They had other concerns. Like whether there were other surprises to be found. So before anything else, they checked the bathroom and the walk-in closet. One of them always had the other's back. All clear. They hovered over the bed and took a good long look.

"Yeah, he's pretty dead," said the first cop.

The second one looked up at me and back down at the body. "Is this how you found him?"

"Actually, he was under the covers," I answered. "I pulled them back."

"What about the body itself?" he said. "Did you touch him at all?"

The way he was asking told me he wasn't going to like my answer. "He was facedown at first. I rolled him over," I said.

Immediate frown.

"Why?" asked the first cop, also not terribly keen on my answer.

"I guess to see his face," I said.

"Why?" he asked again. "Did you know him?"

Damn good question. I still had the feeling I did, yet I couldn't figure out how. That was a problem. "Did I know him?" I asked back. Saying *maybe* seemed like a really bad idea given the circumstances. It was the sort of word generally used by people who had something to hide. As it was, I'd created enough of that impression just being there. "No," I said. "I didn't know him."

And like that, I was on record.

There was no follow-up question, nothing that suggested they didn't believe me. Instead, procedure took over. It was time to get the word out. The second cop called in to his precinct, reported there'd been a homicide, and gave Sam's address. When he hung up, he said something to the first cop about hoping for some "first-graders." While I didn't know what that was supposed to mean, I knew he wasn't talking about schoolchildren.

"Jesus, the kid . . . ," I said to myself. A little too loudly as it turned out.

The cops turned to me.

Where's the kid? My first thought was that Sam had taken her son with her. That got interrupted by my own replay of searching the town house. Had I even seen a kid's room? No, I hadn't.

The cops were staring, waiting for me to say something. I started to explain that Sam had a son, a two-year-old. I didn't get into the bit about not seeing a room for him or, for that matter, why his mother would want to turn him into an orphan overnight. I did, however, press the issue about trying to find her.

"All right," said the second cop, the subtext being *if it will make you shut up.* "What does she look like?"

I described Sam Kent. Five foot six. Thin. Blond hair, past her shoulders if worn down.

"Any idea where she might have gone?" he asked next.

"No."

"Any idea what she might be wearing?"

"No."

"And you think she's taken sleeping pills?"

"I do," I answered with a quick nod. The caveat came after. "Like I said, though, I can't know for sure."

The second cop called his precinct again and made what amounted to a "be on the lookout" request for anyone on patrol. He also asked that all the emergency rooms in the area be checked. He relayed the information about Sam, right through the part about the sleeping pills, in a dispassionate monotone that suggested a lunch order rather than a life-or-death situation. But I didn't care. It got done. That meant there was still hope.

"C'mon," I was told.

The cops had to see for themselves that there was nobody else in the town house. While the first one took me downstairs and kept a watch on me in the foyer, the second went room by room. Upstairs, downstairs, the basement. A full sweep.

I stood there in silence for a moment with the first cop. As he began to tap his foot on the marble floor, I glanced around, looking at nothing in particular. I was thinking of Sam and where she might've gone . . . of her son and whether he'd gone with her . . . of her husband and where the hell I knew him from. Frustration on every front. I still didn't have any answers.

Pop! Pop! Pop!

I suddenly heard the sound of gunshots out on the street. I spun on my heels toward the front door and was about to hit the deck. The cop, meanwhile, didn't flinch.

"Firecrackers," he said calmly. "It's Hackers' Night."

It took me a moment. First, to calm down. Second, to get my calendar and jargon in order. I realized that it was October 30, the night before Halloween. When I was growing up in suburbia, we called it Mischief Night. Apparently, the urban translation was a tougher-sounding Hackers' Night. Either way, it proved how much on edge I was. Had they been real gunshots outside, I probably would've been screaming about nukes.

The silence settled back in. I was growing increasingly impatient.

"Isn't there something more I can do to help you guys?" I asked the cop.

He gave another foot tap on the marble. "There's going to be plenty you can do," he replied. "Just not with us. In a few minutes, the detectives will get here, and you can give them your full cooperation."

"Of course," I said. Another question occurred to me. I think I was simply desperate to know at least one answer. "There's one other thing," I said.

"What's that?"

"I was about to call 911 when you guys showed up there in the kitchen. How'd you know to come—did a neighbor call?"

The cop hesitated. As if he was deciding whether the answer

was any of my business. "An alarm," he said finally. "Silent, obviously. You must have tripped it."

"But the front door was open," I said.

"It wouldn't matter so long as the system was on." He motioned with his head up to the ceiling. There in the corner was a small white box fronted by a translucent stamp-size piece of glass. It had a red tint. "Motion detectors," he said.

I nodded. And wondered.

We were joined just then by the second cop. "Nothing," he said, referring to his search of the town house.

"Good," said the first cop. He glanced at his watch. As if on cue, the foyer and surrounding rooms were transformed into a disco of red and blue flashing lights. While the neighborhood was spared the sound of sirens at 3:00 AM you didn't need them to know. Things were about to get extremely busy.

The homicide detectives had arrived first. Two of them. They were followed almost immediately by a couple of EMTs and two additional detectives from the Crime Scene Unit—jackets emblazoned accordingly. Soon thereafter two guys from the morgue showed up. The only solo act was from the district attorney's office, a young Irish-looking kid who, much to my surprise, didn't say a single word to me.

Were that only true of those homicide detectives.

After checking out the bedroom upstairs and huddling for a few minutes with the two cops, they approached me and introduced themselves. That was the difference right there. The two cops had been intent on being just that—two cops. The "first one" and the "second one." Never any names. They didn't need to introduce themselves; they didn't need to get to know me. The homicide detectives, on the other hand, were most eager to make my acquaintance.

FIFTEEN

Dr. Remler, I'm Detective Joseph Trentino, and this is my partner, Detective Frank Lopez."

I looked at the two of them. It was clear we weren't about to shake hands. Instead, quick nods all around. Trentino, fortyish, was average height, stocky, and square-jawed. He wore thick-rimmed glasses and clearly didn't give a damn about the fact that he was losing his hair. It was combed back, not over, with no attempt made at filling in what once was. Throw in his deliberate voice and the message was unmistakable: Detective Joseph Trentino was a no-bullshit kind of guy.

Ditto for his partner, Frank Lopez. While slightly taller, thinner, and—thanks largely to his full head of hair—younger looking, Lopez was no less straight to the point. Mind you, it was never approaching rudeness with the two of these guys. Just matter-of-fact. Whether that was merely a job persona or embedded in their genetic code, I couldn't tell. Safe to say, though, neither man was voted class clown back in high school.

The first question was simple, open-ended, and expected. "Why were you here?" asked Trentino. Of course, what he was really saying to me was this: *Okay, buddy, there were two people discovered in this town house. You and a dead man. Now why don't you go ahead and make us believe.*

I did my best.

I told them everything I could about why I was there. How Sam was my patient. About the phone call from her. Rushing to the town house and frantically searching. Everything right up until I was told to freeze.

The two detectives listened. Took a few notes. Gave nothing away as to their thinking. Then came their follow-ups. Trentino fired off the first few.

"At what time did you say Ms. Kent called you?" he asked.

"The exact time I couldn't tell you," I answered. "But it was around two thirty."

"How do you know?"

"At some point in the cab ride over here I looked at my watch for the first time. By then it was a little before three," I said.

Trentino scribbled something in his pad. "You say the front door was open when you got here?"

"Yes."

"The door to the master bedroom was locked, though?"

"Yes."

"You kicked it in?"

"Yes."

"Once inside you saw the victim there on the bed, right?"

"Yes—well, actually no," I said, quickly correcting myself. "I saw what looked like a body underneath the covers. As I told the officers, I pulled them back. The covers, that is."

"And there was the guy staring right up at you, huh?" said Detective Lopez, jumping in.

I gave Lopez a brief, wary-eyed look. There was a chance it was an innocent assumption on his part and he didn't know. Perhaps the cops hadn't said anything to them about my touching the body. There was also a chance the detective knew exactly what he was doing.

Testing me.

"As I also told the officers," I said, "I rolled him over. He was originally facedown."

Lopez grimaced slightly. It was all that was needed to echo

loudly what the cops had told me earlier: moving the body was a boneheaded move. Given, of course, that I was telling the truth in the first place—something the two detectives were clearly trying to determine. Said Lopez, "Did you think there was a possibility the guy was still alive?"

"Not really," I said.

"So you rolled him over because . . ."

I shrugged. "I'm not sure, to be perfectly honest. It's not like I really thought about it. I just did it."

Trentino flipped back a page in his notes. He was trying to find something. He found it. "I see you told the officers that you don't know the victim," he said, still staring down at his pad. He didn't say anything after that. Neither did I. A beat later, he looked up at me.

"I'm sorry, was that a question?" I asked, buying myself a few more seconds.

"I suppose technically it wasn't," he said with a half-smile, the first of its kind. "Let me try again. Did you know the victim?"

The lesser of two evils. It was pretty much what I was choosing between. Very quickly, no less. Stand by my earlier statement even though it wasn't necessarily the case. Or explain as convincingly as I could that, on second thought, there was a chance I did know the guy—a chance only because I couldn't remember how or in what context. Talk about a backward predicament. Tell the whole truth and, in the grasp of contradiction, risk being seen as not telling any of it. Versus a potential lie that would go a long way in protecting my credibility. My head was swirling.

"No, I didn't know the guy," I said.

And like that, I was *really* on record.

More questions followed. One after the other. Mostly about what Sam had said to me on the phone. The exact words she used. Her phrasings. Any clues she might have given about where she went. Rat-a-tat-tat. From there the focus shifted to my forehead. The gash. No sooner had I explained again about hitting my dresser drawer than Detective Trentino flagged down an EMT who was walking by. He wanted the guy to examine me. Check if maybe I needed stitches.

"Let's see if we can't clean away the blood there on Dr. Remler," said Trentino.

The EMT obliged. He got up real close to me, toe to toe, and firmly grabbed my head. He leaned left and looked; he leaned right and looked. His professional opinion was then summed up in one, heavily Brooklyn-accented word. "*Naaaaaah*," he said. Translation: I didn't need any stitches. With some damp clothtype thing and a cotton swab on a stick that looked as if it belonged ringside, he wiped and dabbed away the blood. Once the wound was clear, two butterfly bandages were peeled back and applied.

"Good to go," said the EMT when finished.

What a great idea, I was thinking. Being able to leave. Going home, going to bed, and waking up to discover this was nothing more than a very active bit of REM sleep. Come Thursday at four o'clock I'd open the door to the reception area of my office and see Sam Kent there waiting for me. Alive and well. Moreover, alive and well on the way to a better life for herself.

That's how it was supposed to be. Not this. This was crazy. I'd seen a bloody death, had guns aimed at me by twitchy hands, and was being given the third degree as a possible suspect—if not probable.

It all added up to a headache the size of Montana. Parts of Wyoming thrown in as well. The adrenaline that kicked in with Sam's phone call had run its course. In its place now was staggering fatigue. I looked at my watch while stifling a yawn. Quarter to four. And all was far from being well.

"Guys, can I have a word with you for a second?"

Trentino and Lopez had just resumed their questioning when the first cop approached, wanting a quick conversation. He pulled the two detectives aside. I watched and waited as the cop filled them in on something. A minute later I was told what it was.

A few things actually.

"We've had a chance to confirm some facts," Trentino said. "You'll forgive us that we couldn't just take you at your word." I got another half-smile from the detective. That made two. "For starters, as you claim, a Samantha Kent does indeed live here. Though it turns out Kent is her maiden name. Did you know that, Dr. Remler?"

"No, I didn't."

Trentino continued: "Her husband's name is Conrad Birch. Or should I say *was* because that's him upstairs all right."

Conrad Birch . . . Birch . . . Birch. I repeated the name over in my head, relieved it didn't immediately ring a bell.

"Finally, there's this," said Trentino, bringing his hands to his hips. "It looks like you are who you say you are, Dr. Remler. Your practice checks out, and your home address checks out. But I guess you already knew that."

It was about all I knew, though, that night.

"So, for the time being, Dr. Remler, we've only got one other thing to ask you," said Trentino. "Which is, you're not planning on leaving town anytime soon, are you?"

I was waiting for that third half-smile. It didn't come. He was completely serious. A strong piece of advice disguised as a simple question. "No," I said. "I have no plans to leave town."

"Good," he said. "Then why don't you go home and get some sleep."

I blinked a few times. A modicum of disbelief. "You mean I can go?"

"Yes, that's right. You can go," he said.

I stood there . . . not going. Instead, I was thinking. The knee-jerk relief from the guy-in-the-wrong-place-at-the-wrong-time portion of the night had again faded fast. "What about Samantha?" I asked.

"We've got people looking for her," said Lopez.

"Just the same, I think what I want to do is stick around for when you find her," I said. "Better yet, I'd really like to help in the search."

"I'm sure you would, Dr. Remler, and we appreciate that," said Trentino in a manner that suggested otherwise. "But the best thing you can do for everyone's sake is to go home, get some rest, and be available for us. When we find Ms. Kent, you'll be among the first to know."

"Maybe we could get a sketch drawn," I said. "Better yet, there's got to be a picture of her around here somewhere."

All three of us instinctively looked around the foyer. Lots of artwork but no pictures.

"We'll take a look around the house again, and I'm sure we'll find something," said Lopez. "Even if we don't, your description will be good enough."

"Are you sure?" I asked. "I can help you look. Maybe there's also some other clue we missed."

"We've got people on it, Dr. Remler," said Lopez.

I wasn't about to talk these guys into anything. "All right," I said, acquiescing. "Let me give you my home phone number then."

"It's okay; we'll get it," Trentino told me.

"It's unlisted, though," I said.

"Not to us," he replied.

And there it was. That third half-smile.

I said good night to the detectives. Good morning would've been more accurate. Walking out of Sam's town house I could see the first hint of dawn illuminating the sky. A new day. Halloween, actually. But also a Monday, I realized. Christ. In about three hours I was supposed to be sitting in my office listening to someone talk about their fears and frustrations. "Oh, yeah?" I could say smugly, glaring back at my patient. "Let me tell you about *my* problem . . ."

I walked Sam's neighborhood anyway.

A few blocks in every direction, including a brief foray into Central Park. I couldn't go home without at least giving it a shot, long as it was. No matter how much I wanted to find her, I dreaded the thought of what I'd find if I did. Whatever optimism remained in me was spent on devising plausible happy endings. Sam had been helped by someone on the street. A jogger. A doctor. Hell, a jogging doctor. She was in a hospital somewhere, her stomach pumped and vital signs holding steady. When the cops had checked with all emergency rooms earlier, her paperwork had been overlooked. Misplaced. Hardly out of the question for a New York hospital.

Dawn made itself official. People were beginning to trickle out of their buildings, their complexes, their caves; the go-getters off to get a jump on the workweek. I looked at them and the spring in their step. I had no such spring. My step was a day behind. The last few hours felt like a year.

I held on to the hope but gave up on the search. A needle in a big city. The streets belonged mainly to the cabs at this hour, and I raised my hand to hail one. The ride home saw maybe two red lights. The driver stopped for both.

Back home at last. The coat flung on the hallstand, the keys tossed in the ceramic bowl atop the sofa table. I checked the answering machine. Maybe Sam had tried to call me again. It wasn't blinking.

I went to the kitchen and washed my hands. My blood was still on them. I poured a finger of bourbon and stared at it. Though not for long. Two gulps. Three, tops. A quick empty glass.

I returned to the living room and sat down on the couch. I got up from the couch. I looked out the window. I picked up the phone.

Mila once told me that the older she got the less sleep she needed. "It's my body's way of telling me there'll be plenty of time for that soon enough," she'd said. I thought of her words as I dialed. The contented place from which they came.

It only rang once before she answered. Her voice was clear although quiet. She was already up.

"Mila, it's David," I said.

I told her nothing of what had happened or where I'd been. What she heard was that I wasn't feeling well. My appointments would have to be canceled. Dr. Remler was taking a sick day.

She didn't pry. She didn't press. She didn't do or say anything differently from the other times I'd phoned her with news of being under the weather. Still, I knew she could tell. This was Mila. My Mamka. Instinctually, she could read between the lines, hear beyond my calm demeanor. It wasn't a head cold; it was something else. Something I couldn't explain right then, but later when I was ready.

"I hope you feel better," she said.

"Thank you, Mamka."

I hung up and poured myself another finger of bourbon. Then another after that. Despite my exhaustion, I knew it was the only way I'd ever get any sleep. Simply closing my eyes wouldn't cut it.

Waiting for the desired effect from the alcohol, I thought about the detectives, Trentino and Lopez. The questions they asked and the questions they didn't.

Their focus was clear. They'd concerned themselves strictly with the events of the evening. Not once had they asked about Sam as a patient or what her motive might have been. They only wanted to know what had immediately led up to Conrad Birch's getting killed. Again, I was left wondering. A broken record playing havoc on my memory.

Where did I know him from?

Nowhere closer to an answer, and having achieved the proper numbness from the bourbon, I was finally ready to sleep. I shuffled off to the bedroom. Down the hallway, through the door, and—*Jesus*. I stopped cold, staring at my bed. The covers. Under the covers. The shape of what I thought was . . . impossible. It couldn't be. She couldn't have. I rushed up and pulled them all away. The comforter. The sheets. Until I could see with my own eyes.

That she hadn't.

Sam Kent was not to be found in my bed. Only in my thoughts. I was officially seeing things.

SIXTEEN

Again, it was the phone that woke me. Ringing in my bedroom. Ringing in my head. I rolled over to face a cluttered nightstand. Spare change, folded receipts, a glass of water from at least two days prior, and books that were all dog-eared around fifty pages in and would most likely remain that way. Somewhere buried among all that was also the phone. Still ringing.

A clumsy reach for it and a groggy hello.

"Dr. Remler?" the voice said.

"Yes."

"This is Detective Trentino. We met—"

"Yes . . . last night."

The connection faded for a second. A stretch of static.

"—ear me?" was all I heard.

"What's that?" I asked.

Static gone. "Can you hear me, Dr. Remler?"

"Yes, that's better," I said.

"Good. Listen, we were wondering if we could have a few more minutes of your time."

"Uh, sure," I answered. Then, with a jolt: "Wait, is there any news about Sam?"

"That's what we want to talk to you about," said Trentino.

Not a good sign, I thought. My voice tightened. "Why can't you tell me now?"

"We *can* tell you now, Dr. Remler. We're actually standing outside the door to your apartment. We tried knocking and ringing the bell but—"

"I was asleep. I'm sorry."

"More than okay."

I looked at my watch. It was almost noon. "Give me a minute; I'll be right with you," I said.

In my haste, I put on the same pants, sweatshirt, socks, and sneakers I'd had on the night before. The only addition was a baseball cap for the bed head. That and a swig of Scope. My morning breath was bad enough. I was pushing afternoon breath.

I went to let the detectives in. "Sorry about that," I said as I opened the door.

"No problem," they both replied. Two monotones that made stereo.

We stood there in the entryway for a moment. Nothing was being said. What I wanted was obvious—news about Sam. What wasn't obvious was who was going to break it to me. Trentino looked at Lopez. Lopez nodded back to him. The unspoken language of partners. I couldn't read it.

I also couldn't wait any longer.

"So, what is it? Did you find her?" I asked, bracing.

"We found her, all right," said Lopez.

I exhaled. "You mean she's okay?"

"Not exactly," he said. "Her husband's dead."

Granted. "But she's alive?"

"Very much so."

The two detectives did some more of that unspoken partner language thing. This time, though, I noticed a slight air of bemusement as they exchanged glances.

"So where was she found?" I asked.

Trentino took it from there. "That's the thing, Dr. Remler.

She found *us*. Right when she returned home this morning . . . from a trip to Boston."

My face probably said it all. Instantly perplexed. The words I spoke were surely redundant. "I don't understand."

"Neither do we," said Trentino. "However, we do know this. She was definitely in Boston last night. All weekend, in fact."

"That doesn't make any sense," I said.

"No, it doesn't. Certainly not in relation to what you've told us. But here's where it really gets weird," said Trentino. *"Samantha Kent says she's never even met you before."*

SEVENTEEN

Disbelief and sudden deafness. They went hand in hand.
I was standing there in my apartment not more than three feet away from Detectives Trentino and Lopez as they told me about Sam. I could hear them perfectly. Every word. Yet the one word that kept coming out of my mouth was this: *What?*

What were they talking about? What did they mean Sam had been in Boston? And what was this about her saying she'd never met me before?

"We're talking about Samantha Kent here, right?" I said, suddenly not taking anything for granted. "Five foot six. Thin. Blond hair, past her shoulders?"

"Actually, Dr. Remler, the Samantha Kent whom we met, the one who lives at Fifty-six West Eighty-first Street, is a little taller," said Trentino.

"Do you have a picture of her?"

"No, not on us," he said.

"But she's blond and thin, right?"

"Yes, she is."

"Okay, so I was off a bit with her height."

"That depends," said Lopez, jumping in. "Would you say four-plus inches was a bit?"

I did it again. *"What?"*

"The Samantha Kent we talked to—the Samantha Kent married to Conrad Birch—is five foot ten, easy."

"That's impossible. There's no way she's that tall."

"Perhaps you simply never noticed," said Trentino. "That's possible, wouldn't you say?"

I admitted it was. "But what's with this stuff about Boston?"

"Samantha Kent was checked in at the Ritz-Carlton on Arlington Street on Friday, Saturday, and Sunday night. She was there for some weekend conference—"

"The Children's Aid Society, I'm pretty sure," said Lopez, interjecting again.

Trentino nodded. "Yeah, that's what it was. Anyway, we've got people from the conference, as well as hotel employees, confirming they saw her there. Hey, do you think I could have a glass of water?"

As segues went, that one was pretty strange. Almost bizarre. "Huh?" I uttered.

"I'm sorry," said Trentino. "It's just that's it's been a long night, not to mention morning. I'm very thirsty; would it be possible for me to get some water?"

My answer was "Sure." My look at him was "You've got to be kidding." "I'll be right back," I said, heading for the kitchen. Once there, I pulled a glass from the cabinet and began filling it up at my Poland Spring cooler.

"Nice kitchen." From over my shoulder. Lopez's voice.

I turned to see that the two detectives had decided to keep me company. Regular pals. "Here you go," I said, handing Trentino his glass of water.

"Thanks. So how long have you lived here?" he asked.

"Three years."

He scratched his chin. "It's a nice neighborhood. I've got a cousin who lives not too far from here."

What was this—small talk? It was time to steer the conversation back to Sam. Or was that plural? *Sams*.

"Detectives, in light of everything you've told me, I think I should see for myself this woman you're talking about."

"You mean, the real Samantha Kent?" asked Lopez. In the short time I'd known both detectives it was clear that while both had Jack Webb on the brain, Lopez also possessed quite the sarcastic streak.

I ignored the comment and the inference that I was either crazy or lying or both. "Don't you agree we should arrange a meeting?" I asked.

"Yes, that meeting should happen," said Trentino. "Though, as you might imagine, she's pretty shook up right now and not exactly taking visitors."

"Particularly someone she doesn't know," added Lopez. "Excuse me, *claims* she doesn't know."

"That's kind of the whole point now, isn't it?" I said, getting used to Lopez's shtick. "To clear up all this confusion."

Trentino ran a hand through what little hair he had left. "Like I said, Dr. Remler, we'll arrange for you to see her."

"Good," I said.

"Hey, did you know you're missing a knife?"

I turned to Lopez, who'd asked the question, and followed his gaze to the thick wooden block by my stove. I saw what he was talking about. There were seven knives for eight slots in the block. I was about to answer with the likes of "No, I didn't know that" when, in a flash, I realized what was going on.

So much for polite conversation.

"What are you saying?" I asked, my tone implying I knew exactly what he meant.

Lopez walked over to the block and slowly pulled out one of the knives, examining it. "I was simply asking whether you knew there was a knife missing from your set. That's all. Why, what are *you* saying?"

I eyed them both. Really seeing them for the first time.

We all may have been wearing the same clothes as when we first met, but it was clear we'd come to look different to one another. Very different. The detectives had said as much. Now it was my turn. There was a fine line between being foolishly disagreeable and standing up for yourself, and I was about to teeter on it.

"Detective Lopez, you and I both see a knife block with seven handles protruding out of it, plus an empty slot," I began. "But the fact is, you don't know it was a set to begin with. You also don't know that a set isn't made up of seven knives and the good folks at J.A. Henckels saw fit to bestow a bonus slot upon their customers. So when you ask me if I know I'm missing a knife, my question back to you is the same. Do you really know that I am?"

"Dr. Remler, there's no need to be angry," said Trentino.

"Or defensive," said Lopez.

"You're right. The only need I've got right now is for you both to quit with the innuendos. If you've got something to say, say it. If you don't, then don't. Correct me if I'm wrong, but I've been nothing but forthcoming since this whole thing started. I've answered every one of your questions and offered to help in any and every way possible. If what I've told you isn't matching up with what you think you've learned, then let's figure out who's in error."

The only sound for a moment was the white-noise hum of my refrigerator.

"I'm sorry if you've got the wrong impression," said Trentino finally. The tone was calmer, more affable. It was also very forced. "We appreciate your candor, and we're well aware you've cooperated fully with us. I imagine you've gone through a great deal in the past twelve hours, and what we've just told you couldn't have helped matters. To be sure, your confusion right now is our confusion as well. The last thing we want to do is jump to any conclusions. Rest assured, we'll get to the bottom of all this soon enough."

"Yes," said Lopez with a poor attempt at a contemplative nod. "Soon enough."

The two detectives thanked me for my time and told me they'd be in touch. I showed them to the door. I couldn't tell what effect, if any, my sudden bravado had had on them, but before stepping out to the hallway, they each gave me a prolonged look. Fittingly, Lopez took the last word.

"Happy Halloween," he said.

Alone again in my apartment, I returned to the kitchen to make some coffee. There on the counter sat the glass of water Detective Trentino had asked for. *Trick or treat.* It was as full as when I'd handed it to him. The man who'd claimed to be very thirsty hadn't taken a single sip.

Sam Kent. Samantha Kent. Mrs. Samantha Kent.

I picked up the phone and immediately dialed.

EIGHTEEN

His secretary put me through.

"Hey, what's up?" came Parker's voice.

"Plenty," I said. "I need to talk to you."

"So go ahead."

This had face-to-face written all over it. "Not on the phone. Can I come by your office?"

"Yeah, no problem. You okay?" he asked.

"I'm not sure."

"Tell you what, have you eaten lunch?"

I hadn't even thought about food. "No," I said.

"Neither have I. Japanese?"

He could've suggested Canadian food for all I cared. "So long as there's a little privacy," I said.

"I know just the place. Meet me on the northeast corner of Twenty-third and Lex at one o'clock, okay?"

"Okay."

I had scarcely enough time to take a quick shower and throw on some clean clothes (finally) before grabbing a cab down to Twenty-third and Lex. Parker was already there, waiting for me.

"What happened?" he immediately asked, looking up at my forehead and the two butterfly bandages holding it together.

"It's a long story," I said.

"The reason why you needed to talk?"

"Exactly."

"Then come on, the place is right down the street here," he said, starting to walk east toward Third Avenue.

"Where are we going?" I asked.

"You'll see."

Halfway down the block, Parker stopped in front of a single door, painted with a shiny black lacquer. There was no sign. There wasn't even a number I could see.

"This isn't one of those places where you eat the sushi off a naked woman, is it?" I asked. I was only half-joking.

"Yes, that's exactly how I prefer to lunch on Mondays," said Parker, deadpanning. "In fact, Stacy often meets me here."

He led me into the building and down a long, nondescript corridor. At the end was a waiting elevator, cramped, barely lit, and completely mirrored. We rose four floors with me looking at Parker sideways and him enjoying every second of it. The doors opened, and we stepped off.

"Try not to gawk too much," he said in a whisper. "They really don't like it when people gawk."

But I couldn't help myself. Before me was an unusual sight, to say the least, one I couldn't immediately classify. Was it a restaurant? Was it someone's home? It looked like one big lavish living room, albeit with a scattering of tables and a few waiters maneuvering among them. Most of the clientele were eating. Some, though, were merely playing cards or dominoes. In one corner there was a small sushi bar; in the other, two well-dressed old men were sitting in armchairs, reading the newspaper and smoking cigarettes. They were Japanese. Everyone was Japanese. The vast majority at least. As for the few gringo exceptions, they looked as if they could afford to be anything they wanted to be.

I leaned over to Parker, returning the whisper. "I don't suppose this place is in Zagat's, huh?"

"This place isn't even in the phone book."

"So, what makes you so special?"

"My firm handles a few Tokyo clients. This is their Harvard Club, and I've got a guest membership."

A young Japanese man, around thirty and impeccably attired, approached us. Actually, he approached Parker.

"So nice to see you again, Mr. Mathis."

There was no accent. He spoke English perfectly. He shook Parker's hand crisply and with a deferential nod of the head.

"Likewise, Jimmy," said Parker. "Allow me to introduce a very good friend of mine. Jimmy, this is Dr. David Remler."

Parker hadn't really put any extra emphasis on the *doctor* part preceding my name, but his using it was most intentional. While I was never one for soaking up the social status that went along with it, at that moment I wasn't complaining. Whether it made much of an impact I didn't know. The only thing clear was that by virtue of Parker's introduction I too was now getting Jimmy's crisp handshake and deferential nod.

"It's an honor to meet you, Dr. Remler. Welcome."

"Thank you."

Jimmy turned and said something in Japanese to a nearby waiter. The waiter motioned with his head at a table near the wall, and within seconds we were seated.

Parker was right. We had our privacy. Those few who could possibly overhear us didn't even seem to be aware we were there. "All right, so what's going on?" he asked.

"Maybe we should order first," I said.

"We kind of already have."

I'd had enough confusion of late and didn't really need any more. Parker picked up on that pretty quickly. "I'm sorry, I should've explained," he said, chuckling. "This place doesn't have menus. In fact, it doesn't really have a kitchen. It's all rare sushi, no pun intended, and it's all flown in from Japan—from the coast of Kyushu, to be exact. There's only one dish to be had here and that's an assortment of this morning's delivery. Chef's choice, as they say."

"I see. So it must be pretty horrible."

"Yeah, it's the worst you'll ever taste."

"At least it's cheap, though, right?"

"Like they're giving the stuff away."

"Good thing, because you'd never dream of expensing this lunch, would you?"

"The thought never crossed my mind."

It was nothing more than our usual mindless, semicomedic banter, yet it was everything. A reality check, a reassurance, a reminder that everything hadn't gone completely bonkers. Never lose your sense of humor, the saying went. Lose that and for sure they've got you beat.

"So, like I said, what's going on?" asked Parker again.

I knew that the question—repeated, no less—was the premise for our lunch. Still, I sat there for a moment saying nothing. There was so much to tell, and I hadn't really given any thought about how to tell it. Where was I supposed to begin?

I decided the best place was with the part Parker already knew. "Do you remember that patient I was telling you about the other day?"

"You mean the woman with the kid?"

My head immediately dropped. *The kid.* I kept forgetting about the kid. The detectives didn't say anything about him. Nor did I ask. There we'd been in my apartment, quibbling about cutlery and Sam Kent's height, and I didn't even ask about her son. Where was he in all this? Presumably okay, I figured. Though it seemed a lot of my presumptions were now being challenged.

"David?"

My mind had wandered off, trying to picture a two-year-old boy. The innocence. I apologized to Parker, gathered my thoughts, and settled into explaining what had happened as best I could.

I started with Sam's phone call to me and her confession, her enervated tone and my suspicions—another suicide attempt. I ended with the detectives dropping by my apartment unannounced. In between, I reconstructed the order of events, pausing a few times to question if I'd gotten it right or left anything out.

Parker, meanwhile, was doing his very best to wear two hats. That of a friend and that of a lawyer. Being the friend, he showed concern alternating with periodic expressions of disbelief: *Holy shit . . . You're kidding me . . . Jesus.* That sort of stuff. Being the lawyer, he wanted to know the who, what, when, where, and why. And if at any point I wasn't giving it, he'd pepper me with questions.

Somewhere amid the back and forth our meals arrived. Big round plates that weren't prepared so much as art directed. Colors, shapes, textures. Concentric circles of sushi and sashimi that when viewed through a slight squint took on the appearance of an impressionist painting. Despite my not having much of an appetite or being in the mood to enjoy anything, I couldn't deny that it looked amazing and tasted even better. At the very least, my stomach was being cheered up.

We continued to talk as we ate. When I'd fully brought Parker up to speed, he tapped his ivory chopsticks a couple of times on what was now his empty plate. I waited for his low sustained grunt, his vacuum-cleaner noise. It came and stayed longer than usual. Made sense. There was a lot to think about.

"Here's the thing," he said ultimately. "There are two sets of facts, or statements parading as facts: what you know and what you've been told. The first set—what you know—includes only what you can prove. No more, no less. What you've been *told*, on the other hand—the second set—is what's making up most of your story. Especially the confusing parts. You've got your sessions with this Kent woman and you've got the detectives, notably the curveballs they were throwing at you this morning. Again, it's just stuff you've been told." He flung out his hands for emphasis. "First set . . . second set. So right away, you know what you have to stop doing, right?"

I looked at him, unsure.

Parker leaned in. "You've got to stop treating *both* sets like they're the truth. You follow?" He didn't wait for me to answer. "Take the detectives, for instance. When all is said and done they're accountable for the truth only on the witness stand.

Until then it's all a game. Hide and seek. They think you're hiding something, and they want to find out what it is."

"But I'm not."

"Irrelevant. If you were the pope they'd handle you the same way. They'd kiss your ring, but they'd still think you were holding out on them. So that's the first thing, right off the bat. Being able to discern what's for real and what's merely bait."

"The stuff about Sam Kent's being out of town, her saying she doesn't know who I am—you're telling me it might not be true?"

"No. I'm telling you not to believe it simply because you're told it," said Parker. "Example. You said the detectives claimed Sam was definitely at the Ritz-Carlton up in Boston. Bullshit. She *may* have been there, in fact she probably was, but there's no way the detectives have got around to proving that yet. Until they do, though, they'll act as if they have, even tell you they have witnesses. It turns up the heat on you."

"That's legal?"

"It's all relative. Somebody was murdered, which happens to be extremely far down on the list of things that are legal. I think the word for what they do, what the detectives have, is leeway."

"So, what am I supposed to do?"

"Exactly this. Talk to a lawyer," he said. "The visit the detectives made to your apartment—that charade about a glass of water to get into your kitchen, literally and figuratively—was all about one thing. What's more, it's the one thing I'm sure they didn't tell you."

"What's that?"

"They found the murder weapon."

"The knife?" I asked.

"Yep. Now they want to know if it could belong to you. That's your prize for being in the wrong place at the wrong time last night."

"It probably didn't help that I lost my temper with them this morning."

"Don't worry about it. Who wouldn't be upset in that situation? You were tired, frustrated—your reaction was perfectly normal. Again, though, you were playing by their rules, working with their set of so-called facts. They may all be true, but you've got no way of knowing at this point. Like I said, what you've got to focus on from here on out is everything you know for sure, the stuff you can prove. *And it all revolves around your patient.*"

I began to feel it before he finished that last sentence. The looming. A creeping sensation, originating in the gut where a hundred dollars' worth of raw fish was starting to work its way back upstream. It was nausea. It was queasiness.

It was dread.

I knew the road Parker was about to go down. I knew exactly where he was heading. The problem was, I was already there. It was all coming together. And it was all falling apart.

Said Parker, "What you want to do right away is gather everything that establishes Samantha Kent as your patient. For starters, did she pay you by check or credit card?"

I closed my eyes and rubbed the back of my head. "She paid me in cash," I said, barely above a whisper.

"She did?"

"Yeah, she said she didn't want her husband to know she was seeing a therapist. She told me he saw all the canceled checks and credit card bills."

"What about your other patients? Did one of them maybe see her in your office?"

I thought about it. "No, I don't think so."

"Wait—what about Mila? She would've had to go through Mila to get to you, right?"

"E-mail."

"What?"

I was now mumbling.

"E-mail," I said again, a shade louder. "She exchanged e-mails with Mila after first contacting my service. They never actually talked."

"Christ, David, how could—" Parker stopped. He was catching himself. His voice had become agitated, his expression tense. The lawyer hat was starting to piece it together and, in doing so, was threatening to knock the friend hat right off his head. "Sorry," he said.

"It's all right," I assured him. "Let me explain."

I told him about my first session with Sam. Her going on about not giving Mila a phone number because she was moving. Then her tears and the supposed truth. Sam's fear of her husband. *Her fear that she might kill him.*

"How serious did you think she was?" he asked.

"Not enough to report her, if that's what you're asking. She seemed far too levelheaded."

"Okay, keep going."

I did.

It felt so odd at first to be recounting the intimate details of a session to someone else. An instinctive twinge of betrayal. But I got over it pretty quickly. Patient confidentiality assumed the person was actually a patient. Suddenly, I didn't know what Sam Kent was. Or, for that matter, who she was. The one thing becoming increasingly clear was that she wasn't the wife of Conrad Birch. Detectives Trentino and Lopez had indeed met the real one. That much wasn't bait.

"So, what do we got?" said Parker. He was talking to himself as much as he was to me. "You were treating a woman who claimed to be Sam Kent. She's not. You don't know who she really is, nor can you prove she even exists."

"My notes," I said. "What about my notes?"

"That's the problem. They're *your* notes. It's like writing about a UFO. It proves nothing."

I thought of something else. "What about her phone call to me at home; can't we trace the number?"

"Did she call you on your cell?"

"No, landline."

He shook his head. "LUDs only cover outgoing calls."

"Lugs?"

"*LUDs,*" he said. "Local Usage Details—otherwise known as your phone records."

A waiter swooped in and removed our plates. "Coffee?" he asked. We both declined, sitting in silence as he departed.

Then a click in my head, the spark of remembrance. "The party," I said.

"The what?"

"The Kesper Society cocktail party. I told you I was going for Crescent House, right?"

He nodded.

"She was there."

Bingo, said Parker's eyes. "You mean a roomful of people saw the two of you together?"

There was that nausea again. That queasiness. That dread.

"Not exactly," I said, deflated. "She approached me outside on the sidewalk as I was leaving. She was dressed to the hilt and came down the steps of the museum as if she'd been inside."

"But she never was."

"So it would seem."

"How'd she know you'd be there?" he asked.

"I have no idea."

"Actually, come to think of it, she could've read it in the paper. The Kesper people put out a press release naming the different organizations invited—it makes all the gossip columns. She could've seen Crescent House listed somewhere."

I nodded. Never mind that I could count on one hand how many times I'd read a gossip column and still have five fingers to spare.

"Still," he continued, "she had to give you a reason for her being there, right?"

"She told me her husband managed the charitable trust for the Kesper Society."

"Her husband being Conrad Birch?"

"She never referred to him by name."

"She was alone, though?"

"Yes. She said her husband was traveling."

"How convenient."

"Very."

Parker shook his head slowly. "It's pretty damn incredible when you think about it," he said, almost impressed. "I mean, what that implies. The planning, the maneuvering, the—" He stopped again. This time because of the look I was giving him. A look of regret. "What is it?" he asked.

"There's something else."

I'd told him everything. That is, everything from the moment I'd been woken up by the phone call the night before. Consciously or not, I hadn't come clean with the whole story. I hadn't told him what happened after the Kesper party, her coming back to my apartment and making me dinner. How fitting—the *no-name linguine* prepared by the woman using someone else's name.

Parker listened intently to the details of that night, the sexual underpinning being quite obvious.

"Tell me you didn't . . ." His voice trailed off.

"No, I didn't," I said. "She just cooked me dinner."

"But you were attracted to her?"

"Yes," I admitted.

"And she seemed attracted to you, right?"

"Yes."

"Was she ever by herself in the kitchen?"

I thought for a second. "At some point I left to get a bottle of wine."

"I wonder where she put it."

"The wine?"

"No, the knife," he said. "She had to get it out of your apartment somehow."

"You think—"

"More than think. You're missing a knife, all right. The same knife used to kill Conrad Birch."

"Fuck."

"Fuck squared," said Parker. He leaned back in his chair and folded his arms. "Congratulations, David; you're being framed for murder."

NINETEEN

On the bright side, I didn't have to rush back to work. Some bright side.

"Take tomorrow off too," Parker told me. He'd paid the bill for lunch and we'd just said good-bye to Jimmy. The consummate host managed to remember my name. Including the *doctor* part.

"I can't cancel another day," I said, once on the elevator. "If you're worried about my mind-set, Parker, don't. I'll be fine."

"That's not why," he said. "Though, yes, I am concerned about your mind-set. You need to be available for me all day tomorrow in case I decide to set something up with them."

"With who?"

"The detectives."

"What for?"

"To air everything out. Otherwise you're a sitting duck."

We stepped off the elevator and began walking down the long corridor. As we approached the shiny black lacquer door, it opened and two Japanese businessmen stepped inside. We exchanged quick, knowing glances. Secret handshakes with our eyes.

"There are a couple of things you've got to do first," said Parker, once we were out on the street. "The first is to try to figure out how you know Conrad Birch, if at all. That's crucial. If this woman has really done a number on you—and so far she has—the odds are your instincts are right and there's some connection to be made. If we know what it is, I'm confident about going to the detectives."

"And if I can't figure it out?"

"Then we press our luck and wait a bit. They've got you at the scene with an alibi that, so far, you can't prove. They've got the murder weapon, which, not to jump the gun—or the knife, as the case may be—belongs to you. The one thing they don't have, however, is any inkling of a motive. They don't need that to arrest you, but it sure makes the D.A.'s office a lot more comfortable. So my bet is, the detectives will be paying you another visit."

"Do I cooperate?"

"Not anymore," he said. "You're on record as claiming you don't know Birch. You can't give them the chance to pin you as a liar. If they come to talk to you again, don't say a word—simply call me and we'll take it from there. In the meantime, I'm going to make a few calls myself. A couple of friends of mine in uniform might know something about the investigation."

"What else do I have to do?"

"Go over your session notes you took on the woman," he said. "The fake Samantha Kent."

The fake Samantha Kent. It would've been funny if it wasn't happening to me.

"What am I looking for?" I asked.

"Clues, a mistake, anything. Something she said that tips her hand. No matter how clever she's been, nobody's perfect." He raised his forefinger. "On that note, buy yourself one of those minirecorders in case she's foolish enough to call you again."

"Okay. What else?"

"I think that's it," he said. "Oh, on second thought, you should have your forehead checked out. That's a pretty nasty gash. You might need a stitch or two."

"The EMT thought the butterfly bandages would be enough."

"What EMT? You mean at the town house last night?"

"Yeah."

"You didn't clean that yourself?"

"No. The detectives had one of the medical guys take a look at it."

"And he cleaned it for you?"

"Yeah, why?"

Parker thought for a second, ultimately shaking his head. "It's nothing. Don't worry about it."

I didn't believe him. My eyes made that clear.

"Listen, everything's going to be fine," he said. "A little hairy for a bit, but ultimately fine. So just hang in there, okay?"

"Do I have a choice?"

Parker spotted a cab down the street and quickly raised his hand. "Where you heading?" he asked. His office was down near Wall Street.

"Up to my office," I said. "I'm going to check on my notes like you suggested."

The cab pulled up to Parker. "Go ahead, take this one," he offered.

"No, it's okay. I'm going to walk for a bit."

"You sure?"

"Yeah. Listen, thanks for everything. I really don't know what I'd . . . I mean, with everything that's happened, I wouldn't know who else to, you know—"

"David?"

"What?"

"You suck at sentimental."

"Not a strong suit, huh?"

He shook his head, let out a laugh, and opened the door to the cab. "I'll talk to you later, all right?"

"Sure."

I started to walk back uptown. Any hope of clearing my mind in the process was quickly lost. Everything replayed itself. The previous night, the past few weeks. I couldn't help it, couldn't stop it. Every other block seemed to bring a new revelation. Another piece to the puzzle that was the fake Samantha Kent.

My Mystery Patient.

The bit about her nanny. What was her name? Celine? Celeste? I was pretty sure it was Celeste. The conversation on the sidewalk outside the Met after Kesper's cocktail party. Celeste was the reason that dinner had to be cooked at my place. Then, back at my apartment, she was the one supposedly on the other end of the phone taking down my number. My *unlisted* number. It would be needed two nights later when I got the call.

My Mystery Patient.

The favor she asked me. Escorting her down from my apartment and into a cab. She knew it was no favor at all. It was my obligation. As a *gentleman*. She probably had worked out a very crafty way of telling me her address. A little story. An aside. All very natural and all intended to plant the seed—making sure I'd remember when the time came. When I had to rush to her rescue.

Oh, how easy I'd made it for her. She didn't have to tell me anything. I joined her in the cab and went along for the ride. My bid to be the übergentleman. How amazing to think that even then she nearly gave my memory too much credit. I almost couldn't remember the address. But, of course, I'd seen the town house firsthand. She knew I'd find it if I had to crisscross every block on the Upper West Side. And just to make sure, she went out of her way to prompt me about that huge eagle over the entrance. So clever.

My Mystery Patient.

She must have killed Conrad Birch. She must have had a key to his town house. She must have known him somehow. And she must have known the real Samantha Kent would be out of town. I glanced down at my left hand as I continued to walk. There was the coil mark from the stove on the inside of my palm. If that didn't sum it up, nothing else could.

I'd really been burned.

But with all the revelations came new questions. Not to mention a greater urgency to answer some of the ones outstanding. What were her motives? Why did she want Conrad Birch dead, and why was I being set up to take the fall? I was becoming more convinced that I indeed knew Conrad Birch somehow. It would mean she and I both knew him without knowing each other. Yet, there still had to be a connection between the two of us. For some reason she'd sought me out. Chose me to play with.

Why?

I took a few more steps and stopped on a dime. I turned, raised my hand, and marched out into the street looking for the first available cab. I had a feeling I knew where a few more answers were waiting, and it was exactly where I was heading. But the time for walking was over. I was now in a hurry.

TWENTY

It was almost creepy.

The darkness, the stillness of my office. I'd spent hours there alone so many times, and yet this time somehow felt different— as if I were trespassing on my own property. A ridiculous notion, I assured myself. Though hardly a surprise. In relatively short order I'd managed to corner the market on things that were out of whack.

I flipped on some lights and approached my credenza, pulling out a drawer. As it slid along the rollers, the whole piece creaked as if it were being woken up. The file for Samantha Kent wasn't what I went to first. Instead, I went with my gut. Straight to the *B*'s. Baxter . . . Bernstein . . . Bibby. My fingers shuffled past each file and its protruding plastic name tab in robotic fashion. One after the other until . . . there it was.

Birch, Conrad.

I'd known the guy from somewhere, all right. That somewhere being my office. I removed his file, took it over to my desk, sat down, and opened it. As soon as I did I knew why my memory of him was so hazy. There was only a single page of notes in his folder. It was from our first, and what ultimately would be our last, session together. Conrad Birch had been a foot dipper.

On average they occurred one out of every ten prospective patients. Those people who, for any number of reasons, decided not to continue with therapy after their initial exposure to it. Their interest was fleeting, and it was as if they'd dipped their foot in the pool and decided they weren't up for the swim. I'd had enough of them over the years to forget their names and often their faces. But I never failed to take notes on each and every one.

Good thing.

My eyes immediately went to the upper right corner of the page. The date. It had been just over a year since Conrad Birch had sat in my office. I tried to picture him. His clothes or a certain idiosyncrasy. Did he sit on the couch or in the wingback chair? It was no use. Any remnant of that day had been deeply buried. Mostly by time, but also by the horrific image still fresh in my mind and not about to go anywhere. A man drenched in blood and frozen in fear. Conrad Birch, dead in his bed.

I raced through my notes. Once, and then twice. The short, choppy sentences I'd settled into as habit over the years. A kind of shorthand. I called it my psychological yeast—intended to give rise to the big picture. A person in full.

It seemed Conrad Birch had come to me with a problem as common as it was complex. The guy was having an affair, and he was worried. He said he couldn't leave his wife and understood he had to end it with his mistress. However, he feared how she'd take the news. She had a temper. She had a mean streak. He wanted to know how he should handle it.

That was it. The gist of what I'd written . . . other than a single last bullet point: *discussed how best to break with mistress.*

I didn't elaborate on that in my notes. I didn't need to. Like I said, it was a problem as common as it was complex. Few things are more symptomatic of being human than having an affair. "The problem isn't in your head," I'd often say. "It's in your DNA." That didn't make it right. It just made it ubiquitous.

So I probably told Birch what I'd told a lot of people before him. He needed to strike a balance. To be sympathetic to the feelings of his mistress but also firm in expressing his own. To be honest but not to a fault.

I wasn't advocating coldheartedness or deceit, just realism. By definition, breaking anything off in this world—whether it be a relationship or a branch from a tree—caused some type of damage. To accept that was to accept that there were no quick fixes. No magic elixirs. Bottom line: there was going to be some hurting. The goal was to minimize it. Do that and both sides would end up okay.

Of course, in the case of Conrad Birch, he ended up at the morgue.

Was there a connection? Was his mistress my Mystery Patient? A jilted lover seeking revenge? While that suggested a motive for murder, it left unclear why she'd want me to take the fall.

She had a temper. She had a mean streak. That's what he'd said.

I went back to my credenza and flipped through the *K*'s. Kass . . . Kebner . . . Keddilson. My forefinger came to a stop on the newest plastic name tab.

Kent, Samantha.

I returned to my desk and went over what I'd written. Three pages representing two sessions. I was looking for a mistake, a slipup. As Parker put it, something she'd said that tipped her hand.

The problem was, that's all she did. Everything was about tipping her hand. She made me think she was in a disastrous marriage, wed to an emotionally manipulative man. A mother of a young son stuck with no way out because of the taint of a previous suicide attempt.

"I'm here because I want to kill my husband," she'd confessed.

It wasn't possible to lay down your cards any more than that. And all for one purpose. So when she called me in the black of the night, her faint voice telling me that she'd actually gone through with it, I'd *believe*. I'd jump to, a puppet on a string.

I closed the file. Slammed it, actually. The more I read, the more I came to realize what a dupe I'd been. It could've happened to anyone, I tried to tell myself. But there wasn't much consolation in that. It had happened to *me*, and I felt disgusted. No, worse than that, actually.

I felt helpless.

TWENTY-ONE

The slender man with silver hair was putting on his Burberry coat while talking to someone. I saw him as I spun through the revolving doors. Then he saw me. Immediately, he turned on his heels. "*Thank God* you're here, Dr. Remler," he called out.

This from a man I'd never met before.

I had left the office, the two files in hand, and cabbed it back to my apartment. There in the lobby was Robert Gordon, the building's owner. All I'd seen before was a photo of him—the *same* photo—over and over in the quarterly bulletins that updated tenants on the various goings-on in our high-rise. Now, as he approached me, I couldn't help thinking one thing: it was high time Mr. Gordon got a new photo taken. The one featured in those bulletins, clearly snapped sometime during the Reagan administration, had moved well beyond a stretch.

"Robert Gordon of Gordon Holdings," he said, his hand extended.

I shook it and informed him I knew who he was.

"I recognized you from your book jacket," he offered, perhaps in response to my slightly quizzical look as to how he knew it was me.

I nodded and waited for him to continue.

"My goodness, you don't know, do you?" he finally said.

"Know what?" I asked.

"I came down as soon as I was called. This sort of thing has never happened before in any of my buildings, so I wasn't sure about all the legalities. In fact, I even called my attorney to see if they could really do such a thing without your being here."

"Mr. Gordon, I'm afraid I don't—"

"Turns out, though, that a search warrant pretty much entitles them to free rein."

"*A what?*"

"A search warrant," he repeated. "It happened a little while ago. Two detectives arrived, along with a policeman, to search your apartment. They ordered the super, Javier, to open your door. Javier, so you know, called my office immediately and . . . Dr. Remler, wait!"

I was already ten feet gone, heading straight for the elevators. Had there actually been one there waiting, he never would've caught up.

Again: "Dr. Remler, please wait!"

As I hit the Up button, Mr. Gordon stationed himself next to me.

"*When* did you say this happened?" I asked.

"About an hour and a half ago," he said, catching his breath. "That's when they first got here."

"When did they leave?"

"They were in your apartment up until ten minutes ago."

The elevator arrived. We both stepped on, and I pressed for the twenty-second floor.

As the doors closed, Mr. Gordon cleared his throat. "I might mention that when I got here I insisted that one of the detectives show me the search warrant. Not that I'm an expert, but it did look legitimate."

"I'm sure that it was," I said.

"Does that mean you know what this is all about?"

I gave the man a good, long, hard blink. All people were nosy. Some simply took longer than others to get around to it.

"No, unfortunately, I don't," I said in a tone that suggested it was none of his business. He picked up on it. Sort of.

"As you might imagine, Dr. Remler, the building will have to conduct its own inquiry regarding this situation."

I was spared from having to respond by our arrival at the twenty-second floor. The elevator doors opened, and again I was off to the races, leaving Mr. Gordon in my dust like a fifty-to-one shot. For some reason, I expected to see a web of yellow tape down around my apartment. Probably because I'd seen so much of it the night before at the town house. Instead, when I reached my door there wasn't anything to indicate I'd had company, welcome or not. Somehow, that almost made it worse.

Here goes nothing, I thought, reaching for the doorknob.

Nothing, indeed. The door was locked. How thoughtful of the police. God forbid anyone else be afforded the chance to take stuff from my apartment.

I reached for my keys. Again, Mr. Gordon caught up to me.

As I opened the door, I prepared for the worst: Hollywood's version of the search warrant. Drawers turned upside down, clothes strewn everywhere, the obligatory ripped pillow, with feathers still floating in the air. Ironically, Hollywood's version of the search warrant isn't too far off from Hollywood's version of the burglary.

I stood in the doorway and looked.

There were no feathers still floating in the air. In fact, the place looked pretty much as I'd left it. *Pretty much.* When I stepped in and began to eye things a little more carefully, the signs were there. Cushions were rearranged, wall hangings slightly askew. That was just the living room.

The room to check after that was a no-brainer. I walked into my kitchen and immediately saw what I expected. Which is to say, I didn't see it at all. It was gone. I no longer possessed a knife set. They'd taken the entire block of J.A. Henckels. *They.* Who was I kidding? I had little doubt Detective Lopez was the one gleefully wrapping the thing up in an evidence bag. Not that Trentino didn't also have his fun. That full glass of water I'd given him—the one he never took a sip out of—was sitting in the exact same spot on the counter. Only now it was empty.

I was really starting to dislike these guys.

The rest of the kitchen appeared in order, so I made my way back toward the living room. That's where I discovered Mr. Gordon having the time of his life. He was in full snoop mode, poking around the back of my bookshelf as if I were Jeffrey Dahmer and there were former tenants—at least parts of them—floating around in old Mason jars just waiting to be found.

"I keep them in my freezer," I said.

He jumped at the sound of my voice, nearly knocking over a shelf and my complete set of Churchill's *The Second World War*. "Excuse me?" he said, turning to me with a very poor attempt at nonchalance.

"Never mind." I ran a hand through my hair. "Listen, Mr. Gordon, I appreciate your coming here and seeing to this matter personally. Now, if you don't mind, I've got to make a few calls—as you might imagine. So, unless there's anything else I can—"

"No, no, I understand," he said. "I really have to be going anyway."

He didn't move. So I did. I started to walk toward my door, which had remained open.

"I'm just glad I hadn't left before you got here," he added. "I wouldn't have wanted a doorman—or Javier, for that matter—to be the one who broke the news."

I turned back to him. "Nor I, Mr. Gordon. Again, I appreciate all you've done."

He still didn't move.

"Perhaps when things settle down you could ring me at my office and fill me in a little more," he was saying now.

"Absolutely," I lied.

"I mean, I'm sure what's happened here is one big misunderstanding, right?"

The man was inertia.

"Yes, that's exactly what it is," I said. "One big misunderstanding."

He smiled, although I could tell he was far from convinced. Finally, he headed for the door. As he did he reached into his coat and pulled out his wallet. He removed a business card. "Maybe if I could hear from you tomorrow?" he said, handing it to me.

I took the card and ushered Mr. Gordon the last few steps to my door. "Maybe," I told him. He looked as if he wanted to say something more, but my closing the door in his face while quickly uttering, "Thanks again," pretty much nipped that idea in the bud.

Good-bye, Mr. Gordon.

TWENTY-TWO

I poured myself a drink. Then another. After that I picked up the phone and dialed. It was Stacy who answered.

"Hi, David," she said. "He's right here."

Normally, there would've been some chitchat between her and me, but Parker had obviously filled her in.

He got on the line. "Hey, buddy."

There'd be no small talk here either. I got right to it. "The bastards came and searched my apartment."

"I know," said Parker.

"You do?"

"Yeah, I caught wind of it about twenty minutes ago. A friend of mine from downtown. I called your direct line at the office, but I guess you'd already left."

"Yeah, it was a nice surprise to come home to."

"They didn't turn your place upside down, did they?" he asked.

"More like sideways," I said. "They took the knives."

"Makes sense considering that they did indeed find the murder weapon."

"You confirmed that?"

"Yeah."

"So you were right."

"Believe me, I wish I'd been wrong," he said.

"Where'd they find it?"

"In the alley next to the town house. The knife was clean—no blood and no prints—but it was found directly beneath one of the windows of the master bedroom. Given that it's consistent with the stab wounds, we'd be talking about the king of all co-incidences."

"So they can just do that? They can march into my apartment and take my knives?"

"Among other things."

"What do you mean?"

"I don't know yet, exactly. All I was able to find out was that they found something else implicating you besides the knives," he said. "What does it say on the property voucher?"

"The what?"

"It's a piece of paper they're required to leave behind. It lists what was removed."

"I haven't seen it," I said. "Where would it be?"

"It's supposed to be readily visible, but sometimes they like to have a little fun, you know, like taping it to the toilet seat."

"Hilarious."

"Yeah, I know."

I checked in my bathrooms. I checked in my bedrooms. No piece of paper to be found.

"Where else haven't you looked?" he asked.

"Only the library."

Sure enough. On the seat of the chair behind my desk was the property voucher. Holding it in place was clearly an example of "having a little fun." A handpicked book-cum-paperweight taken from my shelf: Dostoyevsky's *Crime and Punishment*.

I read Parker what was on the voucher. Indeed, there were two things listed, except the second item—after the knives—wasn't what you'd call specific: *Misc. Paper.*

"What's that supposed to mean?" I asked. "It could be any-thing."

"That's the point; they don't want us to know yet. Take a look on your desk there. Do you notice anything missing?"

I quickly thumbed through a few stacks of papers. "Offhand, I don't. I'll check more after I hang up."

"Don't worry about it; we'll find out soon enough."

I stared down at the voucher again. "Hey, aren't they supposed to leave behind a copy of the search warrant as well?"

"Actually, no, they're not required to. But I'm sure it's legit. The missing knife from your set would've been ample cause for any judge," he said, before changing gears. "Tell me, did you learn anything at your office?"

"As a matter of fact, I did. I checked my files. Conrad Birch had come to me for a single session a little over a year ago."

"No kidding."

"It gets better. You know what was bothering him? He was having an affair and wanted to end it. Birch was worried about how his mistress would take the news. He described her as having a mean streak."

"You think—"

"It's a definite possibility," I said. "My Mystery Patient was his mistress."

"That would be one hell of a mean streak. Though it would explain a lot, wouldn't it?"

"Yes, except why it is I had to be involved."

"Right," said Parker. "And that was your only involvement with Birch? One session?"

"That was it."

"Nothing else in your notes?"

"No. At least nothing that jumps out at me."

"Okay, now just tell me he didn't pay for the session in cash."

"Wouldn't that be something?" I said with a half-laugh. "But I'm sure it was either by check or credit card. I'll have Mila look into the invoice."

"Not that we're rushing to prove any connection," he said. "I mean, the good news is we know how you know him. The bad news is you told the police you didn't."

"Couldn't we simply explain the circumstances?"

"We could, though I've got to think about that one. They can't subpoena your patient files, so it's a question of how they'd find out."

"I don't want to lie, Parker."

"You also don't want to go to jail."

The mere mention of the word had me flustered. I took a deep breath. "This is really happening, isn't it?"

"I'm afraid so."

"When does it begin to get better?"

He didn't say anything. Never was there a more ominous silence.

"You there, Parker?"

"I'm here."

"What is it you're not telling me?"

Now it was his turn to take a deep breath. "It's like this," he said. "But before you freak, trust me, it's not as bad as it sounds."

"Parker . . ."

"Okay, okay," he said. "Tomorrow, you're going to be arrested for the murder of Conrad Birch."

I started to freak.

He let me go for a bit. As if I were a blue marlin that had just been hooked. I ranted. I raved. I exploded with anger. Only when I started to ramble on about prison and being somebody's bitch did my best friend decide it was perhaps time to reel me in.

"All right, so this is what I've been able to negotiate so far," he began. "I spoke to the D.A.'s office, and the cops are in line with this. They're not going to come and get you. We're going to go to them. That way, there'll be no flashbulbs going off. Turns out, Conrad Birch was a pretty big deal on Wall Street. Did you know that?"

I barely heard what Parker was saying.

"David, I need you to focus here," he said.

He was right and I knew it. I had to try to compose myself.

Bear down and concentrate. This was my life we were talking about.

"A big deal on Wall Street? No, I didn't know that," I said.

"Yeah, well, apparently he—"

"Wait, I *did* know that."

In a flash, the first session I had with Samantha Kent came back to me. Make that, the fake Samantha Kent—a distinction I was having a hard time getting used to. Whoever she was, she'd claimed her husband was a venture capitalist downtown. I'd even asked her if that meant Wall Street. I remembered because of the way she answered. It was a phrase she claimed her husband had often used. *That's where the money is.*

Like that, her duplicity became all the more staggering. She actually commingled fact and fiction. I explained this all to Parker, and we both agreed: the idea of my Mystery Patient being Conrad Birch's mistress was gaining momentum.

"Back to my impending incarceration," I said. How I was managing glibness at that point, I didn't know.

Parker continued, "What I was saying was that we're going to make this as civil as possible. I've promised the D.A.'s office your complete cooperation, and they've promised a meeting. The arrest is going to happen, but what the meeting gets us is an up-close look at what they think they've got on you. It also means you'll be processed faster."

"Is that supposed to cheer me up?"

"Yes, because you'll get a same-day arraignment and won't have to spend a night in lockup. You'll thank me later."

"They've agreed to all this?"

"It wasn't easy."

"And I'm being a dick to you about it, aren't I?"

"I didn't exactly expect you to do cartwheels, so don't worry about it," he said. "Now let's talk about posting bail. How much are you worth?"

"I have no idea."

"Sure you do. Think about it. Stocks, bonds, savings. You rent now, but on the flip side there had to be profits from the sale of . . ." Parker was about to mention the apartment and the lake cottage I'd owned with Rebecca. I knew why he stopped. I could tell what he was thinking. *Probably not the best time to bring up the dead wife.*

But it was too late. I'd started to think about her, and as a result, I began missing her in a way I never had before. It was a hybrid of loneliness and anger, and it had nothing to do with the places we called home. I simply realized that none of this would've been happening if Rebecca were still alive.

"Anyway," said Parker, bulling ahead, "try roughing out a number."

I started doing the math in my head. Royalties from *The Human Pendulum* had proved quite the windfall. "Three and a half million," I ultimately told him. "That's about what I'm worth."

"How much of that is liquid?"

"Close to two."

"Good," he said. "Push comes to shove, I can always secure a bond for you if necessary."

"Thanks."

"Hey, that's what friends are for."

"Yeah, but who would've thought?"

"I know, this is one fine mess, that's for sure."

"No, what I mean is, I always knew you'd be my friend. Who would've thought you'd also be my lawyer."

Silence.

"That's the other thing," he said, his voice hesitant.

"What's that?"

"I'm not going to be your lawyer."

It was yet another surprise in a day loaded with them. "What are you talking about?" I asked. "Is it one of those conflict things?"

"No, it's not that," he said. "I'll be the first to tell you, I'm a really good criminal defense attorney. As cocky as that sounds, it's actually quite the opposite. Because part of what makes me so good is that I know when a prospective client needs something different from what I can offer. Or, in certain situations, something better."

"I think you're selling yourself short, Parker."

"Not in this case. This one's going to be a different animal. High profile. Talked about and written about. Which means you need someone with an equally high profile leading your charge; someone who's more used to playing in that arena. That's what I mean by better."

"Are you sure?"

"Never more so," he said. "I've given it a lot of thought, and I've already made the arrangements. Meet me in the lobby of the Chrysler Building tomorrow morning at nine sharp."

"You're going to introduce me to the guy who's better?"

"No," said Parker. "I'm going to introduce you to the guy who's the best."

TWENTY-THREE

Before going to bed that night, I called Mila to tell her I'd be out another day. At least. I also confirmed what she'd already suspected. It had nothing to do with my being sick.

"Let's just say I wasn't about to make you any *kasicka*," said Mila. The dish was her version of chicken soup. Never mind that it had no chicken in it, nor was it really a soup.

I apologized for being less than honest and further apologized for not being able to give her the whole story. My reluctance to explain everything had as much to do with exhaustion as discretion. I did reveal that the problem related to my newest patient, Samantha Kent. Or, as I told Mila, a woman posing as Samantha Kent. "*Do prdele!*" she exclaimed upon hearing that little twist. While I boasted a most limited Czech vocabulary, I had no problem translating. *Holy shit!*

On the heels of that, I asked Mila if she could dig up the billing paperwork on Birch.

"Is there some sort of connection?" she asked while going through her files.

"Quite possibly," I said, leaving it at that. She didn't press me, probably realizing she'd be told in due time.

"Here it is," she said. "Oh, good, he paid by check. June of last year."

The "oh, good" was because Mila made a copy of all incoming checks before depositing them.

"Do you want me to get it over to you?" she asked.

"No, hold on to it for now. I'll let you know when I need it."

"No problem. Anything else?"

There was, in fact, one more thing. I asked her about those initial e-mails sent by my Mystery Patient. "Any chance you still have them in your computer?"

Mila's initial silence was answer enough. She'd deleted them.

I wasn't surprised. Nor was I terribly disappointed. Given the lengths gone to by my Mystery Patient to live up to her moniker, I highly doubted she would've left an electronic trail. I could almost picture her sitting at one of those public terminals at a cybercafe.

"Sorry, David," said Mila.

"Don't worry about it." I added a few words of false cheer and said good night. I hung up the phone and stared blankly at the wall. It was officially my word against the world.

That night, I got a good, solid twelve minutes of sleep.

At a little past nine the next morning, I met Parker in the lobby of the Chrysler Building, Forty-second and Lex. I would've been more punctual, except I couldn't figure out what to wear. How do you dress for an arrest?

As we rode the elevator up to the forty-fifth floor, Parker gave me a little background about the man we were on our way to see.

"His name is Victor Glass."

He was the managing partner of Edwards, Vode, Isadore & Locke. It was one of the oldest firms in the city, as revered as it was feared. "The founders were ruthless," explained Parker. "Dog kickers, candy from a baby, you get the idea—and just in case you don't, consider the firm's acronym."

He waited as I strung together the first letters of the founders' names. *Edwards, Vode, Isadore & Locke.*

I smiled, amused.

"Of course, that was a long time ago," he said. "They're all dead now. In-house counsel for Hell, Incorporated, if I had to guess."

Which brought him back to Victor Glass.

While Victor was perhaps not the equal of his firm's founders in meanness, he wasn't shaping up to be warm and fuzzy either. Parker described him as a tough-talking, charismatic guy's guy who could go from turning the screws to turning on the charm and back again in a heartbeat. Throw in the fact that he possessed a brilliant legal mind and you had a lawyer who'd managed to win more than 80 percent of his cases. For a prosecutor that would be extremely impressive. For a criminal defense attorney—what Victor was—it was Hall of Fame.

"How do you know him?" I asked.

"We originally met a couple of years ago at some husband-and-wife event put on by the Bar Association. Soon after, I scratched his back on something," said Parker. "Now he's scratching mine."

We got off the elevator and entered the spacious, ultramodern reception area of Edwards, Vode, Isadore & Locke. Not what I expected given the firm's long history. The space was a melding of curves and harsh angles, all of it set off by minimalist furniture, sleek lighting, and bizarre artwork. It was like Frank Lloyd Wright meets Frank Gehry meets Frank Zappa. So much for traditional mahogany.

"They've redecorated," said Parker, looking around. He sniffed. "Pretty recently too."

"It does kind of have that new-car smell, doesn't it?"

We approached a sharply dressed receptionist who pressed a button and announced our arrival into a tiny wraparound headset. Her voice was elegant and practiced. She made a couple of keystrokes on her computer as she waited for a response.

"Okay, thank you," she said into the headset before disconnecting the line. She looked up at us with a pleasant smile. "Mr. Glass will be with you in just a couple of minutes."

We had a seat on what was a park bench made out of leather. Scary thing was, it was pretty comfortable.

Parker reached into his briefcase. "Here," he said, handing me a glossy folder.

"What's this?" I asked.

"Victor's press kit."

I took the folder and stared at Parker with a raised eyebrow. "The man has a press kit?"

"Yep."

"Do you have a press kit?"

"Nope."

I was starting to get the picture.

I opened the folder and began thumbing through the various tear sheets and reprinted articles. The range was astounding. Victor Glass had been featured in everything from the *Harvard Law Review* to *Playboy*. As I looked at his photo in an article from *Esquire*, I realized I'd seen him before. Probably on TV, one of the cable news programs. The name hadn't stuck, but his face had.

Kind of like Conrad Birch.

I kept thumbing through the press kit. For sure, a lot had been written about Victor Glass. Then I came across something written *by* Victor Glass. It was an Op-Ed piece in the *New York Times* entitled "Dumb Justice." The argument was simple. Lawyers have educational requirements. Judges have educational requirements. Why not juries?

It was a fascinating read. Especially the last few paragraphs.

That said, consider this my closing argument:

Ten of the twelve jurors in the O. J. Simpson trial hadn't graduated from college. Should this prevent them from enjoying any of the freedoms in our society? Of course not. Should this prevent them from determining the freedoms of another human being?

You better believe it.

Circumstances preventing one from going to college are perhaps relevant in a job interview—but not the justice system. Too much is at stake. The fact is, education level bears directly on one's ability to reason, including the weighing of testimony and evidence. To deny that is to deny not only common sense, but the existence of more than one hundred independent studies. A "mountain of evidence," if you will.

We require our lawyers and judges to be college graduates. And yet, as demanding as those professions are, what job could possibly hold more responsibility than being a juror?

I suppose being President of the United States is a possibility, but that simply proves the point. Imagine our electing a Commander in Chief who never went to college.

Victor Glass is the author of If Only Jesus Had a Lawyer. *He's an attorney in Manhattan.*

"Just so you know, we fired the decorator," he said.

I looked up to see Victor Glass standing in the reception area. His suit jacket was off, his shirtsleeves rolled back to the elbows. Pretty interesting, I thought—he hadn't sent his secretary, choosing instead to greet us himself. It was a nice touch. The right touch.

Parker glanced around again at the decor. "Aw, it's not so bad," he said, getting up.

"Yeah, if you're Ray Charles," said Victor.

The smartly dressed receptionist tried to contain a laugh as Victor walked over and gave Parker a hearty handshake. Each expressed how good it was to see the other. I stood up, and Parker made the introduction.

"Victor, this is David Remler."

"It certainly is," he said. "I understand this isn't one of your better weeks."

"And it's only Tuesday," I said.

Victor flashed a smile. His teeth were whiter than white. Up until that moment I never quite understood the notion of someone having "movie-star good looks." Suddenly, I understood completely. Trim and fit, his hair combed back, he was the guy you'd normally see *playing* the part of a lawyer in some big movie. Only Victor was the real thing and, if Parker was right, one of the best there was.

And he couldn't have been more than forty.

"Why don't we head back to my office," he said. "We'll talk about what luck we might have with the rest of the week."

"Good idea," said Parker.

Victor gave one last suspicious look around the reception area, his eyes landing on a sculpture in the corner. It was made entirely of spoons. "I don't even want to know what that thing is supposed to be!" he nearly shouted, shaking his head. He then winked at the receptionist, who blushed ever so slightly.

We followed Victor down a long corridor. We took a right and walked another long corridor. Along the way we passed a series of huge paintings. Four distinguished-looking men, one seemingly frowning more than the next.

"The infamous Evil Bunch," said Victor, without breaking stride. "Their portraits got displaced when we redid the entrance. I think they're all pretty pissed at me because of it."

We kept walking. The corner of the building meant Victor's office. He had two gatekeepers. Both sexy librarian types. One a blonde, the other a brunette.

"Hold my calls, Ashley, will you?" he said to the blonde, who was sitting on the left as we passed by. Meanwhile, the brunette on the right got up and followed us into Victor's office.

"You guys want coffee or anything?" Victor asked.

We both declined. Secretary No. 2 turned with a polite smile and left us.

"All right, then," said Victor. He motioned us over to a seating area that included four oversize club chairs. I sat in one and looked around. Along the near wall was a colossal bookcase. Along the far wall was a gigantic credenza. In the corner, in front of a huge panoramic view of the East River, was Victor's massive desk. No wonder the guy seemed larger than life.

We were all seated.

"How's Karen?" Parker asked Victor.

"You mean my ex-wife?"

"Whoa, when did that happen?"

"A few months back."

"I'm sorry to hear that."

"You and my bank account," he said. There was that smile again. "No, I'm just kidding. I wish her well." He picked up a legal pad and a Montblanc from the enormous glass table in front of him. "So enough about my problems."

Parker had already given Victor the big picture, otherwise entitled "How the Hell My Friend, David Remler, Got into This Mess." Nonetheless, Victor wanted to hear it all from me. Start to finish. Beginning with the very first time a woman came into my office and introduced herself as Samantha Kent.

I spoke as calmly as I could.

Along the way Victor cut in with a few questions. He seemed to be operating on two levels. On the surface, he was filling in the gaps—things I either hadn't been clear about or simply neglected to mention. Below the surface, he was putting my story to the test—asking me about the details. What was she wearing at such and such a time? What wine did you drink at your apartment? Things like that. He didn't seem so concerned with my answers as with the way I gave them. Meaning, was I remembering or fabricating?

"And that brings us to our being here this morning," I said, finally wrapping up my story.

Victor jotted something down on his pad, after which he took a moment to review the notes he'd made. Then he looked up at me and stared right into my eyes. "So, did you kill Conrad Birch?"

I was flustered for a moment. Hadn't this guy been listening? "I just told you I didn't," I said with a note of defiance.

"No," said Victor. "What you told me was everything that supports the *argument* you didn't."

The distinction was a little lost on me.

"That's all right," he said. "The question has been asked and answered. Your body language says it all. You didn't kill Conrad Birch."

"Well, it's nice to have my lawyer at least believe me," I said facetiously.

"Yeah, except I'm not going to be your lawyer," said Victor.

I immediately looked at Parker, who up until that moment had been content to sit back and observe. Now he looked as confused as I did.

I threw my hands up. "Doesn't anyone want to represent me?"

Parker was about to say something. Victor followed up before he could.

"What I mean is, I won't be lead counsel," he said. "That is, if we do indeed go to trial."

"Why not?" I asked.

"Because I'm a guy, that's why." He was about to explain when Parker jumped in. He'd caught on fast.

"Because you'll be standing trial for killing a guy, and in your defense, you'll be blaming it on a woman," said Parker.

Victor nodded. "No less, a woman who we, as yet, can't prove exists," he said. "The prosecutor will stack the jury with chicks and make sure they all have a clear view of the grieving widow sitting in the front row."

"Oh" was the best I could muster in response.

Victor continued: "So the last thing you need is some slick guy like me standing up to argue for the entire trial. I'll be there. I won't be silent. And I'll be making sure everything goes as planned. But day in and day out, what you really need defending you is a pair of tits."

"And a great pair at that," came a voice.

I turned to look. We all turned to look. She was leaning against the doorway dressed in a white blouse and a black skirt that came right above her knees. But the most notable thing she was wearing was her confident smile.

My lead counsel had arrived.

TWENTY-FOUR

Speak of the devil," said Victor as she walked in the room. The three of us got up.

"No, Victor, *you're* the devil," she said. She reached Parker first and put out her hand. "I'm Terry Garrett."

"Parker Mathis," he said.

They shook. She turned to me. But instead of extending a hand, she simply looked me over. "Oh, good, you're attractive," she said. "Maybe we'll want a jury stacked with chicks after all."

While I marveled at how she could assess my appearance in a manner so matter-of-fact, so devoid of emotion, that there wasn't even a hint of flirtation, Parker shot Victor a look. *A jury stacked with chicks?* It was the same phrasing Victor had used.

"Am I mistaken, or do the walls have ears?" said Parker.

Victor shrugged his shoulders. "Sorry. It's just that men in trouble talk far more self-consciously when a woman is in the room. Given the specifics of David's predicament—his possible involvement with a female patient—I wanted to make sure we didn't have any filtering up front. Of course, I also didn't want to make you have the same conversation twice." Victor pointed at the speakerphone device on a nearby endtable. "This way Terry's up to speed."

"Big Brother lives," said Parker. "Or, should I say Big Sister?"

"Hey, I just work here," said Terry. "Sue Victor. He's the one with all the money."

"Ain't nobody poor at this place," said her boss.

With that, the four of us sat down.

"Terry is the latest addition to our family. She came to us from Weiss, Stone, and Wilcox out in L.A."

The way Victor said it, I presumed the place wasn't your typical Jacoby & Meyers.

"Excellent firm," said Parker.

"Yeah, well, Weiss still isn't talking to me," said Victor.

Terry smiled. "I think Victor would prefer to think he stole me away. Truth is, I was always an East Coast girl at heart."

"Second in her class at Harvard Law," said Victor.

"Yes, and all my mother wanted to know was who was first," said Terry.

"I think we had the same mother," said Parker.

Terry laughed. Parker laughed. Victor cracked a follow-up joke. I gazed at all three with a face that said "Hello? I hate to break up all the fun, but I'm about to be *arrested* later today!"

They all picked up on the look, and we quickly got back to business. Actually, the "we" didn't really include me. I'd given them the ball, and they were running with it, brainstorming angles and discussing possibilities. For example, whether there were any security cameras in my building that might have recorded my recent comings and goings, and with whom. If so, were the tapes saved and for how long?

On the heels of that, I threw out another idea—finding the cabdriver who took me to the town house that night. Surely he'd remember a guy who paid him an extra five bucks for every red light he ignored.

"I'm afraid it fails as an alibi," said Terry.

She wasn't bothered by the remote odds of tracking down the driver without knowing his name. Rather, what ruled out making the effort in the first place was the fact that every window in Conrad Birch's bedroom had been left open. The cold temperature that night had chilled his body to the point of preservation, effectively extending the time-of-death estimate by a few hours. That would've given me ample time to kill Birch, go home, and come back again via the cab under the pretense of helping my patient.

So much for that idea.

Eventually, my legal troika moved beyond the facts of the case to strategizing how the rest of the day should play out. First up would be our meeting with the detectives and the D.A.'s office. After that, I'd be processed and there'd be the arraignment.

As Terry, Victor, and Parker debated tactics, I sat there quietly, listening. Initially, I'd thought my best friend was going to be my lawyer. Then my best friend had introduced me to the guy he thought was the better man for the job. Then that man had told me what I really needed in my corner was a woman. Pondering it all, I wouldn't exactly describe my feelings as comfortable.

"Are you okay, David?" Terry asked after a bit. I obviously didn't look it.

"As a matter of fact, no," I answered. "I've been sitting here for over an hour, and I'm still waiting to hear one thing. Why a woman would want to pose as Conrad Birch's wife and frame me for his murder."

"*Why?*" said Victor. "David, this might sound a little strange, but that question really isn't relevant. Especially when it comes to keeping you out of jail. So don't worry about why. Making a jury believe it was possible in the first place—that's what we have to worry about."

"Just the same, I'd still like to know. Because it doesn't make any sense."

"I don't blame you," said Terry. "But that's the problem with irrational behavior. Everyone always approaches it looking for a rational explanation." She gave me a slight smile. "I think I got that from a book called *The Human Pendulum*. Ever hear of it?"

"Rings a bell," I told her.

"Which leads me to a question I'm pretty sure I already know the answer to," she said. "In everything you and this Mystery

Patient talked about, I bet you she never mentioned your book, right?"

I thought about it for a moment. "No, I'm fairly certain we never discussed it," I said.

Terry glanced at Parker and Victor before looking back at me. "It's just a hunch, but I'll bet you a million dollars she's read *The Human Pendulum* front to back. If not a few times over."

Victor nodded and then peeked at his watch. "I think it's time," he said.

"You're right," said Parker. He turned to me. "Are you ready?"

"As ready as I'll ever be," I answered. I tugged at my sport coat and brushed a hand on my jeans.

We all stood up.

"Okay then," said Victor, walking over and putting a hand on my shoulder. "Let's go get you arrested."

PART III

TWENTY-FIVE

I think it was David Byrne and his group, Talking Heads, who summed it up best with a simple lyric: *How did I get here?*

The here was New York Supreme Court, specifically a very uncomfortable chair at the defendant's table. To my right was Terry Garrett. To my left, Victor Glass. It was a lawyer sandwich, and I was the meat. Dead meat, perhaps, if you were an odds-maker.

But first, that question again: How did I get here?

It had been seven months since that initial meeting in Victor Glass's office. Seven months since I'd been introduced to Terry Garrett. From that point on it had been a crash course in the American legal system, the old axiom holding true: when it comes to learning the ins and outs of anything, there's no sub-stitute for hands-on experience.

Lesson 1: Beware of free medical attention.

From the spacious confines of Victor's office that first morning, we traveled to a cramped interrogation room at the Twentieth Precinct. It was a glorified closet—eight feet by ten feet if you rounded up. Everything about the room was metal. The furni-

ture. The blinds. Even the lukewarm coffee they offered us had
a metallic taste to it.

Strictly by the numbers, the teams were evenly matched. On
one side of the table were Detectives Trentino and Lopez. They
were joined by an assistant district attorney by the name of
Glenn Hemmerson. He was a thin man, roughly forty, with dark
eyes, big ears, and a haircut that suggested either he or his bar-
ber had served in the military. At the outset, it was explained
that the A.D.A. who'd shown up the night of Conrad Birch's
murder was heavily involved with another homicide case. Hemmerson was taking his place.

On the other side of the table was my team. My gang of three.
Parker, Terry, and Victor. Three-fifty, three-fifty, and five-
hundred an hour, respectively. Ouch. Parker was reducing some
of the sting by giving me the best-friend discount—100 percent
off. Still, even with Parker's being there gratis, I was looking at
a serious legal tab in the making. Enough that when Victor ex-
cused himself for a few minutes to go to the bathroom, I couldn't
help doing the math. The guy was taking a thirty-three-dollar
pee.

Not that I wasn't getting my money's worth.

What became abundantly clear was that Parker had placed me
in very capable hands. Terry was razor sharp and possessed an
unflinching poise. She also, for lack of a better phrase, knew
how to "work it." While the two detectives seemed to care less
that she was very attractive, Hemmerson, the A.D.A., couldn't
get past it. His was a libido on the loose. So whenever Terry
talked, her eyes—long lashes and all—always fixed on Hemmerson. He was too busy loving it to question it.

Then there was Victor.

Never had I seen a guy who could control a room like him.
For sure, he didn't kill 'em with kindness. There was no professional courtesy or smoke-blowing of any kind. Flummery was
not his style. Rather, Victor was arrogant, bellicose, and unrea-
sonable. A real loose cannon. How much of it was an act I didn't
know. What I did know was that it got the job done. He was able

to keep the other side on their collective heels and therefore dictate the meeting's flow—a feat all the more impressive given that he was hardly holding all the cards.

But as much as I derived some pleasure from watching Detectives Trentino and Lopez perform with a little less swagger, there was no denying the evidence they'd gathered. It was worse than I thought. A lot worse.

What I knew going in was bad enough. I was at the scene of the crime for a reason I couldn't prove. Strike one. The murder weapon had belonged to me. Strike two. The facts were indisputable. Were Trentino and Lopez keeping a checklist, the box next to *Did he have the means and opportunity?* would've been heavily shaded in.

Then came this development: motive.

At least a strong indication of what it might be. And where did it come from? The library in my apartment. The *Misc. Paper* of the property voucher finally defined.

It was a typewritten letter—hand signed—that Conrad Birch had apparently sent me a month earlier. As Hemmerson removed a photocopy of the letter from a folder and placed it on the table in front of me, I replayed that evening with my Mystery Patient. Our bumping into each other after the Kesper cocktail party. Her self-guided tour of my apartment as soon as we walked in the door. The playful quips shouted out from my library; how she expected more wood paneling and how if she spotted a pipe rack she'd be making a quick exit. Funny lines. Engaging lines. Buying her the time she needed to plant the letter. To deliver strike three.

I leaned over the table and read it. Victor, Terry, and Parker gathered behind me and did the same. Two short paragraphs with single-line spacing. Conrad Birch was writing to let me know he didn't appreciate the way I'd threatened him. He couldn't wire me the money right away because of a banking error. That's all. There was nothing sinister going on, he stressed in all caps, and I was not to worry. He'd soon clear everything up. Until then, he asked that I remain patient.

"Can you tell us what this letter is all about, Dr. Remler?" asked Hemmerson.

"No, he can't," said Victor quickly before I could respond.

"Can't or won't?" said Hemmerson.

"Both," said Victor. "Not until we get a handwriting analysis on the signature."

Hemmerson smirked. "Fair enough," he said. "But perhaps this is a good time to give Dr. Remler a second chance at a question he's already answered." He turned to me. "Did you know Conrad Birch?"

I immediately looked to Victor, who didn't bat an eyelash.

"Mr. Birch had been a patient of Dr. Remler's," he said. "Albeit for only one session."

"Excuse me?" said Hemmerson, his tone incredulous.

"You heard me," replied Victor. He reached into a folder and pulled out the copy of Birch's check courtesy of Mila.

Hemmerson glanced at it. "Then why did your client lie to the police?" he asked.

"Not revealing the identity of a patient is Dr. Remler's professional prerogative."

"Barring unmitigating circumstances, yes. But the guy was dead. Murdered, I might add."

"That doesn't change a thing."

"Says you."

"Says at least ten different judges in this state, the last I checked."

Hemmerson rolled his eyes. He couldn't tell whether Victor had done his homework or was completely bullshitting. Either way: "Then what about Dr. Remler's so-called Mystery Patient? Why didn't he extend her the same privilege? Why did he so easily offer it up that he was treating her?"

Victor came right back. "Because it was a life-or-death situation, that's why."

"You mean, the life or death of someone he can't prove exists."

"How quickly we forget who actually has the burden of proof," said Victor.

Again, Hemmerson smirked. "It's hardly shaping up to be a burden, if you ask me."

The subject was dropped, if only for the time being, which pretty much underscored the reality of that meeting. The certain inevitability of everything that would follow. For as good as Victor was, his intervention on my behalf that morning could only reap so much. And for all of Terry's skill and grace, she wasn't a magician. She wasn't able to make the mounting evidence go Poof! and disappear. No matter how much my lawyers maneuvered and angled, the road ahead looked very long and exceedingly bumpy.

"One last thing," said Hemmerson. "Would you care to discuss how and why your client's blood was found on the victim?"

Parker wasted no time. It was as if he'd been waiting for the question all along. The savvy hitter sitting on the curveball. "First off, you know that Dr. Remler admitted to incidental, after-the-fact contact with Mr. Birch," he stated coolly. "And as for how you even have a sample of Dr. Remler's blood, well, we'll leave that for the Mapp hearing and the issue of illegally obtained evidence."

I looked at Parker. Terry and Victor looked at Parker. Hemmerson looked at Parker. The only ones not looking at Parker were Trentino and Lopez. That's because Parker was looking at them. Glaring, actually.

"Am I supposed to understand what you're talking about?" asked Hemmerson.

"Why don't you ask your detectives," Parker answered. "When they had an EM technician clean a cut on Dr. Remler's forehead I'm sure they asked permission to retain his blood for analysis, right?"

I remembered Parker's original hesitation when I told him about the EMT. It was a definite, albeit fleeting, look of concern. I called him on it, and he told me it was nothing.

But it was something. He knew what had gone down, how

there was a high sign between the detectives and the technician. He knew that without even being there.

The A.D.A. glanced at Trentino and Lopez, who weren't about to admit to anything. It was pretty obvious Hemmerson didn't like surprises. Especially ones that complicated his job as a prosecutor. Nonetheless, he held his displeasure in check. "It's perfectly good evidence," he said.

Parker shook his head. "Perfectly inadmissible is more like it."

"We'll see about that."

"Yes, we will, won't we."

Terry interceded. "Gentlemen, why don't we move on," she said, all the while locking eyes with Hemmerson. His hard edge immediately softened, and he enthusiastically agreed. The horn dog. He was absolutely smitten. I got the sense that if Terry had said, "Gentlemen, why don't we all take turns kicking Hemmerson in the crotch and then throw him out the window," he would've enthusiastically agreed to that as well.

Meanwhile, Parker turned to me with a quick raise of the eyebrows. A wordless echo of what I was already thinking. Could I have realistically known what the detectives were plotting with the EMT? No. Just the same, the message that he'd begun to deliver over our lunch was now coming through loud and clear. We were playing on a whole other level. One where the rules were not only different but sometimes didn't even exist. I'd have to do my best to adapt and adjust.

In the interim, note to self: *beware of free medical attention.*

Lesson 2: Don't slouch.

Fingerprints. A mug shot. The requisite paperwork. After all the posturing in the meeting, the outcome was what was expected— no minds were changed. I was read my rights and officially arrested. New York State penal law, section 125.25. Murder in the second degree. By the time I was transported to central booking down on Centre Street, the clock on the wall said half past one. I would've looked at my watch for the time except I'd left it with Parker at the precinct. I gave it to him to hold, along with my wallet and key chain. The alternative was having the police put them in some oversize envelope for purportedly safekeeping. Strange how we tend to have "personal effects" only when we're either in prison or dead.

At a little before two I was in a holding area waiting for my arraignment. The good news, thanks mainly to my coming in voluntarily, was that the hearing was happening that same afternoon. The bad news was that after only ten minutes in that holding area I was going out of my mind. Up until that point, the confusion of what was happening to me had been neutralized by a quiet confidence that everything would be cleared up. That "justice" would prevail. Now I wasn't so sure.

And it was scaring the hell out of me.

I looked up in the corner to see a security camera staring back. It reminded me of yet another dead end in trying to prove my Mystery Patient existed: after checking with the management office for my building, Terry learned that none of the security cameras were the kind that recorded.

At around four thirty I was led out of the holding area by a gray-haired, potbellied officer, who guided me down a long hallway into the courtroom and over to a bench along the wall. The officer grunted three times, noises I took to mean "Have a seat." I had one while he remained standing right next to me.

I saw Parker first. He was seated in the aisle on the other side of the courtroom. He gave me a quick smile and a reassuring nod. Thankfully, he wasn't a thumbs-up type of guy because there wasn't enough optimism in the world at that moment to buy in to a gesture like that.

Next to Parker sat Terry. She'd been going over some papers in her lap when she looked up and caught my eye. She too gave me the quick smile and reassuring nod. Then came a signal I didn't understand at first. Terry placed the back of her hand underneath her chin while slowly pushing back her shoulders.

Huh?

She pushed her shoulders back a little more and I got it. *Sit up straight, David.* That's what she was telling me. I glanced down. Sure enough, I was slouching. Rather badly, no less. It was my body's interpretation, perhaps, of how my mind felt. All at once I raised my head and straightened my spine. Terry watched, and when I'd made the necessary adjustments, she gave me a wink. *Much better, David.*

Terry's eyes returned to the papers in her lap, and I was left to wonder. Had I hired a lawyer or a mother? Of course, with a little common sense applied, I understood. Scoliosis concerns aside, I was getting my first bit of coaching on being a defendant. Look good. Look sharp. Look innocent. Take nothing for granted and every opportunity to show you've obviously been wrongly accused.

In other words, good posture mattered. To judges and juries alike.

But at the arraignment it was just a judge. A relatively young one at that. Blond hair, square jaw, and horn-rimmed glasses. In watching him work it was clear that the guy probably didn't know the meaning of downtime. He talked fast and always with his hands, and when someone didn't respond quickly enough he'd prompt them with even faster talking. To suggest he was quick to lose his patience was to assume he had any in the first place. He didn't. Not that I could see. Within five minutes he scolded three different attorneys for not answering his questions as soon as they were asked. It was like sitting through the lightning round of the Due Process Game Show.

A few minutes later I was the next contestant. A court clerk called out my name with a deep voice that featured a perfect blend of apathy and fatigue. My escorting officer reached over and put his chubby hand high on my back, right behind my perfectly square shoulders. He pushed and I stood. We walked over to a thick oak table in front of the judge as Parker and Terry got up to join me. That's when I realized Victor was nowhere to be seen. I barely knew the man, yet I knew enough to know I very much wanted him to be there. *Where the hell is Vi—*

There he was. Pushing through the double door at the back of the courtroom while straightening his tie. He walked toward us with a relaxed gait, his expression calm. In a place jammed with people—lawyers, defendants, various civil servants—all looking as if there was someplace else, anyplace else, they'd rather be, Victor Glass appeared more than just content. He seemed downright at home.

It was my gang of three and me again, but before our feet even came to a stop before the judge, he began firing away. "Do you waive a—"

"Yes, we waive a reading, Your Honor," fired back Victor. He was still ten feet away from the table. In another courtroom he'd just interrupted the judge. In this courtroom, he was basically sucking up to the guy by being expeditious.

Accordingly, what followed was a blur.

Right off the bat, there were a few exchanges between the judge and the A.D.A. Hemmerson, certainly no stranger to how the judge operated, was now talking twice as fast as when we had our morning meeting. He was all business and barely glanced in my direction when summarizing the People's case against me. Hell, he wasn't even stealing glances at Terry.

The judge next asked Victor a few questions. A lot of it was legalese, and given the rate at which it was being thrown around, it might as well have been Portuguese. I simply stood there and concentrated on my posture.

The only disarray arrived with the request from Hemmerson that I be remanded. That term I knew. Victor immediately began singing my praises as a model citizen with no prior trouble with the law. He implored the judge to set bail and at a reasonable amount. Hemmerson countered by pointing out the severity of the crime I was charged with and the manner in which it was carried out—heinous and with blatant disregard for human life, respectively. The public interest *required* that I remain incarcerated.

Victor was about to respond when Parker jumped in with a loud clearing of his throat.

"Your Honor," he said, "Dr. Remler is a psychologist with numerous patients who very much depend on his counseling day in and day out. As you well know, he's guilty of nothing at this moment, so as you make your decision I would ask that you weigh the adverse effects of removing Dr. Remler from the lives—"

The judge interrupted. As it was, Parker had been granted more words than anyone. "You don't think, Counselor, that the patients will flee their coveted doctor once they learn of his predicament?"

Parker smiled. "With all due respect, sir, I imagine it will be quite the opposite."

"Why's that?"

"Simple," he replied. "Misery loves company."

Call it a minor miracle. The judge actually leaned back in his chair and chuckled, if only for a moment. He then leaned forward, grabbed his gavel, and lifted it up. "Bail is set at a million dollars," he announced.

Bang. The gavel came down.

My gang of three and I made a hasty exit from the courtroom as the judge immediately moved on to the next case. Once out in the hallway, I thanked Parker for his timely sense of humor. Terry echoed the sentiment and referred to an article she'd once read that said more than 60 percent of judges have been in therapy. As for Victor, he wanted to know through his whiter-than-white smile if Parker was currently "happy enough" at his present firm. A pretty nice compliment, I thought.

Lesson 3: A grand jury will indict a ham sandwich.

I was out on bail. It was a seven-figure reminder of how that extended trip to a remote hillside village in South America was probably not a good idea. Nonetheless, freedom with a big asterisk attached to it was still freedom. While I didn't know if it was only temporary, it sure beat the alternative. No two ways about it.

Fallout.

A quasi-known person accused of killing another quasi-known person equaled full-scale media coverage in the city. Manhattan was, after all, the capital of both the financial and publishing worlds, not to mention the recognized leader in neurotic behavior, and here was a psychologist turned bestselling author entangled with a lion of Wall Street. By the time I got home from my arraignment after posting bail, there was a throng of reporters and camera crews camped outside the lobby. I could only imagine the look on the face of my dear old landlord, Mr. Robert Gordon, when he heard about that.

At least he wouldn't have to then watch it all on the news. As soon as my cab turned the corner and was met by a parking lot of news vans, I had the driver pull around to the service entrance. I ducked in unscathed.

When I got up to my apartment I had messages from the *Times*, the *Journal*, the *News*, the *Post*, the *Observer*, the *Voice*, and *Newsday*. CNN, CNBC, MSNBC, FOX, and all the local network affiliates had also tried to contact me. I would've arranged for a new unlisted number were it not for Parker's pointing out that reporters could easily get ahold of any number they wanted, private or not. Just like police detectives. "The best thing to do is let your machine pick up everything for a few days. After that, no one will bother you again until the trial," he said.

Until.

Not "*if* there's a trial" or "*should* there be a trial" or any other phrasing that suggested it wasn't a foregone conclusion. In listening to Parker, as well as to Terry and Victor, I discovered there were now three—not two—absolute certainties in the world. Death, taxes, and a grand jury indictment of David Remler.

The hearing was scheduled for three weeks after my arraignment. It was my assumption I'd testify. I assumed wrong. In a lunchtime strategy session back at Victor's office, he explained that no matter how eloquent and persuasive I thought I could be, at the end of the day I'd be a liability to myself.

I asked why.

"Memory," said Victor, swallowing the last bite of his roast beef on rye. "Memory is the Florida ballot of the human skill set. Confusing by design and completely unreliable." He picked up his Fresca and took a sip. "Right now you may or may not be able to recall what's happened in the past month with one-hundred-percent accuracy. But six months from now I'll guarantee you this: something will be blurry if not lost completely. And that's all they need. Say one thing before the grand jury and another at the trial and—Pow!—the prosecutor's got you on an inconsistency. After that you're fucking Pinocchio."

I looked at Victor while mulling over his words.

"Besides," he added. "A grand jury will indict a ham sandwich if presented with one."

And there it was. Lesson number three delivered.

Sure enough, the grand jury voted a true bill, which, in my rapidly expanding vocabulary of legal terms, meant I was indicted. Three days later I was in New York County Supreme Court being arraigned (again) on their indictment—a hearing bordering on the redundant. The only thing new discussed was a motion schedule and possible dates for jury selection. As riveting went, it wasn't. No wonder I'd never seen this part played out on any of those law dramas on TV.

The legal terms kept on coming. One after the other; one day to the next. Discovery demand, Rosario material, omnibus motions. Most I understood when explained to me, while others I simply nodded my head at. Eventually, I was reduced to asking the quintessential junior high school question: *will this be on the exam?* If it wasn't going to impact my understanding of the actual trial, I didn't want to know about it.

A notable exception was the Mapp hearing.

This dealt with the search and seizure of evidence and, as scheduled, was supposed to be the last hearing before the trial.

The first I'd heard about it was when Parker and Hemmerson had their little exchange regarding the method in which the detectives obtained a blood sample from me. Having listened to the way the two talked that morning at the precinct, I'd come to expect some serious fireworks. But the fuse never got lit. It was yet one more lesson learned about our legal system: *sometimes you just have to ask nicely.*

Which was precisely what Hemmerson did in a phone call to Parker a day before the Mapp hearing was supposed to happen. Hemmerson apparently realized that while he had a decent shot at getting the sample ruled as legal evidence, there was a better shot to be taken—that is, to simply ask for a new sample.

Indeed, Parker never said we *wouldn't* willingly provide a blood sample. His issue was with the manner in which one was taken. The unabashed insolence of it. So when Hemmerson called and politely asked for a voluntary sample, Parker told him no problem. The next thing I knew, a paramedic was in my living room sticking a needle in my arm. Oddly enough, he kind of looked like that original EMT guy.

I later asked Parker why he'd made such a stink about it in the first place. "If you had no problem with their having a sample of my blood, why didn't you just let them keep what they had?"

"Because everything communicates, David. Especially with these guys," he said. "What you say and what you don't say, what you take issue with and what you let fly. In this instance it was just a friendly reminder. A little piece of advice."

"Which was what?" I asked.

"Don't fuck with us."

"Oh."

All rise.

The trial, fast-tracked because of its high-profile status, got under way about seven months after the arrest. It was the beginning of May, but you wouldn't know it by looking at a thermometer. What had been an extremely cold and damp spring wasn't done yet, and summer seemed like a long way away.

Marching into the courthouse that first morning, Victor was more than happy to make a statement to the swell of media that had turned out. Having already discussed the case during guest appearances on Court TV, *Imus in the Morning*, and every Live at Five–type news program in the city, he had his talking points honed and well rehearsed.

The district attorney's office had made a dreadful mistake, Victor declared. Their so-called evidence was circumstantial at best. In due time and with due process, Dr. David Remler would eventually walk out of the courthouse a free man. That was the gist.

Listening to Victor, I couldn't help thinking he was born for this type of stage. While all those huddled around him hunched their shoulders and shifted their feet to ward off the morning chill, Victor stood straight and firm. He was eloquent. He was passionate. That you could see his breath as he spoke merely underlined what was already abundantly clear. Victor Glass was breathing fire and ready to go.

It was quite the show.

Who are all these people? That was my first reaction walking into the courtroom. The aisles on either side of me were packed with spectators who, almost in unison, turned to stare. Lovely. If they'd been standing and smiling, I would've known what it felt like to be a bride.

I glanced around at the faces. It was obvious that some of these people were reporters, but as for the vast majority, I had no idea who they were. There certainly wasn't anyone I recognized. Outside of Parker, that is.

He was already seated in the first row directly behind the defendant's table. It was a location that very much represented his involvement in the case—always hovering in the background. A mental spotter. Due diligence. Gap insurance.

I'd first thought Parker was going to be my lawyer. He'd first told me he wouldn't be. We were both wrong. We were also both right. As much as Parker had other clients—paying clients—to attend to, he never strayed far from the thinking and planning that led up to my trial. I didn't need to be a psychologist to know he felt a certain responsibility for his decision to have someone else represent me, and while he never seemed to doubt that decision, he clearly was doing whatever he could to ensure it was the right one. I was thankful. So were Victor and Terry. If two heads on my behalf were better than one, three proved invaluable.

"Stacy wanted to be here, but she had some crisis up at the center," Parker said to me as he sidestepped out to the aisle to greet me.

"Imagine that," I replied. "A crisis at a women's crisis center."

He smiled. "Good. You're loose. It's important to be loose."

"I hope it's not that important because on the inside I couldn't be more uptight."

"As long as it doesn't show, it doesn't matter." He looked around. "Hey, I never asked, were your parents flying in for this?"

"They wanted to, but I told them it was best if they stayed home," I said. "This is hard enough on them as it is. The last thing they need is to fly across the country to suffer through it up close."

Parker nodded as Terry and Victor came over. They wanted to discuss a final detail regarding the opening statement. Parker had been involved with the crafting of it.

A few minutes later a door opened to the right of the bench. The jury was about to be let in. Parker returned to his seat, and the rest of us headed to the defendant's table, but not before Terry gave a pull on my arm and quickly filled me in on the seating chart. "You'll always sit between me and Victor," she said. "That way he and I can both whisper to you if we have to."

We sat down. Terry to my right. Victor to my left. Me in the middle. In the middle of it all.

And you may ask yourself, well, how did I get here?

That's how.

TWENTY-SIX

I sighed. "We're not doing very well, are we?"

Terry looked up at me from the notes she'd been poring over on her desk. The two of us were back in her office. The trial was three days' old. "David, we haven't even stepped up to the plate yet," she said.

"But they sure have. I mean, I feel like we're getting hit really hard."

"That's because we are."

"Oh, good. I feel much better now."

Terry's mouth curled up at the corners. Her cheerful expression seemed a mismatch for the words that followed. "What do you want me to say? This Mystery Patient of yours did a serious number on you. She gave the prosecution a whole lot to work with."

"Then why are you smiling?" I asked.

Her eyes narrowed. A flush of intensity filled her face. "Because it's our turn now."

That it was. The prosecution had rested. Most comfortably, I thought. With their exhibits A through what felt like Z, their extensive serology reports, their handwriting expert who verified Conrad Birch's signature on the letter planted in my library, and their detailed testimony from Detectives Trentino and Lopez, even I was wondering if maybe I did actually kill Conrad Birch. I could only imagine what the jury must have been thinking.

The jury.

"Don't be afraid to look at them," Victor had told me before the trial started. "Make eye contact—don't smile, don't frown—just eye contact. For sure, this will make a few uncomfortable, and they'll look away. Others, though, will welcome it—and these are the ones you want to focus on. To these people, justice isn't decided in their head or even their heart. It's in their gut. So let 'em take a good look at you, okay? Let 'em feed their instincts. "

I nodded. When it came to what went on inside a courtroom, there was little, if anything, Victor Glass didn't have an opinion about. Still, if there was one thing in which he took particular pride it was juries. How to pick them. How to talk to them. How to read what they're thinking. And, as I discovered, even how to look at them. Some men are fond of sports analogies, while others are quick to quote poets and writers; when it came to Victor and juries, it was all about a simple card game.

"Everyone thinks twelve people make up a jury," he told me. "No. Twelve people *sit* on a jury, but it's really only ten who matter. Ten people can talk two people into anything 99.9 percent of the time. Especially when another sequestered night at the local HoJo's lies in the balance. So you focus on ten of them, and from there it's basically a game of gin. Do you play gin, David?"

"Not as much as I drink it."

"It's like this," he plowed on. "The jury pool is the hand you're dealt. Right away you've got your keepers, the people—just like the cards—you know you want for sure. Then the real strategy starts. Knowing who you need and who you'll have to toss to get them. And all along you've got to keep track of what your opponent is doing. Who he's keeping and who he's throwing away. If you're good, he'll play right into your hand. But if you're not careful, you'll play right into his. Of course, all that said, and no matter how much skill you've got, you still need

some luck to win." Victor nodded. "That's gin . . . and that's juries."

I nodded in return. His theory was interesting. But what really captivated me was his conviction. He didn't merely think
this; he *knew* this.

As for Terry's approach to juries, the analogies were more up
my alley. Her frequent allusions to such folks as Freud and Jung
tipped me to her minor at Princeton. Psychology.

"I look at it this way," she'd said on the eve of jury selection.
"By and large, authors are viewed with a fair amount of reverence. One of our objectives in picking a jury, therefore, would be
to select as many people as possible who've read *The Human Pendulum* or, more realistically, have at least heard of it. The prosecution, of course, would have the opposite objective. But here's
the thing: the actual message of *The Human Pendulum* turns all
that thinking right on its head. Your book is about the unpre-
dictability of human nature; it maintains exemplary behavior
isn't cumulative and that we're all susceptible to evil given the
right circumstances. No exceptions, no one immune."

I nodded. "Including the author."

"*Especially* the author," said Terry. "You can't be familiar with
your book without considering the tantalizing possibility that
through the murder of Conrad Birch you've managed to prove
your point."

"So we shoot for a jury of nonreaders; those who aren't familiar with the book, right?"

"Right. We sacrifice reverence for ignorance. Not uneducated
people, mind you—lord knows, that's a sticking point with Victor."

"Yes, I read his O.J. jury editorial."

"One of my favorites," she said. "No, we want smart, all right,
just not *Book TV*–on–C-SPAN smart. And, unless I'm giving
Hemmerson too much credit, our friendly prosecutor will be
gunning for exactly that crowd."

She was right. Come jury selection, one of the first questions
Hemmerson asked the candidates was whether they were famil-

iar with *The Human Pendulum*. Those who were became his instant best friend. Meanwhile, those who weren't became Terry's best friend.

The challenges flew.

But in the end, reality won. The people who made me a best-selling author were few and far between among the jury pool.

"Gin!" declared Victor.

Of the seven women and five men picked—five of them white, three black, three Asian, and one Hispanic—none had ever read *The Human Pendulum*. Only two had ever heard of it.

Never was I so happy to have missed out on some royalties.

Still, Hemmerson had a grand old time with the book just the same. In the three days he took to present the prosecution's case, not one went by without his mentioning it. As he liked to remind the jury, I'd put my premise into practice. I'd engaged in a wicked bit of foreshadowing and tipped my hand to the violent streak that burned within me. His grandstanding reached its peak when, on the trial's second day, he stood directly in front of the judge's bench and loudly announced to the entire courtroom that he'd already contacted the Guinness World Records people. For with *The Human Pendulum* I'd written the world's longest confession.

Quipped an on-air reporter that evening, sans rim shot, "You might say they're really throwing the book at Remler."

TWENTY-SEVEN

I was still in Terry's office lamenting the efforts of Hemmerson and the prosecution when Victor strolled in. He was wearing two pieces of a three-piece suit, the jacket off, his shirtsleeves rolled up neatly to his elbows. "So does he or doesn't he?" was his first question.

He wasn't wondering if I dyed my hair. Does he or doesn't he *testify?* That's what Victor was asking—whether or not I should take the stand.

The risk was that Hemmerson might trip me up, make me contradict myself. He could rile me, unsettle me, make me sweat. Perspiration had a funny way of suggesting guilt. But if I held my own—or better yet, appeared sympathetic—the reward could be a veritable fountain of reasonable doubt.

Does he or doesn't he?

"Tough call," said Terry. "Particularly because Hemmerson has been given a really long leash. I swear, it's like Lomax has never met a defense objection he couldn't overrule."

She was referring to Barton Lomax, the judge, an old and rigid man who didn't seem to sit on the bench as much as grow out of it. In his near thirty years of presiding over cases in Manhattan, he'd proved himself to be many things, according to Victor, none of which were particularly endearing. Lomax was

ornery, caustic, impatient, and wholly intolerant of anyone who
dared challenge his authority.

Terry regarded me for a moment, still weighing the decision
of whether I should testify. "Let's wait and see," she said. "We'll
take a measure of how things are going in a couple of days and
decide then."

Victor didn't hesitate. "Okay, you're the boss."

She put her hand to her ear. "What's that?"

"Cute," said Victor. He turned to me. *"You're the boss*. That's
by far her favorite expression."

"Only when you say it, Boss," she added.

He chuckled and pushed one of his rolled-up sleeves past his
elbow. "Okay, so what else?"

"Witness list," she said. "Let's go over it."

Victor took a seat on an upholstered floral-print chair. It was
mere human-size compared to the seating in his office.

For the next twenty minutes we discussed the array of people
who I hoped would be saving my butt. None were solely character witnesses since my maiden voyage into authorship had
pretty much established character as being irrelevant.

Next up: damage assessment.

It started first and foremost with Detectives Trentino and
Lopez. Big hitters for the prosecution. To watch and listen to
them was to realize how often the two men had taken the stand
over the years. In the exacting atmosphere of a murder trial, they
came across as very cool customers. Selective in their choice of
words, levelheaded in their delivery. When Hemmerson initially
asked each to state his rank, I finally found out what the cop on
the scene had meant when he told his partner he hoped for
"first-graders." As Hemmerson explained to the jury, detectives
were ranked based on tenure and ability. First grade, second
grade, third grade. A descending order. Lopez and Trentino, I'd
discovered, were first-graders. And at the top of their class to
boot.

Hemmerson had both detectives recount all of their conversations with me. Trentino first, followed by Lopez. While it bor-

dered on redundant, the echoing of their testimony furthered the notion that what both men were saying was fact and not merely opinion. I interpreted it as a sign of the times. In the good old days the word of anyone wearing a badge was as good as gospel. Now there wasn't a Joe on the street—or in the jury box—who didn't know about a certain police division called Internal Affairs. Not to mention how they've always got plenty to do.

So Hemmerson seemed to be taking no chances. He'd devised a very tight script, and the detectives were sticking to it with aplomb. Which is not to say there weren't any surprises. Hemmerson made sure to include a few damning tidbits that went beyond the facts. It was like slow-pitch softball. He'd lob a loaded question at Trentino or Lopez, and they'd have a field day.

Example.

"Tell me, Detective Lopez, did you notice anything strange or out of place about the defendant when you visited him at his apartment?"

"I suppose I did," began Lopez. "In my opinion, Dr. Remler appeared a little out of it."

"What do you mean by *out of it*?"

"A little disoriented. Both Detective Trentino and I could smell alcohol on his breath."

"Do you think he was intoxicated at the time?"

"I couldn't say for certain without administering a Breathalyzer. But Dr. Remler was certainly inconsistent in his behavior. At times cooperative but at other times quite abusive."

Hemmerson acted shocked—*shocked!*—by this development. "Did you feel threatened?" he asked.

"That's a relative term for me since I carry a firearm," said Lopez, his chest seemingly expanding. "Suffice to say, I don't believe he was acting in a very rational manner."

And so on.

Of course, Terry was sure to hit back hard on her cross-examinations. By the time she was done with both Trentino and

Lopez, the jury had been made aware that my being "out of it" maybe, just maybe, had something to do with the two detectives having just woken me up. Then she trapped Lopez a bit with his implication I'd been drinking. She asked if he thought it was possible he smelled alcohol on my breath the night before at Conrad Birch's town house. She'd stressed the word *possible*, and Lopez seized on it as if he'd been given a loophole from the truth.

"Possible?" he repeated. "Yes, I think it's possible."

"Then why didn't you administer a Breathalyzer or have Dr. Remler's blood drawn? Your mere suspicion in that situation would've satisfied any court's definition of just cause."

Lopez didn't really have an answer for that. He mumbled something about how hectic the night was and that not everything could get done in a timely fashion.

But still. The accusation had been made. The suggestion planted . . .

The doctor was a drunk.

Trying to fight it was tantamount to the classic denial of having never slept with a pig. No matter how much evidence was presented to the contrary, the jury had already envisioned me rolling in the barnyard mud with Barry White music playing in the background.

If there was a silver lining, though, it was this: I realized I *was* drinking too much. Or, more accurately, for the wrong reasons. First came Rebecca's death, then this trial. In both instances, I was relying on the bottle to dull the pain. The problem was that it threatened to dull everything.

I'd seen too many patients not to know there was a significant chasm between alcohol abuse and alcoholism. Nonetheless, the lesser of two evils was still evil. So it was decided, sitting in the courtroom as a man who'd had carnal knowledge with a pig, that I'd go on an alcohol-free diet for a while. Cold Wild Turkey. Simply put, I shouldn't need four or five bourbons to close my eyes at night.

Now, three days later and sitting in Terry's office discussing the detectives, I'd yet to have a drink.

From that issue to another: Mila.

The poor woman. She so wanted to help me. But she'd been a helpless pawn in my being framed and, as a result, was a key witness for the prosecution. Albeit a reluctant one.

Said Hemmerson in the courtroom, "Ms. Benninghoff, you never actually talked to, let alone saw, this woman whom Dr. Remler was calling Sam Kent, right?"

"I'm sure she—"

"Just yes or no, please, Ms. Benninghoff."

Mila looked up at Judge Lomax as if to say, "Can he do that?" He looked down at her as if to say, "Sorry, but those are the rules."

"No, I never saw this woman," Mila said to Hemmerson.

"Or talked to . . ."

"No. But what I was trying to—"

"Thank you, Ms. Benninghoff. So you never talked to or saw this supposed Mystery Patient, nor did you ever see any payment from her other than the cash Dr. Remler gave you, isn't that right?"

"But you don't understa—"

"*Yes or no*, Ms. Benninghoff."

"No."

"Which means that she very well could've been a fabrication on the part of Dr. Remler, correct?"

"No."

"No?! Why not, Ms. Benninghoff?"

"Because I don't believe David would ever do such a thing."

"Precisely," said Hemmerson, acting as if Mila had fallen for some Perry Mason–like trap. "You trusted him. And he knew you trusted him. Which made it all the more easy for him to accomplish his deception."

That's when Terry objected for what was probably the third time in three minutes. The first two were about badgering the witness. The latest was to point out that Hemmerson hadn't actually bothered to ask Mila a question in that last exchange. Judge Lomax was quick to respond each time. Overruled, overruled, and—small miracle—sustained.

Said Lomax, with more than a hint of sarcasm, "Here's a yes or no for you, Mr. Hemmerson. Do you actually have another question for the witness?"

Hemmerson took the talking-down-to in stride. He'd made his point. "No, Your Honor. No further questions."

"Your witness, Ms. Garrett."

Terry stood up to cross-examine, but the facts were what they were. Mila couldn't prove any more than I could that the only mystery about my patient was who she was and not, as the prosecution would contend, whether she existed. Moreover, getting Mila to assert her belief that I'd never fabricate such a thing— especially to kill someone—would draw further attention to my book. So when Terry walked up to the witness-box and smiled warmly at Mila, I had no idea what questions she'd ask. Turns out there was only one.

"Ms. Benninghoff, the prosecution would have us believe that it was Dr. Remler who sent the initial e-mails to you under the guise of Sam Kent. But if Dr. Remler's objective was to create the appearance of a patient whom he could later claim was Conrad Birch's mistress, why would he make you first believe his patient was a man?"

"I have no idea."

"Neither do I," said Terry before turning to the judge. "No further questions, Your Honor."

At the time, I didn't know what she was getting at. Now, back in her office, she was about to let on.

"They're painting you as a criminal mastermind, David. You not only fooled strangers, you fooled people who knew you very, very well. You were cunning, you were imaginative, you were brilliant. So you know what we have to do, don't you?"

"What's that?" I asked.

Terry grinned. "We've got to show them they're right. That you are in fact a criminal mastermind."

Confused, I looked at her, while Victor laughed out loud.

"I like it," he said. "I like it a lot."

"What do you think, David?" she asked.

"I think I have no idea what you're talking about."

"*You got caught!*" she said.

Victor chimed in. "It's the one thing the prosecution hasn't delivered on. If you're so clever, how come you were dumb enough to get caught so easily. Approach it like that and the jury starts to wonder if maybe the real mastermind isn't on trial."

"Don't you see, David? If we can make them wonder, we can make them believe," said Terry, her intense look returning. "That your Mystery Patient is very much for real . . . and very much at large."

TWENTY-EIGHT

Parker reached for the check, and I immediately yanked it out of his hand. "You've got to be kidding me," I said.

Parker glanced at Stacy, sitting to his side, before looking back across the table at me. He shrugged. "What do you mean?"

"After all your pro bono work on my behalf, do you really think I'm about to let you also buy me dinner?"

"He's got a point, honey," said Stacy with a wink. She shook her head in mock disappointment. *"I knew I should've gotten the lobster."*

It was Friday night, and the three of us were at the Manhattan Ocean Club. The dinner had one rule: no talking about the trial. For the most part we stuck to it. Thankfully, the combination of dim lighting and a preponderance of tourists meant no one really recognized me. The media coverage in the city had continued to be unrelenting.

I laid my credit card down, and the waiter swooped in to pick it up.

"You know, I could probably get the things postponed," said Parker.

"Don't be silly," I said.

The "things" were a series of depositions Parker had to attend in the coming days on behalf of one of his clients. They were going to keep him from being at my trial.

"I could maybe go," said Stacy. "It's been pretty much under control at the shelter the past couple of days."

I laughed. "You are without a doubt the worst liar in the world," I told her. "If Crescent House is any example, things are never under control at your shelter. Don't even think of skipping out in the name of moral support."

Stacy turned to Parker. "Am I really that bad of a liar?"

"The worst," he said.

"What gives me away?"

"Your face. It tends to pucker when you're bullshitting."

"Pucker?"

"Yeah, like you're eating a lemon."

Stacy looked at me. I nodded slowly in agreement.

"Great," she said, mostly amused. "Corroborating testimony."

"Ooh," said Parker. "I love it when she talks lawyer."

That got him a smack on the arm. "Speaking of Crescent House, though," she said, turning back to me, "what's been the fallout there with you and the trial?"

"You know how therapists are," I said. "Everything is layers. The official line is that I'm innocent until proven guilty. The unofficial line is that until the verdict I should scale back my involvement with the place. Somewhere between minimal and nonexistent."

"How enlightened," she said.

"Tell me about it. Though on one level—or should I say layer—I don't blame them. The push is on to expand, so everything is about funding. Somehow, having a suspected murderer on the board is putting a little damper on donations. Imagine that."

"You'd think in some perverse way it would be a draw," said Parker.

"Funny, I said the exact same thing to Bennett Larson the other day. He's the front man for Crescent House when it comes to money. Anyway, he's all concerned that Arnold Kesper is going to pull back his donation."

"How much did he give?"

"A million."

"Are you serious?!" said Stacy. "I've got to get my center on the guest list."

"Be careful what you wish for," I said.

"Why, is the guy really that much of a wacko?"

"Actually, yes—he was relentless about my testimony in the rabbi trial. But I guess I'm referring more to that night in general for me."

"You mean, when you foolishly invited your Mystery Patient back to your apartment?"

Parker laughed. "Geez, nice tact, honey."

I had to laugh as well. Stacy was rarely, if ever, so blunt. "Yeah, seriously, stop beating around the bush, will you?"

"Hey, sometimes it just takes a woman to tell it like it is," she said with a smile. "That reminds me, though—about that night—wouldn't your doorman have seen you walk in with her?"

"He did, but he can't remember what she looked like," I said.

Parker shook his head, disgusted. "Yeah, we questioned the guy, but he was clueless. He said he had enough trouble keeping track of the actual residents."

I was about to crack a joke connecting lobbies to lobotomies when I saw something out of the corner of my eye. A man walking toward me. An amazing coincidence. Not more than a minute after mentioning how Arnold Kesper had grilled me about the rabbi, here was the prosecutor in that case coming to a stop at our table.

Ethan Greene.

"Technically, I'm not supposed to be talking to you," he said with a slight chuckle.

"I know. Consorting with the enemy," I said back.

We shook hands, and I introduced him to Parker and Stacy. Parker and he knew of each other but had never met.

"So, is there anything you can do for your star witness?" he asked Ethan.

"I feel bad," he replied. He looked at me. "I know I owe you one, but unfortunately, this isn't exactly a situation where I can return the favor."

I told him I understood, which I did.

"As it is, Hemmerson and I aren't exactly the best of buddies."

"Why's that?" I asked.

"No tales out of school," he said. "Let's just say we don't always see eye to eye on things." He chuckled again. "That and the fact that I used to kick his ass in racquetball. The man doesn't like to lose."

"I get the sense," I said.

"From what I know, though, you're in pretty good hands, David."

"I've got Parker to thank for that."

"Only if we win," said Parker.

Ethan nodded. "Terry Garrett knows what she's doing. And as far as Victor Glass is concerned, he knows what everybody is doing."

Ethan glanced over his shoulder at the table where he was sitting. There was a young woman, alone, taking a sip of wine.

"Is that your wife?" I asked.

"Someday, if I play my cards right."

"Then you better not keep her waiting."

We shook hands again. He squeezed a little harder this time. His eyes looked almost mournful. "You know I'm standing here telling myself you didn't do it," he began. "But what's ironic is how everything that makes me do that is everything you yourself wrote about—and ultimately debunked. What's a guy supposed to do?"

"How about wishing me luck?"

"That I can do," he said. "Good luck, David."

"Thank you; I appreciate it."

Ethan left and rejoined his girlfriend. Moments later, the

waiter returned with the credit card slip. A tip, a total, and a signature. We were free to go. But Parker, Stacy, and I simply sat there in silence. We'd done a pretty good job of avoiding trial talk. Somehow, though, bumping into Ethan made it feel as if that's all we'd been discussing.

Stacy to the rescue. So she thought.

"Do you want us to swing by tomorrow night and pick you up first?" she asked me.

I looked at her, puzzled. "For what?"

"Cassandra's party," she said, the "*Hello? Where have you been?*" implied. "Don't tell me we've got to talk you into going again."

"No, you won't have to be doing that," I said.

"Good," said Stacy.

"No, not good," said Parker, getting the picture.

Where I'd been was on trial for murder. Apparently that was reason enough for Cassandra Nance to drop me—a once permanent fixture—from her well-heeled guest list. I was now persona non grata of the Upper East Side cocktail set.

"I wasn't invited," I announced.

"That can't be," said Stacy with a dismissive wave.

"Is this where we're supposed to say it was probably just an oversight?" asked Parker.

I nodded. "Yep."

"Any chance you'll believe us?"

"Nope."

"Oh, c'mon you guys," said Stacy, not fully ready to accept my social pariah status. "There's a very good chance the invitation simply got lost in the mail."

I looked at her sideways. "Do you honestly believe that?"

"As a matter of fact, I do."

I started to laugh.

"*What?*" she demanded.

That only made me laugh harder.

"Oh, shit, I was puckering, wasn't I?"

*   *   *

In a show of support for me, and to protest the grave injustice I'd suffered, Parker and Stacy boycotted Cassandra's party the next night. They went to a movie instead. Wanting to keep my third-wheel tendencies with them in check, I declined their invitation to go along.

Over Chinese takeout in my kitchen, I couldn't help thinking about my chance meeting with Ethan Greene. It was indeed an amazing coincidence.

But that's not where it ended.

A couple of hours after downing my fortune cookie, I flipped on the late local news. The top story was about a murder in Queens. The second story was about a suicide in Upstate New York.

I sat there bewildered as the anchorwoman spoke of the "rabbi murder trial that had riveted the city" the previous year. The screen then switched to footage of the rabbi and, after that, the woman he'd been found guilty of killing. When the anchorwoman's face returned, she took a brief and polished pause.

"Tonight," she said, "that rabbi is dead."

It was an apparent suicide. Though only in a jail could a man found dead alone in his locked cell garner the word *apparent*. Lest there be any doubt, "sources" reported that the rabbi had left behind a suicide note. In it, he confessed to his crime. He had, in fact, murdered the woman.

There was one more thing.

The screen switched again as the anchorwoman handed off to a male reporter who was standing outside the Butler Correctional Facility upstate in Wayne County. With the prison fences as a backdrop, he explained how the rabbi had apparently "ended his life."

In a most ironic twist—the operative word truly being *twist*—he'd killed himself in the very same fashion that his defense lawyers had tried to pin on his victim. Suicide by self-garroting.

With a shoelace and a spoon, the rabbi was off to make peace with his God.

I continued to watch the news up through the sports and the

weather. Not that I could tell you who won what game or if it was finally going to get warmer for the start of the week. When that same anchorwoman told me to stay tuned for *Saturday Night Live*, I turned off the television and went to bed. I didn't know exactly how to feel.

So, in the end, I felt nothing.

TWENTY-NINE

Are you surprised to see me?" she asked.

I'd just come out of the men's room at the courthouse that Monday morning. It was a little before 9:00 AM. In a matter of minutes the first witness for the defense—*my* defense—was going to be called. Stopping briefly by an exposed radiator to tie one of my wingtips, I felt the tap on my shoulder. When I turned around, there she was. Smiling.

I looked right at her . . . and smiled back.

"Actually, I'm delighted to see you," I said.

It was Emily Morgan. Fittingly, my Monday, nine o'clock. She was a seventy-four-year-old widow who had lived in the same rent-controlled apartment off Lex and Eighty-eighth for more than thirty years. I'd known her for the past four. If anyone threatened my premise for *The Human Pendulum* it was her. She was a genuine sweetheart.

"Do you realize, David," she said, looking about the long hallway, "that in all my years in this city I've never once set foot in this building?"

"Consider yourself fortunate," I replied.

"You know, come to think of it," she said, "I've also never eaten at Tavern on the Green."

"I'm afraid you're not missing much there either."

"Really? All those lights; it looks so pretty from the outside."

She was just getting warmed up. I readied myself for another loose segue—something Emily Morgan excelled at—and it came. For the next minute I heard about the one and only time she rode in a horse-driven carriage around Central Park. That begat another minute about her niece, Jennifer, who rode horses out in New Canaan. Before I knew it I was hearing that the remake of *The Stepford Wives* had been filmed in that town.

I discreetly glanced down at my watch. Endearing as Emily was, I was about to be officially late to my own murder trial.

A quick good-bye and thank-you for her support was followed by a near sprint to the courtroom, my heels slipping slightly on the polished floor with each stride. I pushed through the doors, resumed a walk, and fixed my eyes on where I needed to be—the empty chair between Victor and Terry. I took a seat and, like a schoolboy, apologized to them both for running late.

After twenty seconds of discussing the plight of the rabbi, I was back on my feet again, standing as Judge Lomax was announced. It was then, out of the corner of my eye, that I saw her.

Sam Kent. Samantha Kent. Mrs. Samantha Kent.

The real one.

For the first time, I was seeing her in person. There'd been a couple of pictures in the papers, and as a result, I'd gained a sense of what she looked like. Yet, it was a very detached, almost *sur*real sense. As much as our lives had suddenly intersected, I didn't really know much about her.

What little I did know came from the brief stories accompanying those newspaper pictures. That and what was relayed to me by Terry based on statements Samantha Kent made to the police, and other Rosario material. Taken together, one thing was clear: my Mystery Patient had done her homework. Posing as Samantha Kent, she appropriated far more than a name.

Being an only child.

Growing up in Larchmont, New York.

Attending Brown.

Even the former job as a buyer for Bergdorf's.

Of course, how she knew all this could've stemmed more from pillow talk than research. Over the course of their affair, Conrad Birch could've simply told her things about his wife. It didn't matter. Either way, my Mystery Patient had really got into her role.

One thing she didn't appropriate, though, was the family business. I could see why—it didn't play into the sympathy card. As pointed out in the *Times*, Samantha Kent was the only child of Archibald Kent, founder of Kent Oceanic. They made most of the world's cargo ships and a hell of a lot of money in the process. At age seventy-seven and a widower, "Archie" Kent supposedly had a net worth of $4 billion. That made Samantha one serious heiress.

But given what my Mystery Patient did and didn't lift from Samantha Kent's life, it was what she flat out made up that proved most pivotal. Two things in particular.

One was the nanny, Celeste. As I eventually discovered, Samantha Kent and Conrad Birch never had a nanny. The reason was simple. Because, two, *there was no kid*. They were child-less. The two-year-old boy at the center of everything—the pending custody battle and, ultimately, the desire to kill Birch— was a complete fabrication.

Which meant that along with the pictures I'd already seen of the real Samantha Kent, I was able to add one more. A portrait of a woman in a state of disbelief. Especially when it came to my alibi.

She'd said she didn't know her husband had ever seen a psy-chologist. Considering what Conrad Birch told me in that one session we had together—that he was cheating on his wife—I was inclined to believe her. Accordingly, I saw no reason to dis-pute that she'd never seen me before. My status as an author stretched only so far.

So what *did* Samantha Kent know?

The answer was this: all the things that guaranteed Terry would never call her to the stand. Samantha Kent knew that she came home one morning from a trip to Boston to learn her husband had been brutally murdered. She knew that the knife used to stab him repeatedly was a knife I owned or, should it be said, once owned, since I could no longer account for it. Finally, she knew that a letter signed by her husband had been found in my apartment and that it strongly suggested I had a motive. It was bad enough to have Detectives Trentino and Lopez spell that out for the jury. To have a grieving widow do it yet again was suicide.

I was now staring at her.

The real Samantha Kent was more blond than she appeared in any picture I'd seen. Her hair was now different too. It fell straight to her shoulders, parted on one side and angling across her forehead. She was also thinner in person, with pronounced cheekbones that practically gave shade to the rest of her face. In a world where wrinkles were now optional, a woman's age was a difficult thing to peg. A safe bet was forty, forty-five at the outside. In total, she was attractive, although in a way that suggested she was once far more so. The difference between mannered and effortless, I suppose.

That was what I saw. But it wasn't what I was staring at. These things about her—her physical presence—I looked at and noted. However, what caught my attention, and held it, was something more. Something . . . *intangible*. A certain poise, a stoic demeanor, a chin held high. A reserved nature that set her off without appearing cold. It took a little bit before it all came together for me. What I was looking at in Samantha Kent was wealth.

Not diamonds and pearls. That was rich. Wealth was altogether different. In my profession, I'd been able to get up close to a host of people who possessed a great deal of money. Learning a thing or two about them couldn't be helped. The simplest and broadest observation was that there were those who disguised their money and those who flaunted it. In either case, it was like a coat they'd decided to wear or not wear. A matter of choice. Conscious. Deliberate.

Then there were the select few who seemed to have no

choice. For these people, money was not a coat. It was more like a coating. Ethereal-like. An air. An aura. And that's what made it wealth. Because, no matter what, it couldn't be bought. Instead, it was seemingly genetic, embedded somewhere in their double helix. Disguising it was impossible; flaunting it was redundant—not to mention wholly out of character. It was beyond their skin. It was beneath their skin. In other words, it was everything about them.

And everything about the real Samantha Kent said wealth. Real wealth.

I kept staring at her.

She was clearly not happy to be sitting there that morning. It was evident in the way she blankly stared ahead from her first-row seat, looking at nothing and no one. Having some experience myself as a surviving spouse in a courtroom, I could almost hear Hemmerson stressing to her the importance of being at the trial. The emotional impact it provided. Then again, that her first appearance wasn't until that morning made me think a compromise had been struck. *At least be there when the defense is making their case. Your sitting there can only make it harder for them.*

My thoughts segued. A natural progression, really, as opposed to the likes of dear old Emily Morgan. Unfortunately, what was natural also proved to be quite depressing. I was thinking back to my wife's death, reliving the loss. How prematurely and unfairly Rebecca's life had been taken away. I grew up believing I knew what justice was. I really grew up when I realized there wasn't enough to go around. Too many bad things happened for no good reason. There was nothing we could do about it and, far too often, no one to blame. Life was a tangle of circumstances. Unpredictable. Out of control. Like a speeding car on a slick road with a young kid behind the wheel.

I kept staring at her.

Then, in a fraction of a second, she turned my way. Our eyes locked. Total awareness of each other and more than ample time to appreciate the circumstances. The real Samantha Kent was staring right at me. It couldn't have been more than a few seconds, but it might as well have been a lifetime. And if the weight of her gaze was any indication, she didn't like what she saw.

Could I really blame her?

A lot of people had been telling her that I was the guy who murdered her husband. Police detectives, prosecutors, various pundits in the news media. Now here I was to prove them all wrong. Or at least create enough reasonable doubt to that effect. And the kicker? For my defense, I was pawning everything off on a heretofore nonexistent woman who was having an *affair* with her husband. Jesus. If I were Samantha Kent, I'd hate my guts too.

I was staring at her again.

I'd looked away, but here I was looking back. I couldn't help it. I felt this strange curiosity, a peculiar interest. Then I felt pain. It was Victor Glass's foot meeting my ankle with a swift, forceful kick. My eyes left Samantha Kent and found Victor's waiting for me. He whispered through his blinding smile. "Stare at her any more, and you'll start creeping the jury out."

He probably had a point. But still. "Did you have to kick me?" I asked.

I expected a "sorry." Instead, Victor simply nodded. "As a matter of fact, I did," he replied.

THIRTY

You may call your first witness, Ms. Garrett."

Terry stood from her chair to my right and adjusted her suit jacket with a slight tug. She moved her eyes across the jury with a warm smile. She doled one out to Judge Lomax as well. "Thank you, Your Honor," she said. "The defense calls Dr. Hans Lenbakker."

And so began Operation Brilliant Idiot.

A succession of witnesses called in strategic order. One to show my uncompromising genius in plotting a complex murder. The next to show how utterly stupid I was in trying to pull it off. Then back to someone for my genius. Followed by another one for my stupidity. And so on. Back and forth. Brilliant and idiot. Repeated enough times to make the jury get the underlying point. I was neither smart enough nor dumb enough to commit this crime.

Dr. Hans Lenbakker was sworn in. He took a seat in the witness-box and promptly folded his legs. He wore a dark-brown suit with a blue-striped tie. While his gray beard was neatly trimmed, he had just enough of that Einstein rumple about him to suggest formidable intelligence.

"Thank you for being here today, Dr. Lenbakker," said Terry, walking up to him.

"You're very much welcome," he answered. Despite having spent the past ten years in the United States, his German accent was still prevalent. It made each word seem deliberate and thought out.

Terry had the doctor give a brief history of his educational background and professional credentials. By the time he got to his current stint as director of the Smithsonian's Artifact Authentication Board, I could tell the jury was suitably impressed.

"Your Honor, the defense would ask that Dr. Lenbakker be deemed an expert witness," said Terry.

Lomax nodded.

As a chemist, Dr. Lenbakker had come to specialize in demarcating the decaying properties of both organic and inorganic matter. His specific area of expertise was the dating of paintings, along with paper- and parchment-based writings. From the Hitler diaries to purported rough drafts of the Articles of Confederation to the latest claim of a never-before-seen Shakespeare play, Dr. Lenbakker was almost always called in to render his opinion. Few, if any, saw fit to disagree with him.

Now here he was with what amounted to a layup.

Terry strode back to the defense table, opened a folder, and removed a page of loose-leaf notepaper that was sheathed in clear plastic. She approached Dr. Lenbakker with it.

"I'm showing you what's been marked defense exhibit A," she said to him. "Do you recognize it?"

"Yes."

"How so?"

"I've examined it."

"That was a couple of weeks ago, correct?"

"Yes."

"Is it in the same condition today as when you first saw it?"

"The construct of the paper and ink are, of course, a little older," he said with a small, knowing grin. "But other than that—yes—it's in the same condition."

With that, Terry began reciting aloud my notes on Conrad Birch. Our one session together. The admission that he was having an affair. The feeling that he couldn't leave his wife and the fear of having to break it off with his mistress. "*Fear*," Terry repeated. She lingered on the theme, listing off my bullet points of short, choppy sentences that said the mistress had a temper. A mean streak. Terry looked up at the jury and continued, "Dr. Remler then writes that Conrad Birch had, and I quote, *overwhelming concern for how mistress will react.*"

She walked over and handed the plastic-covered page to Dr. Lenbakker.

"As you know, Doctor, these are notes that my client has offered as being a record of his one and only session with Conrad Birch," she said. "Based on your examination of the document, and in your expert opinion, when were they written? Last month? Last year?"

Dr. Lenbakker scratched his chin, the quintessential smart-person hand gesture. "Much longer than a year, most definitely. Closer to two years, in fact. The breakdown of the ink particles alone would heavily support that. The oxygenation—something we call *rusting*—would all but guarantee it."

Terry turned around and faced the jury. "So, Dr. Lenbakker, let me ask you this. If Dr. Remler had intended to fake the fact that he once treated Conrad Birch in order to construct an alibi, what you're saying is that he was brilliantly planning to kill Mr. Birch for nearly *two* years?"

"Objection!" shouted Hemmerson. "First off, the murder itself was over seven months ago. More important, Dr. Lenbakker has been called to verify ink, not the intentions of the defendant."

"Sustained," said Judge Lomax. "Ms. Garrett, what your client may or may not have been planning to do is for the jury to decide."

"I'm sorry," she said. "I just thought Dr. Lenbakker might have an *ink*ling."

Most of the jury giggled, along with the rest of the courtroom.

Terry turned to the witness-box. "Thank you, Dr. Lenbakker." He handed her back the page, and she officially entered it into evidence. "I have no further questions, Your Honor."

"Your witness," said Lomax with a nod toward Hemmerson.

The assistant D.A. stood up but didn't move from behind his table. "We have no questions for Dr. Lenbakker."

"Very well, then. Ms. Garrett, your next witness."

Terry had barely made it back to her seat. "Your Honor, in the time since the cross-examination of Detectives Trentino and Lopez, the defense has realized additional questions for them pertinent to our case. Given their presence in the courtroom today, I'd like your permission to call them back to the stand."

Hemmerson began to make an objection, but Lomax quashed it with a raised palm.

"I'll allow it," he said, though his expression suggested he wasn't a big fan of the request either.

Meanwhile, I suppressed a smile. Terry had told me it was extremely common for detectives to attend the trials of their cases beyond the days they were testifying. A vested interest sort of thing. Nonetheless, neither she nor Victor was about to bank on it. So they let drop to a reporter the day before that they had a surprise witness lined up. Predictably, that reporter later asked the detectives if they knew who it was.

"The defense calls Detective Joseph Trentino," announced Terry.

Surprise.

In the back of the courtroom, the detective lumbered to his feet and sidestepped past his partner, Lopez, out to the aisle. He couldn't have looked more bothered. A trip to the dentist held more joy. As Trentino began walking up, Terry pivoted on her heels to face the bench.

"Your Honor, I'd like to ask that Detective Lopez not be present in the courtroom for Detective Trentino's testimony," she said.

Lomax eyed her.

"The reason is that I want both of their recollections as opposed to a joint one."

This time, Hemmerson was up on his feet objecting before Lomax could even blink. "Your Honor," he said, steaming, "this request by the defense amounts to an accusation of collusion by the detectives and, therefore, perjury. Not only do I ask that you deny the request, but I also demand an apology from Ms. Garrett."

The brief chortle in the courtroom was from Victor. First day of the defense's case and Terry had quickly got under Hemmerson's skin. No longer the pretty attorney he wanted to sleep with, she was just one more defense lawyer trying to make him look bad. The difference being she appeared to be having more success than most.

Lomax mulled over Terry's request and Hemmerson's objection. A few seconds later, he was asking Detective Lopez to go stretch his legs for a bit. The way the guy got up and left the courtroom went beyond dentist. A trip to the proctologist was more like it.

As for his partner, Trentino, he finally made it up to the stand. Apparently, swearing to tell the whole truth before God has no expiration date during a trial because the guy wasn't sworn in again.

As he sat down, Terry immediately did a little recapping. If someone had happened upon the proceedings at that moment, he would've presumed Terry was working for the prosecution. Her questions dealt with my being in the wrong place at the wrong time. But where Hemmerson had left off with the detectives, Terry kept going.

"Detective Trentino, let's look at the big picture for a moment. You've got a psychologist at the scene of a crime who explains he's looking for a patient of his. He tells you right away his patient has confessed to killing her husband. Only it turns out the husband is not her husband—he's someone else's husband. What's more, the patient has been pretending to be that someone else, that is, the husband's real wife. Sounds pretty confusing, doesn't it?"

"Yes, it does."

"Almost hard to believe, huh?"

"Yes."

"I mean, if I were trying to make up an alibi, I certainly wouldn't choose one as far-fetched as that. Would you?"

Hemmerson quickly objected on the grounds that it called for speculation. Terry countered that the detective had heard many alibis in the line of duty and that he was uniquely qualified to comment on the viability of the one put forward by her client. Fair enough, Judge Lomax must have thought. He instructed Trentino to answer the question.

Said the detective, "As alibis went it didn't seem very plausible. No, it wouldn't have been my choice."

"In other words, if Dr. Remler were fabricating his alibi, he'd been pretty stupid about it, right?"

"Those are your words, not mine."

Terry nodded. "What if I said Dr. Remler could've been smarter about making up an alibi if that was indeed what he was doing? Could those be *our* words, Detective Trentino?"

He rolled his eyes and took a moment. "Sure, okay . . . yes, he could've been smarter."

"Good. Thank you," she said. She paced a bit without saying anything. "Now let's go back to that fateful night in the Birch home when the police first found Dr. Remler. He was coming up from the basement, correct?"

"I wasn't there, but that's what the initial two officers on the scene reported."

"Do you know what Dr. Remler was doing in the basement?"

"No, I do not."

"You never asked him?"

"Like I said, I didn't arrive on the scene until the crime had been reported."

"I'm not sure I understand," said Terry. "You didn't ask him because you weren't the first to arrive on the scene?"

Trentino's forehead was starting to crease. Frustration with a touch of stress. "No, I didn't ask him that directly, I suppose, because he'd told us he was searching for his patient."

"Ah, the alibi," said Terry, a finger raised in the air. "And you believed it—what Dr. Remler was telling you?"

"At first."

"In fact, he said that he had searched every room in the Birch town house, isn't that right?"

"Yes, he said that."

"And do you still believe that?"

Trentino thought for a moment. This was a verbal sparring match, and he seemed very intent on not getting roughed up. *Where is this lawyer broad going with this?*

"Did you hear the question, Detective?" she asked after a stretch of silence.

"Yes, I heard the question," he snapped. "The answer is, I don't know."

Terry, somewhat incredulous: "You don't know if you believe him?"

"That's right. I don't know."

"Maybe this will help," she said, turning to the jury. "Dr. Remler's fingerprints were found in practically every room in that town house—*every* room—including the basement. That would be pretty consistent with someone who was looking for someone else, wouldn't it?"

Hemmerson objected. "I fail to see the point of this line of questioning," he said. The toss of a life preserver to his suddenly flailing detective witness.

Judge Lomax squinted at Terry. "Ms. Garrett, could you either get to your point or move on, please?"

"Your Honor, my point is simple. The prosecution would have us believe that my client plotted and carried out a complex murder. But if that were the case, it would've been pretty stupid of him to leave his fingerprints all over the place. Unless, of course, my client is telling the truth, which is what I'm trying to prove—that Dr. Remler truly was looking for his patient that night, and that she truly did kill Conrad Birch."

"Hell, you can't even prove she exists."

Terry froze for a moment. Her look was genuine surprise as

the words seemed to echo in the courtroom. When she did move again it was to turn to Trentino. Slowly. The seasoned detective had let his emotions overtake his brain, if only for a moment. He'd blurted out something without thinking, and while it may have been true, it also played right into Terry's hands. So before the judge or anyone else could intercede, she seized the moment.

"You're right, Detective. And why is it we can't prove she exists? Because that's exactly what she wants. It's how she intends to get away with this murder. You think she's make-believe, but I've got news for you, that's what she's *making* you believe. She's manipulating you just like she did Dr. Remler. But as opposed to my innocent client, you're helping her get away with it!"

Hemmerson's face now had the color and shine of a Red Delicious apple. He objected on so many levels that even the stenographer looked up with amazement. Grandstanding, witness badgering, incendiary language. "Detective Trentino is not on trial here!" he shouted.

Lomax promptly scolded Terry for her tactics. He also reminded Trentino that he was on the stand to answer questions and not to inject commentary. In other words, *If you had kept your trap shut, buddy, maybe she wouldn't have given you such an earful.*

Said the judge, "Do you have any further questions for the detective, Ms. Garrett?"

"No, I don't," she said.

Lomax looked at Hemmerson and asked if he wanted to re-question Trentino. He didn't. The quickness of his answering no suggested he was in damage-control mode, the best move being to get his detective off the stand as fast as possible.

"You can step down," said Lomax.

Trentino did, but not without casting a cold stare on his least favorite woman in the room. Terry could've easily turned away, but didn't. She returned the stare and then some. I looked over at Victor, who was suppressing another chortle. He turned to me with a beaming smile. "That's my girl," he whispered.

I nodded with a quick smile of my own. The proud boss was

reflecting on the prowess of his recent addition to the firm and his decision to make her lead counsel on the case.

As soon as I had that thought, I had another. What if there was more to it than that? What if, in the exuberance of the moment, Victor had let slip the true extent of their relationship? *That's my girl.* My mind raced with the idea that he and Terry were an item. He was a good-looking guy; she was a good-looking woman. He was recently divorced; she was single. They worked together and knew each other to be smart and talented. It was more than conceivable.

And I didn't like it.

The reason should've been because of the possible complications. I was on trial for murder and could ill afford a lovers' spat or quarreling of any nature jeopardizing my defense. No matter how professional two people could claim to be, if they were personally involved, there was no way their private lives—especially when troubled—could remain on the sidelines. Life didn't work like that. People didn't work like that.

Yet, that was the last thing I was thinking about. Truth was, I simply didn't want Terry to be seeing someone. Not Victor. Not anyone. You'd think the prospect of spending the rest of my life in jail would've made all other interests a distant second. But there I was. Watching Terry shoot daggers back with her eyes at some pissed-off detective and wondering how it happened. That a crush had crept up on me.

I told myself I was crazy. Then I changed my mind. *Pitiful* was the better word. It hadn't been that long since I'd taken an interest in a woman, and she ended up framing me for murder. Now here I was having thoughts about my attorney. Had the absence of companionship finally caught up to me? Was I that starved for attention?

The day continued. Adding insult to injury, Terry didn't call Trentino's partner to the stand next. In fact, she didn't call him at all. Getting Lopez booted from the courtroom was a way of distracting the jury. She was making them consider the possibility that the two detectives were indeed in cahoots, railroading the defendant regardless of the facts. Between the nightly news and practically every prime-time cop show, one could hardly rule it out.

Instead, Terry continued with her strategic list of witnesses. Back and forth. There was the coroner who testified that Conrad Birch was definitely asleep before he was stabbed. This meant less of a struggle for the killer, if any at all. Very smart of me.

Then there was the policeman who had found my knife—the murder weapon—in the alley directly below Birch's bedroom. I obviously must have thrown it out the window to get rid of it. Very stupid of me.

Unless, of course, it wasn't me.

Unless, of course, *she* wanted the knife to be discovered.

Back and forth. Back and forth. Terry proceeded with her witnesses, sowing the seeds of reasonable doubt with a deft and efficient hand. Slowly but surely, my Mystery Patient seemed to be coming to life in that courtroom. Some of the jurors were even nodding their heads.

"I don't think you'll need to take the stand," Victor whispered at one point.

Yes, indeed. Operation Brilliant Idiot was rolling right along. Brilliantly.

But then the wheels fell off.

THIRTY-ONE

I t was their one and only rebuttal witness.

The defense had rested, my case made. And without my having to assume the risk of testifying. The time was a little before three on a Wednesday. Hemmerson stood from his chair and, looking nowhere but directly at Judge Lomax, announced, "Your Honor, the prosecution calls Gabrielle Dennis."

On either side of me I could hear Victor and Terry utter in unison: "*Who?*"

We all turned and saw a bombshell of a young woman get up from her aisle seat in the back of the courtroom. She looked to be in her mid-twenties, with long, blond hair and an incredibly top-heavy figure that left little doubt as to where she stood on the issue of breast implants. If she wasn't wearing such a tight blouse with her short skirt, maybe it would've been harder to tell.

"What do you think?" Terry asked in a whisper. I may have been sitting right next to her, but I knew it wasn't me she was talking to.

"Don't know," said Victor, his voice even softer. "But that reminds me, I've got to renew my subscription to *Playboy*."

The young woman walked past our table and up to the witness stand. As she was sworn in, Victor's tone took on a "but seriously, folks" register. "Safe to assume we're not going to like this," he said. "Should we ask for an offer of proof?"

Terry shook her head. "If it was any other judge besides Lomax, maybe."

"Then get ready to pounce," said Victor.

She nodded and began to quickly jot down a note. Victor, meanwhile, opened his briefcase and took out his BlackBerry. He began to quickly type. Presumably an e-mail to someone. As to who it might be I had no idea.

Hemmerson approached the young woman. "Could you please state your name for the court?"

She leaned in to the microphone. "My name is Gabrielle Dennis."

"You're here today, Ms. Dennis, because you knew the victim, Conrad Birch, correct?"

"Yes, that's right."

Hemmerson took a few steps back, almost as if he was clearing the way. "And in what capacity did you know Mr. Birch?"

She didn't hesitate for a moment. "I was his mistress."

The courtroom immediately launched into a collective murmur with a few scattered gasps. Lomax quickly asked for order but didn't get any. He demanded it a second time, and everyone began to quiet down. That's when Terry pounced. "Your Honor, we've had absolutely no advance notice of this witness and, given her claim, the timing of her appearance is dubious at best."

Hemmerson jumped right in. "Your Honor, the timing is not only genuine, it's also quite logical. Ms. Dennis only became known to the D.A.'s office yesterday evening, and only because of the intense media coverage this trial has been receiving. She heard news reports of what the defense was claiming and believed it was her duty to come forward."

The judge instinctively looked at Terry. He apparently knew a good tennis match when he saw one and was content to let the issue play out a little more. Sure enough, Terry was ready with her next shot.

"Is the prosecution claiming that they themselves haven't had time to vet this witness?" she asked incredulously.

"Justice is a twenty-four-hour-a-day operation," said Hemmerson with a smirk. "We've had ample time."

"But still not enough time to inform the defense. How convenient. Or is a better word *desperate*?"

Hemmerson threw a nasty look at Terry before addressing the judge again. "Your Honor, if you let me proceed, you'll quickly discover this is a legitimate witness. Not only that, Ms. Dennis has information that I believe will alter the course of this trial."

That last remark had baseline winner written all over it. Lomax raised his hand as if to say, "Enough." He leaned back in his seat, scratched his head of gray hair, and declared that the questioning of the witness could continue. Hemmerson had won the point. Seemingly, the momentum of the match had swung back in his favor.

All eyes returned to Ms. Gabrielle Dennis on the stand. Actually, with a glance at the jury, I realized that the eyes of the five male jurors probably never left her. And given what she had to say, it was clear that she was a bombshell in every sense of the word.

"When did you first become involved with Conrad Birch?" Hemmerson asked her.

"About two and a half years ago."

"How did you meet?"

"We worked out at the same gym."

"Where was that?"

"Max Fitness," she said.

"The one down here near Mr. Birch's office, correct?"

"Yes, a few blocks away."

Hemmerson nodded as if he were hearing all of this for the first time. "Do you remember who initiated your meeting each other?" he asked.

"Not exactly. It was kind of mutual. We were on treadmills next to each other one day. I was having a problem with setting a program, and he offered to help."

"And you seemed to hit it off from there?"

"I guess so."

"In terms of a sexual relationship, though, would you say he initiated the affair?"

She paused for a moment. "Well, again, we were two consenting adults. But, yes, I'd say that's accurate."

"Did you know he was married?"

I expected a pause here as well from Ms. Dennis. Not so she could determine her answer but because of how the answer might make her look. I was wrong. She answered immediately.

"Yes, I knew he was married. He told me he was."

Right then, I realized something. *Christ.* Samantha Kent was sitting through all this, wasn't she? It was bad enough for me. Her level of discomfort had to have been something else entirely. I'd done pretty well not to look over at her since Victor's initial swift kick to my ankle, but I couldn't help it. My only other "cheat" that day had been during the morning when I stole a quick glance to confirm she was indeed sitting in the same seat she'd been in for the past week. She was.

Except now she wasn't. She wasn't in that same seat or any other. I was actually relieved. She certainly didn't need to hear the testimony of Gabrielle Dennis. There was sympathy and there was sadistic. Perhaps Hemmerson had had the decency to send Samantha Kent home during the lunch recess.

He continued the questioning of his surprise star witness: "How long did the affair last, Ms. Dennis?"

"About nine months."

He turned to the jury. "So you first became involved with Conrad Birch about two and a half years ago, and the relationship lasted for about nine months, correct?"

"Yes, that's right."

"The reason you're here today is because of news reports that told of how the defense was blaming the murder on a supposed Mystery Patient who was Conrad Birch's mistress, and that—"

"Objection!" shouted Terry.

"Sustained," said Lomax. He didn't even wait to hear Terry's

208 HOWARD ROUGHAN

grounds. "Mr. Hemmerson, let's refrain from hearsay and the suggestion of blame in the media or by anyone else."

"My apologies, Your Honor. I'll be more careful." He turned back to his witness. "Now, Ms. Dennis, suffice to say, you became aware of the defendant's claim that Conrad Birch had been a patient of his and told him of having an affair, correct?"

"Yes."

"According to the defendant's handwritten notes, this affair took place roughly two years ago, which would seem to coincide with the time in which you were involved with Conrad Birch, right?"

"Yes."

"Furthermore, you've read and heard in news reports that the defense is suggesting this mistress was Dr. Remler's Mystery Patient, is that correct?"

"Yes, that's right."

"So I have to ask you then," he said with a bit of dramatic pause, "have you ever been a patient of Dr. David Remler's?"

She looked directly at me, her face nearing anger. "No, I have not," she said.

"Have you ever even met him before?"

"No, I have not."

"Which is why you came forward, isn't it?"

"Yes. I didn't think it was fair."

Hemmerson turned back toward the jury again. "You wanted to set the record straight. Right a wrong, if you will. Even at the risk of personal embarrassment."

"Like I said, it just didn't seem fair."

"Okay, we'll leave it at that, Ms. Dennis. In my opinion you've displayed some real courage in coming forward, so let me try to wrap this up. Tell us, how did the affair end?"

"Not very well. At least as far as I was concerned."

"What do you mean by that?"

"Conrad told me he couldn't leave his wife."

"You were hoping he would?"

"All I knew was that I loved him."

"Do you think he loved you?"

"He said he did. But again, he also said he couldn't leave his wife. So I figured, what was the point?"

"You ended the affair, then?"

"Technically, yes. Though the way I saw it, I didn't have much of a choice."

"Thank you, Ms. Dennis," said Hemmerson. "I have no further questions, Your Honor." He walked back to his seat. Actually, it was more like a strut.

Judge Lomax: "Your witness, Ms. Garrett."

Terry glanced at her watch. Instead of getting up, though, she asked her first question right from her seat. "Ms. Dennis, where did you and Conrad Birch usually do it?"

"Objection!" shouted Hemmerson. He sprung from his chair so quickly it nearly tipped over. "She's trying to demean the witness!"

"I'll rephrase the question," said Terry right away. She stood and walked a few steps in front of the defense table. "Ms. Dennis, where did you and Mr. Birch conduct the affair?"

She blinked a few times incredulously, but eventually answered. Not very loudly, though. "Mainly in hotels."

"I'm sorry, could you please speak up?"

Gabrielle Dennis glared at Terry Garrett. This was not shaping up to be a beautiful friendship.

"I said, mainly in hotels," she answered, her voice terse.

"Could you name one of them for us?"

With barely a beat in between, she did. "The Wall Street Inn."

"Did you ever pay for a room there?"

"No, Conrad did that."

"Did you ever see him pay by credit card?"

"I never saw him pay at all," she said. "I mean, I know he paid. We just—"

Terry interrupted. "You just didn't want to be seen together in public. I understand. So it's not like anyone ever really saw you together, right?"

"We were discreet, yes."

I glanced over at Victor, who was checking his BlackBerry. He pressed a key on it and looked to be reading something. Meanwhile, Terry looked at her watch again. This time she was quite deliberate about it. "Now, Ms. Dennis, let's talk about your breakup with Conrad Birch. You said he told you he wouldn't leave his wife, is that right?"

"Yes."

"Did that make you angry?"

"I was upset."

"Were you perhaps more than that?"

Hemmerson objected. He wanted to know what Terry was getting at. So did Lomax. He asked her to get to the point.

"Let me put it this way," she said. "Ms. Dennis, would you consider yourself to have a temper?"

"I'm not sure I know how to answer that."

"Yes or no would be fine."

"I can get mad about things, if that's what you mean."

"Not exactly. What I'm asking is that if someone described you as having a mean streak, do you think it would be an accurate assessment?"

She mulled the question over. "No, I don't think it would be."

Terry nodded. "Would it surprise you then that Conrad Birch told my client he thought that's exactly what his mistress had?"

"No, actually, it wouldn't."

"Why's that?"

"Conrad had a tendency to exaggerate. Sometimes even lie. He was having an affair, after all."

"I see," said Terry, now looking at the jury box. Specifically, the women sitting in it. "So someone having an illicit affair is more likely not to tell the truth. That's interesting, because you were also having an illicit affair."

"But—"

"At least, that's what you're claiming here today." Terry had talked right over her. "Tell me, Ms. Dennis, what do you do for a living?"

"I'm an actress."

Terry paused. The answer was an unexpected windfall. The implication of someone playing a part. "Are you currently working right now?"

"No, I'm not."

"When's the last time you did work?"

"Well, I'm also a waitress."

"I see. But in terms of the acting, when's the last time you got paid to do that?"

"Maybe six months ago."

"Maybe?"

"It could've been longer. It was for a commercial; I can't really remember the exact date."

"As for other acting you've done, is there anything we might have seen you in?"

Hemmerson objected. "Is this a courtroom or the Bravo channel?"

Lomax tended to agree. "Let's keep it moving, Ms. Garrett. It's getting late."

Terry's face lit up just a shade. It was as if Lomax had said the magic words. "I agree, Your Honor, it is getting late. In fact, given that, combined with the surprise nature of the witness, I'd like to request that we adjourn until tomorrow morning."

Lomax looked at his watch. The clock on the wall was behind him. It was ten of five. Close enough for a full day he apparently thought. He picked up his trusty gavel. "Court is in recess until tomorrow morning at nine."

Bang.

Gabrielle Dennis and her gravity-defying figure stepped down as the rest of the people in the courtroom gathered their things and stood. Terry walked over to Victor and me.

"Did he e-mail you back yet?" she asked Victor with a nod toward his BlackBerry.

"Yeah. He's starting on it right away."

I looked at the two of them. "Starting on what? Who's *he?*"

"You'll see," said Victor.

THIRTY-TWO

His name was Anthony Magnetti, but Victor called him "The Magnet." The reason was simple, he explained. The guy could pull almost any information about anyone right off his computer. Or perhaps more accurately, he could pull it right off everyone else's computer.

"There are hackers, and then there's The Magnet," said Victor to me, with a straight face no less. As he continued with the hyperbole, he seemed unaware he was talking about the guy the way a kid talked about a superhero. It got to the point that I was fully expecting to see a skintight bodysuit and cape come walking through the door.

So much for expectations.

The man who showed up at Victor's office after we returned from court was not about to inspire a Saturday-morning cartoon. Anthony Magnetti, aka The Magnet, was easily three hundred pounds and, at around five-and-a-half-feet tall, didn't really hide it very well. So, thankfully, there was no skintight bodysuit. There was also no cape. He did, though, have something hanging down his back: a ponytail.

"The Magnet has arrived!" exclaimed Victor, getting up from behind his desk. The two hugged like old friends. As was protocol, Victor's secretary (the brunette) hovered in her high heels until her boss could inquire about a drink preference.

"Coffee, please. Light and sweet," said The Magnet.

The Magnet.

I hadn't quite persuaded myself to call him that when Victor made the introduction. Thankfully, he wasn't one of those types who invoked the phrase "but my friends call me . . ." For some reason, people who did that made me a little nervous. As if meeting a guy who, according to Victor, had done work for both the CIA and the Mossad wasn't reason enough to be nervous.

"David, meet The Magnet."

"Anthony Magnetti," he said, sticking his hand out.

"Hi, Anthony," I said, shaking it. "David Remler."

The guy was somewhere between geek and hip. His thick black glasses were countered by a black leather biker jacket. And the aforementioned ponytail hung in stark contrast to a somewhat nasally voice. Perhaps tipping the scales in favor of hip was his relaxed, easygoing style. Truth was, I'd never really met a laid-back geek.

Victor returned to his desk for a moment. "Let me just buzz Terry."

Terry had been in her office checking her voice mail. While we waited for her to travel down the hall, we settled into Victor's big club chairs and engaged in small talk. Victor expressed his continued frustration with the anemic Knicks, while The Magnet reported that he was a few days away from cracking the Pentagon's new internal file encryption code. To each his own.

Victor's brunette secretary returned with The Magnet's coffee. She placed it down with a coaster on the glass table in front of him without making a single decibel of noise.

Terry arrived.

"Hey, Anthony," she said, walking in. "Three cases since I've been here and three dates with you. People are going to start talking."

"Good," he said. "I'll be able to tell you what they say—a buddy of mine is teaching me wiretapping."

I only had to know the guy for a few minutes to know he was serious.

Terry warmly shook hands with The Magnet and sat down in the fourth and final club chair. Let the briefing begin.

That's what it was in a nutshell. From the moment Victor first e-mailed him, The Magnet had been busy digging up anything and everything he could find on our surprise witness of the day. Gabrielle Dennis . . . the woman claiming to be Conrad Birch's mistress.

"Okay," said Terry. "The possibilities are as follows. One, she's the real deal and is telling the truth. Two, she's a plant—"

"Or, should we say, *im*plant," cracked Victor.

"Yeah, they were kind of out of proportion, weren't they?" said Terry.

The Magnet put his coffee down and flipped back a page on his notepad. "Gabrielle Dennis's breast enlargement surgery was performed here in Manhattan four years ago on January 14 by Dr. Rueben Stolzmier at a cost of six thousand four hundred and eighty-seven dollars."

The office fell silent for a moment.

Then, like a ringmaster, Victor shouted with a wide grin, "The Magnet, ladies and gentlemen!"

I couldn't help asking the question. Perhaps it had to do with my own sense of patient privacy. Or maybe it was just wide-eyed curiosity. "Anthony, how could you find that out?"

He looked at me, all three hundred pounds of him, and answered, "You think you want to know, but trust me, you don't want to know."

"In fact, David," said Victor, "for the record, you're not even at this meeting."

Oh.

Terry continued: "As for the third and final possibility, it's this: Gabrielle Dennis is trying to jump-start her career."

I knew that as far as Terry was concerned this was a very real possibility. While she hinted at it in her cross-examination, it wasn't until after court adjourned that the theory picked up considerable momentum. That's when we stepped outside to see Gabrielle Dennis do anything but shy away from the media. Quite the opposite. She seemed to revel in it. The publicity. The limelight. The hope that a producer or two was watching on TV.

"I have my suspicions," said Terry. "Let's not get ahead of ourselves, though." She turned to The Magnet. "Tell us what you've got, Anthony. What's the deal with the gym?"

He flipped back to the first page of his notes and scrolled down a bit with his finger. "She and Birch were both members during that time," he said. "The gym uses a MagSeven card-swipe system to ID people and chart usage patterns for staffing. The data pools centrally with all its other branches behind a weak-ass virtual network perimeter, so tracking their visits was easy."

"Stop showing off, Anthony," said Terry with a smile.

The Magnet smiled back and cut to the chase. "As I was saying, Gabrielle Dennis was much more of a regular at the gym than Conrad Birch."

"And in terms of overlapping?" asked Terry.

"Only eighteen times from the first date you gave me. Though ten of those occurred within one month."

"Let me guess," said Victor. "January."

The Magnet chuckled and grabbed his hefty gut. "The most common New Year's resolution—and one I've clearly never kept."

I smiled. I liked a guy who could laugh at himself.

"Okay, so Gabrielle Dennis and Conrad Birch could've met as she claimed they did," said Victor.

"Or that's just the way she knew about him," said Terry. "What about the Wall Street Inn, Anthony? Or any other hotels?"

"Birch had four credit cards, plus a corporate card from his firm," he answered. "Not a one showed any Manhattan hotel, including the Wall Street Inn."

"I'm assuming he would've paid cash. Credit cards are too much of an infidelity trail," said Victor. "Not that I'm the voice of experience on that or anything."

"Of course not," said Terry.

Damn. There it was again. That nagging feeling Victor and Terry were involved. *Had he really just winked at her when he said that, or was that me imagining it?* The only thing I remained certain of was that I didn't want it to be true.

The Magnet checked his notes again. "As for restaurants, particularly receipts that suggest two people, there isn't anything to indicate Birch wasn't with his wife. While there's a concentration near his office, most of those were with his corporate card."

"What about the girl's finances?" asked Terry.

"What finances?" said The Magnet with a smirk. He flipped a page forward again on his notes. "Gabrielle Dennis gives new meaning to *struggling actress*. She had—and still has—one checking account with Chase. Barely in the black with three overdraws in the past three years."

"No lump-sum payments or steady increase in deposits during the time she claims she was with Birch?" asked Victor.

"No. The only money going in was from her waitressing job and the occasional royalty payment for a commercial she did that ran for two flights—twenty-six weeks."

I watched as Terry and Victor seemed to be going over their mental checklist of questions. What they'd covered and what they hadn't. Terry's face had that click of realization.

"What about any run-ins with the law?" she asked.

The Magnet shook his head. "No police record, no pending lawsuits, no judgments . . . nothing," he said. "She hasn't owned a car for five years, so there's not even an outstanding parking ticket."

Victor stood up and walked over to his windows. The sun was setting, and the sky had taken on a streak of orange along the horizon. "So, what I'm hearing is this," he said, his back to us. "Nothing that's out-and-out suspicious on the one hand, versus on the other hand—"

Terry jumped in. "Nothing in her testimony today that she couldn't have picked up from television or the newspapers."

"Exactly," said Victor.

The Magnet reached for his coffee. "Out of curiosity, have you checked the autopsy report on Conrad Birch to see if he had any moles or beauty marks you could call her on?"

"I thought about that," said Terry. "I checked and he didn't."

Victor turned around. "What else, Mag'? Anything you found that we haven't gone over?"

"I got into most every drugstore chain. She had a prescription for Xanax a year back with three refills, but who hasn't, right?" He scoured his notes some more. "Oh, I almost forgot. There is one other thing," he said. "It's far from a smoking gun, but it does make you wonder a little more about her real motivation."

"What is it?" asked Terry, sitting up in her chair.

"Her phone records," said The Magnet. "Two days ago, Gabrielle Dennis placed a few calls to EpicOne Media."

I had no idea who they were, but both Terry and Victor apparently did.

"How many exactly?" asked Victor.

"Three."

"Was it to someone's direct extension?"

"No, it was the main line every time."

"We could still track it down, I suppose," said Terry.

"Tough, though," said Victor, still by his windows. "Even if we did, they're not the most cooperative folks on the planet. Plus, they're not terribly fond of lawyers."

"You wouldn't be either if you got sued every other week," said The Magnet.

I felt as if I were watching a foreign movie without subtitles. "Who or what are we talking about?" I asked.

"Sorry, David," said Victor, sitting back down. "EpicOne Media publishes the *National Tabloid*."

No further explanation was needed. The paper they were talking about made the *Enquirer* and the *Star* look like the *Times* and the *Journal*. A monkey and a keyboard got it right more times than they did.

"Well, the notion that she's trying to sell her story certainly hurts her credibility," said Terry. "But it doesn't exactly prove the story wrong now, does it?"

The Magnet shrugged. "Like I said, I didn't think it was your smoking gun."

"Though it's not bad as far as ammo goes," said Victor. He looked at his watch and then up at Terry. She nodded.

"On that note, why don't we let you go, Anthony," she said.

The Magnet pushed off the arms of his club chair with a slight grunt and stood. His feet shuffled as if to absorb all of his weight. As we shook hands, I thanked him for his efforts. It felt weird. I didn't know what exactly had been accomplished or what would come of the information he'd dug up. Nor how it would be used, if at all, and whether it would save me. He was helping David Remler, but there was very little about it that felt personal. It was clear that John Doe would've received the same treatment. He was there because that's what he did. "Just doing my job," he might have said.

And while the difference was that he got paid to do it, I couldn't help noticing the parallel. "Just doing my job" was the humble mantra of a superhero.

There are hackers, and then there's The Magnet!

Victor gave him another hug, and Terry volunteered to walk him out of the office. "Back in minute," she said.

Victor and I sat down again as they left.

"Did I tell you he's done work for the CIA and the Mossad?" said Victor, with a nod toward his door.

"Yeah, you mentioned that," I said.

"For all I know, Magnetti's not even his real name. Ironic, isn't it? Such a private man being the great invader of other people's privacy."

I didn't respond. It wasn't the most comforting thought given that I'd become a party to it.

"Yeah, I know," said Victor, reading my mind—or perhaps my body language. "But it's like plutonium. You can use it for good or you can use it for evil. I happen to think proving your innocence is a good thing."

I told him I agreed, although the acronym of Victor's firm—*Edwards, Vode, Isadore & Locke*—was surely a joke waiting to be made. Ultimately, I elected to keep it to myself.

"You want a drink?" asked Victor. He stood and headed for his wet bar, which was adorned with crystal decanters filled with liquors that were no doubt aged for some ridiculous amount of years.

"No, I'm all set," I lied. Few things sounded better than a drink at that moment. Fortunately, one of those things was the sound of my mental Magic Marker crossing off another day on my mental "how long it's been since I've had a drink" calendar. Ten days and counting.

Terry returned.

She sat back down, kicked off her heels, and put her feet up on the glass table. Victor finished pouring what, of course, had to be my poison of choice—bourbon—and joined us. For a few seconds we simply all stared at one another.

"So, what are we thinking?" asked Terry.

"Fifty-fifty Gabrielle Dennis is telling the truth," said Victor. "Though if she's lying, I'd put all my money on Terry Garrett making her crack tomorrow."

"That's a big *if*," she said.

"Yes, it is," he agreed.

More silence ensued. Victor polished off his drink. Terry bit her lower lip. I simply sat there and waited. Putting my fate in other people's hands required more than trust, I'd learned. It also required a great deal of patience.

There was a rap on the door. Both of Victor's secretaries were standing there. The blonde and the brunette. "All right if we head out, Victor?" asked the blonde.

Victor nodded. "Yes, thank you," he told them. "Have a good night."

They smiled in sync and wished us all the same before turning on their heels to leave.

When they were out of earshot, Terry kidded, "Do you *really* need two secretaries, Victor, or is it simply the male-power-trip thing that I think it is?"

"Oh, it's definitely the male-power-trip thing," he said, grinning. "Sometimes one woman just isn't enough." He started to laugh.

"Holy shit!" exclaimed Terry. "Of course!"

Victor and I both looked at her. *What?*

She had that click of realization on her face again. Only it was more pronounced. "I just figured out what we have to do tomorrow," she said.

With that, Terry stood up from her chair, rubbed her temples, and began to explain. When she was finished, Victor had only one thing to say.

"What the hell are you two still doing in my office when you should be rehearsing?"

THIRTY-THREE

The next morning, Terry rose to her feet in the courtroom and informed Judge Lomax that, having reconsidered, she had no further questions for Gabrielle Dennis. "Instead, Your Honor, I'd like to call Dr. David Remler to the stand."

Does he or doesn't he?

"I do," I told the clerk with my right hand raised. The whole truth and nothing but.

Lomax motioned for me to be seated. Terry approached and, despite her game face, managed to give me a reassuring nod.

Here we go.

"You begged me to put you on the stand, didn't you, Dr. Remler?" she started.

I smiled like I was supposed to. "I don't know about begged," I replied. "It was more like *strongly urged*."

The quip brought a smattering of laughter from the back of the courtroom.

"Either way," said Terry, "I had no intention of having you testify. I mean, we've all seen those television law dramas where those crafty prosecutors trip up the innocent defendant."

"Objection!" cried out Hemmerson. "That's a gross mischaracterization."

"That my client is innocent or that you're crafty?" cracked Terry.

"That's enough, Ms. Garrett," said Lomax. He turned to Hemmerson. "I'm going to take it on faith that the jury is aware of the types of TV programs being referred to here and how they are fictional in every way." He shifted his eyes back to Terry. "That said, Ms. Garrett, I won't have you baiting the prosecution. Or, for that matter, trying my patience. So, in other words, cut it out."

"My apologies, Your Honor." She walked a few steps toward the jury while still talking to me. "The point I was trying to make was that up until yesterday, in all honesty, I felt we'd done a pretty good job of proving your innocence, Dr. Remler. That's why I made the decision not to have you testify in your own defense. But then we heard from a young woman named Gabrielle Dennis." She paused. "Prior to her appearance here, had you ever seen her before, Dr. Remler?"

"No, I hadn't," I said.

"There's no way she's the woman who became your patient— the one claiming to be Samantha Kent—is there?"

"No, it's not the same woman."

"You're sure of that?"

"Absolutely, yes."

"So, seeing Gabrielle Dennis testify yesterday that she was involved with Conrad Birch during the time he told you he was having an affair . . . well, that must have come as quite a shock," she said. "A real incriminating witness brought forward by the prosecution. If Gabrielle Dennis was not the patient who framed you, then who are we supposed to believe? You or her?"

Terry's tone sounded almost combative. As if she was somehow turning on her own client.

God, she was good.

It made my response sound that much better. "Actually, I think the logical choice is to believe both of us."

Terry cocked her head. "How do you figure that?"

"With all due respect to the prosecution, I think they've done me a favor. They've treated me as if I've been lying through my teeth from the very beginning. Lying about everything," I said. "But with Gabrielle Dennis, they proved I was telling the truth about Conrad Birch, that he was, in fact, an adulterer."

"Yes," said Terry. "But they're obviously trying to suggest that because his mistress wasn't your so-called Mystery Patient, you, in fact, have been lying."

I looked at Terry. She looked back at me. It was as if we were both looking at Victor's secretaries again. The two of them, walking away from his office the night before.

"Really, the only thing the prosecution has proved is that *one* of his mistresses wasn't my patient," I said calmly.

"What are you suggesting, Dr. Remler?"

I reminded myself of the advice Terry had given me. *Talk as if you're at some shrink conference, David, instead of a courtroom.*

"As a psychologist," I began, "I've seen countless examples of both men and women who've had more than one extramarital affair at the same time. In the case of Conrad Birch, therefore, I'm not really surprised at all by yesterday's developments."

Terry pursed her lips and nodded. "So, in other words, once you're not a one-woman man, who's to say you're a one-*mistress* man?"

"Exactly," I said. "But what's also key is that, at least with the patients I've treated, there's an utter reluctance to admit it."

"Why do you think that is?"

"Ultimately, I see it as a societal boundary. While we continue to frown on those who have affairs, we nonetheless have come to accept it as commonplace. To hear that someone has cheated on a spouse rarely shocks us, when you get right down to it."

"But the prospect . . ."

"Of two affairs simultaneously? It's fair to say that the stigma is more than double."

"But Conrad Birch sought your counsel, Dr. Remler. He told you about his affair. Are you saying such a stigma would prevent him from telling you about an additional affair?"

"The short answer is yes," I said. "Though in the case of

Conrad Birch we have to remember the purpose of our meeting in the first place. He was concerned about ending a relationship with a woman who had a mean streak. Guilt never really came into play."

"But again, the prosecution has claimed you've fabricated this whole story right down to your patient notes written nearly two years ago. What do you make of that?"

"It would mean I not only had tremendous patience in plotting a murder but was also the recipient of tremendous luck. I somehow guessed that Conrad Birch was having an affair."

Terry again walked toward the jury box. This time she went all the way to the far end of it and turned around—as if she were the thirteenth juror. "In other words," she said, "you're not only a psychologist but, unbelievably, a member of the Psychic Friends Network."

Again, there was a smattering of laughter from the courtroom. The difference this time being that most of the jurors were contributing to it.

Terry looked up at Judge Lomax. "I have no further questions, Your Honor."

Before she could even get back to her seat, Hemmerson had stood and fired his first shot. "Dr. Remler, I'm going to try my best to not do you any more *favors* here, okay?" The sarcasm was anything but subtle. "Tell me, the knife used to fatally stab Conrad Birch over fifty times, who did that belong to?"

"If you're asking whether it was in my possession at the time of the murder, the answer is no."

"Actually, that's not what I'm asking. Very simply, was it your knife, yes or no?"

"Yes."

"Yes, it was your knife," Hemmerson repeated. "And the letter that clearly stated how your relationship with Conrad Birch was more than doctor and patient, and that was, perhaps, more than a little incriminating . . . this letter signed by Conrad Birch—a signature that no one in this courtroom disputes—where was it found?"

"I'm told it was found in my apartment," I answered.

I looked at Terry and Victor, who were both discreetly shaking their heads. Terry had warned me about being overly coy with Hemmerson, how it would only make me appear to be skirting the truth. The prosecutor was about to prove her right.

"I'm sorry, Dr. Remler, is it now your contention that the letter was not found by the police in your apartment?" he asked.

I got with the program. "No, that's not my contention. That letter was found in my apartment."

"You also don't deny you were at the scene of the crime, correct?"

"Correct."

"That your alibi for not being the murderer is that you were coming to the aid of a patient—a woman you cannot prove exists, correct?"

I stared at Hemmerson and tried to keep my composure. It wasn't easy. I was starting to think that if there was an Oscar for assholes, he'd be up for the Lifetime Achievement Award.

"Is that correct, Dr. Remler?" he repeated. "You cannot prove she exists."

"Yes, that's right."

Hemmerson did his own walk toward the jury. "Now, if I understand you correctly, you'd like us to believe that Conrad Birch was the Don Juan of Manhattan, that he had a whole harem of women."

"That's not what I said."

"No, you're right, you suggested he was having more than one affair at the same time. That's an awfully convenient argument, especially at the eleventh hour of this trial, don't you think?"

Terry objected. "Argumentative, Your Honor."

"Sustained," said Lomax.

"Withdrawn," said Hemmerson. He remained standing near the jury box and continued. "The fact is, you can't prove Conrad Birch was involved with more than one woman any more than you can prove your Mystery Patient exists. Do you disagree with that?"

"No, I don't."

"And as far as your contention, based on your alleged notes, that Conrad Birch was having an affair, didn't you just tell the court minutes ago how prevalent infidelity is in our society?"

"I believe I said the acceptance of it was commonplace."

"Yes, just like the occurrence of it. In fact, would you dispute the many studies out there that say at least fifty percent of all married adults have engaged in an extramarital affair?"

"I'm not familiar with these studies," I said.

Hemmerson walked back to the prosecution's table and lifted a stack of papers in the air. "Well, I'm familiar with them, Dr. Remler. Would you like me to read from some of them?"

Hemmerson practically turned to Terry in anticipation of her objection. Before she could say the word, he withdrew the question. The guy was in a groove.

"Dr. Remler, are you aware that of the seventeen hundred and eighty-four stabbings reported in New York City last year, seventeen hundred and three of them were committed by men?"

"No, I didn't know that."

"Yet, you claim it was a woman who must have stabbed Conrad Birch, correct?"

"Yes."

"Despite the fact that over ninety-five percent of all stabbings are perpetrated by men."

"No, not despite. I've simply explained what happened the night Conrad Birch died—my version of the events that took place."

"Yes, you certainly have, Dr. Remler. And if you ask me, it's quite an *unbelievable* version at that." He turned crisply to Lomax. "Nothing further, Your Honor."

THIRTY-FOUR

Question: when is a tie the same as a win?

Answer: when your attorney says it is.

At least that's what I was hoping. Terry, for her part, seemed pretty sure about it.

The two of us were sharing a cab heading back uptown. Terry was returning to her office, and I was going home. Victor had stayed behind at the courthouse to talk to someone. "Chat the guy up" was how he put it.

As the buildings and storefronts passed my window in a blur, I couldn't quite figure how Terry managed to sound so upbeat in the wake of my testifying. Sure, I came across decent enough when she was asking the questions. She'd prepared me well, and I'd managed to remember all of my lines. As per Victor, I'd even made a lot of eye contact with the jury. But any sense of relief, any twinge of optimism, all but disappeared with Hemmerson and his cross-examination. To put it simply, I thought the guy had me for lunch.

"Not so, and here's why," said Terry, shaking her head. "Hemmerson may have rubbed your nose in the evidence, but there was nothing new to be learned. The jury's already heard it all."

"What about that little statistic about men and stabbings?"

"It may be true, but it also plays right into our hand. Again, you're being framed. Your Mystery Patient chose a murder method that further points the finger at you and away from her. It's just one more dot to connect in our closing argument."

"I suppose that makes sense."

"It definitely makes sense. More important, though, what stood out today was how Hemmerson didn't really go after you on the multiple-mistress angle. He danced around the thing but didn't touch the psychology of it. He knew it wasn't his turf. That means, in spite of his chest-pounding with the evidence, what we've got is a jury contemplating the very real and—key word here—*reasonable* possibility that Conrad Birch had more than one affair going on."

"So Hemmerson *didn't* have me for lunch?"

"Light snack, maybe," she said. "But you scored points too. That's why I called it a tie. And, let's face it, a tie is as good as a win."

I looked at Terry blankly. This wasn't the first of her rationales to have a head start on me. "I was with you right up until 'let's face it,'" I said.

She grinned. "It's all about expectations, David. When jurors watch a prosecutor go after a defendant, they're looking for the knockout. That's the way people are, and that's the way the law is set up. It's all about absolutes. You're either innocent or guilty, and in either case, the verdict has to be unanimous. By holding your own with Hemmerson, it's as if he's the one who failed."

"Perception-based reality," I said.

"Exactly. The onus was on him to score the knockout, not the other way around."

I remained staring ahead at the cab's Plexiglas. A solid ten seconds of silence passed. Then, tongue in cheek: "This conversation is just an elaborate attempt to cheer me up, isn't it?"

"Pretty much," she said, playing along. "Did it work?"

"A little bit, actually."

"Good. I'd hate to think I've lost my touch."

We'd had a full thirty blocks of conversation about the trial, ending with a long laugh. When it died down, I realized there were another thirty blocks before Terry would get out at the Chrysler Building. I decided to change the subject. Simultaneously, so did she.

"I'm sorry, go ahead," I said.

"No, that's all right," she said. "You first."

"I was just going to ask if this was what you always wanted to do. Practice law, that is."

"Uh-oh, you're not going to analyze me, are you?"

"Not unless you tell me your demanding parents forced you to go to law school."

"No, that was entirely my doing. I basically knew I wanted to be an attorney since I was twelve and a half."

"And a half, huh? Sounds like you remember the exact moment."

"I do. It's when I saw Paul Newman in *The Verdict*."

I started to laugh. "That's so weird."

"Why?"

"Because I wanted to be a psychologist ever since I saw Judd Hirsch in *Ordinary People*."

"You're kidding me."

"No. From that day forward it was my mission to help all the Timothy Huttons in the world."

"Yeah, but didn't you think it was the mother who really needed the analysis?"

"You're right, except I had a huge crush on Mary Tyler Moore growing up, so I was probably in denial on that."

"Wow," said Terry. "Two impressionable young people letting Hollywood dictate their entire future."

"It's the stuff of congressional hearings, if you ask me," I said. "Though, what's pretty amazing is that we both followed through on it."

"You have, perhaps. I've still got a ways to go."

"What do you mean?"

"The super-duper big plan was that I was going to represent the poor," she said.

"If it's any consolation, that's what I'll be when I'm done paying you and Victor."

She laughed.

"Seriously," I added. "What happened to your plan, if you don't mind my asking?"

"Nothing. It's still there—just revised. As much as I want to do 'low-income law,' I realize I don't necessarily want to live like the people I'm representing. I'm not a martyr, and I like to shop as much as the next gal. So the revised plan has me doing 'high-income law' for about ten years. That should pay the bills for happily ever after."

"I'm impressed."

"Don't be. I haven't done it yet."

"You will."

Terry gave me an appreciative look. Eyes that said thank you in a very real way. In that moment we weren't lawyer and client. It was a little awkward. Because we both knew that lawyer and client was exactly what we were.

The cab pulled up to the northeast corner of Forty-second and Lex, right in front of the Chrysler Building.

"It's time to be brilliant," she said. She was referring to the crafting of her closing argument.

"How much of it have you written?" I asked.

"About two-thirds."

"That's good. You're almost done."

"Yes, except the one-third remaining is the heavy lifting—the part that's supposed to make twelve people say 'not guilty.'"

I tapped my index finger on my temple. "Tell me, please, that you have it all right up here."

"Piece of cake." She winked and offered to give me some money for the cab. I declined.

"You need to save up for when you don't make three hundred and fifty bucks an hour," I said.

*   *   *

I went home, later climbing into bed that night without having a drink. Eleven days and counting. My alarm was set for eight the next morning. At seven forty-five, my phone rang.

"Hello?"

"David, it's Terry."

Her voice was anxious.

"Is something wrong?"

"I'm not sure, to tell you the truth," she said. "I got a call five minutes ago from Judge Lomax."

"What's up?"

"He wouldn't say, exactly. He was calling to tell me he wanted all counsel to meet in his chambers at nine thirty. And if that's not strange enough, he specifically asked that you be there as well."

"Is that normal?"

"It's the opposite of normal."

"What do you think the reason is?"

"I really don't have a clue. I just called Victor to let him know, and he has no idea either. The only thing Lomax would say was that *something highly unusual has happened*."

PART IV

THIRTY-FIVE

Judge's chambers. Nine thirty on the dot. All were assembled.

I'd met Terry and Victor out in the hallway first. Victor, who clearly possessed an extensive grooming regimen to begin with, nonetheless looked to have applied an extra spit and polish. His impeccable wardrobe was represented by a dark navy suit that featured an added accessory—a red silk handkerchief that sprang from his breast pocket like an origami flower.

As for Terry, she struck me as having also spent a few extra minutes in front of the mirror. Her preference for minimal makeup was still evident, although there seemed to be a little more attention to detail. Something with the contrast in her eyes, I thought. Her hair, normally worn down, was tucked back neat behind a black barrette, the sheen of which matched her perfectly tailored blazer and skirt. Assuming we all have a favorite outfit hanging in our closet, I was pretty sure I was looking at hers.

So what was my excuse?

"You missed a button," Terry said to me right away.

I looked down, and sure enough, the shirt beneath my tie was bunched up around my stomach. It was actually the buttonhole I'd missed. Or skipped, as it were. I made the correction.

"There we go," she said. "Much better."

I nodded. Then I immediately threw back my shoulders and straightened my posture. She smiled.

"So, what's our best guess?" I asked.

"Problem with a juror," answered Victor. Though as fast as he said it, he basically ruled it out. "Only that would hardly qualify as 'something highly unusual,' as Lomax put it. Plus, he made the call himself."

Terry turned to me and translated. "Normally, a clerk or a secretary would make the call in that situation. Not the judge."

"My gut tells me it's something that personally involves him in the case," said Victor.

"Can't imagine what that would be, though," said Terry.

Victor glanced at his watch. "Neither can I. But it's time to find out."

The two turned and began walking. I fell in line right behind them. While my lawyers had no idea what was in store for us in Lomax's chambers, they at least knew how to get there. We hung a left at an intersecting corridor and continued all the way toward the end. Along the way, we passed a court officer who gave Victor a nod of recognition and the okay for all of us to proceed. The second-to-last door on the right, with a partially torn sign that read PRIVATE, was where we went in.

I looked around. There were people milling about, every one holding some type of file or other paperwork. We passed a few offices with the doors open, and I stole quick peeks. A woman putting on a robe to the left. A guy on the phone to the right with his feet up on the desk, a brass gavel paperweight in his hand.

Welcome to backstage of the legal system.

Lomax's chambers were at the very end of the hallway. His door was also open, and the three of us stepped inside. Lomax wasn't there, but already seated and waiting were Hemmerson and the two other prosecutors who'd been assisting him. A young man and woman. The only talking they'd done in the courtroom was in the form of hushed whispering into Hemmerson's ear. The young woman looked smart and poised. The young man looked as if he was maybe an hour out of law school.

"Hello, Glenn," said Victor.

"Morning, Victor. Morning, Terry."

Hemmerson turned to me with a slight nod, which, all things considered, was more than I would've expected. Up until that point, the proceedings hadn't exactly been congenial. The contempt seemed to be flowing freely back and forth across the aisle, and Hemmerson's entire demeanor left little doubt that he had it in for me. But good.

Then again, I suppose that was his job.

It felt strange to have that thought. In fact, as I took a seat on the couch to the side of Lomax's desk, everything seemed to feel a little strange. For a few minutes, no one was playing his or her part. The personalities, the battle lines, the maneuvering—they were all on hold. We were merely six people sitting in a room and waiting.

Don't get me wrong. The apparent trace of civility hanging in the air had only so much of a mollifying effect. To think for a second that it was all strictly business with Hemmerson, that he had no choice in his deep dislike for me, was to miss the big picture. No matter what, I couldn't ignore one inescapable and very human truth. When a guy is trying to put you away for the rest of your life, *it's always personal*.

Besides, the jerk was making eyes at Terry again.

Well, kind of. If Hemmerson was a horn dog out of the courtroom and a eunuch inside one, judge's chambers were turning out to be a curious middle ground. The attraction had resurfaced, but it was being expressed in a far more subtle manner. You'd have to be sensitive to it in the first place to pick up on it. In other words, you'd have to be me.

Any further grumbling to myself about Hemmerson was halted by the rigid heel-to-toe of Judge Lomax entering his office. In one hand was a coffee mug, in the other an ominous red folder. For sure, no one was looking at the mug.

Lomax took a seat behind his cluttered desk and began making room for the folder. "Are we all here?" he asked, head down and shuffling some papers.

"Yes," said Hemmerson.

"Yes," said Terry.

Lomax looked up for the first time. His tired eyes were searching, and immediately it became obvious whom they were searching for. The defendant. When they found me sitting on the couch to his left, I tried to gauge his expression, but the old man was wearing one serious poker face.

He hit a button on his phone and leaned in to the speaker. "Eunice, could you come in here, please?"

Lomax shuffled a few more papers, and as he did I glanced around. I'd been focusing so much on the players in the room that I'd neglected to take in the room itself. *Neglected*. Now there was a fitting word. The worn furniture and overall dated decor had been overrun by the dust and freestanding piles of yellowing *Wall Street Journal*s. It was the office that time forgot. Not to mention the cleaning lady.

A slender, gray-haired woman who was presumably Eunice entered the office with a stenograph machine. One of the old ones, of course. She took a seat behind Lomax without acknowledging anyone. No eye contact whatsoever.

Said Lomax, "I want there to be a transcript of this meeting due to the unorthodox nature of what's about to occur and the unavoidable impact it will have on this case."

Eunice typed away, her fingers a near blur.

As for the rest of us, no one moved. I don't think anyone even breathed. Intentional or not, the judge had managed to display a fine flair for the dramatic.

Make that a very fine flair. That's because when Eunice stopped typing, there was only one sound left in the room. It was Lomax tapping his fingers on that red folder before him.

What the hell does he have in there?

THIRTY-SIX

Finally, his fingers stopped tapping.

After giving Eunice a glance over his shoulder, Lomax began. "For the record, the defendant, Dr. David Remler, is present in addition to his counsel. Also present is the prosecution team." He turned to me. "Dr. Remler, what I'd like you to do right now is describe for us physically the woman you claim was your patient. You've stated that she introduced herself as Samantha Kent, correct?"

I exchanged a quick glance with Terry, who, despite looking equally as confused as I, nonetheless gave me a slight nod. *Go ahead, David.*

"Yes," I answered while clearing my throat. "Though she actually went by 'Sam' with me."

"And her physical description?" asked Lomax.

I thought for a second. My description of the woman I believed was Sam Kent was already a matter of record. The judge was asking a question he already knew the answer to. Lawyers did that. Where was this going?

"She was around five foot six. Thin. Blond hair, past her shoulders if worn down," I said.

That's when Lomax opened the red folder.

Barely. He slid his hand in and pulled something out. A rectangle. It was a photograph. A color Polaroid, to be exact. He held it up to me. "Dr. Remler, is this the woman you described?"

The picture and his question happened so fast that the first reaction from the rest of the room was no reaction at all. Hemmerson, along with Terry and Victor, seemed almost paralyzed by what was clearly a most unexpected turn of events.

The paralysis would prove short lived, however.

"Your Honor!" exclaimed Hemmerson. "With all due respect, what the hell is going on?"

Lomax raised his palm. "It will all become clear in a minute or two," he said. His expression was tough to peg. While slightly peeved by Hemmerson's tone, he also appeared to be slightly amused. The look of someone who anticipated a certain response from another person and then got it in spades.

Meanwhile, there was the photograph. I leaned forward and studied the image for a bit. It was of a woman standing on a city street corner in broad daylight. I assumed Manhattan, but I couldn't tell. Sure enough, she was thin, medium height, with blond hair about shoulder length. Incredible. Everything matched the description of my Mystery Patient except for one thing.

It wasn't her.

There was fast temptation, I have to admit. Given my predicament, a possible life sentence hanging in the balance, the thought crossed my mind to yell out, "Eureka, that's her!" For so long I'd been unable to prove her existence. Now, suddenly, here was the chance to make believers of them all. Tell a lie to serve a greater truth. Yeah, there was temptation all right.

"No," I said. "That's not the woman."

"Are you sure?" asked Lomax. "Take a good look."

I already had. "Yes, I'm sure that's not her."

I could tell Victor and Terry didn't know precisely how to react to my answer, though disappointedly certainly appeared to make the most sense. Despite the overall confusion about what Lomax was doing, this much was clear: had the woman in the photograph been my illustrious, yet elusive Mystery Patient, the defense of Dr. David Remler would've taken a considerable turn for the better.

All the more reason why Hemmerson looked happy. Or was it relieved? His smile was more shaky than confident. Nonetheless, it was still a smile. The prosecution had obviously dodged a bullet.

But wait.

There would be another shot.

Without saying a word, Lomax returned the photograph to his red folder and took out a second one. This one wasn't a Polaroid. Nor was it one of those standard four-by-sixes the local drugstore pumped out. This photograph was square, maybe five by five. He held it up to me as he'd done the first time. I stared in disbelief.

Eureka.

There she was. My Mystery Patient. Thin, medium height, and blond hair about shoulder length. Except this time it was definitely her. The fake Samantha Kent. No need to lean in for a closer look. Although the shot was taken at night, there was plenty of light around her. She was wearing a long black dress and a red shawl draped over her shoulders.

"Dr. Remler?"

My eyes had gone wide. The jaw had dropped.

Lomax raised his voice a level and tried again. "Dr. Remler?"

I needed to say something if only for Eunice and her trusty stenograph machine in the corner. The transcript had to make official what everyone watching me had already gathered.

"That's her."

"Are you—"

"Yes, I'm sure. That's definitely her," I said.

The initial shock of seeing the photo quickly gave way to the perplexing realization of where it had been taken. There she was, standing on the sidewalk all aglow under a streetlamp before some very recognizable steps. The ones leading up to the Metropolitan Museum of Art. Venue for the Kesper Society cocktail party.

Which meant . . .

"What is it, Dr. Remler?" asked Lomax.

He was staring at me. No, it was more like he was studying me. He obviously had picked up on my expression—a look of putting one and one together in my mind. Turned out, he knew exactly what I was thinking.

My Mystery Patient wasn't standing alone.

Like a magician, Lomax revealed that the photograph in his hand was only half a photograph. The other half had been folded back, neat and straight, the crease invisible to the eye. With a flip forward, the picture became complete. My Mystery Patient and me. Standing side by side.

How did Lomax get ahold of this?

It was surely everyone's first question, though that's where the similarities ended. There'd been a flip-flop in circumstances. An upending of emotions.

Hemmerson was no longer smiling. Sudden unease had taken root on his face through a crisscross of wrinkles. As for the young duo supporting him, they knew just enough to appear very concerned.

Cut to Victor and Terry. Their assumed disappointment was now the look of marvelous opportunity. The defense of Dr. David Remler had indeed taken a turn for the better.

"Your Honor, I demand an explanation!" barked Hemmerson.

Lomax was flashing that half-peeved, half-amused expression again. "First of all, calm down, Counselor," he said. "Second, listen to what I'm about to tell you without interrupting me." He swung his eyes over to Victor and Terry. "That goes for all of you."

So began the explanation.

"When I returned here to my chambers yesterday after court was adjourned, there was a FedEx envelope waiting for me. Judges don't normally open anything they're not expecting. However, the sender was listed as NYU Law School, where I'm a guest lecturer. That was good enough for me. I opened the envelope.

"Inside was a photograph and a typewritten note." Lomax went to his red folder again and pulled out a piece of paper. Presumably, the note. "There was only one sentence, and it read as follows," he said, his forefinger pointing down at the words. *"Dr. Remler is telling the truth."*

Lomax took a deep breath, almost as if he were daring Hemmerson or anyone else to interrupt. No one did. Yet.

He continued: "Naturally, the contents of this envelope gave me considerable pause, first and foremost because of where the envelope came from. Or at least where I thought it came from. I went about contacting several people I know at NYU Law School, none of whom had any knowledge of the envelope. Nor were they able to trace it to anyone on campus.

"That's when I called FedEx. According to the tracking number, the envelope was mailed from one of their midtown locations. Paid for in cash. Beyond that, there was nothing more they could tell me. So, at this time, I have no idea who the mailer of this envelope is."

"Excuse me, Your Honor."

Lomax threw Hemmerson a cold stare. "What did I tell you about interrupting?"

Apparently not enough.

That brief exchange smacked of a father scolding a son, and it underscored what was becoming very evident. Lomax had relied on his near thirty years of experience as a judge in calling this meeting and in determining what role he'd play. Especially up front. As such, he was determined to keep it a one-man act.

Hemmerson apologized, somewhat sheepishly, and Lomax went on. The second photograph was still in his hand.

"Putting aside the anonymity of the sender for a moment, the primary issue for me as it relates to the trial is the consequence of my having seen this picture. Which brings us to what I'm sure Mr. Hemmerson wanted to interrupt me about. I showed two photographs to Dr. Remler. Yet, I stated there was only one in the envelope sent to me."

Hemmerson nodded. Other than that, not a peep out of him.

Said Lomax, "The reason for this is simple, albeit unconventional. Before I can entertain a host of conspiracy theories, the law requires that I first assume Dr. Remler is innocent. In doing so, I also have to assume he had nothing to do with sending me this photograph.

"But if that's the case, what I can't assume—or rather, what I can't rely on as proof—is Dr. Remler's mere word." Lomax picked up the first picture he showed me. The Polaroid. "Which is why there's another photograph. In other words, I needed a control group."

I blinked a couple of times, somewhat stunned.

The guy had been testing me.

"Yesterday, not long after receiving the envelope, I had Eunice here go out on the street with an instant camera we keep in the office. I asked her to find and take a picture of a woman who fit Dr. Remler's description of his alleged patient. This way, I could know that Dr. Remler, a man whose freedom lies in the balance, wasn't simply being an opportunist." Lomax stopped and examined the shot briefly. "I think Eunice did a very nice job, by the way."

I glanced at Eunice as she recorded Lomax's compliment. She gave the ever-so-slightest of smiles. Safe to say, for this woman it was a veritable tidal wave of emotion.

"Anyway," said Lomax, "you've now seen how I've utilized that photograph, as well as the one sent to me. You've also seen how Dr. Remler responded. I suppose, for some of you, my actions might challenge your sense of a judge's prerogative. While I'll give both sides an opportunity to register their opinion, please keep one thing in mind. From a legal standpoint, I've already done my homework on this."

The judge leaned back in his chair and put his hands behind his head. It was the body-language equivalent of *Bring it on*.

No surprise. Hemmerson brought it first.

Like a windup toy that had been twisted a few times too many, he fired off question after doubting question. The key one was this: "How do we know the defendant himself or someone representing him didn't mail you the picture? If that were the case, your control group would be rendered meaningless."

Terry gave me a quick stare to make sure I kept my mouth shut. While my instinct was to defend myself—deny I'd done any such thing—I'd been hanging around lawyers enough by then to know better. I saw what she and Victor saw. It didn't matter that Hemmerson had essentially accused them of sending the picture as well. We had the best possible person to defend us. The judge.

Said Lomax, "While it's conceivable Dr. Remler and/or his counsel sent me the picture, it begs the question as to why they waited until now. Because if you look closely, you'll see it wasn't taken recently. In fact, it was taken many months ago. Right around the time of Dr. Remler's arrest."

Everyone leaned in toward the photograph.

"Is there some kind of date printed on it?" asked Hemmerson.

Lomax shook his head coyly.

"Then how could you know that?"

"Because I happen to be a fan of Mark Rothko," he said. That hardly cleared anything up, and he knew it. Lomax pointed with his forefinger. "You see that swath of red in the background? That's the banner for what was the Rothko exhibit. I know because I went to it. Two days before it ended—*last October*."

And like that, Mark Rothko became my favorite artist of all time.

Meanwhile, a stymied Hemmerson cut his losses on that angle and immediately moved to another. "Your Honor, be that as it may, your leeway as a judge in this situation also permits you to ignore the contents of the envelope."

"It does indeed," replied Lomax, putting the picture down. "The problem with that, however, is twofold. First, someone out there knows I received the picture. If I choose to disregard it, it doesn't mean everyone else will."

Hemmerson squinted. "Who else are you referring to?"

"The press, for starters. Who's to say they won't get the same anonymous envelope in the mail. Then what? No, I'm more comfortable tackling this situation head-on as opposed to waiting for possible fallout elsewhere."

Hemmerson was dumbfounded. "How on earth could you let the threat of media exposure dictate your actions?"

Lomax shook his head. "You're missing the big picture, Counselor. It's not the press that ultimately has me concerned. I said the problem with ignoring the envelope was twofold. It's the second fold that has me concerned." He picked up the picture again. "If this woman was indeed Dr. Remler's patient, it means she's still at large. Hell, even if she wasn't his patient, she's still out there. Only by finding her will we know for sure. Whether she's a material witness, suspect, or innocent bystander, we need her to be found. Ignoring her doesn't make her go away."

So much for dumbfounded. Now Hemmerson looked genuinely panicked. *"Are you suggesting what I think you're suggesting?"*

"It's no small hassle for me either, I assure you. But yes, I'm suspending the trial. A further police investigation is needed. And, if I may make a suggestion, they might want to start by showing this photograph to Samantha Kent. The real one. Maybe she'll recognize the woman."

Hemmerson began to pace. It was as if he was trying to defuse his anger with every step. It half worked. While he didn't scream, his tone went beyond deliberate. "And if it turns out this whole damn thing was a hoax—or worse, some desperate attempt to prevent a guilty verdict, what then?" he asked.

"Then we start again," said Lomax.

"But don't you see? That's a win-win for the defense."

"That's odd," interjected Terry, clearly unable to resist at that point. "I thought this was about justice, not who wins or loses."

Hemmerson gave her a sarcastic nod. "Thanks for the civics lesson, Counselor."

"I'm serious. You don't win if you put the wrong person behind bars."

"I don't put anyone behind bars. That decision, in case

you've forgotten, is made twelve people at a time. The jury is your justice."

"Then why don't we show them the picture and see what they think?"

"Very funny."

"Why not?" asked Terry. "You're contending the picture doesn't prove anything. If you believe that, why couldn't a jury?"

"Hey, you know, maybe you're right," said Hemmerson sarcastically. "But first, why don't we all take a polygraph to make sure no one here was involved with that picture. Shall we have your client go first?"

"Okay, that's enough," said Lomax. "The jury isn't seeing the picture, and no one's taking a polygraph."

Victor cleared his throat. "Sorry to interrupt, Your Honor. Can I suggest one thing that perhaps *should* happen?"

"Go ahead."

"I don't know what your intention is regarding the dismissal of the jury, but I'd like you to wait at least a day."

"What for?"

"So Samantha Kent can see the photo before the news media gets wind of the suspended trial," said Victor. "I'd hate to think this mystery woman would know something was up before we possibly got a positive ID on her."

It was a good point, and the judge knew it.

"I see," he said. He looked at Hemmerson. "Does the prosecution have a problem with that?"

Hemmerson rubbed his temples. "With all due respect, sir, on my list of current problems relating to this case, that one kind of pales in comparison."

"I'll take that as a no," said Lomax. He proceeded to act out a cough. "Now if you all don't mind, I'm feeling a little bit under the weather." He turned back to Eunice. "Would you please instruct the bailiff that today's session will be canceled due to illness?"

Again, Eunice gave the ever-so-slightest of smiles.

Lomax glanced at Victor, who nodded. "I appreciate it, Your Honor," he said. He cracked a smile. "I do hope you're feeling better soon."

There was no further conversation. No polite chitchat to be had. Terry, Victor, and I simply stood and thanked Lomax for his time. All things considered, it was the most appropriate figure of speech. *His time.* I didn't have to know much to realize that a younger judge, one with fewer years on the bench, would've been hard pressed to do what Lomax had done.

In Hemmerson's opinion, perhaps, what had occurred represented a beleaguered judge in the waning days of his career. A guy who simply stopped caring about the system.

But that certainly wasn't my opinion. What I saw had nothing to do with a judge's apathy. Quite the opposite. I saw a man who, after a lifetime of experience, fully understood the system. Embraced it. And knew, if need be, he could lean on it a little more. Just like an old friend.

For that, I was forever grateful.

THIRTY-SEVEN

It wasn't quite a celebration that night, though it shared many of the same telltale signs. Smiles, jokes, laughs, drinks, and more drinks. There was even a toast.

"To the Phantom Photographer!" said Victor, raising his glass. We all readily drank to that.*

Victor, Terry, and I had been joined by Parker and Stacy. We were camped out in the cushion-lined confines of the very swank Bar and Books down on Hudson Street. This, after having had dinner next door at Mi Cocina.

In listening to Victor, I couldn't help saying the words over in my head. *The Phantom Photographer.* Amazing, really. In a trial in which the central character was known as my Mystery Patient and a supporting role was being played by a hacker dubbed The Magnet, I suppose it figured.

Surrounded by lawyers, I had to ask, "Have you ever had a case like this?"

Parker, Victor, and Terry shook their heads in unison.

Meanwhile, I knew enough about how my mind worked to

---

*Mine happened to be of the Diet Coke variety, but I hardly gave that a second thought. Day twelve and, despite being surrounded by every alcohol imaginable, it was the least tempting day of them all for me. Credit my "stay of execution" from Judge Lomax. The sense of relief proved greater than any possible urge lurking within.

know there was no use trying to stop it. The "it" being my compulsion to speculate on who took the picture. And, just as important, *why*? What was his or her motive? I had no doubt that sending the picture to Lomax was an attempt to help me, but it seemed highly unlikely that that was the purpose of taking the picture in the first place. What, then, was the original motive for tailing me like that? Or was it even me who was being tailed?

Naturally, I wasn't alone in pondering these questions. From the moment we left the courthouse that morning, Terry and Victor were equally as stumped. By dinner, the list of confounded included Parker and Stacy. Inevitably, there reached a point when there was little left to say. Because there were no real clues to speak of, our speculation had its limits.

"I think we'll know eventually," remarked Terry, putting a bow on the subject not long after we sat down at Bar and Books. Though she knew as well as anybody that her suggestion was based on wishful thinking more than anything else.

So while the conversation moved on to other topics, my mind stayed put on who could've snapped the picture. Yes, if there was an assumption to be made it was that the person knew either me or my Mystery Patient. But taking that for granted did little to narrow the field. All bets were off. It could've been anyone.

The truth of this statement became clear to me when, in my stone-sober state, I found myself looking at Parker and Stacy. Of course, to think for a moment there was a possibility that one or both were behind the camera that night at the Kesper cocktail party was to abandon all of my senses.

What the hell. I asked them anyway.

"Yeah," said Parker right away. "It was us. And in case you were wondering, I was also on the grassy knoll."

Stacy kept a straight face and nodded. A regular comedy team.

"Yeah, well, can you blame me?" I said.

Parker raised an eyebrow. "You mean, for being paranoid?"

"It's not really paranoia if he suspects we did something nice for him, is it?" asked Stacy.

"I don't know," said Parker. "I'm not the psychologist here."

"That's a really good question, though," said Terry, chiming in. "I've always associated being paranoid with suspecting the worst of someone. What is it, David, when you inherently suspect the best of someone?"

I thought for a second before answering. "It's either one of two things," I said. "Love or ignorance."

"Funny, I always thought they were one and the same," joked Victor.

Terry gave him an elbow. "Spoken like a true divorced man."

"Ouch. Hurt a guy, why don't you?"

"Just the ones who can take it."

"Oh, in that case, I'm flattered," he said facetiously.

"Speaking of hurting a guy, how did our man, Hemmerson, react to today's events?" asked Parker.

"Not very well," said Terry.

Victor chuckled. "Somewhat of an understatement, wouldn't you say, David?"

I nodded.

"Parker, you should've seen the way Terry and Hemmerson got into it toward the end," said Victor. "It was beautiful."

Terry shrugged. "I couldn't let Lomax do *all* the heavy lifting for us."

"Absolutely not," agreed Victor. "You got in at the right time; well done. In fact, on that note, allow me to propose another toast." He put his arm around Terry. With his other, he picked up his glass. "To Terry Garrett and her excellent work in *People versus Dr. David Remler.*"

"Hear, hear!" we all said, or some equivalent thereof. As we clinked glasses, I couldn't help watching Victor's hand give Terry's shoulder a squeeze. It immediately became the most overanalyzed squeeze in history. Was it sexual? Just friendly? Sexual disguised as just friendly?

I was staring at Terry's shoulder—postsqueeze—when I felt

something. It was her eyes. She was looking at me looking at her shoulder. I looked up and our eyes met. She smiled briefly, and I looked away like a nervous schoolboy.

Terry leaned forward in her chair and rested her drink on the table. "Thank you, Victor," she said. "But truth be told, the real credit goes to one very special FedEx envelope."

"Trust me, Terry, if you hadn't been doing such a good job in the courtroom, odds are Lomax would've sat on the photo," said Parker.

"I agree," said Victor. "The toast stands."

We continued to talk, tell stories, and laugh for a while longer. Stacy, who was brilliant at the nonsolicitous solicitation, got Victor to pledge money to her women's crisis center on behalf of his firm. In addition, Terry offered to throw in some pro bono work.

After joking that he and Stacy should leave before anyone changed their mind, Parker looked at his watch. "Seriously, though, it is getting late."

The rest of us put up a mild protest and urged them to stay for one more round.

"Really, we'd love to," said Parker with a mock sigh. "Except, unlike *some of us*, I actually have to be in court tomorrow."

He and Stacy stood, and we said our good-byes.

Then there were three.

Victor, Terry, and I took ourselves up on that idea of one more round. Never mind that I'd already drunk about an entire liter of Diet Coke. We continued to have a good time. Certainly there was nothing outwardly awkward about the situation, but I'd be lying if I said there wasn't a part of me that was determined not to leave the two of them alone.

As it turned out, it was Victor who left Terry and me alone. He'd spotted someone he knew toward the front of the bar. In his words, an "old chum from law school." "Be right back," he told us.

Then there were two.

A few seconds of silence passed.

"Are you having a good time?" Terry asked.

"I am," I said. "I hope it doesn't look otherwise."

"Not at all."

More silence. Noticeable this time. Finally . . .

"We're not, by the way," she said.

"Excuse me?"

"Victor and me. We're not an item."

I looked at her blankly. At least, that was the look I was going for. With any luck she wouldn't think she'd just answered the foremost question on my mind.

"Oh, *puleeeze*," she said.

So much for that facade. "Okay, maybe I was wondering a bit," I admitted.

She grinned. "Way to hang tough under cross-examination."

"It was your four-syllable *please* that did me in."

"Yeah, I learned that one living out in L.A.," she said.

"So why are you telling me this, that you and Victor aren't an item?"

"I thought you wanted to know. Turns out I was right."

"I see. You were merely setting the record straight."

"Exactly." She looked up at the ceiling. "Though now that I think about it, if Terry Garrett were to marry Victor Glass, I wouldn't have to get new monogrammed towels."

"Do you actually have monogrammed towels?"

"No."

"I didn't think so. You don't strike me as the type."

"I bet Victor has them, though."

"Probably," I said. "You also don't strike me as the type who would take another man's name."

"Ah, that's where you're wrong."

"Really?"

"If only for the children. A mommy and daddy should have the same last name."

"So you want kids?"

"I do," she said. "Don't tell anyone, but I already have the name picked out."

"*The* name?"

"Yes. It's going to be the same name whether it's a boy or a girl."

"I'm afraid to ask."

"Did you ever read *To Kill a Mockingbird*?"

"Sure," I said.

"I want to name my first child Atticus."

"You better pray for a boy."

"What about *Atty*?" she said. "That could be a girl's name."

"Not if you ever want her to like you."

"You think?"

"Maybe not. Though good luck finding one of those mini license plates with her name on it."

"I think she'd be able to deal."

"I suppose," I said. "But she'd have to be tough like her mother."

"Maybe this is a good time to tell you that it's all just an act with me."

"An occupational necessity is what you're going to tell me, right?"

"Exactly. In my spare time, I'm Jell-O."

"You don't expect me to believe that, do you?"

"It's true," she said.

"I mean, the part about you having spare time."

Terry laughed and took another sip of her drink. She rested it back down on the table and looked at me as if trying to make up her mind about something.

"What is it?" I finally said.

"Do you mind if I ask you a personal question?"

"Go ahead."

She crinkled her mouth. "Did you and your wife want children?"

As soon as she finished the question, she regretted it. All because of my expression. There was no way I could hide my discomfort. It was as if I could feel the sudden pallor in my face.

"I should've known better," she said. "I'm sorry."

"Don't be," I told her. I took a breath. "It's just that when my wife died, she was four months' pregnant."

Terry grabbed her forehead. "Oh, god."

"It's okay."

"David, I didn't . . ."

"Really, it's okay. How could you know?"

The answer was she couldn't. Still, she clearly felt awful. Her eyes began to well up.

"C'mon, Garrett. Don't go Jell-O on me!"

The line got a slight smile out of her.

"That's better," I said. I was about to take another shot at levity—something about lawyers always asking the tough questions—when I happened to look down at my hand. To think, I didn't even feel it.

Her hand was on top of mine.

She'd obviously been caught up in the moment, and as soon as I saw it, she saw it too.

"Sorry," she said, slowing lifting her hand.

"Again, with the apologizing."

"No, that was stupid of me. I mean, it wasn't really intentional, but it was stupid of me all the same."

"What if I said it wasn't?"

She blinked slowly. "Then I'd remind you that you're my client. It's like you and one of your patients. It's not ever supposed to happen."

I immediately slouched. "Now *I* feel like the idiot."

"Why?"

"Because it almost did happen with me."

"Your Mystery Patient? That was different," she said.

"Thanks, but I'm afraid you're just saying that."

"No, think about it, David. For all intents and purposes, you were seduced. That was part of her plan. Moreover, she knew it would work because you were vulnerable having lost your wife. She took advantage of you emotionally."

Terry's last sentence launched the quickest of flashbacks. That guy. His theory. Tangible versus intangible—the true difference between men and women. I could see him so clearly, his tan-out-of-season existence. Pompous Nathan looking at me incredulously at Cassandra Nance's party. His question. *Can you honestly say that you've never been taken advantage of emotionally by a woman?*

I guess I no longer could.

"Still," I said to Terry. "I feel like some pathetic guy who falls for any woman who gives him the time of day."

She rolled her eyes. "Wow, that makes me feel really special."

"You know what I mean. Besides, you're the one telling me you're not interested."

A coy smile. "I never said that."

"Oh, really?"

"I was merely pointing out the circumstances of our relationship."

"You mean, attorney and client."

"Exactly," she said.

"But if the circumstances were different?"

She stared into my eyes and said nothing. She didn't need to.

"Of course, they're not different, are they?" I said.

"No."

We both took a moment.

"You're right," I said. "It would be wrong."

She nodded, and I nodded back. Rational minds were prevailing. We were absolutely, positively doing the right thing.

If only it felt right.

"Maybe the only thing wrong is the timing," I said.

"Maybe. But I can't think about that—or, more specifically, you in that way—and represent you at the same time."

"Well, that settles it," I said. "You're fired." I laughed before she could ever think I was serious. "How about this, though? We'll make a deal. When this whole thing is over and, hopefully, I'm not heading off to jail, you and I have dinner."

"Are we actually plea-bargaining for a date?"

"I suppose we are, yes. So, what do you think?"

"I think we have a deal," she said.

"Good. Should we have a written contract drawn up or some-thing?"

"No. Oral contracts are enforceable in this state."

I extended my hand. "Then we'll shake on it."

Terry glanced over at the bar and put her hand in mine. When I squeezed, she pulled me forward.

"What are you doing?"

"Taking a chance," she said.

We were face-to-face, inches apart. Terry leaned in and put her lips onto mine. We kissed.

"There's a bad oral contract joke to be made here, isn't there?" she said as we returned to a safe attorney/client distance.

"Probably," I said. I was stunned that she'd just done that. But I also couldn't have been more happy about it. "You do realize your boss is twenty feet away, don't you?"

"Keenly aware of it," she said.

We both looked over at Victor, who had his back turned to us. His "old college chum" turned out to be a fetching young blonde. To his credit, they did appear to be getting quite chummy with each other.

Terry shrugged. "Well, there go my monogrammed towels."

THIRTY-EIGHT

Limbo.

There was no better way to describe the feeling. A measure of relief trying to fend off a greater measure of apprehension. As nice as it was not having to wake up and go to court, I couldn't help thinking how much harder it would be if I eventually did have to go back. Priority number one: not getting my hopes up too high.

Resuming some semblance of a life in the meantime—that was priority number two. I didn't have to be a psychologist to understand that the key to doing that was going back to work. It was so simple. Take my mind off my problems by focusing it on the problems of others. Both good for me and good for them. Fact was, I'd left all of my patients in limbo.

Which was why a good number of them had decided to leave me.

I remembered how the judge at my arraignment predicted such an outcome based on my "legal troubles," and yes, there was nothing like being tried for murder to put a little crimp in my professional reputation. But that wasn't the true cause of the exodus. Rather, it was this: while there were certain things New Yorkers could abstain from for a while, a weekly mental-health fix didn't seem to be one of them.

So it was. When the doctor was away, some of the patients did stray.

On the flip side, Parker's response to that arraignment judge had some truth to it. Misery did indeed love company in my situation. Sure enough, my remaining patients expressed a stronger faith in me than ever before, and I actually picked up a few new ones. Go figure. Despite returning to the Swiss-cheese schedule of appointments that had marked the early days of my practice, I was heartened that there weren't more holes than there were.

"Fuck 'em!" said Marcus.

No doubt my Thursday, three o'clock wasn't about to bail on me. Marcus Owen, the hostile sculptor, was back in full force. He even came with surprising news.

"I've decided to put the American Blind Spot to bed," he announced.

More surprising was the reason why. Marcus had finally traveled outside of the country. He'd left American soil and ventured across the Atlantic.

"This earth, this realm, this England," he intoned in what could best be described as a Shakespearean dinner-theater accent.

"Really?" I said. "How was the trip?"

He shook his head. "Man, did I ever have a shitty time. Now I know why we were all in such a rush to leave that country in the first place."

"Wasn't your cup of tea, huh?"

"Hell no," said Marcus. "Nor was it my crumpets, my kippers and bangers, or my disgustingly warm beer." He shook his head again. "Then, of course, there's Prince Charles."

This should be good, I thought.

"I mean, he seems like a smart enough guy and all, but when push comes to shove, don't you get the feeling he's got the backbone of a marshmallow Peep?"

"A what?"

"Think Easter."

I nodded. "So, basically, you're saying the trip made you re-examine the whole Blind Spot thing?"

"Yeah. Having walked among the Brits, it didn't seem right to dwell on the shortcomings of Americans anymore."

"That's a little odd given that many people find their culture to be far more civilized than ours."

"*Civilized?*" he repeated back incredulously. "David, polite as they may be, the fuckers barely have resealable milk."

And that's when I realized—sitting there with Marcus and listening to him rant. I, David Remler, had missed my job.

The session ended soon thereafter, leaving me a few minutes to make some notes in Marcus's file. Not that I actually made any. I wouldn't call it dwelling, but it was hard not to sit there and think about who had been my next patient. My Thursday, four o'clock.

"Knock, knock," she said.

I looked up to see Mila poking her head into my office. Right on time. Instead of meeting every other Tuesday at five as we usually did, she'd asked if we could make a switch. She also wanted to turn it into a weekly meeting for a while because with my being out of the office, the bills and other business-related issues had piled up.

"No problem," I'd told Mila. "When do you want to do it?"

"How about Thursdays at four?"

"Sounds good."

Her motive couldn't have been more transparent, but I didn't care. Mila obviously thought that filling the hour my Mystery Patient had occupied was in my best interest. Who knows? Maybe it was. Either way, it was a very Mamka-like move on her part, and for that alone, I wasn't about to say no.

I waved her in. "*Rád te vidím,*" I said like a student who'd done his homework.

She nodded with approval. "It's good to see you too," she said.

Ever since her testimony at the trial, Mila had felt terrible. She so much wanted to help me, and the mere thought that she couldn't drove her crazy. Worse, with the cutthroat and manipulating questioning by Hemmerson, her testimony had managed to hurt my case.

"I think that prosecutor guy is a total *buzerant*!" she informed me.

I was going to ask what that meant. On second thought . . . "I don't want to know," I told her. Suffice to say, she was never going to knit Hemmerson a sweater.

After I assured Mila about a dozen times that she'd done nothing wrong and that it was me who should be apologizing for getting her into that situation, her guilt began to subside. She was able to ask me for an update without getting emotional. Until, that is, the update became news of my trial's suspension. There was no stopping her tears of joy on hearing that.

"So, what's going to happen now?" she asked, taking a seat in front of my desk.

"First, the police are showing the picture to Samantha Kent today to see if perhaps she recognizes the woman. Obviously, we hope she does."

"What if she doesn't?"

"The police release the picture to the press. It's printed in every local newspaper and gets shown on every newscast. Odds are somebody out there will recognize her."

"You would think so."

"Of course, finding out who she is—that's one thing. Catching her might very well be another," I said. "I imagine she might already be someplace far away. I certainly would be if I were her."

"You never know," said Mila.

I looked at my watch. I realized that most of the day had passed without hearing from Terry. She had told me she'd call once the police had visited with Samantha Kent. Instead of having her come into the station, they were going to show the picture to her at her apartment. The new one. It was no surprise she'd moved to a new address given what had happened at the old one.

I thought about ringing Terry. I decided to wait a little while longer. Maybe there was a delay in getting to meet with Samantha Kent. She wasn't home or something like that. Whatever the reason, that Terry could've simply forgotten to call me didn't enter my mind.

What a difference a kiss makes.

In the meantime, there were indeed some checks to sign with Mila. Rent, electricity, and the like didn't have much sympathy for my limbo status. In addition, there were some of my books to sign. The stash that Mila kept at her apartment had been depleted. In light of the publicity generated by my trial, *The Human Pendulum* had become a hot commodity for collectors. Scary to think how many were hoping that I'd be sent up the river. Call it perverse economics. A guilty verdict would do so much more for the value of a signed copy than an acquittal.

At about a quarter to five, Mila left my office. With nothing more to do there, I started to pack up for the day. It was right as I was putting on my coat that the phone rang.

"Good, you're still there," she said.

It was Terry.

"I was starting to wonder if—"

"Yeah, I know," she said. "Apparently things took a little longer than planned."

"But Samantha Kent was shown the picture, right?"

"Yes, she saw it."

"And?"

"She didn't recognize the woman."

"Not at all?"

"Nope. She had no clue."

"Damn," I said.

"Tell me about it. That would've certainly been the shortcut home."

"So, how come it took all day?" I asked. "Did Samantha Kent stare at the picture for three hours or something?"

"No, the delay came after. Your buddies, Trentino and Lopez—who, by the way, aren't the happiest of campers in light of this picture—decided they wanted to show it to some of the neighbors from the old town house as well as some of Birch's coworkers. I couldn't really argue with that."

"No, it makes sense."

"Unfortunately, we got the same result. No one recognizes your Mystery Patient. The moniker lives on another day."

"What now?"

"Exactly what I said. You're going to see the picture of her on your eleven o'clock news tonight."

"That fast, huh?"

"Yep. Combined with the suspension of the trial, I wouldn't be surprised if it's the lead story."

"For once, publicity we want."

"A nice change of pace, isn't it?"

"Yeah," I said. "Can I ask you a silly question, though?"

"No, David, you won't be in the picture."

"You're scaring me now," I said through a laugh. "How'd you know I was going to ask that?"

"Woman's intuition," she answered. "The photo will be cropped pretty much like it was when Lomax first showed it to us. The only difference is that it will be slightly magnified and computer enhanced so it's clearer."

"The police are doing that?"

"At our insistence, yes. Like I told you, they haven't been too happy about all this. It makes them look bad, and we all know they don't like to look bad."

"They are cooperating, aren't they?"

"Just enough so no one can prove otherwise. Trentino and Lopez are still convinced you're guilty and that you're somehow behind the picture."

"Jesus, did they actually say that?"

"No. Woman's intuition again. They really didn't have to spell it out; their body language did all the talking. But don't worry, starting tomorrow the phone tips should start pouring in."

"You really think so?"

"You'll see. The public loves a manhunt. Kidnappers, snipers, you name it. The fact that, in this case, it's a woman—and a good-looking woman at that—only makes it sexier."

"Described that way, it sounds like a TV reality show."

"Because that's what it is," she said.

I chuckled. "God bless America."

"Exactly. Then again, I can name at least fifty countries where you'd already be serving a life sentence."

It was a sobering thought.

We ended the call by agreeing to speak the following morning. The last thing Terry explained was the wording the police were providing for the news media. The upshot being that "people having any information about the identity and/or whereabouts of this woman in the picture are to call the following 800 number." That was typical language. Of curious note, however, was what language wouldn't be used. My Mystery Patient was not to be labeled a "possible suspect." Rather, "the authorities believe she might have valuable information regarding the death of Conrad Birch."

Yeah, like maybe why she killed him.

That night, sitting on the couch in my apartment, I tuned in to the late local news. With some quick channel-flipping, I saw that, sure enough, it was the lead story across the board. There was a full-screen picture of my Mystery Patient with the anchorperson reciting almost word for word the language Terry had gone over with me. In a nice touch, the phone number to call spelled out a mnemonic-like catchphrase. 1-800-FOR-TIPS.

If there was such a thing as brushing your teeth optimistically, I was doing it soon after the news. I even gargled optimistically. This was good, I thought. It felt right. I undressed for bed, embracing the possibility that this was the beginning of the end. A happy ending.

That's when I got the call.

THIRTY-NINE

Did you miss me, David?"

I stood there stunned. There was no need to ask who it was; I knew right away. It was her. My Mystery Patient. Late at night and calling me again. Only this time she sounded a lot more awake.

"Because I certainly missed you."

I wanted so much to yell. To scream and curse. To give in to my anger and unleash my rage. From the start, she'd played me for a fool, and I'd played right along. Which was why, when I finally opened my mouth, I remained calm. Because only a fool wouldn't recognize that I was being given a golden opportunity—to learn something for real about the fake Samantha Kent.

And to get it on tape.

The minirecorder that Parker suggested I buy was right there in the drawer of my bedside table. All set and ready to go, ready to prove once and for all that this woman actually existed. Quietly, I grabbed the recorder and lifted it to the top of the phone by my ear. With a slow press of my thumb, we were rolling.

"I take it you watched the news tonight," I said.

"Oh, c'mon!" she scoffed. "You're not going to scream and holler at me first?!"

"It's tempting."

"But let me guess, the shrink in you says not to, right?"

"Something like that."

A sigh. "Yes, I watched the news tonight," she said. "I've got to tell you, if I'd known I was being photographed, I would've smiled more."

"I doubt you're smiling now, though."

"The way I see it, David, you're either smarter than I gave you credit for, or you're the recipient of some incredibly dumb luck. I tend to think it was the latter."

"Call it what you want. The fact remains, you're going to have a hard time shopping at your local supermarket tomorrow."

"I know, what a shame," she said, amused. "I could've cooked dinner for the two of us again." She started to laugh.

"You really think this is funny?"

"Why, you don't?"

"Actually, in a way, I find it kind of ironic," I said. "Being framed only to be saved by a picture."

She snickered. "Is that what you think you are? *Saved?*"

"Let's put it this way: I'd much rather be me right now than you."

"I wouldn't be so sure, David. Life is full of surprises."

"You've certainly proved that."

"Precisely my point," she said. "People never know as much as they think they do."

"Starting with your real name, in my case. Of course, you could fix that right now."

"What, and spoil the mystery?"

"At least tell me this. Why me? Why set me up?"

"That's easy. Murder one-oh-one. The best way to cover your tracks is to lead everyone to somebody else. And who better—who more *deserving*—than the smug psychologist who turned Conrad against me?"

"What are you talking about?"

"You know exactly what I'm talking about." She lowered her voice, making it deep like a man's. It was a creepy tenor. *"My therapist thinks this affair is destructive. My therapist thinks I really should end this and try to fix my marriage.*"

I listened word for word, my mind racing. On the heels of her initial cryptic patter, this was an avalanche of revelation. The suspicion all along had proved right; my Mystery Patient was indeed the mistress. Or at least one of two mistresses if a certain buxom blonde was telling the truth at the trial. Quick mental note: *follow up on that.*

But not yet. More pressing was the motivation. Her reasoning.

What she'd told me was at once startling and familiar. It seemed that Conrad Birch had done what so many before him had done—pawned off the guilt of a difficult life decision by essentially blaming the therapist. Textbook, really. The poor patient who's rendered powerless. Pushed into it. At the mercy of his doctor's advice. It was so common in my profession that we had a name for it, silly as it was: the Shrink Rap.

Still, to hear it all from her at that moment was no less a jolt. My Mystery Patient wasn't the only one who'd set me up. Conrad Birch had as well. And they'd both done an awfully good job of it.

She continued: "Tell me, David, what's it like to have so much power over people's lives?"

"I should ask the same of you."

"No. What I've done is simply give you a taste of your own slick medicine. I saw how you work firsthand, remember?"

"What? That I tried to help you, at least the 'you' whom you pretended to be?"

"You were playing God, and a self-serving one at that," she shot back. "I'm curious, do you move in on all your vulnerable female patients?"

"You're telling me that wasn't part of your plan? To make me attracted to you?"

"Well, widowers do tend to be very lonely," she purred. That was followed by a snicker. "Yes, it was very much part of the plan, but it really worked because of something else I knew—

that you're either too arrogant or ignorant to consider the consequences of what you do for a living. The oh-so-sacred advice you dispense as you sit there in your little cocoon of an office, shielded from the real world. That's why you had no problem telling Conrad what you did."

"I didn't turn him against you," I insisted. "He used me as his foil."

"Bullshit."

"Christ, don't you see? He was trying to take the easy way out. I never told him those things."

She snickered again. "I love that you actually expect me to believe you."

"Is it so hard? What, you'd rather believe the guy who suddenly left you and went back to his wife? Think about it," I said. "Can you honestly tell me he never misled you up until that point?"

"He lied to me plenty of times. That's why I killed him."

I glanced at the recorder in my hand, the tape spinning. Never mind why she felt the need to go to such extreme measures. Her prison psychologist could take that up with her.

"That's right. He lied to you. Perhaps even more than you knew," I said. I was going back to my mental note and the supposed second mistress. "You followed the trial, didn't you?" She didn't respond. I could tell she knew where I was going. "Another woman came forward claiming she was the mistress, did you know that?"

Silence.

"I said, did you know that? Because if she was telling the truth, it means he was lying to you that much more."

"Even more of a reason to kill him then."

"Yet you'd still take his word over mine?"

"It looks that way, doesn't it?"

"But what about—" I stopped. I realized I was trying to make a rational argument to someone who completely embodied the irrational. What was the point? I had what I needed. She'd basically admitted to everything. Not believing the tape would be to think I got some woman to read a script for me over the phone. That would be a tough sell to a jury, and Hemmerson would be the first to admit it.

Irrational, yes. But the thought occurred to me quickly. *After being so clever, could she suddenly be so dumb?*

It was as if she'd read my mind.

"So, did you get all of it?" she asked, void of any emotion.

"All of what?"

"You've got a lousy poker voice, David. You were recording the conversation, weren't you?"

"No," I lied. "I wish I were, though."

She laughed. "Funny thing is, even if you're lying, you're still telling the truth."

I glanced at the recorder again, a knee-jerk reflex. The spindles of the tape continued to spin in unison. "What's that supposed to mean?" I asked.

"It's like I told you, life is full of surprises. Want one more? Here it is." She paused. "I'm not done yet."

I was silent. There was nothing I could say, and she knew it. The moment was hers.

"First, I took care of Conrad. Now it's time for that bitch of a wife he ran back to," said my Mystery Patient. "Tonight, she dies."

Click.

FORTY

So much for remaining calm.

The last time I was on the phone with this woman, she told me she'd killed Conrad Birch. She may have lied about being married to him, but she sure was telling the truth about the killing part.

Now she was telling me Samantha Kent was next.

Never mind what I knew as a psychologist. There was no need to factor in the years of observing people. Nor did it matter that, almost by definition, mistresses harbored a profound resentment for the wife of the man with whom they were having an affair. In weighing the threat to Samantha Kent's life, between idle and real, the only thing I needed was the image of her husband stabbed to death. Covered in blood. His face locked in terror and forever embedded in my memory.

All the more reason why I gripped that recorder so tight in my hand as I hung up the phone. Yes, the threat was real. It was as real as she was. Something the tape would prove once and for all.

There were calls to make, a murder to stop, but first things first. I pressed rewind and waited a few anxious seconds. I pressed Play and listened for the sound. Her words. My evidence.

I got neither.

What I heard was a sharp, piercing whistle amid static.

In a fumbling panic, I rewound the tape further. I got the same sound; nothing of our conversation. I checked the batteries. Fidgeted with the volume. Ejected the tape and put it back in. When none of that worked, I ejected the tape again and flipped it. I was running out of remedies.

Funny thing is, even if you're lying, you're still telling the truth.

It didn't make any sense when she said it. Now it made all the sense in the world. There were no remedies. I told her I hadn't been recording the conversation. I thought I was lying. I wasn't. The truth was, I hadn't recorded anything. For sure, not anything of use.

And she'd made damn certain of it.

As to how, I didn't know yet. But as I pressed Play one more time—my face a blended red of anger, frustration, and disgust—that sharp, piercing whistle coming out of the recorder sounded more and more like her laughing at me.

I had asked myself the question: after being so clever, could she suddenly be so dumb? The answer was no. She was more clever than ever. It was me who couldn't have felt more dumb.

"911 emergency," the operator said.

As soon as I made the call, I wondered: what the hell was I going to say? That a woman's life had been threatened by another woman, only I didn't really know who the second woman was, let alone the address of the first?

"Hello, is anyone there?" the operator asked.

"Yes, I'm sorry," I said. "I've made a mistake. Again, I'm terribly sorry."

I hung up and ran to my kitchen, where I had Terry's home number written down on a pad. I looked at the clock on the stove. It was past midnight. Maybe she was still up. If not, hopefully she wasn't a sound sleeper.

After four or five rings, Terry answered. Her groggy and muted "Hello?" left little doubt that she'd been sleeping. She was barely awake when I started to tell her what had happened. Needless to say, she was wide awake by the time I finished.

"Stay right there by the phone, and I'll call you back," was all she said.

"But—"

She hung up.

There was no hesitation in her voice. No mulling over what to do. At least none that required my feedback. Terry was off and running, and I was left waiting. I was glad I'd called her and ever thankful she was there for me. Still, I felt little relief. Someone's life was in jeopardy, and there was only so much I could do to help. Worse, what if there was nothing anyone could do? A race against time held out hope. But what if it was already too late?

What if Samantha Kent was already dead?

Fourteen days and counting. I thought I'd known temptation over the past two weeks. Ha. Those were mere twitches compared to my seizurelike desire to have a drink at that moment.

Suddenly, I wished I'd already acted out the cliché. The one where I put the exclamation point on my decision to stop drinking by emptying out my entire liquor cabinet in one full and melodramatic sweep. In the made-for-television movie, the camera would be looking up from the (rock) bottom of the trash can as all the bottles came crashing down. Absolut Symbolism.

Yes, that would've made it a bit easier. Instead, my liquor cabinet was not only full but right there in my kitchen. A few steps and a couple of rationalizations away. I could've emptied it out, all right. One swig at a time.

I walked over to the cabinet and opened it. Then I closed it. Empty-handed.

Thankfully, it was my desire to avoid the other cliché that proved stronger. Setbacks and relapses were so common that they seemed almost an expected and necessary part of the recovery process. Somewhere along the line, we forgot how powerful shame could be as a deterrent. I was determined to remember.

Better to wait by a different phone.

I returned to my bedroom and sat down on the bed. Five minutes passed. I leaned back against my headboard. Ten minutes passed. I grabbed one of the books off my bedside table. This one was dog-eared at page fifty-two. Twenty minutes later, and I hadn't made it beyond page fifty-three.

What's going on, Terry?

I looked at the phone and willed it to ring. It didn't. A half hour had gone by without hearing back from her. Good enough reason, I thought, to give her a call. Stupidly, I'd left her number back in the kitchen. Just what I needed, one more walk past the liquor cabinet.

It didn't matter. The desire to drink had been trumped this latest time by the desire to know what was going on. I grabbed Terry's number and returned to my bedroom. I dialed and waited.

She didn't answer. I got her machine. There was a slim chance she was there and couldn't pick up for some reason. On another line or in the bathroom, perhaps. But there was no denying the much better chance. She'd left.

She'd gone to Samantha Kent's apartment.

I pushed back the thought—the fear, really—that Terry would ever be so foolish as to go alone. No way. She called Victor. She called the police. She maybe even tried to track down Detectives Trentino and Lopez. Surely, that's the way she'd handled it.

I left a message on her machine just in case. I tried not to sound too worked up. At best, I half succeeded.

Another ten minutes went by. I was officially stir-crazy. I thought about calling the local police precinct and doing my best to explain. Anything besides sitting there and waiting.

Finally, the phone rang. I answered in a heartbeat.

"David, it's Terry."

"Where are you?"

"Samantha Kent's apartment building," she said. "I need you to get over here."

"Where is it?"

"Ten-thirty Park Avenue, on the corner of Eighty-fifth."

"Terry, what happened?"

"I'll explain when you get here."

"Why can't you tell me now?"

"Trust me that I can't, okay? Just get over here as fast as you can—and bring the tape recorder."

She hung up before I could say another word.

FORTY-ONE

The corner of Eighty-fifth and Park as fast as you can, please."

Sitting in the back of the cab for the short trip to Samantha Kent's new address, I couldn't help reflecting on the parallel. The certain symmetry. After she lost her husband, Samantha Kent moved from the Upper West Side to the Upper East. When I lost Rebecca, I did the very same thing. I even relocated my practice there.

In terms of actual distance, the move was barely a move at all. But on the island of Manhattan, where millions of people squeezed their lives within twenty-two square miles, a little distance went a long way. Especially if it involved the crossing of Central Park. For those seeking a fresh start, entire oceans didn't offer as much promise as did that patch of green.

At least two blocks before reaching Samantha Kent's apartment building, I saw the red-and-blue dance of flashing lights and immediately assumed the worst. The night was already eerily reminiscent of that original night. Both were initiated by a phone call. Now I feared both would end in murder. The same person responsible.

The lights belonged to a total of two police cars. As I got out of the cab, I looked for an ambulance. I looked for a morgue wagon. I saw neither. They could've easily come and gone by that point.

Terry and I saw each other almost simultaneously. She was inside the lobby, much of it visible through the large glass double doors of the entrance. Before I could go in, she came out and took me by the arm, pulling me to the side.

"Good news and bad news," she said. She was talking fast. "The good news is nothing happened. No one tried to kill Samantha Kent tonight."

I did a quick exhale. "What's the bad news?"

"The same thing. *No one tried to kill Samantha Kent tonight.*"

I gave Terry a sideways look.

"What I mean is, you've got two detectives inside thinking you cried wolf."

"Trentino and Lopez?"

She nodded.

"They think I fabricated this?"

"The thought more than crossed their minds. As I told you, they weren't terribly impressed by that photograph. Now with this . . ."

"How could they honestly believe I made up that phone call?"

"The same way they believe you killed Conrad Birch," she said. "Did you bring the tape?"

"Yeah." I reached into my pocket and pulled out the recorder. "Like I said, she must have done something—used a device, maybe—because she knew I couldn't record her. All you hear is a high-pitched whistle."

I pressed Play so Terry could listen to it. I watched her grimace at the shrill-like sound.

"She definitely did something, all right."

"Any idea what?"

"Offhand, I don't know. But, generally, where there's a will there's a gadget."

"Maybe the police will have an idea."

She shook her head. "This tape is strictly between us for now. It doesn't help you, and given the mind-set of Trentino and

Lopez, it probably hurts you. Besides, it's the only copy. You never hand cops the only copy of anything."

"We need to have it checked out though, don't you think?"

"Definitely. Tomorrow we'll get Anthony on it."

I threw her a blank stare. *Anthony who?*

"The Magnet," she said. "If he can't figure out what happened with the tape, he'll know someone who can."

I started to put the recorder back in my pocket.

"On second thought, why don't you let me hold on to that," she said.

I handed it over. In doing so I had my first chance to focus on Terry rather than what she was saying. I'd woken her up from a deep sleep, made her scramble, and here she was in jeans, an old sweater, and no makeup looking as attractive as ever.

"What?" she said, noticing my slightly extended gaze.

"Nothing."

She cocked her head, not buying it. Still, I thought it was the wrong time for me to be anything but her client.

Instead: "No, I was simply thinking how relieved I am. Half of me thought Samantha Kent would already be dead when I got here."

"Half of me thought the same thing."

"Which reminds me, why couldn't you fill me in over the phone?"

"Sorry about that," she said. "Right when I called you, Trentino and Lopez wandered over within earshot. Intentionally, no doubt. I didn't want them to hear anything, good or bad."

"How'd you get in touch with those two in the first place?"

"I didn't. Victor did."

"You called Victor?"

"Didn't have to. He was lying right next to me."

I froze. Terry laughed. I shook my head, slightly embarrassed. There went my just being her client.

"Oh, you should've seen your face," she said with a playful push on my shoulder. "*Yes*, I called Victor—right after I hung up with you. I wanted him to be the one to call the police."

"Why?"

"Because he's a better alarmist when need be. In fact, as we speak, he's upstairs in Samantha Kent's penthouse apartment trying to get her to consent to police protection."

"Do you think she needs it?"

"Probably not. Given our killer's star turn on the eleven o'clock news, she's probably en route to a faraway place. If she wasn't already there, of course. That said, better safe than sorry."

"I agree."

"Yeah, except Kent has refused the protection."

I was about to ask why, but I stopped myself. I already knew why.

I was why.

Terry watched me realize all this and nodded. "Needless to say, you've never been too high on her list."

"Unless we're talking about a shit list, I suppose."

"In that case, after tonight you've locked up the number one spot for even longer."

"She's ticked off, huh?"

"One way to put it."

"Who wouldn't be? She thinks I killed her husband."

"Yeah, the Mystery Patient idea was never really a big hit with her," said Terry facetiously. "Hence, her nixing the protection."

"Still, can't the police do it anyway?"

"No, not without consent. What's more, it's not like they're really pushing it on her given the circumstances. If anything, they'd rather keep an eye on you."

"Let 'em."

She smiled and looked at her watch.

"Are we waiting for something?" I asked.

"Yes, the real reason why you're here. You have to give a statement."

"Oh, great."

"Don't worry about it. Just tell them exactly what happened minus the part about you recording the conversation."

"What if they ask if I did?"

"Fat chance. But if they do, tell them yes. They'll ask if you have the tape with you, and you can tell them no." Terry patted her pocket where she put the recorder. "This way you won't be lying," she said. "At that point, I'll step in and tell them we'll have to make a copy before we can hand it over."

Two seconds later, Victor poked his head out from the entrance.

"There you guys are," he said. He came over, shook my hand, and then shook his head. "You got fucked with tonight."

"It's been going on a little longer than just tonight," I said.

"Very true." He looked at Terry. "You holding the recorder?"

"Yep."

"We'll get to the bottom of that tomorrow," he said. "I'm thinking The Magnet could probably help us."

"I'm thinking the same thing," said Terry. "Any luck with Samantha Kent agreeing to the police protection?"

"That's a big no-go," said Victor. "Though she did volunteer to sue your ass, David."

"Did you inform her that all my money is already going to your firm?"

He chuckled. "No, but I should have. Seriously, though, the woman wanted to press charges."

"For what?" asked Terry incredulously.

"Harassment."

"That's ridiculous."

"No kidding," he said. "Though as I live and breathe, let it be known that our detective friends were considering it."

Terry rolled her eyes. "What'd you tell 'em?"

"That they had bigger fish to fry. Of course, that's when Lopez pointed out that David was that same fish."

"I really love those guys," I said.

"Speaking of which," said Victor. "If we're out here any longer, they'll think we're plotting something sinister." He turned back toward the entrance. "C'mon."

FORTY-TWO

Terry and I followed Victor inside the lobby of the building, where Trentino and Lopez were waiting. I expected them to look somewhat unhappy. I was wrong. They looked *extremely* unhappy.

"Let's make this quick," said Trentino with a pronounced scowl. Combined with his square jaw and thick-rimmed glasses, the look actually approached threatening. At least to me.

Not so to Victor. "If you'd like to make it really quick, Detective, we can skip it altogether," he said with a sarcastic grin.

Lopez glared at me. "You mean, like pretend the phone call never happened?"

"Oh, that's good," said Terry back to him. "Because you certainly wouldn't want to reveal your bias in the investigation now, would you?"

I stood there watching the sparks fly. I knew it was late. How late was becoming abundantly clear.

That's when a cooler head prevailed.

"Excuse me, would one of you happen to have any aspirin?"

We all turned to the voice. It belonged to the distinguished-looking doorman. Slender, gray-haired, and easily in his sixties, he was sitting behind a desk along the wall by the entrance. The way he posed the question, we knew what he really wanted. It wasn't aspirin. It was peace and quiet. In a polite yet pointed manner he was very cleverly asking us to shut up already and get on with it.

Which was precisely what we did.

I began telling Trentino and Lopez exactly what had happened. The phone call and what was said—her wanting to kill Samantha Kent as well as the stuff about why she set me up. Her whole Murder 101 speech.

That's when I realized how much of a favor that doorman had done me.

As the detectives listened, with Trentino taking notes, there was no eye-rolling. No snickering. Not a single expression of disbelief. When Lopez asked me whether or not I'd been drinking prior to getting the call, neither Victor nor Terry jumped down his throat. I calmly answered that I hadn't been, and that was the end of it.

Amazing. With a simple question, the doorman had shamed everyone into civility. We were courteous. We were respectful. We spoke in hushed tones.

Then all hell broke loose.

It started with the doors of the elevator opening, though that's not what everyone heard first. Rather, it was the yelling that made us all look up in unison. Her yelling.

"You son of a bitch!"

Samantha Kent was coming right at me, finger pointed. Her stride was adamant, her face a compression of outrage. When our eyes locked, she was a good twenty feet away from me. And I still felt the need to step back.

The rest happened so quickly I could only recall pieces. Visual and verbal snippets. She was screaming at me, calling me a murderer.

"You can't fool me, you fucking asshole!"

She was wearing a robe. It was long. Her hair was pulled back. She was wearing only socks on her feet. She yelled some more. Then she ran.

"I swear to God I'll kill you!"

Trentino and Lopez cut her off before she could reach me. At first they simply acted like a fence, letting her rant and rave without allowing her to get closer. But she wouldn't let up. The heiress railed against the two detectives in a way that belied her slender frame. Her anger was making her stronger. The screaming became louder.

"Police protection? Ha! The only protection I need is from you!"

I was shocked. I think we all were. The Samantha Kent from the courtroom—the composure, the stoicism, the unyielding poise of considerable wealth—had succumbed to raw emotion. The night's events had triggered her breaking point, and we were all there to see it.

I was shocked, yet I understood. A tantrum, a tirade, whatever you wanted to call it. There was no shortage of terms. As tempting as it was to say she'd simply gone crazy, I'd made a living off knowing otherwise. Samantha Kent was simply acting like a human being.

Not that the distinction really mattered in the needed calm of a Park Avenue apartment building at two in the morning. Ultimately, the detectives had had enough. The fatigue alone of trying to contain Samantha Kent was taking its toll. Trentino and Lopez dug in their heels and began forcing her back toward the elevator. If she wouldn't quiet down on her own, a thick, metal, noise-suppressing box that could return her to where she came from was the next best thing.

Samantha Kent disappeared into the elevator with the detectives and, within seconds, so did the commotion. A hushed quiet resumed. I exchanged weary glances with Terry and Victor. Then I peeked over at the distinguished-looking doorman who'd watched and heard it all. As I caught his eye, there was little doubt in my mind that we were both thinking the same thing.

We could've all used some aspirin.

I walked home. Terry and Victor each offered to share a cab with me, but I declined. I needed the air. I needed some space.

It was nearing three in the morning, and the streets of Manhattan certainly offered more of both than usual. On some blocks not a single person passed me. When I did see people, none of them had smiles. The smiling people, it was safe to assume, were all snug in their beds sleeping. Happily.

With air and space to spare, I tried to focus on what I really needed. Some answers. More than ever, my Mystery Patient had left me wondering.

Why did she call? Why did she tell me what she did? To that point, every one of her moves had a purpose. So why did she say she was going to murder Samantha Kent that night and not do it?

I thought of what Terry had said.

Given that her picture had been plastered on the local news, our killer wouldn't likely stick around the city. If indeed she was hightailing it for parts unknown, the phone call may have been nothing more than an elaborate "Fuck you!" Perhaps the threat against Samantha Kent was simply a reminder of how much control my Mystery Patient still had over me. Even in her absence, she had me pegged.

I remained her pawn.

The mere thought of that word brought me back to my days at Columbia and one of my psych professors. I could picture him so well. The unkempt hair, rimless glasses, and pilling sweaters of Dr. Alvin Wexler.

An avid chess player, to put it mildly, Dr. Wexler held the game up as a metaphor for practically everything. Our hopes, our dreams, our fears, the infield fly rule, you name it—they all could be better understood, he seemed to think, through a better understanding of chess.

Predictably, Dr. Wexler's obsession and its spillover into his teaching became tiresome and, eventually, somewhat annoying for all of us who were his students. Even so, as I walked those last few blocks to my apartment, I found myself recalling something Dr. Wexler had told me.

The context was an after-class conversation. I'd received a B minus on a case-study analysis I thought I'd nailed. I approached Dr. Wexler, wanting to know why I hadn't received a higher grade.

"That's easy," he told me. "You only saw what was in front of you."

When I asked what he meant, he asked me—surprise—if I played chess.

"A little," I lied.

"Then you can appreciate its paradox; how it's a game of infinite possibilities defined by a finite set of movements. That's why, ultimately, chess is played in your head and not on the board in front of you," he said. "The board represents the finite. Your head represents the infinite. If you only play what you see, you'll never win. The point is, to excel in chess—and in anything else for that matter, including this class—you have to imagine. You have to see beyond what's in front of you."

He eyed me closely, trying to gauge whether I understood. I said nothing, but my face showed obvious confusion.

"In other words, Mr. Remler, your paper proved only that you'd read the case. But those who scored higher proved something more. That they'd read *into* the case. They used their heads and saw beyond the facts presented. Their analysis went deeper, and so must you next time."

I pushed through my building's revolving door and into the lobby. Walking by the doorman, who was fast asleep at his desk, I stepped onto the elevator and hit the button for my floor. The entire way up I continued to hear Dr. Wexler, his words resonating, the meaning sinking in. As I stared blankly up at the floor numbers, the realization hit. All along, I'd been staring blankly at the chessboard.

It was time to start using my head.

FORTY-THREE

A little over fourteen hours. That's how long it took. From the moment I stepped off the elevator to the moment I made that fateful determination. A little over fourteen hours.

The first three were spent copping barely enough sleep to get me through the day at the office—six sessions I didn't dare cancel. On the heels of the trial and my prolonged absence from the troubles of others, I was intent on adopting the de facto postal carrier motto. Neither snow nor rain nor late-night phone calls threatening murder would keep me from showing up to work.

Offering my complete, undivided attention, however, was another story.

As my nine o'clock discussed her boyfriend's inability to commit to anything besides sex, I mentally replayed the conversation with my Mystery Patient.

Then, for a few minutes during my eleven o'clock—a middle-aged man who, in recounting a dream, was convinced his overdue library book represented his fear of death—I considered any and all conceivable motivations for the phone call itself.

And while my three o'clock professed reaching a newfound understanding of why she'd recently divorced ("mutual professional jealousy"), I tried to figure out what, if anything, I was overlooking.

Yet it wasn't until the end of the day, after my four o'clock had left, that I managed any answers. One big answer, really. Alone in my office, sitting behind my desk, staring at the wall ahead of me. A little over fourteen hours later, it occurred to me.

I was being set up again.

My Mystery Patient had every intention of killing Samantha Kent. She'd merely lied about when. The reason was simple. She also had every intention of making me the prime suspect. *Again.* The night before was all about laying the groundwork.

She calls. I cry wolf. Everybody comes.

The wolf's not there. Everybody goes home.

Those were the facts. That was the chessboard—there for everyone to see. Except now I was onto her game. I saw the move to come.

It was the one in which Samantha Kent turns up dead . . . and everybody comes looking for me.

No, I told myself. I wasn't going to let it happen.

All along I'd done the expected. The right and rigid mind of a psychologist. That's what made me an easy mark. I was so logical, so predictable.

Except this time I'd come up with an idea. A crazy idea. Foolish. Stupid. Ridiculous. Something I'd never normally do.

Which was exactly why I decided to do it.

FORTY-FOUR

I dialed from my office. The phone rang a half a dozen times before someone finally picked up. "Ten-thirty Park Avenue," said the man.

I was hoping it wouldn't be the same doorman from the night before. It wasn't. While maybe around the same age, this guy sounded less polished. His voice was huskier, a little gruff.

"Yes, hi, this is Fiorillo Florist over on Madison," I said. "We've got a delivery for one of your residents, her name's Kent . . . Samantha Kent. Could you please tell me if she's at home right now?"

It was a simple question, but as I expected, it threw the guy off balance for a second. As if I'd asked him for the time, only in Brazil.

He cleared his throat. "Whatever you've got for her, drop it off and I'll make sure she gets it."

"Normally, that's what we'd do, but my customer insisted that this be hand delivered."

I listened to a heavy sigh. It was a prelude to sarcasm. "Yeah, well, *normally* we don't give out information on the whereabouts of our residents."

"Sure, I understand," I said, without any attitude back. That would've been a dead end. Instead, I eased into a more regular-

Joe accent. "Here's the thing, though. This customer of mine plopped down three hundred bucks on the bouquet, and he doesn't want it sitting around. So, I tell you what, just let me know if she's home right now. If so, I'll send someone over, and you can take it from there."

Another heavy sigh. Different register, though. This one hinted at a reluctant acquiescing. Sure enough, after all the air had been expelled from his lungs, the doorman gave me a break. "Yeah, she's here," he said.

It was all I needed to know.

The next call was to Hertz. Early evening on a Friday meant limited availability. "You've got two choices," said the clerk, a rather depressed-sounding woman. I asked if by two choices she meant two categories of cars. Stupid me. "No," she said. "I mean, literally, we only have two cars left."

Fifteen minutes and a ridiculous day rate later, I was behind the wheel of a beat-up white Hyundai Accent. I could've gone with the "much nicer Mercury Marquis," or so I was told, but it was also much bigger. I needed small.

The better to land a parking space.

That's what it was all about. At least as a start. Which was to say, I didn't figure on taking advantage of the car's free unlimited miles. I wasn't leaving Manhattan. I wasn't even leaving my zip code. My destination was less than twenty blocks north of my apartment. Ten-thirty Park Avenue. Home to Samantha Kent and her penthouse apartment. Where I knew she was.

The rest was simple. Find a parking space across the street from her building, one that offered a good view of the entrance. Then do three things—sit, watch, and wait.

Actually, there's never been anything simple about finding a parking space in Manhattan. The one I ultimately got took forty minutes of being double-parked with my hazards on. In fitting fashion, the car leaving happened to be the one that I was blocking.

It was a tight squeeze. Even with the Hyundai, I was practically kissing bumpers front and back. With the engine off, I made a quick call from my cell to the same doorman, only now I could actually see him. Chances were slim that Samantha Kent had left while I was in transit, but I had to make sure. "Sorry to bother you again," I said to the guy after reminding him of our earlier conversation. "My delivery person is running late. Ms. Kent is still there, right?"

She was.

Like that, my weekend plans were settled. If Samantha Kent was heading out, I was following her. If she wasn't, I was staying put. Either way, I'd still need to eat, but that wasn't a problem. I was in the takeout capital of the world, after all. With a little explaining over the phone, the city was my menu. If a restaurant could deliver to the front door of an apartment, they could certainly deliver to the front door of a parked car. "It'll be the third one from the corner on the left. A white Hyundai." To the delivery guy on his bike, coming to me was actually easier. No dismount was required.

All the same, I ate light. The last thing I wanted was to be off searching for a bathroom when Samantha Kent decided to go out. Or, worse, when my Mystery Patient decided to drop by. For sure, a coffee and a bran muffin were out of the question. The idea that such a thought represented both good thinking and comic absurdity wasn't lost on me. But I didn't care. I had my reasons for being there, and that's all that mattered. It was a gamble, and I was betting on the come . . . that my Mystery Patient would come to kill Samantha Kent.

In the evolution of the species, this was what supposedly separated humans from the rest of the animal kingdom. Intuitive reasoning, right or wrong. In short, a monkey would've never been sitting where I was sitting.

Though after eight hours in that Hyundai, I was beginning to wonder if perhaps the monkey wasn't the smarter beast. That aching, no-sleep joint pain had settled in, as had the boredom. I would've killed for a book on tape. Worst of all, I was beginning to question what the hell I was doing. I couldn't help thinking again about that Talking Heads lyric, *How did I get here?* The difference this time being that not only did I know but it was entirely my doing.

Still, I kept my eyes trained on the entrance to that apartment building.

Part of it was stubbornness. Part of it was a continued gut feeling. Mostly, it was because if I wasn't doing this, I'd be doing nothing. And the thought of that bothered me more than any fatigue I might have felt.

Dawn.

With it came a calculated risk. A nap. Two hours to try to offset the effects of the previous twelve. The word *refreshed* didn't really come to mind when I awoke. However, I was in good enough shape to carry on.

I watched joggers and dog-walkers and a few people out to get the paper and some coffee. As the address suggested, Ten-thirty Park Avenue was a well-to-do building. White-glove. The residents were a blend of new money and old, though the latter seemed to dominate. Old money loved old buildings, and the one I was staring at appeared to date back to the horse and buggy.

At eight, with the sun fully up although hidden by clouds, a new doorman came on duty. This one was younger than the others, which is to say he could've been my father as opposed to my grandfather. Having seen four of these guys to that point, the common bond, besides an AARP membership, seemed to be their whiteness. Caucasian didn't begin to describe it. One after the other, I was bearing witness to the Aryan doorman race.

Nine thirty.

A cab pulled up. Cabs were tricky. It was difficult to see who was getting out of them. They also blocked my view. I craned my neck to get a glimpse of the new arrival. It was a man. I watched as he—

Christ.

Out of the corner of my eye. Walking toward the entrance. Big black sunglasses. Large shoulder bag. A long raincoat with a high collar. She was looking straight ahead. Inconspicuous. Incognito.

No one would've recognized her. Including me.

Were it not for one thing.

The Yankees cap. Gray flannel. New but styled to look old. The same cap she had on in my office that first day. We'd even talked about it, albeit briefly. Her uncle used to take her to games as a kid, she told me.

It all came rushing back—flooding me, my head, the car, everything in sight. I knew it was her. My Mystery Patient had come to make her move.

And I was going to stop her.

FORTY-FIVE

My hand swung toward the Hyundai's door, blindly reaching for the handle. I felt and found it, pulling hard while beginning to push. My shoulder leaned in, and I barreled out of the car. I looked. My eyes quickly fixed on her as she was turning into the building's entrance. She was all that I saw.

Until it was too late.

I had tunnel vision. What I really should've had was oncoming-traffic vision. I heard the screeching skid of tires, and the rest was a blur. The front of the van, the impact, the pavement. When I opened my eyes again, I was flat on my back looking up at an overcast sky.

Then came the pain.

Fast, fierce, and in a continuous loop from my knees to my hips. I lay there motionless. A couple of people came rushing over. They stared and gawked and were no doubt asking me if I was okay. But I couldn't hear them. Their voices were static.

Another person joined the circle hovering over me. A young man. He was gripping his forehead with both hands, and in what little of his eyes I saw peeking through, I could tell he was no mere onlooker. He was the driver of the van.

My muddled gaze traveled down from his face to something he was wearing. It was a smock, white with orange and green lettering across the chest. I couldn't read it at first. I blinked and squinted, trying to force the words into focus. When I had, I couldn't believe my eyes. The smock said "Maxine's Bouquet."

Irony of ironies. I'd been hit by a florist.

The voices were getting louder now, clearer. It was a full-fledged commotion all around, with me still lying there motionless. Thus, the question everyone wanted to know. "Are you able to move?"

I didn't know. I continued to look up at the people around me. The jogger, the dog-walker, others. "Try wiggling your toes . . . try wiggling your fingers." They all seemed to be talking at once, telling me the same thing. All save for the delivery guy from Maxine's Bouquet. Hands still gripping his forehead, he was mumbling to himself and anyone else willing to believe him. *"Out of nowhere . . . He just jumped in the middle of the street out of nowhere."*

That's when I saw the person standing next to him. The doorman from Samantha Kent's building had come out to see what had happened. Like the others, he was staring down waiting for me to move.

I moved, all right.

The sight of him sucked the fog out of my head in an instant. The woman in the gray flannel Yankees cap. My Mystery Patient. She was on her way to Samantha Kent's apartment. And I wasn't. At least, not yet.

The crowd gathered around me had wanted some toe- and finger-wiggling, but I gave them much more. Faster than you can say "TV evangelist," I jolted up and climbed to my feet. *Hallelujah.*

Not really. It may have looked like a miracle, but it sure didn't feel like one. The pain was excruciating and no longer limited to my knees, thighs, and hips. The whole body was taking part.

I was far from healed, yet I was off just the same, pushing past people and straight into the entrance of Ten-thirty Park Avenue. I didn't look back. If I had, I'm sure the faces would've all been the same, awash in surprise and baffled curiosity. They'd seen a new twist on the hit-and-run accident and, in the process, acquired one more notch on their "only in New York" belts.

"Hey!" I heard behind me.

While everyone probably wanted to know where I was going, especially in such a rush, there was one man who *needed* to know. The doorman. Between a sprint and a hurried walk was my limping jog—right through his lobby.

"Hey!" he shouted again.

I reached the two elevators and smacked the Up button. Call it a break or call it an idle Saturday morning; either way, one of the doors opened immediately. Before stepping on, I took a quick glance over my shoulder. The doorman had chugged into the building and was heading right for me. I could've stopped and explained. I could've told him what was going on. But there was simply no time.

I pressed PH and the door began to close. In the last second, through a vertical sliver no more than two inches wide, I caught a glimpse of the doorman arriving too late. His very white face was very pissed off. "Sorry," was the best I could get out of my mouth.

It dawned on me that I should've told him to call the police. It also dawned on me that it would've been redundant. If they weren't already on their way because of the accident, they certainly were going to get the call now.

Up went the elevator. A moment to catch my breath—and to realize again how much pain I was in. Yet I knew I was lucky. Had the van driver been any slower on his brakes, I would've been dead for sure.

But was I too late? Would Samantha Kent survive as well?

Halfway up to the penthouse floor, all thoughts turned to the prospect of what lay ahead. I didn't know what to expect or how I'd react. I wasn't armed, whereas my Mystery Patient probably was. All I had, maybe, was the element of surprise. Again, if it wasn't too late.

The elevator door opened.

Haste or no haste, my first move was not to move at all. I had my back against the wall by the panel of floor buttons. Anyone stepping on wouldn't see me until I could see them. Far better than the other way around.

Except no one stepped on. Quickly, I held the door and peeked around it. I saw a square foyer, sparsely decorated. No one there.

I got off the elevator and listened. There were two apartments, three o'clock and nine o'clock. Hearing nothing, I started left, when over my shoulder I heard it. A crash. Something breaking. I turned on my heels and rushed to the opposite door.

Shit, it's going to be locked.

But it wasn't. A clumsy twist of the brass knob and I was in.

Immediately, I heard a scream, raw and guttural. There was grunting and what sounded like gasping for air. It was all coming from down the hallway in front of me. As fast as I could, I ran. Twenty, maybe thirty feet, past a kitchen and a dining room. The noise—the struggle—getting louder as I got closer. Until it was all right in front of me.

What I saw first was the knife. The long, steel blade, raised in the air and angled straight down. It was trembling. *They* were trembling. Standing toe to toe, Samantha Kent fending off the downward thrust of my Mystery Patient. Their arms were extended, locked at the elbows, but of the two of them, only Samantha Kent's legs were buckling. She was fighting a losing battle. Pain, fear, panic, and anger. Her face said it all.

For a second I froze. The adrenaline of the moment had rendered my lungs spent, my chest wall on the verge of collapse from the relentless pounding of my heart.

Do something, David.

I didn't think. I reacted. Head down, teeth gnashing, I charged across the room and tackled high. Her Yankees cap went flying. So did the rest of her. As we tumbled and headed toward the ground, I tried to spot the knife. Had it dropped? Was it still in her hand? I couldn't see it.

I also couldn't see the wall. My momentum had taken over, and I careened right into it. The impact was hard enough. On the heels of being tattooed by that delivery van, the feeling was agony. If I didn't already have a few cracked ribs, I did now.

The knife. Suddenly, I saw it. It was lying on the ground maybe a yard away. But so, too, was my Mystery Patient. She rolled left, then right, woozy from our collision.

Get the knife, David.

I pushed off the wall and onto my knees. I was dizzy. The room was spinning. Wait—there were *two* knives in front of me. Two of everything. I shook my head and blinked hard, but it was no use. The double vision remained. Two knives—one real the other not. How fitting. Unfortunately, it was the fake Samantha Kent who knew which one was real.

Her body stretched, and her hand reached. I couldn't stop her. She started to get up. Like a punch-drunk fighter, I did the same. I was back to seeing one of everything again, but what I saw didn't bode well. My Mystery Patient was standing before me with the knife gripped in her hand.

She said nothing. I said nothing. For the longest second of my life, the only exchange was a look. Hers was half disbelief. The other half I couldn't discern. For sure, mine was a hundred percent dread. I took a breath and winced. Complete physical torment. Any notion of the weaker sex no longer applied at that point. Especially when she was the one holding the knife.

You're a dead man, David.

She lunged.

At least, that's what I thought. But it wasn't a lunge. It was a bullet ripping through her. In the back and out the front. Thirty-five caliber. Fired from a gun held tightly in the hands of Samantha Kent. The one and only.

The blast was a cannon, a rocket, a supersonic boom. Given the utter silence it interrupted, there could've been nothing louder. As the echo bounced all about the walls, the body of the woman I'd once known as my patient went rigid. Then it went limp.

She fell to the ground as the blood seeped from her stomach. It was soaked up like a sponge by a beige carpet, and for the first time, I noticed where I was. Where we all were. It was the living room.

Though not for my Mystery Patient.

She was dead.

FORTY-SIX

As soon as Samantha Kent pulled the trigger and quite possibly saved my life, she collapsed to the floor. At first I thought maybe she'd been stabbed at some point while defending herself, the loss of blood finally taking its toll. But as I rushed to her side there was no blood to be seen. No signs of a knife wound. While she was out cold, she was definitely breathing. My best guess was that she'd fainted. Pure mental and physical exhaustion. I could hardly blame her.

"Freeze!"

Man, did that ever sound familiar. This time, though, I knew the drill. Slowly, I turned to face two cops with their guns drawn, and slowly I put my hands up—and kept them there. There was no reaching for my wallet. No sudden movements of any kind.

Right behind the two cops were two paramedics. Together, they all thought they were responding to an accident, a guy hit by a delivery van. They certainly didn't expect to arrive on the scene and learn from a ticked-off doorman that said guy had decided to make a mad hobble into his apartment building. Up to the penthouse, no less. Of course, that was nothing compared to their hearing the gunshot while stepping off the elevator.

So there I was. One dead woman, one unconscious woman, and me.

I can explain everything, officers . . .

Luckily, I didn't have to. As one paramedic confirmed the death of my Mystery Patient, the other waved some smelling salts under Samantha Kent's nose. She came to. She was shaky, she was groggy, and a little dizzy, for sure. But she was also something else.

Thankful.

Ignoring the paramedic's advice to remain lying down for a few more minutes, Samantha Kent rose gingerly to her feet. As tears began to trickle down her cheeks, she walked right over to me. I lowered my arms while the cops lowered their guns. The woman who less than forty-eight hours earlier had screamed at the top of her lungs that she wanted to kill me now wanted to hug me.

"Thank you," she said softly.

I hugged her back. "Thank *you*."

She squeezed a little tighter, and I nearly fainted myself from the pain—all courtesy of my rib cage. The paramedics made it clear there was a hospital and an X-ray machine in my immediate future. But even more immediate was the cops' need to figure out exactly what had happened.

We went into another room, a den, away from the grisly image of death sprawled on the beige carpet. That's where Samantha Kent did her best to explain. Beginning with the phone call she'd received the day before.

It was from a woman claiming to work in the Human Resources Department of Conrad Birch's firm. The woman said she needed the spousal signature on some documents so the final dividends from Birch's 401(k) money could be paid out. Rather than ask her to make the trip all the way downtown, the woman offered to come by Samantha Kent's apartment the next morning since she herself lived not too far away over on Second Avenue. A time was set. Nine thirty, Saturday morning.

Like that, my Mystery Patient was in.

"She looked so normal when I opened the door," said Samantha Kent. "I led her back to the living room and offered to make some coffee." She started to tear up again. "I never even made it to the kitchen."

Prompting her to turn around was what she described as a rustling noise. "I don't know, it wasn't loud or anything, yet for some reason it made me glance over my shoulder. Thank God I did."

What she saw was the woman pulling a large knife out of her shoulder bag. "Then the next thing I knew she was charging right at me." Samantha Kent shuddered as if reliving the moment. "The rest was a blur. Somehow I was able to grab her arm as she tried to stab me. Reflexes, I guess. It wasn't like I had time to think."

She described the struggle, the way she tried to fight off the woman. She remembered thinking she was surely going to die. "I wasn't as strong as she was. I didn't know how much longer I could hold her off. And then . . ." Samantha Kent looked at me with more tears. She couldn't finish the sentence.

I finished it for her. "That's when I showed up, I guess."

The cops turned to me. Up until that point they hadn't made the connection. I wasn't the guy they'd seen on the news; she wasn't the woman they'd read about in the papers. But with their eyes going from her to me, it was like a one-two punch. It knocked everything into place.

"You're that psychologist," said one of the cops, his finger pointing.

I watched the other cop as he looked at Samantha Kent. He didn't say anything—wisely so—though I could tell what he was thinking. *And you're that murdered guy's wife.*

Putting it together, both turned in the direction of the living room, where the paramedics were assisting the guys from the morgue wagon. Almost in unison, they asked the same question.

"And is she . . . ?"

I nodded. "Yes," I said. She was her. My Mystery Patient.

I began to explain how it happened that I was there. Hearing myself talk, I realized how strange it must have sounded. Perhaps even unbelievable. Yet, there I was standing in front of them, and there had to be a reason. When I finished giving it, the looks were priceless. They knew I had to be telling the truth. Who on earth could ever make something like that up?

One of the cops cracked a small joke to that effect, and in the first real moment of levity, everyone allowed for a brief chuckle. Mine turned out to be the briefest. Laughing hurt like hell, and there was no way to hide it.

"You should really go to the hospital," Samantha Kent said.

The two cops agreed, saying they could fill in any blanks on their report later. They called to the paramedics in the living room, who promptly came over to the den.

"We'd like you to go as well, Ms. Kent," said one of them. "As a precautionary measure."

She'd have nothing to do with it. "I'm okay," she said. "What I'd really like is to answer any further questions you might have, officers. Then I'm going to pack a suitcase, check into a nearby hotel, and call my Realtor. Would any of you gentlemen like to buy an apartment?"

Her tone, calm yet determined, left little doubt that, for her, a trip to the hospital would be a waste of time. She was indeed okay. Physically, for sure, and seemingly mentally as well. Despite her brush with death, what was clearly evident was a desire to put not just the events of that morning behind her but everything that had led up to it. She'd lost her husband and had to contend with a murder trial in which the prospect of his infidelity was discussed openly. If finally getting on with her life meant having to pull the trigger herself on his killer then so be it. At least, that's the sense I got.

One thing for sure, though, I was incredibly grateful she owned a gun. I was about to say as much when I caught myself. Sure, odds are it was registered, but maybe it wasn't. Whatever the case, the cops hadn't broached the subject yet, and I wasn't going to be the one to bring it up.

"Sorry, sir, it's mandatory."

That was the response to the expression on my face as a stretcher was brought into the apartment for me a minute later.

I didn't argue. I climbed aboard and let the paramedics strap me in. The last pull on the tether by my feet was like the last horse entering the starting gate. Immediately, we were off.

"Can you do me a favor?" I said to one of the guys as we wheeled out onto the street toward the ambulance. "Do you see that white Hyundai over there?"

He looked. "Yeah."

"Can you grab the keys from the ignition?"

"No problem," he said. "Lock it up, too, right?"

Never mind that the condition of the car itself was one big antitheft device. "Sure, thanks," I told him.

An hour later, X-rays at Lenox Hill Hospital showed the extent of my injuries to be three broken ribs. "A hat trick," claimed the doctor who examined me. Though not exactly younger looking, he wore a baseball cap and had a Pearl Jam T-shirt peeking out from under his white jacket.

"So, what now?" I asked.

"Nothing," he said. "Avoid comedy clubs, Shiatsu massages, and all middleweight title fights, sanctioned or otherwise."

"There's nothing that you do?"

"Nothing the body doesn't do better and faster by itself."

"Not even an Ace bandage?"

"Nope."

"What about the pain?"

"Yeah, that I can do something about." He buried his head in his clipboard and made a few notations. "Wait here and a nurse will get you a Percodan prescription and send you packing."

Here was a curtained-off area of the emergency room. Privacy unless you actually wanted to have a conversation with somebody. Listening to the managed chaos around me—a less than harmonious dialogue of medical terminology and people complaining—I realized I should probably get in touch with a few people and fill them in. That's when I also realized I left my cell phone back in the Hyundai. Good thing the car was locked after all.

The need to pester a nurse for a phone was instantly abated

by a familiar voice right outside the curtain. "Paging, Dr. Remler . . . Dr. Remler."

"C'mon in, Parker."

And Stacy right behind him. The two of them maneuvered around the curtain and immediately shook their heads upon seeing me.

"*What the hell were you thinking?*" asked Parker, only half kidding.

"Shut up, honey," Stacy told him through a smile. She came up and kissed me on the forehead. "My hero!" she gushed.

"That's more like it," I said.

"The nurse told us you had three broken ribs. Do they hurt?" asked Stacy.

"Only when I breathe."

I filled them in on what had happened. They could hardly believe it. Then I asked how they'd heard.

"Terry called me," said Parker. "She should be here momentarily."

"How'd she know?"

"Apparently a reporter buddy of Victor's was monitoring the police band looking for tomorrow's story. He found it, all right. He called Victor, who's actually out in Connecticut playing golf. Victor, in turn, got in touch with Terry."

As if on cue, she poked her head around the curtain. "Oh, thank God!" she said. She was clearly a little more than my lawyer at that moment, and I watched as Parker and Stacy pretended not to notice.

I told the whole story over again to Terry. Parker and Stacy hardly minded. Even after hearing it for a second time, they still couldn't get over it.

Neither could I, really.

It was one thing to have the idea, to think I'd finally got inside the head of my Mystery Patient. It was entirely another to find out I was right.

"So after all this, who was she?" asked Stacy.

Parker looked at me. I looked at Terry. Terry looked at all of us. Blank stares all around. I'd been wheeled out of Samantha Kent's apartment before the determination could be made, let alone the question asked.

"You'd think she'd have some identification on her," I said. I was quick to correct myself. "On second thought, maybe not."

"Either way, we'll know soon," said Terry. "I'll make some calls in a little bit."

Half of me wanted her to make those calls right away. The other half reassured me that after waiting this long, a little longer wouldn't kill me. An interesting choice of words given the morning I'd had.

So, if only for a bit more time, my Mystery Patient would remain a mystery. The difference now being that I was certain she had no further moves to make. It was a terrific feeling that I could sum up in one word.

Checkmate.

There was just one problem, though. Something I didn't know.

There was more than one game being played.

PART V

FORTY-SEVEN

Her name was Haley Morgan.

Age thirty-two.

Only child of Adam and Shirley Morgan. Both deceased.

Lived by herself in a studio apartment in Chelsea.

She did a few small acting jobs and some modeling, mainly catalog stuff. In lean times—which is to say, most of the time—she worked as an office temp through an agency. That was the hook. A little over two years before, she'd been assigned for a few months to a Wall Street investment firm. The same firm where Conrad Birch worked.

End of story.

At least as far as the papers and local news broadcasts were concerned. All combined, that was the gist of their reporting. In the twenty-four hours after my leaving the hospital—and in between a steady diet of Percodan and sleep—I took it all in.

"But there's more, isn't there?"

I looked across the table and watched Terry react to my question with a knowing smile. Two days after the fact, and we were having our agreed-to "when this whole thing is over" dinner.

"Yes, there's more," she answered. "The press haven't gotten ahold of her rap sheet yet."

"Meaning, she has one?"

"Yep. Two priors. One for cocaine possession, the other for theft of a doctor's prescription pad," she said. "Sad thing is, Haley Morgan was a smart girl. Graduated from Vassar."

It made sense. Her plotting went a little beyond community college.

"Did you get all this extra stuff from The Magnet?" I asked.

"No, from her actual police file. As you might imagine, those guys are pretty tail-between-the-legs on this one. The more they feed us, the less we'll rub their noses in it publicly. At least that's what they're hoping."

"What about Hemmerson?"

"He left a message on my voice mail at work. He did his best to sound gracious, even said he wanted to buy me a drink."

"What a guy."

"Tell me about it."

"Any chance you'll hear from Trentino and Lopez?"

"The same chance you will," she said. "Somewhere between slim and none."

"Big surprise."

"I know." She tapped her forehead. "That reminds me, though. Victor mentioned he was going to call you. Did you hear from him?"

"Yes, a congratulatory call. He told me what I did took guts, and I told him that *stupidity* was probably a better word. We settled on *tenacious*. In the end, however, it was semantics. As Victor put it, all that mattered was the result."

"He's very Machiavellian that way," she said. "Though he does have his Miss Manners side as well. He wrote Samantha Kent a note on behalf of the firm. I think that was a nice touch."

"I agree. What did the note say?"

"I don't know exactly. As it turned out, she almost didn't even get it. Victor had it messengered, only to find out she's not living in her apartment anymore. Finally, after some coaxing, a doorman revealed she'd checked into the Drake."

"Yeah, she did say something about going to a hotel. Can't blame her, I guess."

Our waiter returned. We'd sent him away twice already with the apologetic albeit ubiquitous "We need just another minute." At the risk of loitering indictments, we decided to order.

The restaurant was the Blue Water Grill down in Union Square. Live jazz, fresh seafood, and, thankfully, very patient waiters. I went with the pan-roasted Mahi Mahi, while Terry opted for the lobster. Showing off her crustacean expertise courtesy of her eleventh-grade oceanography class, she proudly took me through all the lesser known yet edible parts. There was the slender but worthwhile meat to be found in the uropods and telson at the very end of the tail, as well as the tomalley.

"The what?"

"The green stuff here in the torso that no one eats except crusty old men and me," she said.

"Sorry I asked."

In between, Terry filled me in on her recent chat with The Magnet. Out of sheer curiosity, she'd called him with a small follow-up question. She wanted to know how Haley Morgan was able to prevent me from recording our telephone conversation.

Explained Terry, "It's called a sprayer."

"Are you sure that's not another part of a lobster?"

She grinned. "According to Anthony, it's this small device that emits a high-frequency pitch preventing the magnetic recording of any fiber-optic transmission."

I looked at her and laughed. "You just made that up, didn't you?"

"Hey, for all I know, Anthony made it up, but I doubt it. He sounded pretty sure of himself."

"A sprayer, huh?"

"I don't think they sell them at Kmart. Anthony did say that while they're relatively new, they're also readily available on the Internet."

"What isn't these days? Nonetheless, it strikes me as pretty odd that someone like Haley Morgan would know about a device like this, let alone, have one," I said.

"I know. Though stranger things have happened."

"Like everything else she did, right?"

"Exactly."

I took another bite of my Mahi Mahi, assuming there was nothing more Terry had learned from The Magnet.

Wrong.

"There's something else," she said. "Apparently Anthony did a little checking on his own into Haley."

"Unsolicited, huh?"

"A cross between professional and morbid curiosity is my guess."

"So, what did he turn up?"

"Perhaps a better understanding of her motivation."

"Concerning me?"

"No, Conrad Birch," she said. "About a year ago, Haley had an abortion."

I nodded with slow understanding. It might explain why Haley hated him so much. Also, why she chose to make a child the centerpiece of her deception.

Still.

"It might not have been Conrad's kid," I pointed out.

"There's always that possibility," said Terry. "The far greater possibility, however, is that it was."

I couldn't disagree. "For certain, this is something Samantha Kent should never know."

"She never will."

Our plates were cleared and the table brushed free of crumbs. A touch of symbolism perhaps since it was right about then that Terry and I both realized this was supposed to be a date and not a debriefing session.

She was no longer my lawyer.

I was no longer her client.

The conversation moved from the past to the future. What was to what might be. The two of us.

Usually couples got the background down about each other—hometowns, hobbies, number of siblings—before any emotional connection was struck. With Terry and me it was the opposite. The trenchlike experience of the trial, the time vested in a shared effort, had allowed our feelings to shape and then bond. Straggling behind were the basic facts.

One of them, my widower status, Terry knew. Rather than shy away from it, though, she tackled it head-on. She had no problem discussing my emotional connection to someone else, and what could've been a minefield in the first steps of our relationship turned out to be the most meaningful exchange we'd had so far.

For the first time, I was able to talk about Rebecca without going on autopilot. I wasn't telling the story about some poor guy who'd lost his wife. Rather, I was sharing with Terry the one event in my life that had affected me more than any other.

Which was precisely why she wanted to hear it.

Watching her listen to me and then follow up with the right questions, I knew she understood this was a part of who I was. There was no changing it. She could either feel threatened by the prospect of competing with a ghost, or she could simply just feel for me.

Her choice was clearly the latter, and by virtue of that, I knew I was finally ready to move on with my life.

I held Terry's hand as we walked a few blocks after leaving the restaurant. I didn't let go during the entire cab ride back to my apartment. We kissed in the elevator. We kissed outside my door.

We stood facing each other in my bedroom.

"I haven't done this for a while," I said.

She stepped out of her heels and smiled. "How long is a while?"

"A few years."

She started to unbutton my shirt. "That's a while all right."

I started to unbutton her blouse. "Oh, good, you've put me right at ease."

She undid my belt. "Would you like me to draw a diagram or something?"

I unzipped her skirt. "No, the mechanics I remember. It's the nuances I might be a little rusty on."

"Sounds like you're about to give a piano recital."

She reached behind her back and unfastened her bra. It fell slowly off her shoulders.

"Well, the hands do play an important role," I said.

Terry lifted one of mine and placed it on her breast. I looked into her eyes, not wanting to blink. She was beautiful. Radiant. The more I stared at her the more comfortable I felt. There was no pain. No broken ribs. No reminders of a life I'd been afraid to let go of.

She gently pressed her body against mine, whispering in my ear. "I think this is going to be good," she said.

FORTY-EIGHT

The word had got out, and out of the woodwork they came—the people from my not-too-distant past who'd managed to keep their distance.

There were the former patients who wanted to return. There were the other tenants in my building who no longer had to look away when walking by me. There was even an invitation.

Not only was Cassandra Nance asking me to one of her parties, she was throwing the whole shindig on my behalf. She called to make sure I was free on the date she had in mind. As for my willingness to be the guest of honor, it was simply assumed.

What a hoot it was to tell her I couldn't make it.

"You mean, you're busy that night, David?"

"Actually, no," I said casually. "I have no plans."

Then there was my esteemed literary agent, Debra Walker Coyne. To be fair, she had no aversion to talking to me during the whole ordeal. She'd phoned on a few occasions to discuss business—foreign licensing of my book, that sort of thing—and each time she never failed to ask how I was doing and express her support.

Nonetheless, I couldn't help harboring a cynical suspicion that she had it all worked out in her head. Guilty or innocent, I was a good book in the making. And like those collectors who in-

undated Mila during the trial with requests for signed copies of
The Human Pendulum, Debra had to have known that guilty
meant a lot more money than innocent. My next book would
surely generate greater buzz were it to be composed in a jail cell.
Not to mention that with all the excess time on my hands, I'd
doubtlessly deliver the manuscript faster. Like I said, though, it
was merely a cynical suspicion.

Cut to the Grill Room at the Four Seasons. Her usual table.

"So, how's my favorite bestselling and now truly famous author
doing?" said Debra, standing up to give me a kiss on the cheek.

While there'd be no jail-cell memoir, my next project would
still fetch a handsome advance. Supremely conscious of my six-
figure legal tab, I grudgingly accepted her offer of lunch that
Friday.

"Good to see you, Deb."

"Better to see you, David."

I sat down and unfolded my napkin.

She leaned in. "I knew there was no way you could've
stabbed someone fifty times over," she said matter-of-factly.
"Your writing style is far too succinct for that."

She launched into her PEZ-dispenser laugh, whipping her
head back with a loud cackle. I joined in, though at a tenth of
the volume, if only to be polite. Then, for fun, I began staring at
the knife next to her plate. When she ultimately caught on, she
threw her head back again, this time for so long and with such a
sustained laugh I was convinced a piece of candy was going to
present itself from her larynx.

"See, that's why your next book has got to be about this whole
experience," she said, finally calming down.

"I don't know," I said. "I'm not sure this is something I really
want to capitalize on."

"What are you talking about? That's the American way!"

"You say that like it's a good thing."

As if to change the subject while making sure to stay right on
it, she started to ask me about some of the players involved. The
detectives, my lawyers, the grieving widow. Most notably, and

not surprisingly, she was curious about Haley Morgan. My Mystery Patient.

I told her what I knew, which wasn't much. Even less, given that I kept the information about Haley's abortion to myself. It was really just a recitation of what had already been reported.

Debra frowned. "Did you at least find out if the police discovered anything where she lived?"

"Like what?"

"Like anything that could help you in your book."

"You mean, the same book I told you I don't want to write?"

"That's the one." She leaned in. "Seriously, if you want to know the truth about a woman, all you have to do is rummage through her closets."

"I don't think that's an option."

"Maybe, maybe not. But you really should inquire with the police. I'll bet you they've gone through her apartment."

The thought had never occurred to me, and my blank expression said as much. Debra continued, "This woman nearly ruined your life, David. Just from a professional standpoint, aren't you the least bit curious about her?"

We ordered and ate, and all along Debra kept up the full-court press on my writing about the ordeal. As she paid the hefty bill for lunch, I figured the least I could do was promise her I'd think about it.

After saying good-bye, I began walking uptown along Park Avenue. I still had plenty of time before my two-o'clock session—a young advertising copywriter who couldn't understand why nobody liked him.

The sidewalks were packed. It was one of those beautiful spring days that got everything right. Blue sky and sun, a gentle breeze weaving in and out of every block. The whole city was room temperature.

Just from a professional standpoint, aren't you the least bit curious about her?

The more I walked, the more Debra's words echoed in my head. She'd asked a good question. In fact, it was better than she probably realized. That's because I'd asked the same question myself. Repeatedly. Only to suppress the answer every time.

But no longer.

As much as I wanted to leave Haley Morgan behind and get on with my life, I now realized I couldn't. Too much had happened. She may have been dead, but like it or not, her impact was living on. And it didn't take a rocket scientist to figure out why.

No, it took a psychologist.

Haley had singled me out and made me her victim. The incredible anger I felt because of that had blocked any other emotion I might have felt for her. With her gone, however, the anger was starting to dissipate. Regret was creeping in. It was all culminating in a thought that truly underscored why I did what I did for a living—that of all the places in which to work, I chose other people's minds.

The thought? If only she'd been my patient for real. If only Haley Morgan had come to me as Haley Morgan.

Maybe she couldn't have been helped. Maybe her pain was too intense. All I knew was I'd never know for sure. Which was precisely what was consuming me at that point. Because I wanted to know *something*. Something more. And until I did, there'd be other words echoing in my head as well.

No one can have more control over your life than you do.

What happened to me from the moment Haley walked into my office had proved otherwise, to put it mildly. Sure, on the surface, I'd assumed control again. But deep down my grip felt tenuous. As tenuous as my understanding of Haley.

She was *still* my Mystery Patient—and until I changed that, there'd always be a part of me that felt helpless.

I came to a corner and a DON'T WALK sign. As I stood there waiting, I happened to glance over at some benches in front of an office building. Sitting on the nearest one were two older men deep in thought and staring at what was between them. A chessboard.

I took out my cell phone and dialed.

FORTY-NINE

Ethan Greene looked at me as if I had three heads. "Do you realize what you're asking me to do?"

"Yes," I said. "A favor."

"No, you're asking me to break the law."

"It's a small fracture at best."

"Since when did you become the legal expert?"

"Since you dragged my ass into court to help you win your case."

Ethan took a sip of his beer. We were at the end of the bar at Hurley's near Rockefeller Center. When I rang him up, he told me he'd been meaning to call and congratulate me.

"Good, now you can do it in person," I said.

He was hard pressed to say no.

My favor, however, was a different story. Ethan was having a much easier time telling me no on that.

He knew the police had indeed searched Haley's apartment, at the very least for an address book or something else that could help them notify a family member. Hardly a gimme given that she was an only child and her parents were dead. Ethan also knew that until the proper arrangements were made for her belongings, Haley's apartment would remain as she left it, undisturbed.

And he had every intention of keeping it that way.

"Listen," he said. "I know you're saying I owe you, but—"

I cut him off. "No, those were *your* words. Right after the rabbi was found guilty and right before all the newspapers labeled you the rising star of the D.A.'s office."

"Yes, and if anyone in that office ever found out I did this for you, I'd be the rising star who crashed and burned," he said.

"That's not going to happen."

"I'm glad you're so confident with my career."

Our back-and-forth was reminiscent of when he was trying to persuade me to testify at his trial. He was relentless. I was determined to be the same.

"One more thing," I said. "Remember when you threatened to subpoena me if I didn't cooperate? I found out you were bluffing. You can't subpoena an expert witness. What's more, I should've been paid for my time."

He let go with a guilty smile. "You've done your homework."

"*Lived* it, is more like it."

He polished off his beer and immediately ordered another. I was starting to think my best bet was to get him drunk. Meanwhile, I'd barely touched my Diet Coke.

"C'mon, Ethan, you're the only one who can do this for me."

He rubbed his temples. "Assuming for a second I get you into her apartment—and I'm not saying I'm going to—what is it you intend to do?"

"I just want to look around."

"For what?"

"I don't know exactly. Something that can help me better understand what motivated this woman."

"Her own words weren't enough for you?"

"I realize it sounds a little bizarre, but I just have a feeling there's more to know."

"What are you telling me, this is a hunch?"

"Not quite that random. I spent a lot of time with her," I said.

"Yes, as she was *pretending to be someone else.*"

"I realize that, but I have to believe parts of her—the real her—managed to slip through. I just want to know what those parts are."

"But what if you're wrong? What if there's nothing more to know?"

"If that's what I find out, fine," I said. "It's the not knowing either way that's bothering me."

"So snooping around Haley's apartment is going to give you, what, some sort of closure?"

"That's one word for it."

"Don't you understand, though? You've already got your happy ending."

"Do you see me smiling right now?"

Ethan went to his beer yet again. A big swig this time instead of a sip. He emptied the glass and set it down hard on the bar. "Okay," he said. "But you didn't get the key from me."

"I won't tell a soul."

"No, *literally*, you won't be getting it from me. You'll have it, but it won't touch my hands at any time."

I thanked him profusely and asked when I could be expecting it.

"Tomorrow, two days tops."

"Shit, I was hoping for this evening."

"Yeah, and I was hoping to play guard for the Knicks."

The next morning, a little after nine, I was in my apartment reading the paper. The doorman buzzed up. He said there was a package for me. Normally, he would've been able to sign for it but not in this case. Two minutes later, there was a loud knock on my door. I opened it to see a bike messenger with dreadlocks and dark wraparound sunglasses. He asked me if I was Dr. Remler.

I told him I was.

"Sign here, mon," he said. He handed me a clipboard that had a pen on a string taped to it. I signed. He reached into his backpack, taking out a small manila envelope. He gave me the envelope and was off. "Have a nice day, mon."

Sure enough, he looked nothing like Ethan Greene.

FIFTY

Inside the envelope were two keys and the address. The keys—one for the entrance to Haley's brownstone and the other for her apartment—were shiny without a single scratch. Definitely copies. The address was typewritten right down to the notation that it was a walk-up. There was no handwriting anywhere, and the paper was indistinguishable. Given the advances in DNA testing, I wouldn't have been surprised if Ethan had had someone else lick the envelope.

I left right away.

The cab dropped me off on Eighteenth Street, midway between Ninth and Tenth Avenue. I unlocked the brownstone's heavy glass door and strolled in as if I lived there. Looking around the foyer, though, I was pretty glad I didn't. While far from a rat hole, it had nondescript down to a tee. Everything seemed gray. The only real color came from the assorted Chinese takeout menus scattered by the mailboxes.

I headed up the stairs as quickly as I could. The accumulated media coverage had left my existence hovering somewhere between quasi- and downright recognizable, and I was loath to be spotted. Being in Haley's building couldn't exactly be chalked up to coincidence.

Arriving on the third floor, I immediately saw what I'd expected to see but didn't after my apartment had been searched. A web of yellow tape. It was strewn over, across, and around her door with all the care of a hurricane. But the message was loud and clear: keep out.

For a moment my feet froze.

Only for a moment, though. I'd simply come too far to succumb to second-guessing. Quickly, I took out a pair of gloves from my pocket. They were the thin latex kind that nurses and doctors use. I'd picked them up at a medical supply store near Lenox Hill Hospital. Of course, doing so was nothing short of paranoia. Ethan hadn't told me to wear them, and it wasn't as if anyone had any reason to be taking fingerprints.

Still, on they went.

I walked up to Haley's door, maneuvered around the yellow tape, and slid the key into the lock. With one twist I entered her apartment and the ethical ambiguity that went with it. Gray like the foyer below.

It was a small studio. It was also a mess. "Lived-in" would've been the polite phrase, but that only made it more creepy given the circumstances. Haley Morgan didn't live there anymore. She didn't live anywhere.

At first, I simply stood in the middle of the room and did a slow three-sixty. A bed, a bookcase, a chest of drawers, a sofa, a boom box, a kitchenette. Scattered clothes, magazines, and a few empty Evian bottles. A framed Picasso print leaning up against the wall.

Forget the fact that I didn't know where to begin. I didn't even know what I was looking for.

But I was intent on finding it.

For the next twenty minutes or so, I poked and prodded. I scanned the spine of every book on her bookshelf. I half expected to see *The Human Pendulum*, but didn't. They were all novels. Beach reads, mainly.

I checked Haley's one closet. It made the rest of the place look spotless. Suitcases and shoeboxes crammed the shelf above the crush of hanging clothes. A fan, a humidifier, and an over-stuffed hamper took up the floor.

I stepped back and turned, facing the rest of the apartment.

The more trivial the items I saw, the more I realized where pay dirt might lie. A diary, for instance. A yearbook, even. But neither was anywhere to be found.

I began to think of my conversation with Ethan. His questioning me. *But what if you're wrong? What if there's nothing more to know?*

Word for word, I remembered my answer. *If that's what I find out, fine. It's the not knowing either way that's bothering me.*

I sat down on Haley's sofa and wondered if I really meant it. Could I leave and be satisfied? Could I just walk away now and never look back?

Much to my surprise, the answer came quick.

The answer was *yes*.

Maybe it was the same thing that brought me there—all my years as a therapist. I'd learned the hard truth: that there is only so much you can do to help someone . . . including yourself.

Or maybe it was the other thing Ethan had said to me, the perceptiveness of it finally kicking in. *You've already got your happy ending.*

I stood up, took a breath, and headed for the door. Yes. I was simply going to walk away. But just for the hell of it, I took one look back.

The next thing I knew, I was on an airplane.

FIFTY-ONE

The seat-belt sign lit up, and the captain announced we were starting our descent. The temperature in Atlanta, he said with typical cockpit-calm, was a comfortable 72 degrees.

On the way to the airport I'd made the call on my cell. "A courtesy call" is what I claimed, posing as a telemarketer. I asked if her name was Evelyn Stark. She said it was. She also said she wasn't interested in whatever it was I was selling. In the middle of my thanking her for her time anyway, she hung up. Perfect.

I'd got what I needed. Confirmation. The knowledge it was actually her, Evelyn Stark.

Haley's birth mother.

It was hard to believe. In Haley's web of lies there was a strand of truth. She was indeed adopted, just like she told me. Only when she told me, she was posing as Samantha Kent.

It all had become clear with a simple card. A Hallmark with flowers on the front and the words *For My Daughter* written in an ornate script. The card was inside a yellow envelope, a corner of which was peeking out from beneath a jewelry box on Haley's chest of drawers. When I was looking straight on from a few feet away, it was barely visible. When I was looking back from the doorway of her apartment, it was practically neon.

The message inside was brief. At the same time, it spoke volumes.

And hinted at even more.

> To my daughter Haley,
>   It means so much that you've found me after all these years. Thank you for forgiving me. I won't tell anyone what you've told me.
>   Love,
>   Evelyn

Immediately, I'd flashed back to the rest of the conversation with Haley about her mother, my describing how making contact could be a good thing. Again, real advice for a real situation in an otherwise complete lie.

But what really amazed me was the idea that it perhaps sank in. It was such a paradox. The warmth of reconnecting with her birth mother amidst the brutally cold murder of Conrad Birch. Not to mention my being framed for it.

Then there was the last line on the card. *I won't tell anyone what you've told me.* Could it be—had Haley really discussed what she'd done? Had she been seeking someone who might understand? It seemed so unlikely. Then again, so did her taking my advice. All I knew for sure was I'd be leaving Haley's apartment the same way I arrived.

Wanting to know more.

And pointing me in the right direction was the front of the envelope in the upper left-hand corner. There I saw one of those return address stickers that charities include with their solicitation mailings.

Ms. Evelyn Stark
114 Traeger Mill Road
Griffin, GA 30224

It was all I needed. Three-plus hours and one Delta Shuttle later, I was renting a car at the Atlanta Airport. Anything but a white Hyundai, I told the agent.

The free map at the counter got me to Griffin. A gas station attendant got me right to the house. It was a tiny ranch with narrow concrete steps. She opened the door for me without asking who I was.

"Ms. Stark, my name is Dr. David Remler."

It took only one look at her to know it wasn't small-town trust that had blindly opened the door. The woman standing before me in a worn, faded blue robe had the hardened gaze of someone who had nothing left to fear. If I was there to rob, rape, mug, or murder her, so be it. It would've simply been the final act of an unkind life. Yes, it only took one look at her to know—this was the woman who'd put Haley Morgan up for adoption.

And now I was about to tell her Haley was dead.

"Ms. Stark, I'm here about your daughter."

"My daughter?"

Her cold stare said it all—I knew something I wasn't supposed to. "Yes, ma'am," I said. "Your daughter, Haley."

She squinted. "What'd you say your name was again?"

"David . . . Dr. David Remler."

"What kind of doctor?"

"I'm a psychologist."

"Haley never said anything about a psychologist. Is she a patient of yours?"

The irony of the question was lost in how it was phrased. Present tense. She had no idea Haley was dead.

"Ms. Stark, I'm afraid I have some horrible news for you."

The cold stare remained fixed on me as I told her. Initially, there was no reaction. She stood still, unblinking. Finally, she asked when it happened and where. "Last week and in Manhattan," I said. She nodded and fell silent. I expressed how sorry I was, and she nodded again.

"I'm going to make some coffee," she announced.

She only made it one step. The cold stare gave way to weakened knees, and she nearly collapsed to the ground. I caught her just in time, and she clung to me as if I were her capsized boat. The tears started and she cried, the sound muffled against my shirt.

"Come, let's sit down," I said.

I practically carried her to a couch that was in a wood-paneled room to my immediate right. There was a television on in the corner. Matlock was saying something in a courtroom.

After a few minutes, Evelyn Stark began to compose herself. I knew that meant one thing. She was going to want the details of her daughter's death. I'd have to edit, I told myself. But there was only so much I could leave out. The story didn't exist without me. Nor was there any polite spin on the troubles that besieged Haley Morgan.

The questions got asked, and I did the best I could. With each answer, Conrad Birch became far less the victim and far more the villain. Given that he used me to dump Haley, the least I could do was use him to lessen the blow with her mother. Evelyn Stark didn't need to know the extent of her daughter's actions, and what I did tell her was always couched in Haley's being wronged herself.

Still, on the heels of hearing that her daughter was gone, the sordid details of how it happened—no matter how parsed— threatened to make a very bad situation worse. That's when I decided to steer the conversation more to Haley's life as opposed to her death. Admittedly, my motivation wasn't a hundred percent altruistic. I was looking for some answers of my own.

"So you obviously got to know Haley," I said.

"Only since last year."

She explained how she'd always wondered about her daughter. The life she was leading and whether she was happy. There were times, said Evelyn, that she wanted to try to find her, except she knew it was the wrong thing to do. If they were meant to meet up one day, then it would have to be Haley who initiated it.

Lo and behold, she did.

"Last fall she called me," said Evelyn. "A few weeks later, she came here and paid me a visit. I haven't had too many happy days, but that for sure was one of them."

She managed a smile. So did I—but only to a point. The fact remained that whatever good this reunion did for Evelyn, it did nothing to change Haley. She still did what she did.

"Did you talk much to your daughter after she came down here?" I asked.

"A couple of times," she answered. "Once before the holidays and once after."

I pressed her. "Did Haley ever say anything about being involved with a married man?"

"No."

"Nothing about a bad relationship?"

"No."

"Did she seem angry about *anything*?"

"Not really."

With each shake of Evelyn's head, I became more disheartened. I'd felt so strongly about tracking down this woman and talking to her, so strongly that there was something to learn. Especially given that Hallmark card, something I didn't want to let on that I'd seen.

But still.

"Ms. Stark, if you don't mind my asking, what *did* you and your daughter talk about?"

I asked the question mainly out of frustration. It was clearly none of my business. Given the news I'd brought, I wouldn't have been terribly shocked if Evelyn Stark had asked if there wasn't maybe a plane I needed to catch. I'd almost started to apologize, but then she went ahead and answered.

"We talked about a lot of things, you know, trying to make up for the lost time. It sounded like she was raised by a good family and all. She went to college, and she told me about some of the modeling she'd done. I could see how that was. She was very pretty." Evelyn stopped as if remembering something. "Would you like to see the picture?"

"What picture's that?"

She explained that Haley had brought a camera down with her, and they'd taken some photos using that "thingy where you could press a button and then hurry in the picture." A week later, she said, Haley mailed her a copy of one of the shots.

Evelyn got off the couch and went to a cluttered bookcase that was by the TV. As the credits for *Matlock* were beginning to roll, she pulled down a small box from the top shelf. "I keep it in a special place," she said.

She walked back over to the couch and opened the box, taking out a picture. She handed it to me, and I looked. At first what I saw was two women smiling, a mother and daughter reunited. They were sitting on the same couch I was. Behind them was a window. It was nighttime.

"This is really nice, Ms. Stark," I said. "Something I'm sure you'll cherish."

I was about to give the picture back when my hand froze.

That's when I saw it.

FIFTY-TWO

Three sets of two numbers separated by a couple of back-slashes. That's what I saw. A simple date printed in the bottom right-hand corner of the picture. The same date Conrad Birch had been stabbed more than fifty times.

Hackers' Night.

I was sitting still and running out of breath. I asked Evelyn if the date was right. Perhaps the camera had been programmed wrong, the internal calendar never set correctly.

"No," she said, looking at the picture again. "That's when Haley was here. It was the night before Halloween."

"Are you sure?"

"I remember because the next day, before she left, she went to the market and bought me some candy to give out to the kids."

I blinked a few times. *The next day?* "You mean Haley spent the night here with you?"

"Yes."

"The *whole* night you're saying, right?"

"Yes, why?"

My head was dizzy. It didn't make sense. If Haley was down in Georgia, she couldn't have been up in Manhattan. Then again, whoever said she was? Certainly not her. She could've called me the night of the murder from anywhere. Now it was all making sense.

Haley Morgan wasn't working alone.

"Ms. Stark, I have to ask you a favor," I said, trying to remain calm. "I need to borrow this picture for a day."

As the words left my mouth, I realized how insane I must have sounded. On the heels of telling this woman that the daughter she gave up for adoption was dead, I now wanted to take the one and only picture she had of her.

"Where are you going with it?" she asked.

"Home to Manhattan. I promise, though, that I'll overnight it back to you on Monday."

She hardly looked convinced. "It's not that I don't trust you—"

"No, I understand," I said. "But what I haven't told you is why I need the picture. I'm going to be showing it to the police."

"Why?"

"Because I think it proves your daughter didn't actually kill anyone."

The change in her face said it all. I suddenly represented a shot at redemption for Haley. Never mind that, at best, the picture proved her daughter was an accessory to murder as opposed to an actual murderer. If it meant my getting the picture, it was a point that didn't need to get made.

"You say you promise to send it back?"

"Yes, Ms. Stark. You have my word."

I apologized again for having to be the bearer of such bad news and assured her I'd be in touch to explain everything better. Then I hustled out of there. Picture in hand.

I hurried back on the road heading toward the airport. There was a plane to catch, but more important, there was a phone call to make. To Terry. I'd tell her what had happened, and she'd tell everyone else, beginning with the police. They needed to know right away that the case wasn't closed. There was a killer at large. Which meant Samantha Kent might still be a target.

I grabbed my cell and glanced at my watch—six twenty-five.

I dialed Terry at her apartment. The good news about the hell I was about to catch for making this trip behind her back was that she was probably going to forget we had eight o'clock dinner reservations.

Three rings . . . four rings. *C'mon, Terry, be there.*

She wasn't. I left a message on her machine to call me as soon as possible and tried next to reach her on her cell. As it rang I looked over at the passenger seat. Four by six, the faces of Haley Morgan and her mother smiling back at me. Amazing. Once again, it was a photograph that was turning everything upside down.

"Hi, this is Terry, please leave a message."

Not picking up at home; not picking up on her cell. *Damn, where is she?*

I next tried Victor. I called his home and then his cell, both with no luck. Despite it being Saturday, I also called his office. When I got his voice mail, I remembered Terry mentioning his taking a vacation. I couldn't remember if this was when it was.

I drove another mile thinking of what to do. The knee-jerk move was to call the police, maybe even try to get ahold of Detectives Trentino and Lopez. They never believed me before. Now they had to. In my mind I went over what I'd tell them. That I'd gone to see Haley Morgan's birth mother and—

Shit.

I could see their faces. Hear their questions. Why was I visiting the mother? How did I find out who she was and where she lived? I'd have to give them answers while at the same time protecting Ethan. I'd have to lie.

Or.

Better yet. Cut out the middlemen. At least for the moment. I'd call Samantha Kent directly. She'd undoubtedly be surprised to hear from me, and she'd undoubtedly start to panic once she heard what I had to say. But I'd do my best to calm her down. "If no one has gone after you yet, chances are they never will." That's what I'd say. In a real soothing tone, too. Then I'd casually suggest she double-lock her door, slide a dresser against it, and immediately hide under the bed.

"What city, please?"

"Manhattan . . . the Drake Hotel."

I got the number and called, asking for her room. It rang eight times before switching to voice mail. I quickly acknowledged in my message that I'd be the last person she'd expect to hear from and gave my cell number. Stressing the importance, I told her to call as soon as she could. As I hung up, a horrible thought. What if Haley's partner had already got to her?

At least Delta Airlines was home. While waiting for some-one—*anyone*—to get back to me, I called to reserve a seat on the next New York flight.

"There's one leaving at nine forty tonight," said the agent.

"Nothing earlier?"

"There's a seven thirty, but that's in less than an hour."

I looked at my watch again—six thirty-five. She was right; there was no way I'd make it. "The nine forty it is then."

I hung up and was about to call another airline for an earlier flight. My cell rang. "Hello?"

"Dr. Remler?"

It was Samantha Kent. Thinking she might have called in for her messages, I immediately asked where she was.

"Why?" she asked, her tone hesitant.

"I'm sorry, but this will all make sense in a minute."

"I'm here at the Drake. I was on the other line," she said. "Is there some sort of problem?"

"Not yet," I said. "But something's happened. It's a long story, but the bottom line is that Haley Morgan didn't kill your husband."

It took her a second. *"What?"*

"The night Conrad was murdered, Haley wasn't anywhere near Manhattan."

"What do you mean? Where was she?"

"In Griffin, Georgia."

She sounded thoroughly confused. "Where?"

"It's about forty miles south of Atlanta. That's where Evelyn Stark lives—she's Haley's birth mother. Haley was staying with her that very same night."

"How do you know?"

"Because I just came from there."

"You're in Georgia?"

"Yes. Like I said, it's a long story."

"Wait a minute, I don't understand," she said. "If Haley Morgan didn't kill Conrad, who did?"

"That's the question. She must have been working with someone."

"But who?"

"I don't know. It could've been any—"

"Oh, my God, David."

On a dime, her voice turned. Confusion to concern.

"Samantha, what is it?" I asked. The moment had instantly put us on a first-name basis.

She didn't say anything.

"Samantha?"

"She said she wanted to apologize to me."

"Who did?"

I could almost feel the phone trembling in her hand.

"That woman from the trial," she said. "Gabrielle Dennis."

The other mistress. Maybe. Deluded publicity hound or the real thing, we never knew. When it no longer mattered, we didn't care. Now the smart money was on accomplice. Somehow working with Haley, she came forward *posing* as the mistress to try to derail my defense.

"What do you mean? Did you talk to her?" I asked.

"She called me," said Samantha. "She was crying, telling me how awful she felt about everything."

"When was this?"

"Yesterday. She said she wanted to tell me in person how sorry she was."

"You didn't . . ."

"No, I told her that couldn't happen. I obviously want nothing to do with her. Except she was so persistent. Now I'm afraid."

"Does she know where you're staying?"

"Yes," she said, her voice quavering. "I had all the calls to my apartment automatically forwarded here to the hotel." She was sounding more and more terrified. "What should I do?"

I was about to tell her to call the police when I heard a beep on the line. It was my call-waiting. I figured it was Terry. Thank God. "Hold on a second, okay?"

I switched over and was right. "We're still on for dinner, aren't we?" came Terry's voice, chipper.

"Not exactly," I said. "Where are you right now?"

"Walking out of the gym. Why? What's wrong?"

I told her as fast as I could. I also told her I had Samantha Kent on the other line. "She's scared to death," I said. "I was going to have her call the police."

"Let me think for a second."

"Do that; I'll be right back." I clicked over to say I'd been talking to Terry.

"What did she say?"

"She's thinking," I said. "I wanted to make sure you were still there."

"I am, but it's the last place I want to be."

"I don't blame you. Hold on one more time, okay?"

I clicked back to Terry. "I have an idea," I said. "Samantha doesn't want to be by herself right now—"

Terry interrupted. "I think I had the same idea. I don't want to call the police until you're back here with that picture. In the meantime, you were thinking she should go to my place, right?"

"Exactly."

"Okay, give her my address and tell her I'll be there myself in fifteen minutes."

"Good, thanks," I said. "I'll come straight there after I land."

I got back to Samantha and filled her in on the plan. Right as I finished, my cell cut off. *Shit.* My battery was toast. So much for checking other flights. I had no choice but to floor it and try to make that seven-thirty Delta flight.

After spending the next twenty minutes violating every possible speed limit there was, doing a near tuck-and-roll from my rental car, and storming the ticket counter to check in, I caught a break at the airport security station. A Saturday-night lull. It was sparse with passengers, and I was able to zip through and sprint for the gate.

"Wait!" I yelled out as I saw an attendant sealing up the Jetway.

Never mind that the door nearly hit me in the ass. I ended up on the right side of it. That seven-thirty flight to New York took off with me on it.

A very impatient two and a half hours later, I arrived at Terry's brownstone address in the West Village. I buzzed and promptly heard the return buzz of the front entrance unlocking. Hers was the entire top floor of the three-story walk-up. I took the steps two at a time.

As I approached her door, left open for me slightly, I gave a pat to the breast pocket of my shirt. That's where I'd put the picture of Haley and her mother. It hadn't gone anywhere, but I was checking just the same.

I walked into the apartment and immediately saw Terry sitting on the couch in her living room. I started to smile.

I stopped midway.

Then everything went black.

FIFTY-THREE

Y ou couldn't leave well enough alone, could you?"

Those were the first words I heard when I opened my eyes. They were being spoken by Samantha Kent.

"No, you had to go ahead and play junior detective."

She was sitting at a small table in Terry's kitchen. Legs crossed, lit cigarette in hand. Slowly, she shook her head.

"And look where it got you."

On the floor, to be exact. Facedown, arms and legs tied together with duct tape like a roped steer. Next to me was Terry in the same position. The gash on her forehead I saw when I'd walked into the apartment was caked with dried blood. No telling how long I'd been knocked out.

"So, what do you have to say for yourself, David?"

It was a rhetorical question. The strip of duct tape over my mouth made sure of it. Terry's mouth was covered as well. There'd be no screaming for help.

I was still groggy, but the big dots were easy to connect. Haley Morgan had been working with someone, all right. Though, as partnerships went, confounding didn't begin to describe it. A man's mistress and the wife he was cheating on. Score one for the ladies.

But how on earth?

I tried to lift my head higher off the floor to get a better look at Samantha. Immediately, I cringed in pain. It was no longer the ribs. If the piece of cookware sitting atop the table next to her was any indication, I'd taken quite the blow to the head from a saucepan. A Calphalon, no less.

"*Mmmmph*," I said.

It was the best I could do through the duct tape. But that was the point. To get Samantha to remove it. I was quickly borrowing from the psychology of hostage negotiations. First things first—establish a dialogue.

"*Mmmmph*," I said again.

She looked at me with a pensive smile, weighing what to do. Curiosity versus caution. "You've got something to say, David?"

I nodded.

"Of course you do. So many questions, so few answers. Quite the surprise we've got going on here." She leaned forward. "You're not going to do anything stupid now, like yell, are you?"

I shook my head.

Samantha got up from her chair. Before walking toward me, however, she picked up the saucepan. Just in case.

In one motion she grabbed the tape and ripped it off my mouth. She seemed to enjoy watching me wince. For a moment she stood there, hovering with the Calphalon. But I wasn't screaming. Not from pain, not for help.

"Are you okay?" I immediately asked Terry.

She nodded.

Samantha sat back down and resumed her cigarette. "Now what would you like to ask?"

I summed it up in one word. *"Why?"*

She glanced at Terry before fixing her gaze back on me. "That is the question, isn't it—why? Why did I want Conrad dead? Why would I seemingly team up with the woman he was fucking? And why—yes, *why*—were you the fall guy?" She looked at her watch and acted out an exaggerated frown. "But as much as I'd like to stick around and fill you in, I'm afraid I'm a little short on time."

I glanced at my bound hands and feet. "Funny, I was thinking the same thing."

She smiled again. "A morbid sense of humor; I rather like that. Conrad had one as well."

"Before you killed him."

"*Yes*, before I killed him."

"All because he cheated on you."

She drew off her cigarette. "Were this only about hurt feelings."

"What, then?"

She was about to answer but stopped. "Oh, you're good, David," she said. "It's quite a trick, being able to make people open up to you."

"The only trick is listening," I said. "But in this case, I'm not sure I buy what I'm hearing."

"You really think this was a crime of passion?"

"What else could it be?"

"Try money."

I didn't follow. She was an heiress. "You mean, like an insurance policy?"

"You could call it that," she said. "The problem is it expired early last year. Right on our tenth wedding anniversary."

I now followed. She was talking about a prenuptial agreement. Clearly, as successful as Conrad was, his bank balances were no match for the Kent family fortune. "There was no infidelity rider?" I asked.

"Ah, you mean a *bad-boy clause*? Yes, it was in there, but it didn't carry on. So to speak. I originally wanted it extended past the ten years, but in the legal give-and-take, that was the give for getting the ten years in the first place. His lawyer had been pushing hard for seven."

"Sounds like it was true love from the start for you and Conrad."

"Yeah, well it wasn't officially my money at risk."

"How much did he stand to make off you?"

"About seventy million," she said coolly. "Of course, he stood to make a lot less if he was dead."

Talk about a morbid sense of humor.

"So instead of paying Conrad, you preferred to kill him?"

She looked at me like a disappointed schoolteacher. "First off, we're talking about *seventy million dollars*. Second, there are more sympathetic figures than Conrad hanging on the wall in the post office. And were she still alive, Haley Morgan would've backed me up on that."

Now we were really getting into it. And the longer we talked, the better chance I had to think of something. An angle. An approach. A way out.

Keep the dialogue going.

"You and Haley—somewhat of a strange partnership, don't you think?"

"Actually," she said, "I tend to think that was the beauty of it. I mean, it turns out there's something indeed more dangerous than a woman scorned. *Two* women scorned."

"In Haley's case, because Conrad broke off the affair, right?"

"Again, were it only about hurt feelings," said Samantha. "Haley was angry all right, and when she showed up on my doorstep, her intent was to turn my world upside down. But as for me, all I could do was stare at her black eye."

"Conrad hit her?"

"Yes, right after she confronted him."

"About what?"

"The drug he secretly slipped her for a few days after she told him she was pregnant. The bastard. I know you're not *that* kind of doctor, but I suspect you've heard of mifepristone."

I had. It was now more commonly known as RU-486.

Christ.

Samantha continued, "The doctor found traces of it in her blood. Right after she lost the baby. Needless to say, she was ripe for revenge."

Okay. "But murder?"

"Admittedly, it wasn't her first impulse. That's why I supplied her with an additional five hundred thousand reasons to go through with it. Half up front, half on the back end, and all payable in cash. It was a lot of money for someone who didn't have any—especially with her sugar daddy having left. Really, I think the hardest part for her was believing I also wanted Conrad dead. But again, there was the matter of the seventy million."

"So, what went wrong?" I asked.

"With what?"

"Haley ended up wanting to kill you."

"It certainly looked that way, didn't it? No, the only thing she wanted that morning in my apartment was the balance of her money. That, and to get out of town as soon as possible. I, naturally, had other plans."

"Killing her, you mean."

"She *was* fucking my husband, after all. Besides, she got made. Her picture was everywhere." Samantha took a final pull off her cigarette and stubbed it out on the table. "I must say, though, it was like she had eyes in the back of her head."

Suddenly, I could envision it all. Samantha going after Haley. Using a knife—Conrad's murder weapon—so it would appear to be the other way around. But somehow, Haley sensed the ambush. She turned just in time. A struggle ensued.

Then I came rushing in.

Samantha clapped her hands slowly. "You really saved the day, David."

I could see Haley's face now. I could see her eyes. They were staring into mine at the moment she picked up the knife from the living room carpet. I was sure she was going to lunge at me. Now I knew otherwise. The scene was like a Rorschach test, only with a right answer. For what I was really looking at in that split second was a woman trapped.

In the promise of a lie.

And when the bullet ripped through her body another split second later, Samantha had made sure it would stay that way.

"How's the session coming along so far?"

I squinted at Samantha. "Excuse me?"

"This . . . what we're doing here," she said. "You're trying to turn this into a session. Get the facts first and then get inside my head. Maybe, just maybe, talk your way out of this. Nice of me to play along so far, don't you think?"

"Here I thought you were just showing off."

She gave me an amused nod. "I could see why Haley thought you were so engaging." She reached for another cigarette. "Of course, the feeling was mutual, wasn't it?"

Intent on letting that one go, I watched her light up and waited. There was one more big dot to connect. Me.

"Given what you've said about Haley's being pregnant, I'm beginning to think Conrad never used me as a foil with her."

"You're right. She never knew Conrad had even seen a psychologist. But I did."

"How?"

"I saw the one thing I made sure Haley never gave you— *proof of purchase.* I happened to stumble across the check Conrad had written you for his first session. Problem was, I never saw another."

"Because there never was another session."

"Exactly. Only I couldn't know that for sure. So months later, when the prenup expired and I learned about Haley, you became a serious loose end. Had Conrad been seeing you on a regular basis, there was no telling the things you knew. Were he suddenly to die, I could ill afford to have you coming forward and somehow implicating me. As it was, he ended up saying plenty in just your one session."

"He intended to break off the affair."

"No, what he really intended was to establish that *impression.* If I was to find out about the affair while the prenup was still enforceable, his lawyers would drag you into court to show his conflicted state of mind. Maybe instead of seventy million he'd end up with thirty-five."

"So I was being used by everybody."

"Nothing personal on my part, rest assured. I didn't even know you."

"Which unto itself was instrumental to your plan."

"Yes, but that paled in comparison."

"To what?"

"Your book." She laughed. "What a premise—good people doing bad things for seemingly no apparent reason. *Hell, David, it was like you were asking for it.*"

"So you had no problem framing me? It was that easy for you?"

"There you go turning the corner, making this a session," she said, shaking her head.

"Let me just ask you another question, though."

Samantha looked at her watch again, this time for real. "I'm afraid I've indulged you long enough. There's another question to be asked, but not by you. It's mine." She rubbed her chin, her eyes darting back and forth between Terry and me. "*What am I going to do with you two?*"

If only I thought she was actually mulling it over.

Fat chance. This was the woman who'd made sure to bring duct tape to the party. Hell, and I'd invited her. I find out Haley Morgan wasn't the one who killed Conrad Birch, so who's the first person I tell? The one who did. Fifty times over with my J.A. Henckels, no less.

I glanced over at Terry, whose eyes showed the same fear I was feeling. No, Samantha Kent wasn't really wondering what she was going to do with us.

FIFTY-FOUR

Can't use my gun now, can I? They'd trace the bullets for sure."

Samantha took another long drag off her cigarette before putting it out on the table next to her last one. Scary thing was, she looked no different than she had at the trial. The icy stare. The calm demeanor. What better to disguise cold-bloodedness than wealth?

"A knife? Not with Haley no longer around."

She stood up and walked over to me, the strip of duct tape in her hand. She slapped it back on my mouth and secured it with a slow, hard press of her thumb. My talking privileges had been revoked.

She turned to the stove. It was a gas stove. She turned a knob. From the corner of my eye I could see one of the front range tops light up with a blue flame. I watched as she blew it out. The pungent smell of gas began to fill the kitchen.

"Yes, we're going to have to keep the hands squeaky clean on this one."

Samantha proceeded over to one of the lower cabinets and opened it. She knelt and stared for a moment before reaching in. Out came a square, metal baking pan.

"I suppose there's a chance the police will ask why you called me earlier, David."

She stepped over Terry and me to the sink and turned the faucet on. She hummed while filling the pan up with some water.

"I'll tell them, of course, you were inviting me over for dinner with your new steady."

My mind got there before she did. The gas, the metal baking pan, the water to jack up the pressure. There was only one place Samantha was heading next. The microwave.

"Shame, I had other plans."

She slid the pan in, slammed the door shut, and punched a few buttons with her perfectly manicured forefinger. The microwave lit up with a soft glow amid a mechanical hum.

"Otherwise they'd have to get *three* sets of dental records."

There'd be no more lingering. No more Q & A. After all that, Samantha simply smacked her hands together twice before looking down at us with a very sick grin.

"Bon appétit, guys."

Out the door she walked. She was gone. And in about five or six minutes Terry and I would be as well. I'd only taken one chemistry class in high school, but it was enough to know we were smack in the middle of a time bomb. That metal pan was destined to spark and catch fire, turning the microwave into a pressure cooker. Aided by the boiling water, the latch would eventually give, blowing the thing open right into the gas-filled room.

Boom.

I turned to Terry. Our eyes met. I wanted to tell her everything was going to be all right. I couldn't—and it had nothing to do with the tape being back over my mouth.

The gas had become so thick I could taste it. I glanced up at the microwave, barely making out the edge of the baking pan. It was banging around on a rotating plate, the rattling noise like nails on a blackboard.

Fuck.

I looked back at Terry. We couldn't talk, but we needed to communicate. More than that, we needed to think fast. Somehow we had to get free and out of that kitchen. Only there was no way we could do it on our own. We needed help.

That's when I saw her eyes go wide. She thought of something and, with a jerk of her head, tried to tell me. At first all I could figure out was that, whatever it might be, I was closer to it. She motioned again. It was the cabinet next to the stove. Vertical from the ground up. There was something in there, she was trying to tell me.

I could barely move. But barely was better than nothing. With a rocking-horse motion I began to inch closer to the cabinet. The rattling of the pan in the microwave getting louder and louder.

Hands behind my back, I stretched and leaned, my fingertips just catching the front panel of the cabinet. Except the handle was too high. I dug my nails into the edge of the door until I could get a grip on it. I tried pulling it open once and couldn't hold on. I tried again. Bingo.

Inside were some dish towels and oven cleaner, a bag of dry sponges and tinfoil.

I turned back to Terry. *What am I looking for?*

She rolled her eyes around in circles. *Huh?*

She rolled them some more. *Oh!*

The tinfoil. The *roll* of tinfoil. Specifically, the serrated metal edge on the box. The next best thing to a knife.

I'd started to reach for it when I heard a loud popping and looked up to see the first spark. Time was running out.

I fixed on the box again. It was propped on a shelf, midway up the cabinet.

I got it and pulled, clinging to it while I rocked back to Terry. She was beginning to gag from the gas, her coughs trapped in her taped-over mouth. *Pop!* Another spark lit up the microwave with an orange glow.

She tried to meet me halfway. We were back to back. She pushed her hands out, exposing as much of the tape around her wrists as possible. I angled the box, serrated edge down, until I had it aligned. Then I sawed. As fast as I could. Above us the microwave groaned, its walls beginning to feel the inexorable push. It was only a matter of seconds.

Frantically, I kept sawing as Terry tried to force the cuts in the tape with all her might. It was working. It just wasn't working fast enough. I had to take a chance. I dropped the box and grabbed her wrists, feeling for the tape. If I could turn the cuts into tears we had a shot. If not, we were surely dead.

C'mon, David!

I gave it everything. All I had and all I had to live for. Until, with a sticky rip, the tape gave. Terry's hands were free. She immediately pushed herself up, rising to her bound feet and lunging for a drawer. She pulled out a pair of scissors and cut between her ankles, dropping back down on the floor to do the same for me. As she hurried to release my arms I looked over at the microwave, its clock ticking away. Smoke was billowing out from the edges, thick and black. The pan was completely on fire.

With one last yank, the rest of the tape gave, and I sprang to my feet. Terry made a move for the microwave, but I swooped her up before she got there. The Off button wasn't going to do squat. There was no stopping it now. Our only hope was getting as far away as fast as possible.

We sprinted out of the kitchen and into the living room, nearly tripping with every stride. I remember heading into a hallway. As for the rest, it was a blur. The floor, the walls, the ceiling, they all shook. The noise was deafening. The sheer force of the explosion slammed into our backs, practically lifting us off the ground. Were it not for Terry's last-minute pull on my arm, we would've been engulfed in flames.

The pull led to a dive and a crash landing in the bathroom. Amid the toppled walls and shattered glass, it was probably the thick porcelain tub we fell next to that saved us. We were bruised and we were bloody. But we were alive.

I held Terry tight in my arms. Our bodies intertwined and our eyes locked.

"*Mmmmph,*" she said.

Oh, and the duct tape was still on our mouths.

With a silent count of three we both ripped the strips off, easing the sting with a long kiss.

"So," I said, when we finally took a breath. "Do you still want to look at that picture of Haley and her mom before we call the police?"

FIFTY-FIVE

We're going to have to change the ending from there."

"Why?"

"Every studio will balk; it would never test well," he said. "It's not *satisfying* enough."

"It sure was to me," I said.

Kevin Daniels smiled and ran a hand through his unruly brown hair. He was back for the first time since he'd left for Hollywood. The belly of the beast. In the interim, the *culturally retarded wayward whores destined to make feel-good-movie johns out of all of us* had finally bought one of his spec scripts. He was officially a screenwriter. Now, only a week after Samantha was arrested and charged with both first- and second-degree murder, he'd flown three thousand miles to meet with me. He wanted to adapt my story.

"All I'm suggesting is a slight change," he said. "Instead of you and Terry calling the police after the explosion, the two of you go after Samantha yourselves. You need to be there when she's finally busted."

Truth was, I wish I had. It would've been great to see. The look on her face. The shock. The disbelief. It couldn't have been much different from *my* face when the truth was learned. When I first saw her for who she really was.

Sam Kent. Samantha Kent. Mrs. Samantha Kent.

There was only one other person who knew Haley Morgan didn't kill Conrad Birch, and that was her mother. And there was only one other person who knew she knew. Samantha. I'd conveniently supplied the name, the town, the state—everything she needed to track the mother down. So after bidding Terry and me a fond farewell, Samantha was no doubt off to Griffin, Georgia, to pay a visit to Evelyn Stark. She was going to make sure the secret died with her. That very night.

She never made it on the airplane.

With one phone call from Terry to the police, patrol cars were dispatched to Kennedy and LaGuardia. The closer of the two airports was the better bet, and sure enough, it was in the waiting area of a gate at LaGuardia that they nabbed her.

Yeah, I wish I could've been there to see the look on her face.

"So, what else can you tell me?" asked Kevin.

We were in my office. He was sitting on the same couch as when he was my patient. I was sitting in the same wingback chair.

"Let's see, what else can I tell you," I said, thinking. I shook my head. "I'm pretty sure that's it."

Technically, I was telling the truth. There was nothing else I *could* tell him. Which is not to say I didn't know more.

After being caught, Samantha had the right to remain silent, but she chose to talk. Her lawyers weren't about to stop her. Their angle was criminal insanity, and despite the premeditation, they felt it was their best shot. Perhaps because it was their only shot. As for me, I couldn't help marveling at what this meant.

She immediately had to be evaluated by a shrink.

Don't ask me how I got my hands on the report. While you're at it, don't ask Ethan Greene either. His days of owing me were over. All I'll say is that the report was filed electronically and logged into a "lame-ass 128-bit encrypted" computer network.

Sorry, but after all that had happened I couldn't resist looking at it.

In the course of two sessions, Samantha managed to be very forthcoming. What better way to bolster her legal strategy? According to her, she felt no remorse. Rather, she believed she was completely justified in doing what she did. And what she did was pretty crazy.

In addition to the things she revealed in Terry's apartment, there were the things she didn't. The little touches and flourishes that rounded out her plan. Answers to the additional questions spawned along the way.

Samantha explained how she slipped out of the Ritz-Carlton in Boston and made the drive down to Manhattan and back undetected. It was a round-trip that fell neatly between the time she placed her wake-up call and when she received it. Beyond that, she attended her conference as normal for the Children's Aid Society and was sure to be seen by lots of people.

There was also her getting Conrad's signature on the letter planted in my apartment. She simply caught him as he was rushing out to work and thrust in his face a stack of things for him to sign. Parking garage renewal, his health club membership check, a card thanking his shirtmaker. "By the third or fourth item, he doesn't bother to read anything," she claimed. "He just scribbles his name and barks out, *Next!*"

Meanwhile, there was Haley. On the night of the murder she had one job. Calling me. It was something she could've done from anywhere. What she obviously didn't tell Samantha was that she'd decided to do it from Griffin, Georgia. Maybe it was happenstance. Or maybe it was the shrewd move of someone who didn't trust her partner all the way. I tend to think it was the latter. Visiting her real mother for the first time doubled as an alibi for Haley. If it ever came to that.

It never did. Only because she shouldn't have trusted Samantha at all.

When the picture of Haley and me outside the museum surfaced, it spelled trouble for both of them. I was supposed to be convicted and sent to jail. Instead, I was free. What's more, as Samantha pointed out, Haley had been "made." The two agreed my Mystery Patient needed to disappear fast. Their definitions of *disappear*, however, differed.

Having Haley call me after my trial got suspended was Samantha's idea. The "sprayer" device they used belonged to Conrad. He apparently was paranoid about people taping his business dealings over the phone.

Threatening to kill "the bitch Conrad ran back to" would further insulate Samantha from any suspicion. At least, that's how she explained it to Haley. In reality, the call was all about her getting away with murder for a second time. *The mistress strikes again.* Were there to be any doubt, Samantha knew I'd gladly come forward and, seeking my own vindication, tell of the phone call I'd received.

Of course, how fast I came forward was of considerable surprise to her. She obviously had no idea I'd be staking out her apartment. It wasn't the way I played chess.

Still, she quickly turned that miscalculation to her advantage. What's more, my showing up that morning most likely saved her life. Her effort to kill Haley had been met with considerable resistance, to say the least. Who knows what would've happened if I hadn't come bursting in.

Amazing.

Haley Morgan. With a knife. In Samantha Kent's living room.

And I had no *clue* what was really going on.

Speaking of which . . .

A few days after meeting with Kevin Daniels, I was walking from my office to the corner deli to grab a sandwich for lunch. That's when a limousine pulled up. At first, I didn't see it. Only when the rear-seat passenger called my name did I turn and look. I stopped dead in my tracks.

It was Arnold Kesper.

His tinted black window was half down, and he was peering out at me. I walked over to the edge of the curb. I had to bend a bit at the knees to make eye contact, and it occurred to me that he probably wanted it that way. It was as if I was genuflecting.

"It's nice to see you again, Dr. Remler."

"You as well, Mr. Kesper."

"Can I give you a lift to wherever it is you're going?"

"It would be a very short ride," I said. "I'm just heading up to the corner."

"In that case, can I delay your arrival there for a few minutes?"

Lest there be any question about what he meant, he opened the door and began to slide over. I stood there for a second considering my options. It wasn't as if I was being offered a ride from a stranger. No, a strange billionaire was what it was.

I got in.

The first thing I noticed was that this wasn't the limo that took my date and me to the prom. This was a feast of burled walnut and the softest leather I'd ever felt. To either side were plasma screens and LCD monitors, all brandishing the latest news and market figures. Across from us sat the same petite and humorless-looking minion who'd ushered Kesper around the night of his cocktail party. She nodded slightly before going back to some paperwork in her lap. As for the food-taster, he was nowhere to be seen.

Kesper watched as I took it all in. "If you've got to deal with New York traffic, you might as well enjoy the ride, right, David?"

"I imagine so."

"You don't mind if I call you David, do you?"

"Not at all."

"Good."

I expected to hear in return that "Arnold" was okay by him. I should've known better.

He continued: "On the subject of rides, it's fair to say you've had quite a wild one in the past year or so. First the rabbi trial and then one of your own."

"You heard about that, huh?"

"It was hard not to," he said. "Yes, I was quite intrigued by the whole Samantha Kent affair. No pun intended, of course."

"What did you think?"

"Do you mean whether I first thought you were guilty?"

"No, that's not what I meant."

"Sure it was," said Kesper.

He was right.

"In that case . . . ," I said.

"What did I think?" He flicked a piece of lint from his trousers. "Well, to be perfectly honest, at first I was rather indifferent to your plight. Guilty or innocent, you seemed to face a predicament that was similar to the rabbi's. Two men asking to be taken at their word. Except you didn't believe the rabbi, did you, David? So perhaps it would've made sense if I didn't believe you."

"Mr. Kesper, I'm not offended if you had your doubts."

"I appreciate the understanding, but as I said, my feelings were more indifferent than anything else. That is, until I heard the news."

"About the rabbi?"

"Yes. You were right; I was wrong. The man was indeed lying. Guilty as sin, as I think you put it."

"Lucky guess, perhaps."

"No, you saw the situation for what it was, while I saw it for what I hoped it wasn't. In the end, your vision proved to be far more enlightened than mine."

He nodded at his minion, who nodded back. She reached to her side and picked up an envelope, handing it to me.

"What's this?" I asked.

"Something I no longer need."

I opened the envelope. Inside were pages of contact sheets plus their negatives. In every picture was the same person. Me.

Me walking into my office.

Me hailing a cab outside my apartment building.

Me exiting a Starbucks.

"One of the trappings of preposterous wealth, David, is the ability to do almost anything you want. Including finding out almost anything you want to know about anybody. Usually, I'll only have a person surveilled for business purposes. Occasionally, though, I'll do it for sport." He smiled. "There are people who, for one reason or another, fascinate me. You were such a person because of your role in the rabbi trial and the book you'd written. It made me curious about the kind of man you really are."

"You mean whether I have any skeletons in my closet."

"That's one aspect, yes. I won't lie to you there. Though I can assure you I'm not one to root for skeletons. I don't get my jollies from observing human weakness. Rather, I simply think it's better to know than not know."

"In other words, it gives you leverage."

"You could say that."

I sat there groping for a proper reaction. I wanted to be angry, wanted to lay into Kesper for his arrogance and disrespect. But most of all, I wanted to thank him. Because I knew what he'd done.

Behind the last contact sheet was an enlargement of one of the shots. I recognized it instantly. It had been taken the night of the Kesper Society cocktail party. Presto—my Mystery Patient and me standing outside the Metropolitan Museum of Art.

"I very much enjoyed meeting you in person that night," he said. "Your representative at Crescent House did well by me."

"Bennett Larson?"

"Yes, like a good moneyman he didn't ask why I wanted you there. He just made sure you were."

And I thought it had been the phrenology head Bennett sent to Kesper that had won us the invitation. Again, how could I be angry? Kesper's orchestrating our meeting netted Crescent House a million dollars.

I continued to stare at the picture, flashing back to that night as well as to when I saw it for the first time. In the chambers of Judge Lomax.

Said Kesper, "I don't want you to think I was holding out on you, David—letting you twist in the legal-system wind, as it were. It was only after I heard about the rabbi's confession note that my indifference to your situation changed. That's when I took a second look at the pictures I'd arranged to be taken. Miracle of miracles, there you were with the woman who fit your description."

"How did you know Judge Lomax would do what he did?"

"I didn't. But I figured sending him the photo would be a good first move. As it turned out, it was the only one needed."

"It certainly turned things around," I said. "For that I can't thank you enough." I slid all the pictures back into the envelope. I started to hand them to Kesper.

"No, those are yours to keep. Or dispose of, whichever you prefer. Like I said, I no longer have a need for them. I know exactly what kind of man you really are." Arnold Kesper extended his hand. We shook. "Good luck, David."

"Thank you," I said. "Thank you for everything."

I reached for the door handle.

"Oh, I almost forgot," he said. "I have something else for you."

He nodded again at his minion, who opened a file next to her on the seat. She took out another manila envelope, this one smaller, and handed it to me. There was no writing or markings on the front. I began to open it.

"Actually, why don't you do that outside," he said.

"Oh . . . okay, sure."

I stepped out of the limo, which promptly took off once I had both feet on the curb. I watched it disappear into the traffic before looking back down at the envelope. I opened it.

Inside was a check made out to Crescent House. It looked very much like the one for a million dollars that Arnold Kesper had already given us.

Except this one had an extra zero attached.

EPILOGUE

Three years later.

It's got all the trappings of an official happy ending but forgive my reluctance to call it that. Life, for all its wonders, has a nasty habit of reminding you that you're never *really* in control. I used to tell my patients otherwise. Now I don't do that anymore.

I'm still a practicing psychologist. I've got a full load of patients again—no more Swiss-cheese schedule. Mila remains my *Mamka*, and as for her Czech language, I continue to make strides. At least that's what she tells me. For all I know, I probably wished her a happy Hanukkah on her last birthday.

As for Samantha Kent, she'll be celebrating all her remaining birthdays behind bars. Life without the possibility of parole. Not a single one of the jurors in her trial bought into the insanity plea. Interestingly enough, as pointed out by Victor, they were all college graduates.

Much to the consternation of Debra Walker Coyne, my esteemed literary agent, I never wrote a firsthand account of what happened to me. Instead, I was content to let Kevin Daniels take his crack at the story. I must admit he wrote a pretty good script, and the ending—changed as it was—certainly shaped up to be more "satisfying" for the popcorn set. After the script was shopped around for months and months, a studio finally bought it. There was even talk of Tom Cruise playing me. But alas, in true Hollywood fashion, it was just talk. After floundering in development for a time, the project is now in turnaround.

"Them's the breaks," said my new bride.

Normally, Terry's falling for a guy she'd represented in a murder trial would've been an extremely bad career move. Except she always knew her career was changing. Or maybe the right word was *evolving*. As of a year ago, she said good-bye to the world of criminal law to oversee the expansion of Crescent House to other cities. Owing to Arnold Kesper's additional ten-million-dollar donation, there've already been a few ribbon-cutting ceremonies. With more to come.

However, Terry won't be able to make the next one, which takes place in Chicago in a few weeks. Rules are rules. You can't fly when you're beyond seven months' pregnant.

We don't know if it's a boy or a girl. As for what we do know, Parker and Stacy will be the godparents. Also, we have the name picked out. In an effort to come up with a more kid-friendly unisex name while still giving a nod to Terry's favorite book, we've decided on Harper Lee Remler. The nursery is ready and waiting.

Which brings me to one final thing.

A little while back, Terry found a loose key of mine. It was a safe-deposit-box key. She asked what it was for and I told her, no hesitation. We've had that type of relationship.

I shared with her the story of the list my first wife, Rebecca, had made when she was pregnant, and how I'd found it after she died. Terry asked what was on the list, and I told her. I still had it memorized.

She listened and nodded. A lesser person would've left it at that. My past would've remained my past, and that list would've remained in that safe deposit box. But not Terry. She's never worried about living in anyone's shadow. Which is why she'll never have to.

When she asked me if I'd get the list from the bank, I didn't know why she wanted it. Two days after I gave it to her, I found out. That's when I walked into the nursery and saw the list framed and hanging on the wall. "It's what *every* child should be taught," she said.

> *To love.*
> *To laugh.*
> *To laugh some more.*
> *To listen and learn.*
> *To say please and thank you.*
> *To have opinions.*
> *To respect those of others.*
> *To be honest.*
> *To be a friend.*
> *To be yourself.*